A.J. S

A SAGA OF
SHIELDS
AND
SHADOWS

THE AEGIS SAGA

Copyright © 2024 by A.J. Shirley

Cover design by Miblart

Map by Natalia Junqueira

ISBN 979-8-9897874-0-1 (paperback)

ISBN 979-8-9897874-1-8 (ebook)

LCCN 2023924389

https://ajshirleyauthor.com

To my younger self. Thank you for persevering and daring to dream big, no matter how small the world tried to make you feel. I love you, you delightful little weirdo. To all the other weirdos, keep dreaming big and don't shrink for anyone.

The Kingdom of Kōsaten

N E S W

Portland
Butchertown
Hillview
Park Hill
Russell
Audubon
Prospect
Fairdale
Fisherville
Prestonia
Crescent Hill
Hazelwood
Klondike
Auburndale
Wyandotte
Duánzào
The Highlands
Smoketown
Middletown
Fern Creek
Bardstown
Beechmont
Valley Station
Shively
Shakes Run
Nulu
Pleasure Ridge Park
Glenview
Highview
Belknap
Clifton
Avondale
Bon Air
Park Duvalle
Neuburg
Okolona
Lake Forest
Kosmodale
Buechel
Lyndon
Clarksdale
Hustbourne
Spring Mill
Bonnycastle
Springhurst
Bowman
Edgewood
Shelby Park
Anchorage

A Saga of Shields and Shadows Playlist

If you like how music sets the tone in your favorite movies and shows, follow along to a playlist cultivated by the author. Parenthetical numbers in the text indicate when to play each song. If the music is distracting to you, simply ignore the numbers and enjoy the story!

1. "Gods & Monsters" by Lana Del Rey

2. "Get You" by Daniel Caesar

3. "River" by Bishop Briggs

4. "Earned It" by The Weeknd

5. "Desperado" by Rihanna

6. "Like a Star" by Corinne Bailey Rae

7. "Die For You" by The Weeknd

8. "Thinking Bout You" by Frank Ocean

9. "Video Games" by Lana Del Rey

10. "Kiss from a Rose" by Seal

11. "Mad World" by Gary Jules and Michael Andrews

12. "Dark Times" by The Weeknd ft. Ed Sheeran

13. "Gangsta" by Kehlani

14. "Power is Power" by SZA, The Weeknd, and Travis Scott

15. "Love & Hate" by Michael Kiwanuka

16. "i love u" by Billie Eilish

17. "Feeling Good" by Nina Simone

18. "Dangerous Woman" by Ariana Grande

19. "Hrs and Hrs" by Muni Long

20. "Body" by Syd

21. "PILLOWTALK" by Zayn

22. "Control" by Halsey

23. "System" by Chester Bennington

24. "Closer" by Kings of Leon

25. "Killing Strangers" by Marilyn Manson

26. "While We're Young" by Jhené Aiko

27. "Sugar Pink Moon" by ilselena

28. "PrimeTime" by Janelle Monáe ft. Miguel

29. "For Lovers Only" by Maxwell

30. "Perfect" by Ed Sheeran

31. "Witchy Woman" by Eagles

32. "Pink Matter" by Frank Ocean

33. "Moon River" by Frank Ocean

34. "Mood" by dvsn

35. "Strange Fruit" by Billie Holiday

36. "In the End" by Linkin Park

37. "lovely" by Billie Eilish ft. Khalid

38. "Way Down We Go" by Kaleo

39. "Best Part" by Daniel Caesar ft. H.E.R.

40. "Say It" by Ne-Yo

41. "My Immortal" by Evanescence

42. "Sweet Dreams" by Marilyn Manson

43. "Chains" by Nick Jonas

44. "Believer" by Imagine Dragons

45. "Heathens" by Twenty One Pilots

46. "Bring Me to Life" by Evanescence

47. "Closer" by Nine Inch Nails

48. "Bang!" by AJR

49. "Ocean Eyes" by Billie Eilish

50. "Til the Cops Come Knocking" by Maxwell

51. "Lost Without You" by Robin Thicke

52. "Royals" by Lorde

53. "Dollhouse" by Melanie Martinez

54. "Castle" by Halsey

55. "Numb/Encore" by Linkin Park and Jay-Z

56. "Hallelujah" by FVR DRMS

PROLOGUE

The Aegis, though not <u>only</u> human, is still very much human. They still have human needs and emotions; they simply have better control over their humanity. Their training prepares them to endure hardship, hunger, loss, and pain—both physical and emotional—without showing weakness. Aegises, however, are fiercely loyal to those they care about and will protect them as they do our entire kingdom. Consequently, to keep their priorities in order, Aegises seldom form personal attachments.

– From *The Epic of the Aegis and the Wanderer* by S.S. (The Shield's Scribe)

Macella knew that the Aegis had arrived well before she came face-to-face with him for herself. How could she not when the other women had made sure she heard? They'd been taunting her relentlessly all day.

Macella didn't really care what any of them said or thought. This was temporary. She needn't make friends or get comfortable. She was here to earn coin and be on her way.

Macella had never looked down on women who made their living selling their bodies, but she never thought she'd be among them. When she'd left home, she had imagined she would find maid work along the way to...wherever Fate was leading her. Macella didn't know where that was, but she knew it was far, far away from the poverty-stricken hovel where she'd grown up.

Nobody had come after her, as she'd known they wouldn't. When you're not the eldest nor the youngest, not sickly or exceptionally talented, not particularly useful but not troublesome, you can disappear in a family of twelve. Macella's parents had likely rejoiced over their luck in having one less mouth to feed.

Unfortunately, Macella soon discovered that maid work was sparse and that nobody seemed eager to take on a woman with her minimal skills and experience. She knew how to care for simple injuries and illnesses, but she was no healer. She knew how to care for and entertain children, but she had no desire to be a nursery maid. She could read, write, and draw well, but the wealthy didn't want secretaries from her station. Hell, they wanted better than her just to clean their skivvies. Macella wasn't highborn enough or pretty enough to get work among those who could best use her skills.

(1) Thus, after several seasons of scraping by, Macella found herself standing in a brothel, awaiting her first customer. It could've been much worse. Macella enjoyed sex and didn't mind at all when her sexual partners came and went. Years of watching her mother's and sisters' near-constant pregnancies had made Macella loathe to imagine herself with babies clinging to her for all her days. She preferred brief trysts that left her free to pursue her own whims.

Of course, that had left her few options in her village. Nobody could survive without a family unit in Shively's harsh terrain, so unless you married, you stayed with your birth family until you died. Macella had never wholly embraced her people's traditions, but she knew that she would not be able to reject the requirement to pair or perish. There had to be more to life than surviving, making babies, and trying to keep those babies alive. There just had to be. All her life she'd felt the tug toward something different. Something more. She believed her Fate had led her to this brothel.

Nevertheless, Macella was still plenty nervous about her imminent debut. She supposed anyone would be a bit nervous their first night trading sex for coin. The others had teased her enough to make sure she'd be at least a little afraid.

"There's an Aegis passing through," Hacienda had drawled loudly, so as to make sure Macella heard her. "I'd bet my tits he finds his way here tonight. Nothing makes a man hornier than killing demons. He will be bursting to bury his sword in some willing lady."

"And since no lady would have him, he's gotta come here and make do with you sad whores!" cackled Esme raucously. The other women joined in the laughter and talk, especially when they noticed that Macella was silent.

"We should give him to new puss over there," Sheena chimed in. She had a pinched look about her that Macella had hated instantly. "Let her pop her cherry on a mongrel."

The others laughed heartily at this and joined in with the many reasons that Macella should bed the Aegis. These reasons all seemed to center on him being too monstrous for anyone else.

"Seeing as we have seniority, we get to pass along unwanted customers from time to time," Hacienda said, straddling a chair across from where Macella sat writing, so that Macella was forced to look at the older woman. "I doubt the Aegis will be too picky and will take whoever won't refuse him."

"He won't mind new puss," Esme added. "It don't matter that you don't half know your cooter from a hole in the wall. He has practice telling whores what he wants because Aegises like things none of us know much about. Nasty, ghastly things."

"They like when you scream or cry or fight." Hacienda smiled cruelly. "They like to take what they want."

"I hear tell Aegises have three penises," Bella stage whispered. "And they can unhinge their jaws like a snake when they eat pussy."

Everyone laughed again. Macella didn't respond, despite how long their wit flowed. She was bothered, but she couldn't show it. She didn't believe everything they said, but everyone had heard disturbing things about Aegises. There had to be some truth in it.

Macella had seen Aegises a few times—cold, strong, silver-haired people with orange eyes and stoic faces. They came to her town looking for recruits among the poor. Many families were willing to give up a few children for the purse the Crown provided in exchange. Macella wondered if she had ever seen this particular Aegis before.

Apparently, the others had foretold correctly when they predicted the Aegis would visit the brothel that night. As soon as he arrived, the teasing started up again. None of the other women could pass Macella without offering "advice" and other inane comments. They gleefully repeated their earlier warnings and outlandish speculation, but Macella refused to respond. As far as she could see, the Aegis was content to drink alone in a corner and wasn't even looking at the whores sashaying about.

So, when Madame told Macella that Aithan of Auburndale had procured a room and requested her services, Macella was rightly panicked. She hadn't truly believed she would be the Aegis's choice. There were all manner of women available, far less green and much prettier than Macella.

Macella was comely enough, with smooth brown skin, an unruly halo of thick hair, and ample breasts, hips, and butt. She could stand to lose a few stone, but she liked her appearance well enough. It had certainly suited her previous sexual partners just fine, but they'd been as sheltered as herself. Aithan of Auburndale had seen much of the world. Surely someone else was more to his taste.

When Macella suggested this to Madame, all she received was a withering look and a room key. She might've tried to persuade Madame, but she could see that the news had already spread, and she couldn't give the watching whores the satisfaction of witnessing her discomfort.

Macella forced herself to walk deliberately, with her head high, as she left the bar and found her way to the Aegis's room. He acknowledged her knock with a grunt. Macella took a deep breath and let herself into the room.

(2) Aithan of Auburndale stood before a looking glass, filling a basin with water. He didn't look up as Macella entered.

Macella studied him. His broad back strained the thin fabric of his shirt as he moved sinuously through his grooming. Macella watched him run his wet hands through his silver hair and splash his face with water. The ends of his long, wavy tresses were wine red. She could see his arresting orange eyes, even though they weren't on her.

Macella stood awkwardly, wondering if she was supposed to just undress or if she should say something bawdy or coy. She didn't know what a regular man would expect right now, let alone an Aegis. Hesitantly, she moved a bit closer, positioning herself against a wall several yards from her customer.

"I heard the other women talking to you about me," Aithan said without any preamble. His voice was deep and gravelly, almost emotionless.

"You...heard?" Macella asked stupidly, then remembered that Aegises had better senses than humans. He must have easily heard the women's passing whispers.

"Hmmm," Aithan answered, his eyes meeting hers in the mirror. "Is this truly your first night?"

"Yes," Macella answered truthfully, but went on quickly, "but I am not a virgin, if that is what you seek. I have had lovers."

Aithan repeated that noncommittal grunt of his. "I do not come to brothels looking for virgins, Macella."

Macella felt a thrill at the sound of her name in his mouth. She didn't know if it was a thrill of fear or of excitement. She didn't bother asking him how he knew her name. Most likely he had overheard it, or Madame had told him, but for all Macella knew, he could read her mind.

"It is not true what they said about me," Aithan continued. "I do not have irregular or monstrous desires. I have a man's needs and a man's appreciation for..."

Aithan trailed off as his eyes moved over her body in the mirror. Macella shivered, almost feeling the heat of his gaze traveling over her breasts, down her stomach, across her hips, and then lingering over where her thick thighs touched.

"I am not a brute," Aithan said. He straightened, finally turning to face her directly.

Macella heard her own sharp intake of breath as she met his gaze.

"I will not force you to do anything you do not wish to do," Aithan stated, his fiery gaze intensifying. "As a matter of fact, I will not even touch you until you beg me to."

Macella's mouth dropped open involuntarily. "You think I'm going to beg you?"

She had meant for it to sound incredulous, but her voice had come out breathier and higher than she'd meant it to. This was not going anything like she'd expected. She could see a glint of amusement in the Aegis's eyes, but his expression remained neutral.

"I suppose we shall see," Aithan replied. Then, in one fluid movement, he slipped his shirt off over his head before turning back to the basin to wash.

Macella used the moment of release from his gaze to catch her breath. She could feel warmth beginning to pool in her belly. His muscles rippled beneath the scarred skin of his back and torso. Macella had never seen such a beautiful body in her life.

"I do not want much in the world, Macella," Aithan told her as he washed beneath his arms. "I have to eat. I like to drink and kill monsters. And I like to fuck beautiful people."

Macella gasped and felt the warmth spreading through her body. Was she actually supposed to feel aroused by her customers? By an Aegis?

"I read people well. Most people are more monstrous than any demon I kill. They reek of greed and fear and lies. The smell is overwhelming." Aithan turned again to face Macella. "You smell like a stream, a crackling fire, an evening breeze, and good pussy. Very, very good pussy."

Aithan let his pants fall to the floor, unashamedly letting Macella take him in. He did not have three penises, but the one he had was plenty. It stood firm, lengthy, and just girthy enough to verge on painful. Macella's vagina clenched involuntarily. She leaned against the wall, letting it support her, since her legs suddenly felt unreliable.

Aithan approached her slowly, his eyes never leaving hers. Macella was grateful for the wall behind her. Otherwise, she surely would've swooned when he stopped mere inches from her—close enough that she could feel his heat and the press of his erection against her skirts.

(3) Aithan leaned toward her, and Macella tensed for the feel of his lips against hers. It didn't come. Instead, the Aegis inhaled, passing his nose over her cheek, past the curve of her ear, and down her neck.

Macella didn't move. His breath felt so good on her skin, awakening tendrils of pleasure deep in her stomach. He continued breathing her in, moving from her neck to her throat and over the swell of her breasts. Without touching her, he slowly lowered himself to his knees. His nose passed near the hollow of her belly before he settled with his face inches from her vagina.

This time, Aithan looked up into her eyes as he inhaled deeply. "Very, very good pussy." He exhaled and Macella felt the tingle of wetness growing between her legs. "I cannot unhinge my jaw like a snake, but I don't need to in order to make you cum in my mouth."

Macella shuddered as the muscles in her stomach clenched. She had never wanted to feel a mouth so badly.

"Would you like me to eat your pussy, Macella?" Aithan asked, his warm breath penetrating the layers of her skirt.

"Y-Yes," Macella stammered, barely able to force the word out of her mouth. She seemed to be using every bit of her energy to hold herself upright.

"Then ask me to eat your pussy," Aithan commanded. "I told you that I would not touch you without your permission."

Macella swallowed hard. She whispered, "Please eat my pussy."

"Hmmm," Aithan breathed against her. "That's not quite begging. Not enough for all the things I want to do to you. You will have to try again. Tell me you want me. Make me believe it."

Macella *did* want him. She wanted him now and she wanted him badly and she didn't care that this was a business transaction. She wanted him.

"I want you, Aithan of Auburndale," Macella panted. "Please. Please fuck me, Aegis."

Aithan smiled and Macella only had a moment to take in how beautiful he was before his face disappeared beneath her lifted skirt. And then there was nothing but sensation. His hands gripped her hips firmly, preventing her from moving away. His tongue moved slowly and patiently, exploring each crevice before dipping inside of her. He hummed contentedly at the taste, and Macella felt a spasm of pleasure ripple up her body. Then his tongue found her clitoris and expertly went to work.

Macella came hard, crying out and gripping handfuls of his hair. Even then, he didn't stop, murmuring into her pussy, asking, telling, commanding her to cum again. Macella did as she was told.

Aithan stood swiftly. Macella's knees had weakened, and she might have fallen were it not for his hands on her hips. Without a word, Aithan slid his hands from her hips to her ass, lifting her effortlessly. He slid into her easily, pressing his mouth to hers as he did so. Macella wasn't sure where her moans ended and his began as he thrust into her, filling her as she'd never experienced before.

It hurt a bit, but the pain was swallowed in the overwhelming, all-engulfing, lavish, maddening pleasure of him inside of her. He held her there, reveling in the feel of his throbbing hardness in her warm softness. It felt amazing and impossible and unbearable. She was going to explode if he held her like this much longer.

"Is that okay?" Aithan murmured against her lips.

"Fuck, god, yes," Macella moaned back. She could feel him smiling.

"Can you take more? Can I go deeper?" the Aegis asked, moving his mouth to trace along her neck.

Macella hadn't realized there was more, but she should've known. She'd seen his cock, and it had been bigger than any she'd ever encountered. She wanted all of it.

"Yes," Macella panted. "Give me all of it. Fuck me, Aegis."

"Hmmm," Aithan hummed against her throat. "As you wish."

He fucked Macella as she never had been, nor imagined she could be, fucked. He fucked her slowly, sliding in and out almost painfully gently, penetrating a little more deeply with each stroke. Each time, she thought he couldn't go any deeper and it couldn't possibly feel any better, and then he did go deeper, and it felt fucking fantastic.

When he finally gave her all of it, Macella felt a delicious weightless sensation deep in her gut. She threw her head back and cried out, her nails digging into his unyielding back muscles.

Aithan growled in a language Macella didn't know and began to move faster. He did it in increments, building speed gradually, while his mouth traced along her neck and throat and across her collarbone. Macella arched her back, but the wall behind her inhibited her movement. She squirmed in frustration.

No doubt intuiting her desires, Aithan pulled her tight against him. Before she could even think, he'd pivoted away from the wall and lowered her onto the pile of blankets and furs without breaking their union. Macella cried out again at the sensations that washed over her at this new angle.

"Okay?" Aithan asked quietly and, in response, Macella thrust her hips up, forcing him deeper.

And then they lost themselves completely, Macella's legs wrapped tightly around Aithan, his face buried in her neck, with one hand gripping her ass, his other entwined in her hair, tugging gently. Macella rode the rhythm of Aithan's deep strokes over wave after wave of pleasure, until she completely shattered. She came so hard she cried tears of joy. The Aegis came with her—she felt his body tremor and his grip tighten as he groaned in that mysterious language. The moment seemed to unfurl like a wisp of smoke, stretching into timelessness.

After, Macella stared up at the ceiling, her mind racing. The Aegis still lay on top of her, his head on her breasts. The silence stretched around them comfortably, spell-like.

"Let me accompany you awhile," Macella said softly, breaking the silence. She felt the rumble of the Aegis's deep laughter.

"An Aegis and a whore traveling the kingdom. We will be ever so welcome wherever we go," Aithan replied dryly.

Macella bristled. "I am more than a whore and, I expect, you are more than a killer, Aithan of Auburndale."

Aithan groaned and propped himself up on his forearms to look at her. Macella met those orange eyes with her own black gaze. She refused to look away.

"You're serious," Aithan said flatly.

Macella gave a curt nod.

Sighing, Aithan rolled off of her to lie on his back at her side. "Macella, there is a reason Aegises do not marry. Our lives are too dangerous and unpredictable to allow room for other responsibilities."

"I am not asking you to marry me," Macella retorted, working to keep her voice even. "My family has been trying to get me married off since I first bled, some nigh two decades ago. It will take more than one good fuck for you to accomplish what they could not."

"Then what do you expect?" Aithan demanded. "You believe we will have glamorous adventures, and you will join me at court for fancy parties?"

Macella sat up so that she could glare down at him. In the low light and the cover of her shadow, his orange eyes deepened to a near-red.

Macella refused to be intimidated. "I expect that it will be nice to have companionship on my wanderings, especially when that companion is a skilled protector. I expect that I will leave this place soon, like I have left so many before it. I expect I will keep going until Fate tells me to stop, because it is Fate that set me on this path and only Fate that can stop me."

"Hmm," Aithan grunted. He studied her carefully.

Macella wondered what he saw.

"I expect that Fate led me to my first and last client tonight and that we were destined to meet, Aithan of Auburndale," Macella finished, lifting her chin determinedly.

The Aegis said nothing for a long moment. Finally, he heaved a deep sigh. "I expect that I am going to come to regret this decision."

Macella felt a surge of triumph, but she tried to look as collected as the Aegis. "I expect you are wrong about that."

(4) Macella leaned over the Aegis and planted a kiss in the soft hair of his chest. Then she kissed each one of the taut ridges of muscle in his abdomen. By the time she reached her destination, his penis was rising to meet her. Slowly, she trailed her tongue around the tip, her eyes finding his again.

"I expect that we are going to have some very good times along the way," Macella murmured. Then she lowered her mouth onto his penis, stopping only when she felt herself begin to gag.

"Fuck," gasped Aithan, his back arching slightly. "I expect you might be right."

Macella marveled at the way his cock stiffened as she worked her mouth up and down its length. It really was a rare specimen of male excellence. She was already beginning to throb at the thought of him inside of her again.

Aithan groaned and lifted his hips. Macella smiled to herself. Clearly, she wasn't the only one eager for round two.

With a final strong suck, Macella lifted herself to her knees. Aithan stared up at her, his eyes burning fire bright. Macella removed her blouse. Aithan's eyes widened slightly as he took her in.

In their haste, they hadn't actually removed any of Macella's clothing for their first round of sex. Consequently, Macella had enjoyed the pleasure of seeing his beautiful naked body in all its glory, while he had felt hers without seeing it fully.

She stood and began to undo the laces of her skirt. Aithan watched, his eyes smoldering. So Macella took her time, undoing the laces slowly before pushing the skirt over her hips and letting it fall to the floor.

"Hmmm," Aithan made a deep, appreciative sound.

It was amazing how many things he could convey with a grunt. Macella felt the compliment warming her skin as his eyes traced her curves. Full breasts, slightly rounded belly, small waist, and wide hips. She turned slowly so that he could see her plump backside as well, earning herself another one of those appreciative humming grunts.

When she figured he had seen her all, Macella lowered herself back to the blankets. She straddled the Aegis and took his cock into her hand to position it against her wet warmth. Aithan inhaled sharply, his cock pressing insistently against her.

Slowly, Macella lowered herself onto his waiting girth. She gasped as it filled her. Somehow, each new angle was a glorious discovery. Macella rocked her hips and felt Aithan spasm in response.

Their second coupling was a long and luxurious journey. Each of them seemed to be trying to learn the other this time, discovering the person beneath the labels of the Aegis and the whore. They looked and tasted and caressed as the fire burned low and the sounds of the tavern faded.

When they had finally had their fill, the Aegis held Macella against him. He buried his face in her coils and curls, inhaling deeply. Macella felt a lazy smile tugging at the corners of her mouth.

"Where do you come from, Macella?" Aithan murmured into her hair.

Macella yawned. "North of here a fair distance. My village was called Shively."

"Macella of Shively, since you will be honoring me with your companionship on my journey, I want to make you a vow," Aithan said, his voice low and serious. "I vow to protect you as best I can. I will never tell you a falsehood, even if the truth is painful. I will never hinder you or your Fate. You are not bound to me. You are always free."

"As are you, Aegis," Macella replied sleepily. The last thing she heard before falling into a deep and dreamless sleep was Aithan's monosyllabic grunt. She wasn't sure what it meant this time.

(5) They left early the following morning. The other women gawked and whispered indiscreetly as Macella gathered her scant belongings. Madame refused to pay Macella, considering she'd fed and kept the new girl several days before putting her to work. Macella didn't argue, even though she'd earned her keep with some downright disgusting cleaning tasks over her few days' stay.

Aithan insisted on paying for both the room and Macella's time for the entire night. Macella knew that Madame was impressed, though she wouldn't show it. For their service to the kingdom, Aegises had the authority to require any citizen to provide them food and shelter at no cost. It was obviously a gesture of good will—and perhaps an apology for the loss of her employee.

"I knew you wouldn't stay long," Madame told Macella, her face impassive. "You have that wandering look about you."

"I am following my Fate," Macella replied, lifting her chin. "I know I have a grand purpose, and I am going to find it."

Madame sighed heavily. "You are a smart woman, Macella. I would not expect you to be foolish and reckless enough to link your Fate to one such as he."

The Aegis stood near the front door, his face as stoic as ever. Madame gestured to him with a curt nod. Macella heard murmurs of agreement from the watching women. Aithan's expression didn't change, but Macella bristled and squared her shoulders.

"You are not the first to doubt me, and I'm certain you will not be the last," Macella said, her voice loud and clear. "There is not much room in small minds for those of us who refuse to shrink. But I will not make myself small for anyone's comfort. Fate led me here and to Aithan of Auburndale. I am not afraid of where it—or he—will lead me next."

Macella spun on her heel and walked away from Madame without looking back. The murmurs of the whores followed her. She felt their eyes on her as she joined Aithan near the exit. Macella turned to face them one last time.

"I thank all of you for preparing me for my monstrous first client," Macella called to them, keeping her face serious, while she allowed her eyes danced with laughter. "It has been lovely knowing you all, but I must go. This kind of jaw flexibility is just too rare to let slip away!"

Aithan's rumbling laughter echoed in the shocked silence. Macella bowed ceremoniously to the watching women. She walked out with her head high, Aithan chuckling in her wake.

And thus began the Epic of the Aegis and the Wanderer.

Part 1
Baptized in Blood, Forged in Flame

The kingdom of Kōsaten is an in-between place whither the veil between the world of the living and dead has always been thin. These thin places threaten to tear, allowing untold dangers to cross into our realm, intent on destruction. We send our children to a torturous training and transformation, aware that this sacrifice keeps us safe.

Only 10 of every 100 potential Aegises survive the training and transformations. These survivors are no longer our children. They know the unknowable and can do the unimaginable. They've looked into the fires of hell, into the face of fear. No matter their appearance when they began, they leave with the telltale wisdom silver hair and hellfire orange eyes that mark the Aegis.

The Aegis shields us, carrying the weight of our world and the power of the gods on their shoulders. Only the Aegises stand between our kingdom and complete desolation.

Very little is known of the training the Aegises endure. Once they cross the mountains of Smoketown into Duànzào, they are lost to us until they emerge anew. They are no longer members of the families they were born into, but instead, belong to one of the otherworldly Shield Guilds. You can determine an Aegis's guild by the hue of their hair. While all Aegises have hair of silver, the ends of their tresses vary, those colors denoting which hellish deity they faced during the trials. If they survive their encounter, they are thus marked and given magical gifts by these dark gods. While the nature of these gifts is unknown to average citizens, we do know which colors align with which dark deity: Crimson for Lucifer, onyx for Hades, emerald for Apophis, cerulean for Kali, gold for Mictlantecuhtli, violet for Meng

Po. Presumably, there are many other death deities our Aegises may encounter, but with such a low survival rate, we can never know their true number.

There are none so loyal in our great kingdom as the warriors who shield us. We cannot fathom the debt of gratitude we owe the Aegises of Kōsaten. They sacrifice love, stability, companionship, and safety to protect us, despite our barely deigning to tolerate them in return. Imagine our kingdom without their loyal service. If but a few of them were to grow lax in their duties, it could spell the end of our civilization. This scribe has seen the evil awaiting us just on the other side of the veil. I have heard their inhuman cries, smelled the stench of death, and witnessed their bloodlust. Do not doubt that the monsters we fear are truly real and much closer than we wish to believe. Our foes are tireless, persistent, and insatiable. Their only desire is to consume our world. If but a fraction were loosed upon the kingdom, the horrors they would rain upon us would be unspeakable.

– From *The Epic of the Aegis and the Wanderer* by S.S. (The Shield's Scribe)

CHAPTER ONE

M acella did not regret her decision. Her months traveling the kingdom with the Aegis had easily been the best of her life. Everything was new and interesting. Each night, Macella scribbled in her notebook—her most precious possession—chronicling the things they had seen and done. She filled her sketchbook with drawings of all manner of people, plants, and landscapes, unable to believe her luck. She had come a long way from the neglected, over-crowded hovel where she'd spent the first decades of her life. Macella wondered what her mother and siblings would say if they could see her now.

The Aegis, for his part, seemed surprised by how much he enjoyed having her as a companion on his travels. More and more often, Macella caught him smiling and even laughing. She saw that it amused him to watch her discover new things, and he liked when she questioned him.

She suspected he'd thought she would be daintier. He didn't know that years of want and neglect had hardened her and made her resilient. Whether they slept in a bed or on the ground, whether food was plentiful or rationed, whether they were welcomed or scorned, Macella never complained. She did her best to make herself useful and to learn all she could. She had never liked being a burden, and she had no intention of being one to Aithan of Auburndale.

(6) The first night they spent outside was beautiful. They had traveled all day, hardly talking, simply enjoying the journey. They made camp for the night in a field of tall grass, their camp shielded by nature: a cliff base at their backs, boulders on several sides, and a river below them. Macella knew that Aithan had carefully chosen the spot for safety, as he always did, though he would sense any approaching threats long before they were any danger. Macella had a suspicion that he also used his magic to ward the camp. She wondered if he'd always done that, or if he considered the extra layer of protection necessary now that she was with him.

The night was pleasant. A warm breeze rustled the grass and caressed Macella's skin. She spread a blanket on the ground and lay on her back, staring up at the multitude of stars. They were so clear; they somehow felt closer than they ever had before. Macella had always loved the night sky, but she'd never seen it like this.

Aithan returned from the river, his hair wet around his shoulders, the crimson ends appearing nearly black against his bronze skin, the silver hair on his bare chest glistening in the moonlight. He smiled when he saw Macella lying in the grass. After laying his wet shirt out to dry, he joined her on the blanket. Macella could feel the warmth of him, though they weren't touching, and could smell his rich, smoky scent. She hadn't known she could be this happy.

"I love the stars," Macella said quietly. "They're so full of stories."

Aithan hummed thoughtfully. "Tell me one of them."

Macella smiled to herself. "Once there was a beautiful nymph called Callisto."

She told Aithan of Auburndale the familiar tale of the nymph with whom Zeus had fallen in love. Ever jealous of Zeus's many infidelities, his wife, Hera, transformed Callisto into a bear. Zeus and Callisto's son nearly killed Callisto, mistaking her for an actual bear. Before Arcas could murder his mother, Zeus placed them both in the sky.

"Zeus was a real ass," Macella said after she finished. "It is bad enough he was so faithless, but he never protected his lovers from Hera's wrath. And what if Callisto did not wish to be stuck in the sky?"

Aithan hummed contemplatively. "Irrational ideas seem logical when the safety of those you care about is at stake. I can understand wanting to tuck someone away where nothing bad can touch them."

Macella heard a wistful note in Aithan's voice that she did not quite understand. Perhaps he had lost someone dear to him. She slid a little closer to him, feeling the warmth of his skin against hers.

"I guess as prisons go, the stars aren't so bad," she acquiesced.

"How did you become such an accomplished storyteller?" the Aegis asked, surprising Macella with the sudden change of subject.

"When there are ten children in a small home, they become adept at entertaining themselves and each other," Macella replied. "I told these stories to put the little ones to bed. My little sister Lotta always begged for one more after all the others had fallen asleep. Sometimes, I would sit outside at night with my mother and older siblings after the littles finally went down, washing clothes or doing some other chore to prepare for the next day. They would often ask me to tell them stories to pass the time. It was the only time they really listened to me."

"Hmmm," Aithan said. "Fools."

Macella laughed. "I did not mind. I love stories. My imagination has long been my dearest friend."

The Aegis was silent for a while. Macella listened to their breathing mingling with the other sounds of the night—the river lapping at stones, insects singing their strange little songs, occasional calls from other nocturnal creatures. She thought the conversation was over, but then Aithan spoke again.

"Did you enjoy caring for the little ones?" Aithan asked quietly.

Macella smiled to herself. "Sometimes. They could be sweet and funny. Usually, though, it was just another chore."

"Do you want children of your own?" Aithan asked, his voice monotone.

"No," Macella answered immediately. "I have never wanted to be a mother."

From the day of her first blood, Macella had faithfully consumed contraceptive herbs each month. She would never risk adding yet another hungry mouth to her family's household.

The Aegis grunted. "You are still young. You may yet change your mind."

Macella bristled. "I know my own mind, Aithan of Auburndale. I cannot foresee the future, but I cannot fathom changing my mind on this any more than I might change my skin. Not everyone desires the traditional roles expected of them."

"No," Aithan answered. "I don't suppose they do."

Again, they grew quiet. The stars waited.

"I cannot," Aithan said finally, in a quiet voice. "Aegises are unable to conceive. I do not believe that I want children, but I was not allowed to make that decision for myself."

Macella inhaled sharply. She had not realized this truth, but she should have. Aegises did not marry nor beget children. This was known. But that they *could* not was not so widely circulated.

"I do not want children, but I would not like to have my choice taken away," Macella said. "I am sorry that your choice was taken from you."

"I swore to you I would never hinder you or stand in the way of your Fate," Aithan said slowly, his voice gruff. "I meant it. If your desires change, I will never fault you or interfere."

Suddenly, Macella understood what he wasn't saying. If she wanted children, he could not give them to her. If she walked away from him because of it, he would understand.

"I grew up in a place where there seemed to be as many starving children as there are blades of grass in this field," Macella replied. "If—and that is a formidable if—I should ever want to be a mother, I know there are many ways to become one. Why would I create more when there are more than enough motherless children across Kōsaten to satisfy my desires?"

Aithan exhaled heavily. Macella didn't know if she had answered well, but she had answered truly. She could still see the faces of the thin, neglected children of Shively. She remembered the children in the back of the Aegis's cart, sold by desperate parents and never seen again. She would never make a baby when she could help those already born into this cruel world.

(7) Without another word, Aithan rolled onto her, crushing his mouth against hers. Macella was surprised but kissed him back fiercely. His tongue was warm and insistent in her mouth. She could feel the warmth spreading to her belly. She moaned, tangling her hands into his wet hair, and pulling him closer to her.

Aithan shifted his weight so that he could slide a hand beneath her skirt. Lightly, he brushed his thumb over her clitoris. Macella moaned again as he pressed his first two fingers firmly against her labia, feeling the wetness already escaping. His appreciative hum sent shivers down Macella's spine.

Aithan pulled away from the kiss. Macella gasped for breath, staring up into his burning eyes. Aithan brought his hand to his mouth, licking his thumb and fingers, before sliding his hand between her thighs again. He rubbed her clit more firmly with his wet thumb, simultaneously slipping two fingers inside her. He swallowed her whimper of pleasure in another kiss.

As he massaged her clit with his thumb, he pressed his fingers deeper inside her. He moved his fingers in a beckoning motion, and Macella could feel the pressure deep in her pelvis, somewhere above and behind the place he was so expertly caressing with his thumb. Before long, Macella felt herself coming apart under his touch. The stars seemed to flare brighter as she climaxed, her cries muffled by the Aegis's mouth still on hers.

After she came, Aithan slid his fingers free and placed them in his mouth. He repeated that appreciative hum, briefly closing his eyes, as if savoring the moment.

"You taste amazing," Aithan whispered. And then he was undoing his pants and thrusting inside of her, and she was floating in an endless starry sky.

"Can you use that dagger on your thigh?" Aithan murmured afterward, his head on Macella's stomach, his hand tracing lazy patterns on her thighs. Macella's skirt was bunched up around her waist, a dagger in a sheath on a leather strap clasped around her thigh.

"Point and poke?" Macella replied drowsily, running her fingers through Aithan's wavy silver hair. "It was a gift from the blacksmith's daughter. She made it for me with her own hands as a nameday present."

"Hmmm," Aithan grunted thoughtfully. "That is a fine gift."

"It is," Macella answered. "Except for when it is a pity present to soften the sting of rejection. She broke up with me the day after she gave it to me. Her brother had made a better match for her with one of his mates. He and I never liked each other much."

Aithan grunted again. "I doubt her brother ever knew someone better than you. But it sounds like he did you a favor. It sounds like stupid runs in that family."

Macella chuckled. "Perhaps, but I don't bear her any ill will. I told you—I was not keen on getting married. Elinor knew it as well as anyone. And this dagger is the nicest thing I own."

"Well, then, you should know how to use it," the Aegis declared. "Funny, I don't recall you wearing it the night we met."

Macella laughed quietly. "Of course not. I was working. Besides—what chance would a dagger have given me against an Aegis? Was I going to sever one of your three penises?"

Aithan's laughter rumbled low in his chest. "Your training begins tomorrow. Tonight, I make you grateful that you left my member intact."

And he took his time, making sure Macella appreciated every inch.

CHAPTER TWO

It was a good thing he wore her out and she slept heavily, because the morrow began an addition to their long rambling days (8). Each morning, and again in the evenings, Aithan of Auburndale taught Macella to defend herself in close combat and to wield her dagger. Macella didn't possess any innate fighting skill, but she approached her training with her normal defiant persistence.

It was hard. Though he was a good teacher and certainly avoided using his many advantages over her, Aithan still exhausted Macella. He was so exceedingly strong and fast. Macella's muscles ached constantly, and her fingers blistered.

Yet Macella never complained. She was just too delighted with her new life to care about trivialities. She made a soothing salve for her blisters (and coaxed the Aegis into letting her rub it onto a few of his neglected wounds). After their evening sessions and meal, Macella would write in her journal while Aithan secured their camp.

When they were near a pond or stream, they would rinse their clothing and bathe. Macella never tired of watching the Aegis rinse the dirt from his glistening skin. She loved to catch water in a bowl and then watch it cascade over his hair and back as she helped him rinse. Then they'd lie on their blankets in the warm evening breeze, Aithan using a soft cloth to massage her sore muscles as he patted her dry.

When there was no water for bathing, Macella wiped herself down with scented oils. When she'd first done this, the Aegis had seemed awed. She explained that they were often without clean water in Shively, and this was a common hygiene practice.

"I have encountered others with the same custom," Aithan replied, his eyes blazing, "but none who smell like you. The oil seems to somehow enhance that irresistible scent of yours."

He had taken the oil from her then, taking over the process. His strong hands worked the oil into her skin so pleasantly, Macella thought she would melt. The way the Aegis touched her was so different from anything she had ever experienced. He seemed as awed by her as she often was by him.

Macella didn't know where they were headed, but Aithan always seemed to. Sometimes they would pass through a town or village, and they would have a night under a roof. Macella soon saw the double-edged sword of the Aegis's life. Seldom were townsfolk happy to see him. Though they mostly avoided open hostility, people were as cold and distant as they could reasonably manage. Usually, though, when they realized Aithan was only passing through, they grew kinder, eager to offer any services that would send him on his way more quickly.

"They're afraid of me," Aithan told Macella on the first night they spent in a borrowed bed. "An Aegis only comes when danger looms. My presence is a bad omen."

"But you come to save them from the danger!" Macella protested. "Surely they can see that?"

"Fear makes people irrational," Aithan replied. "They are afraid of what might come through the fissures, but they rarely have to see or encounter real monsters. I am a tangible threat, so I am the easiest target for their fear. Some believe we cause the danger."

Macella huffed in exasperation. "Why would anyone think that?"

"Do you know how Aegises determine where they are needed?" Aithan asked quietly.

Macella rolled toward him, studying his profile in the firelight of the small room. Aithan did not often talk of the inner workings of the Aegises, and Macella didn't push, though she was extremely interested in understanding more about them. She shook her head and waited for him to go on.

"We sense it," Aithan said simply. "We are connected. We are of both worlds. So, when a rift opens, it calls us. And so, we follow the call and close the rift, and kill anything that comes out before it closes."

"That means," Macella said slowly, "that you might arrive before the inhabitants are even aware of the danger?"

"We *always* arrive before the townsfolk are aware of the danger. It is our duty."

"Oh," Macella said simply. Everything made more sense now. The Aegis came first, then the monsters. Of course, people would fear their arrival.

It wasn't long before Macella had the opportunity to experience this fear firsthand. It happened quickly. Macella and the Aegis were setting up camp one night when Aithan suddenly went very still. It was a few moments before she noticed his rigid posture.

"Aithan?" she said gently. When he didn't answer, she approached him. His back was to her, so she circled in front of him, instinctively giving him a wide berth.

Macella was glad Aithan had told her more about the ways of Aegises, but even still, she was frightened by what she saw. The whites and pupils of Aithan's orange eyes had completely disappeared. It looked like flames had filled the space where his eyes should be. His head was lifted, and his nostrils flared as if trying to catch a scent. For the first time since she had met Aithan of Auburndale, she could see why Aegises were considered inhuman.

It lasted only a few moments before his eyes cleared. Slowly, Macella stepped closer to him. When she moved, his eyes snapped toward her, a low growl in his throat.

"Aithan? Are you okay?" she asked tentatively.

The Aegis inhaled deeply, and his eyes seemed to clear so that he could really see her. "Macella?"

She exhaled in relief and closed the space between them. "What's happened?"

"There is a new rift to the west. We will leave early and travel fast. We should reach it in four days."

Macella nodded and began to move away, but then felt his hand on her arm. She turned back to him and was surprised to see the expression on his face. It was pained and intense.

"What—" she began, but Aithan placed two gentle fingers on her lips.

"Please don't ever look at me like that again," Aithan said, his voice hoarse. "I would never hurt you, Macella. Please do not ever be afraid of me."

Macella was surprised. She knew he was used to being feared and assumed from his demeanor that it didn't bother him. Carefully, she took the hand touching her mouth and kissed his open palm.

"Okay, Aegis. But you have to tell me more about your ways. You have to prepare me for the things I don't know about you."

Aithan relaxed and pulled her to him. He buried his face in her hair, inhaling deeply. "I am not used to having someone around. I will try."

CHAPTER THREE

Thus far, their travels had been leisurely, but now the Aegis set a grueling pace. There was no time for fighting lessons or lovemaking. Rather than walking, Aithan acquired horses. Macella's family had never owned horses—they couldn't afford them—but she learned how to ride quickly because she had no choice. Even with the fear and urgency, she thrilled at the new experience.

As Aithan predicted, they neared a town called Hurstbourne in only four days. It was larger than any she had seen so far and was obviously a relatively wealthy township. Because of the anticipated reactions to the Aegis, Aithan decided that Macella should enter the town on her own. He would follow in a few hours when night fell.

Macella had no problem getting a room at the inn, and the townsfolk seemed fairly friendly. To pass the time, Macella spent her day drawing in the town square. She set out a basket and was pleased to make a few coins drawing quick portraits for some of the fine ladies milling about.

Near the end of the day, one such woman returned with a proposition. Since she had learned that Macella would be in town for a few days, she wished her to teach an art class for the local children. Once the woman assured Macella that she would pay for her services, Macella agreed. The woman, Lilliana, offered Macella space in her home for teaching and promised to arrange everything.

(9) When Macella returned to the inn that evening, it was full of whispers. Apparently, an Aegis had arrived. Macella feigned interest, trying not to be angered by the wild stories the locals spread amongst themselves. It infuriated her that these people could not see and appreciate what Aithan was doing for them—for the kingdom.

Macella washed up and went to a nearby tavern for her evening meal. The talk of the tavern was the same, except in lowered voices. Macella soon saw why—the Aegis was sitting alone in a corner. Just as the first time she had seen him, he was drinking alone, ignoring the stares and whispers. The tables nearest him were conspicuously vacant in the bustling tavern. Aithan did not look at her, but his head turned slightly in her direction when she took a seat a few tables away. She wondered if he had seen her, smelled her, or sensed her with his preternatural gifts. Probably all three.

Macella wished she could join him, defying the whispering townsfolk. She would walk right over to him and kiss him on the mouth in front of everyone. That would shut them up. Or give them something better to talk about.

Macella was staring so intently at Aithan's mouth, thinking about all that he could do with those lips, that she was surprised when his mouth quirked into a smile. Macella looked away, her cheeks hot. Of course, she wasn't the only one staring, but she was the only one who had caught that quick sign of mirth.

Not for the first time, Macella wondered if he could read her mind. She looked at the Aegis again, focusing her mind entirely on him. *Aithan, I want to fuck you*, she thought intently.

The Aegis coughed suddenly, almost spitting out the swallow of ale he had just taken. He turned his orange eyes on her for the first time, giving her a slightly reproachful look.

We will discuss this later.

Macella heard Aithan's voice as clearly as if he had spoken aloud. This time, it was her turn to choke on her ale. Aithan looked slightly amused before looking away again. To anyone who had been watching, it would look like the stranger woman had been staring at the Aegis and he had frightened her when he caught her eye.

Macella did not look at him again. She ate her meal, chatting occasionally with locals who had heard about her drawing skills and that she was going to teach an art class. The gossipy townsfolk informed Macella that Lilliana DuPree and her husband were the town's wealthiest couple and that they lived in a grand house on the edge of town with impressive grounds bordering a dense forest. Apparently, Lilliana loved children, but she was barren. Consequently, she was a generous patron to the town's youth.

"Her husband is the viceroy," said a barmaid, lowering her voice conspiratorially. "But he seems to always have important business elsewhere. I don't put much stock in the local gossip, but they say he has other women he prefers to spend his time with. Women who have given him the children Lady DuPree cannot."

Another patron shook their head disapprovingly. "So, she just rambles around that huge estate alone. She dotes on any child she meets."

Macella thought of her conversation with Aithan. She had no desire to be a mother, but she had meant what she'd said about taking in a child if she changed her mind. There were so many young sufferers across the kingdom.

"Why does she not adopt a child?" Macella asked. "Surely there are many children in need of a loving home—if not in Hurstbourne, certainly elsewhere in Kōsaten."

The other patron shrugged sadly. "Her husband won't hear of it. He refuses to raise a child who is not of his blood. Lady DuPree employees as many struggling parents and orphan children as the viceroy will allow, but if he suspects she is too partial to any one of them, he dismisses them."

Macella frowned. "That poor woman. She must be so lonely."

"I keep mine away from her," the barmaid sniffed. "She's just too strange. She looks at the children likes she would like to steal them away."

The other patron scoffed. "She's just sad and tad eccentric. But she wouldn't harm anyone, especially not a child."

"Hmmmph," was all the barmaid offered in reply.

After her meal, Macella returned to her room. She was not used to spending her nights alone in an inn, but she had always been self-sufficient. She wrote in her journal, read a book from the inn's library, and soon settled into bed. She wondered what Aithan would do with his night.

Macella had just curled up on one side and fallen into a light sleep when she felt a presence in her room. Immediately, she reached under her slip for the dagger on her thigh. Before she could unsheathe it, however, another hand caught hers. The owner of the hand covered her mouth.

"It's me," Aithan said in a low voice. He removed his hand from her mouth but kept his hand on her thigh as he slid into bed behind her.

"I would ask how you got in here, but it seems you have many gifts I do not yet know about," Macella replied in an accusing tone. She felt the rumble of the Aegis's low chuckle against her back.

(10) "We will talk about it after," Aithan promised.

Macella didn't have to ask after what. She could feel his erection against her ass, firm and insistent. "Awfully presumptuous of you, Aegis."

Aithan buried his face in the back of her neck, pulling her tighter against him and inhaling. "I am afraid I've gotten accustomed to *your* gifts."

"Is that so?" Macella teased, squirming against him a little and feeling his penis move in response.

Aithan growled. "Macella of Shively, it has been four days, and if I do not get inside of you, I am going to lose my fucking mind. Besides, you are the one who put the idea in my head at the tavern. Quite literally, actually."

"About that..." Macella began.

"After," Aithan insisted, pulling her slip up above her waist.

His hands greedily roamed over her breasts, stomach, hips, and ass, as he planted kisses along the back of her neck. Macella shivered and arched her back. Aithan slipped inside of her from behind, gripping her waist as he plunged deep. Macella turned her head to stifle her moans in the pillow. It was unusual and exciting having to be quiet. The exhilaration of the secret tryst thrilled through her.

It was quick and quiet, with an urgency that mirrored their first encounter. Still, Macella had already cum twice before Aithan climaxed. The warmth of his breath on her ear as he groaned in that mysterious language almost sent Macella over the edge once more.

Later, Macella rested her head on Aithan's chest, listening to the slow, steady beat of his heart. She knew she needed to get some sleep—they both did—but she couldn't rest without getting answers.

"How long have you been reading my mind, Aithan of Auburndale?" Macella asked in a teasing tone.

"Hmm," Aithan sighed. "That sounds more advanced than what I can do. When we first met, I told you I was good at reading people. I am...very good at reading people."

"Must you always be so reticent?" Macella huffed. She wanted specific information and he had promised to give it to her.

"You have said you saw Aegises in your village, collecting children," Aithan began again. "Did you notice their hair color?"

Macella couldn't imagine what this had to do with mind reading, but she figured she had to let Aithan tell it his own way. "Of course. It was always silver, like yours."

"Yes, but the ends," Aithan explained. "Did you notice the ends? Like how mine are crimson?"

Macella thought back. There had been an Aegis with an emerald-tipped silver afro once. And once she had seen a woman with cerulean-tipped silver waves cut in a severe asymmetrical bob. She had been utterly terrifying, Macella remembered. There was something cruel in the set of her mouth, something hateful in her orange eyes.

"I had not considered it before, but yes," Macella answered. "I have seen green and blue."

Aithan sighed again before continuing. "It is so strange talking to anyone about this. I've never even tried to do so before."

Macella turned her face toward him. He met her eyes in the darkness. Macella wanted him to know that he could trust her. She wanted to know him, even the frightening parts.

"There," Aithan said. "I do not know what you're thinking exactly, but when you looked at me, all focused like that, I got a sense of your thoughts—or the intention behind them. Whatever you were just thinking was sincere and warm and comforting, but I didn't catch any words. At the tavern, however, I heard your words quite clearly."

Macella grinned. "It was an experiment. But what does your hair have to do with it?"

"It is my guild," Aithan replied, choosing his words with obvious care. "All Aegises get the same basic training and gifts. Speed. Strength. Enhanced senses. But we are also connected to the realm of death. As I told you, that is why we can sense the fissures."

Macella nodded, resting her head on his chest again. She ran her fingers through the soft silver hair there, waiting for him to go on.

"There are trials that...align us with a particular guardian of the underworld. We share their blood, and they provide us certain gifts. Any Aegis you see with crimson-tipped hair is in the Guild of Lucifer. We have the gift of what you might call telepathy, but that is not quite right.

"It manifests differently in different Aegises. For me, it helps me to get a sense of people's true intentions. I can send thoughts, as I did today. It works best when a mind is already...familiar to me. I can receive thoughts when someone is focusing and mentally screaming them at me, like you did today. And, if I focus my energy, I can compel people to speak honestly and sometimes persuade them to my way of thinking or acting."

Macella was speechless for a moment. "Have you—"

"No," Aithan said before she could finish. "I have never even tried to compel you. I've had no desire or reason to do so. And...I just wouldn't."

Macella heard and believed the sincerity in the Aegis's voice. "I know you wouldn't," she assured him.

Macella thought of the other Aegises she had seen. She shuddered, remembering the woman with the cruel expression. "What gifts do Aegises with cerulean in their hair have?"

"That is the Guild of Kali," Aithan replied, his voice hardening. "They are utterly fearless, with a talent for war strategy, even greater physical strength than the typical Aegis, and an unparalleled bloodlust. They are also able to inflict pain on others using only their minds. I am surprised you have seen one collecting children—that is not the type of work a Kali Aegis would typically take on. It was likely a punishment for some injudicious behavior."

"She was terrifying," Macella whispered, remembering.

Aithan was silent for so long that Macella thought he had fallen asleep. She was dozing a bit herself when he spoke again.

"Are you still comfortable being...?" Aithan fumbled, uncharacteristically flustered. "If this is too much..."

Sleepily, Macella lifted her fingers to his lips. "I am incredibly comfortable. I asked to know more about you, and you have obliged me. I am grateful. Your telepathy is a part of you, like your expert tongue and gorgeous cock. Besides, I imagine your senses helped you to take a chance on bringing me along."

Macella yawned. She was exhausted, but she wanted to make him understand. Propping herself up on an elbow, she found his eyes in the darkness. Her fingers still rested on his lips.

I am not afraid of you, Aithan of Auburndale, she thought with all of her might. *I want to know you. You will not rid yourself of me so easily.*

Macella leaned closer to the Aegis, staring into his orange eyes. *I am not afraid of you.*

Aithan took Macella's hand, pressing her fingertips more firmly against his lips, before kissing her palm and then pulling her face down so he could kiss her mouth. Neither of them spoke again. They didn't need to.

CHAPTER FOUR

M acella woke to the bright morning sun and an empty bed. She'd known the Aegis would have to slip out before the rest of the inn's inhabitants were up and about, but she was still slightly disappointed. She scolded herself for being…whatever she was being. Macella reminded herself that she was free, and Aithan of Auburndale was free, and that she was chasing Fate, not love or attachment.

Macella refused to think about Aithan's eyes as she walked through the chilly morning air. She was not remembering his arms wrapped around her or thinking of his lips on her skin as she asked a shop owner for directions to the DuPree house. And she most certainly wasn't hoping to catch a glimpse of him as she made her way to the impressive home of Lilliana DuPree.

Macella was steadfastly not thinking of Aithan when she nearly walked right into someone. Surprised, she stopped short. The man standing in her path was about her height with a face like a weasel and an oily smile. A badge gleamed on his chest.

"Well, good morning," he said, looking her over.

Macella did not like the way he was sizing her up. She felt like a bug beneath a glass. She squared her shoulders and returned his gaze shrewdly. This lawman was not going to intimidate her if that was his aim.

"Good morning and excuse me," Macella replied coolly. "My mind was elsewhere, and I did not see you there."

Macella moved to step around him, but he placed a hand on her arm. Macella looked at the hand and then back at its owner. Something in her eyes must have reflected her feelings because he quickly released her.

"I'd heard there was a woman traveling alone through town," he said, smiling in a way that did not reach his beady eyes. "I was meaning to pay you a visit at the inn this morning, just to introduce myself. I'm Sheriff Pete."

"Macella." She did not elaborate. She had no desire to prolong the conversation.

"What brings you to Hurstbourne, Macella?" the sheriff asked, his falsely congenial smile still plastered to his face.

"I am just passing through," Macella replied. "But I'm afraid I am in a hurry this morning. Lady DuPree is expecting me."

The sheriff nodded, though he made no move to get out of her way. "Yes, you will be teaching an art class to Lady DuPree's pets. She is a fine woman. A little odd, but obedient. Respectable."

The sheriff's eyes passed over Macella again. Despite his smile, his gaze was disapproving. Macella heard all of the unspoken suspicions and accusations in his words. It was obvious that he did not consider Macella respectable.

"Yes, well." Macella moved past him resolutely. "As I said, she is expecting me, so I must be on my way."

The sheriff let her pass, his beady eyes crawling over her skin. "Enjoy your morning and your stay in Hurstbourne. I assure you that you'll be safe. I will personally keep an eye on you to be sure."

Macella did not look back, though she heard the threat underlying his words. She had met men like him before, drunk on power and always eager to exert it over those they considered weaker. Hopefully, she would not have to engage with him much during her stay.

Soon enough, Macella reached Lilliana's home on the outskirts of town. The stone structure was artistically crisscrossed with vines of ivy leaves, allowing it to blend with the surrounding forest. Macella thought it looked like a fairy's house—something that had grown along with the rest of the dense foliage. It felt magical.

A servant met Macella at the door and directed her to the garden. She made her way around the house, taking in the beauty of the grounds. It was all as fairy-like as her first impression: flowers and climbing vines, fountains and bird feeders, small creatures and large insects darting around freely.

As Macella reached the garden gate, she heard urgent, hushed voices. Quietly, she moved closer, finding a gap in the foliage. She could see Lilliana DuPree in close conversation with another woman. The young woman was poorly dressed and haggard, her face streaked with tears. She wrung her hands as she pled with Lilliana.

"Please, miss," the woman begged. "I have nowhere else to go. I will do anything."

Lilliana looked to be blinking back her own tears. "Annabelle, you know I cannot disobey the viceroy. He dismissed you. There isn't anything I can do."

To Lilliana's obvious dismay, Annabelle fell to her knees. She clutched at Lilliana's skirts, staring up at her beseechingly. Lilliana tried to disentangle herself, but Annabelle held fast.

"You know that I have no family, no children, no home," Annabelle sobbed. "You gave me work when no one else would bother with an orphaned teenager. My years here have been the best of my life. Please, let me come back. I can work in the kitchens, out of sight. The viceroy does not have to know."

"Enough, Annabelle," Lilliana said sharply, pulling free. "I am sorry, you know I am, but there is nothing I can do. You have to leave."

Annabelle buried her face in her hands, weeping loudly. Lilliana pulled her unwillingly to her feet. Annabelle did not resist as Lilliana pushed her toward the gate.

Macella quickly moved to conceal herself behind the nearby shrubbery. Moments later, a sniffling Annabelle passed out of the garden and made her way across the grounds, away from what had apparently been her home.

Macella moved back toward the gate. She peeked through and saw that Lilliana stood alone, crying silent tears. Macella's heart went out to the poor woman. She waited a few minutes, before making an intentionally noisy approach.

By the time she passed through the gate, Lilliana had composed herself. Macella could still see that her eyes were red and puffy, but she pretended not to notice. Lilliana had set up a cozy classroom in her garden. Several large tables were spread with all manner of art supplies and snacks. Macella had never seen such extravagance.

"This is lovely," she said, moving to set up her easel.

"Yes," Lilliana agreed. "I'd meant for my own children to be taking lessons in this garden by now. But that was not my Fate. Thus, it amuses me to fill it with children from town whenever I can."

"That's very generous of you," Macella replied, unsure what else to say.

Luckily, children began to wander into the garden, and Lilliana rushed to fuss over them. Soon, there were about a dozen children of various ages settled at the tables. There was nothing remarkable about the day of teaching, except for the behavior of the hostess.

Lilliana hovered. She spent the entire morning in the garden with them, her eyes always on the children. She anticipated their wants and pressed them to eat the treats she'd had prepared. She doted on them, petting, and embracing them by turns. Macella saw that most of the children were fairly indifferent to these attentions, but they liked the treats and the art.

Macella was sure Lilliana would leave when the afternoon group of children arrived, but she was wrong. As Macella repeated the same lesson to a new group of children, Lilliana flitted around the garden admiring the children and their work. Macella thought it must be a strange thing to be a rich woman with nothing to do all day.

When only a few children lingered in the garden, eating treats, Lilliana handed Macella a purse heavy with coins and led her through the house to the front door. "How much longer do you think you will be in town?" she asked.

Macella hesitated. She did not know when the rift would appear or what would happen once it did. "Probably a while yet," she hedged.

"Well, you are very good with the children," Lilliana said. "If you decide to stay a longer while, I'd love to talk about opening a proper art school for the poor little darlings."

Macella smiled, knowing that she would rather gouge out her own eyes. "I will keep that in mind."

Macella had gone a fair distance toward town before she realized that she had forgotten her pencil box in the garden. She turned back, as she had plenty of time to do as she pleased, and it was a pleasant evening for walking. When she reached the DuPree estate, rather than bothering Lilliana or her servants, Macella decided to cross through the forest into the garden. She would grab her pencils and get out without having to endure another awkward conversation with Lilliana.

(11) As Macella approached the garden, she saw a large shape near the forest's edge. It seemed to be someone hunched over, but in the fading light and the shadows of the forest, Macella couldn't be sure. Instinctively, Macella slid her satchel to her back and pulled the dagger from its sheath on her thigh.

"Are you alright?" Macella called to the shape.

The figure reared up, and Macella realized it was much taller than she'd realized. It loomed over her, blanketed in shadow. It couldn't be a person. The lower half was all wrong. Macella heard a rasping sound as the creature moved. Her eyes searched for the source of the sound, and then she stopped breathing.

The first thing Macella saw was the scaly tail sliding across the underbrush, rustling leaves as it moved. Then she saw the child lying on the ground, unmoving. And in a horrible moment of clarity, Macella could see the human torso covered in reptilian skin and ending in a snake-like body and tail.

Before she could think, Macella lunged toward the creature, dagger in hand. It was a stupid decision, and the monster had not expected it, which is the only reason Macella didn't die. Instead, her dagger sliced across the creature's white belly. Though the dagger didn't appear to have cut it very deeply, the beast reared and let out an earsplitting shriek. Macella draped her body over the child, waiting to feel the snake strike.

But now other screams were filling the night, and Macella looked up to see the creature disappearing into the trees. Several servants stood screaming in the garden, their eyes bulging. Frantically, Macella checked the child. It wasn't breathing. There was a bloody gash across its throat.

Macella looked into the child's glassy eyes and knew she had been too late. She cradled the child's head and closed its eyes. Her hands came away bloody.

CHAPTER FIVE

M acella didn't know how much time passed with her holding the tiny body. She was stunned into timelessness. This lifeless thing had been an eager, energetic child just a short while ago. It had been eating treats and learning to draw. Now it would never eat or play again.

She had not heard the running footsteps and the cries of the growing crowd. Suddenly, Macella was jerked to her feet, pushed about by several sets of hands, the bloody dagger ripped from her hands. It wasn't until she felt the rope wrapping around her wrists that she realized what was happening.

Macella opened her mouth to speak, but there was a bright flash of light and then a blinding pain. Someone had hit her across the face. She hadn't even seen it coming.

The garden was crowded with people. Macella saw Annabelle among them, along with Lilliana DuPree. A sobbing woman was being supported by several others at the crowd's center. The man who had hit Macella was now being restrained by a few other men. The sheriff had bound her wrists and gagged her as well.

Suddenly, the crowd went silent. The only sound was the sobbing woman, who Macella assumed must be the dead child's mother.

"What has happened here?" said a familiar deep voice.

Macella raised her head to see the Aegis had parted the crowd. He saw her then. She watched as he took in her bound wrists, disheveled clothing, and her swollen cheek. Something bone-chilling entered his face.

Don't, she thought desperately. *You have a job to do here, Aegis. Don't you dare risk it for me.*

For a moment, Macella thought he would ignore her. Aithan stood very still, but it was the deceptive stillness of a coiled snake. Finally, he exhaled, and Macella released the breath she hadn't realized she was holding.

"What happened to this child?" Aithan demanded, his voice flat and emotionless. Several people stepped further back, but no one spoke.

Then Lilliana DuPree stepped from the crowd. She was visibly shaken, her eyes on the tiny body. "This woman—this stranger—taught an art class here in this garden today. When she'd finished, I sent her on her way and went to lie down to rest for a spell. Then I heard screaming. My servants say they came and saw something monstrous. A snake woman. They say it transformed. Into...into her."

Macella tried to catch Lilliana's eye, but the woman would not return her gaze. She only had eyes for the dead child. Macella shook her head violently, trying to plead her case.

"Well, Aegis," said the sheriff, "are you not here to rid us of a hellish threat? What do you know of snake women?"

"Lamia," Aithan replied. "They feed on the blood of children. If a lamia crossed into our realm, it would need a willing host body. A childless woman."

"Do you have children, woman?" Sheriff Pete demanded, giving Macella a violent shake.

She saw Aithan's jaw clench. Macella shook her head at the sheriff.

"Well, that seems settled."

"Nothing is settled," Aithan snapped, his voice cold and hard. "We will not know until we force the creature to reveal its true form. My senses do not convince me that it is this woman. I will first seal the rift, and then I will interview every childless woman in the village."

There were several loud groans from the crowd, accompanied by many more outraged whispers. The Aegis glared at the sheriff, completely indifferent to the angry mob at his back. The sheriff, however, looked uncomfortable. Macella knew that the man was going to be prideful; she could see it in his weak chin and small eyes. This could go very badly.

"This strange woman—a woman traveling alone—shows up in my town and the next thing you know, there's an Aegis. The next day, I got a murdered child," the sheriff spat.

The child's mother sobbed loudly.

Sheriff Pete puffed out his chest and continued. "The way I see it, there's a clear connection between the two. Either this woman is the monster you're here to kill, or she's a murderess that I'm going to hang."

The crowd buzzed in agreement. Macella could feel their fury permeating the air. Her knees felt weak. She might have fallen to the ground if she wasn't being held by the sheriff's men. She saw Aithan's eyes darken to a red orange.

"You will do nothing until my investigation is complete," Aithan growled, prompting the sheriff to take a step back. "I trust you know better than to impede my work."

"Maybe they conspired together!" called a man from the back of the crowd. "She murders, and he gets paid to come rid us of a so-called monster!"

Several voices shouted their agreement. This was turning ugly fast. Macella hoped Aithan could defuse the situation quickly. The longer this confrontation lasted, the smaller the chance Aithan would be able to complete his mission here. And the more likely she would be hanged for murder.

Tell them to imprison me, Macella thought at Aithan, her eyes pleading with him. He only glanced at her briefly, his jaw set. She wasn't sure if he was getting her exact words or just a sense of them, but she refused to give up. *You must give them something to calm them.*

The Aegis sighed almost imperceptibly. When he spoke again, his voice was loud and hard, allowing no argument.

"I am endowed by the Crown to protect the people of Kōsaten from the dangers of hell. I will seal the rift, and then I will interview all of the women, including this stranger. Until I have completed my work, I suggest you imprison her. By sunset tomorrow, I will hand you the head of the lamia, or you can hang whoever you choose, and I will be on my way."

Macella sagged in relief. She knew the sheriff would grasp at this chance to save face while still appeasing his people. Aithan looked hard at Sheriff Pete, who nodded curtly in response. Then the Aegis turned to face the townsfolk. They took a collective step back and their murmurs ceased.

"If anyone here wishes to question my abilities or my honor further, they are welcome to stay and speak with me directly," Aithan said flatly, his eyes traveling over the throng. "Otherwise, I suggest you disperse to your homes."

The townsfolk heeded the Aegis's suggestion. Macella didn't know if it was out of fear or if the Aegis had used his gift to compel them to comply. Perhaps both. Macella watched as the grieving parents followed a wagon carrying the dead child. Mercifully, it had been covered with a blanket.

The sheriff's men jerked Macella forward roughly. Surprised, she stumbled over the uneven ground, unable to catch herself with her bound hands. The men let her fall on her face.

"Get up, you fucking cunt," one of the men demanded, kicking her in the side.

Macella gasped, the pain surprisingly sharp.

Macella heard the distinct snicking sound of a sword being unsheathed. Ignoring her aching ribs, she rolled onto her side and found Aithan with her eyes. His sword was in his hand, his eyes blazing.

Don't you dare! Macella shouted in her mind. *Do your job and let me do mine. I can endure it.*

(12) The Aegis's sword began to glow crimson. Sheriff Pete and his men stared, wide-eyed. Aithan raised the sword.

You promised me, Aithan of Auburndale! Macella's head ached from concentrating on sending her thoughts. *Do not break your oath. Do not stand in the way of my Fate.*

"Vacate the area," Aithan's voice came out in a choked growl. "I have to expose and mend the fissure."

The men complied quickly, apparently not interested in discovering how the glowing blade worked. The one who had kicked her yanked her to her feet, ripping her blouse in the process. Her full breasts threatened to spill out of her corset.

As the man pulled her away, Aithan finally met her eyes. His were blood red, full of rage, and some other, more complex emotion.

Your Fate does not end in Hurstbourne, Macella of Shively, the Aegis said in her mind. *Keep yourself alive or I swear on all the gods I will murder every person in this fucking town.*

Before the men pulled Macella out of sight, she saw Aithan's crimson eyes beginning to glow to match his sword. She didn't have words, so she *felt* at him—putting all of her multitude of emotions into a last desperate look.

CHAPTER SIX

T he trek to the jailhouse was utterly exhausting. Macella ached all over. The cloth gag was cutting into the corners of her mouth painfully. Her tongue and throat felt rough and dry. The lump on her cheek hurt and her side throbbed where the sheriff's goon had kicked her. Macella wanted nothing more than to curl into ball and be left alone.

The men were none too gentle getting her settled into a small cell at the very back of a dank and windowless building. They did not unbind her hands or remove her gag. She dared not even hope for a sip of water. The only relief was being able to sink to the floor and let her sore body rest. She did not care that the floor was just mud and that the whole cell smelled terrible. She closed her eyes.

When she opened them again, Macella didn't know how much time had passed. For a moment, she didn't even know where she was. Then she felt a throb of pain and the day's memories flooded back. How long had she been asleep? The windowless prison offered no clues as to whether it was day or night.

She felt gentle hands on her face. Then they pressed along her spine and prodded her scalp.

"Aithan?" she croaked, realizing her gag had been removed.

"Thank the gods," he whispered. "Can you sit up?"

Macella sat up with Aithan's help. When her vision cleared, she saw that the door to her cell was open. Her guard—the man who had kicked her earlier—was lying on the ground. Aithan crouched in front of her, a look of concern on his face.

"What did you do?" Macella tried to exclaim, but her voice came out in a raspy whisper.

"Relax," Aithan said placatingly. "He is unconscious but unharmed. He will be fine. When he comes to, I will be gone, and you will still be locked up tight. I am doing my job, as you commanded."

Macella flexed her sore wrists, then hissed at the sting. Her skin was raw and raised where the ropes had chafed against it. The ropes were on the ground beside her, uncut and expertly unraveled. Macella might have asked another question, but then, blessedly, the Aegis was holding a cask to her lips. She felt like crying in relief, feeling the water quenching her parched throat. Aithan made her sip slowly and forced her to take a break long before she was satisfied.

"You know you will be sick if you drink too much at once," Aithan said. "I have some broth for you. It has a dulling powder in it. For the pain."

Aithan reached toward Macella's swollen cheek, then stopped himself and clenched his fist instead. He looked away from Macella as he held a bowl to her lips. Macella drank it gratefully, trying to catch Aithan's eye.

"Have you closed the rift?" she asked when she had finished the broth.

Aithan nodded, but still didn't meet her gaze.

"What is it? What's wrong?"

"I sealed the rift, but I have not found the lamia," Aithan said, his voice tight. "The rift must have opened last night. I did not sense it. I thought I had a few more days."

"But you have sealed it now, and you will soon find the monster," Macella replied soothingly.

Aithan barked a bitter laugh. "It will be too late for the child that died today. Too late to prevent this." Aithan gestured at Macella's battered face and torn clothes. He still refused to make eye contact, instead looking past her at a spot on the stone wall.

"I should have been hunting last night, searching for the rift and any crossers," Aithan snarled. "I was in bed when that demon came through."

He did not say "I was in bed *with you*," but Macella heard the unspoken implication. He had been in bed with her when something horrible had entered the realm he was bound to protect. It was his fault. It was her fault.

Macella knew that Aithan would not be placated by empty words or pretty lies. She also knew that terrible things happened all the time and nobody could prevent that. Her entire body hurt, and she wanted to be far away from this disgusting cell. Nevertheless, she also knew she wouldn't change a single decision she'd made that had led her to this point.

(13) "Look at me, Aithan of Auburndale," she said, her voice hard. "You look at me right now."

The Aegis met her gaze automatically, perhaps surprised into complying by her unexpected tone.

Macella met his eyes unflinchingly, lifting her chin a little and sitting up straighter. "Neither of us knows what might have happened if we'd done something differently. Maybe you would have discovered the rift before the lamia escaped and maybe you wouldn't have. We cannot change that. What we can do is make sure that child's death is the last one the lamia will ever be responsible for," Macella continued. "You can blame me, or you can blame yourself, but either way you have to get it together and finish the fucking job."

Aithan looked stunned. Macella figured he had expected her to be weepy or frightened or something else more damsel-like. He clearly did not know her as well as he thought he did. Macella's mother had called her "strong-willed" when in a good mood, using the more truthful "obstinate" or "headstrong" when Macella annoyed her. Aithan of Auburndale had glimpsed this aspect of her character on the very night they first met. Apparently, he needed a reminder.

"I own my choices, Aegis, good and bad," Macella said, holding Aithan's gaze. "I am so very sorry that child is dead. I truly am. But I would not change anything I've done. Not one thing. I am following my Fate. I did not take a beating today just to get hanged tomorrow," Macella finished, giving Aithan her sternest look. "So, you put that gag back in my mouth, bind my hands, lock my cell, and go find that beast."

Aithan was silent for a long moment. Macella refused to look away, though she wondered if she had been too harsh. Or perhaps he could not process her words while he was so angry.

At last, the Aegis spoke. "You constantly surprise me."

Aithan might have said more, but suddenly his head snapped up and he sniffed sharply. The irises of his orange eyes turned crimson and expanded until the whites and pupils disappeared. Macella's heart hammered. Something was wrong.

A door slammed somewhere near the front of the building. The man who had been guarding Macella stirred.

Aithan drew his sword. It glowed crimson, like his eyes.

"Stay here," Aithan breathed, his voice barely a whisper.

He started out of the cell, then turned back to Macella. He pulled her to her feet, careful not to touch her chafed wrists. Almost involuntarily, he buried his face in the hair at the crown of her head and inhaled. It was brief; he was out of the cell before Macella fully realized what was happening. Still, that small moment reassured her. They were okay.

The man on the floor was struggling to sit up, his expression dazed and unfocused. Aithan's back was to the cell, his attention on the doorway. Macella heard a faint rustling sound.

Her memory of the monster paled in comparison to seeing it now. It slithered into the room, that sickening rustling sound seeming to echo throughout the small space. Its scales shimmered gray-green. When it was fully inside, the lamia lifted its front end, revealing lighter scales on its underbelly.

The lamia loomed, nearly twice Aithan's height. Just above eye level, the scales began to transition into shades of ivory as they spread over a woman's torso. The humanoid face was vaguely familiar.

Then the lamia shrieked, and there was nothing familiar about it. Macella clamped her hands over her ears.

The guard jumped to his feet. He glanced between the Aegis and the lamia blocking the only exit, then ran into Macella's cell.

The Aegis bared his teeth and roared back at the lamia. His eyes blazed in unison with his sword. His silver hair gleamed, the ends shining blood red in the sword's glow.

The lamia was incredibly fast, gliding and striking almost gracefully. Aithan, however, was grace incarnate. He matched the beast's every move, evading her strikes while landing his own. The sword seemed to have little effect on the creature, however. It left bloody scorch marks that crackled and smoked, but even as Macella watched, the wounds began to heal themselves.

Macella's guard huddled against the wall, but she moved closer to the bars, staring intently at the creature. "Aithan, stop!"

Macella did not quite know why she'd said that, but she felt like Aithan's attack was going to fail. She did not know how or why. She just knew he could not continue this battle.

"Something is wrong!" she called to him.

Aithan didn't slow his advance or look her way. "I know!"

He spoke into her mind then, his mental voice calm despite the intensity of the battle. *I have to get close and pierce her heart with a silver blade. This is merely a distraction. If she sees the silver blade, she will flee. I would keep her here as I have the advantage in this small space.*

Anxiety bloomed in Macella's chest. She knew that Aithan knew what he was doing, but she couldn't ignore the insistent foreboding. Perhaps these were the nerves associated with watching an Aegis battle a demon.

As the lamia and the Aegis parried and lunged, retreated and attacked, they moved around the small room. Soon, they moved nearer the far wall and away from the exit.

Two things happened at once then. Aithan pivoted around the lamia's strike, spinning into the shadow of her underbelly. At the same time, he pulled a silver dagger from a sheath on his waist. He leapt and Macella saw his arm arcing toward the beast's heart.

At the moment Aithan was evading the lamia's strike, the man in the cell ran. One moment, he was cowering against the wall, the next he was sprinting toward the door.

The lamia saw the fleeing man at the exact moment the Aegis's dagger began its descent toward her heart. She reversed directions to intercept the escapee, her tail whipping through the air. It struck Aithan's side, throwing him against Macella's cell and sending the dagger flying. It skidded across the floor toward the exit.

The lamia saw the dagger immediately. She let out one of those hideous earsplitting shrieks. But instead of fleeing as Aithan had predicted, the lamia lifted up to its full height, coiling in preparation to strike at the Aegis. Aithan struggled to his feet, his sword raised.

"Something is wrong!" Macella yelled again.

Yes, it is, Aithan thought back. *Lamias seldom attack adults unless cornered. She came here intentionally and is not trying to leave. This is unusual. You have to get out of here. I will distract her.*

(14) Suddenly Macella knew what she had to do. She ran out of the cell, slipping in front of the Aegis just as the lamia opened her mouth.

"Lilliana, don't!" she screamed just as Aithan shouted, "Macella, no!"

Aithan yanked Macella back behind him, bracing for the impact of the lamia's strike. But it did not come.

Instead, the lamia hesitated, closing its mouth. It hissed and seemed torn between resuming its attack or listening to Macella. Macella struggled to get around Aithan's restraining arm.

Trust me, Macella thought squeezing Aithan's forearm imploringly. The Aegis didn't take his eyes off of the monster, but his sigh made it clear he had heard Macella's mental voice. He grunted his displeasure but lowered his arm.

"Lilliana, you have to stop it," Macella entreated. Because it *was* Lilliana DuPree, however distorted. "I do not know what this demon promised or threatened to get you to agree to be its vessel, but it was not worth the price."

The lamia twitched, as if trying to advance and retreat at the same time. It hissed in apparent frustration. Macella felt Aithan's muscles tense and knew he was prepared to shield her at the slightest provocation.

"It made you murder a *child*, Lilliana," Macella hurried on. "The same child you'd been petting and praising all afternoon. Drained of blood. Murdered nearly in your own garden."

The lamia twitched again. This time it shrieked in frustration. Macella fought the urge to cover her ears. She held the lamia's gaze. Perhaps it was a trick of the light, but Macella thought its eyes looked more human—the slit-like pupils rounded out.

"Can you imagine its mother's pain, Lilliana?" Macella demanded. "You know what it is to want a child so desperately that you ache at night. You know the despair of being denied your chance at creating life. But can you even begin to fathom how it would feel to be given that child, only to have it taken from you? To have it *murdered*? To see its lifeless bloodless body lying still and broken on the ground?"

This time the lamia did retreat, as if Macella had struck it. It made a sound somewhere between its shriek and hiss. Macella was certain its eyes were clearer now.

"It will make you kill again," Macella told her. "It will make you kill child after child until your agreement is completed. Will you be happy with the cursed child I am sure it has promised you? Will you be happy with your ill-begotten offspring knowing how many grieving mothers you've left in your wake?"

The lamia opened its mouth again. This time, the hiss sounded like a word. "Nooooooooooooooo."

Macella could almost make out Lilliana's voice. She didn't know how long the woman could overpower the demon. She needed to act fast.

"Lilliana, let the Aegis stop her," Macella beseeched her. "Let him protect Hurstbourne's children. Do not let it use your body to murder any more of them."

Macella definitely heard Lilliana's voice in the hiss this time. "Yessssssssssssss."

"Now!" Macella said to Aithan.

The Aegis dove for the dagger, rolling forward when he'd grabbed it, and using his momentum to carry him into a crouch. The lamia bucked and writhed. Lilliana was losing control.

"You can do this, Lilliana! You must!" shouted Macella. "Hold steady!"

Another shriek rang through the air as the lamia turned toward the Aegis. For a moment, Macella thought Lilliana had lost. Then the creature stopped abruptly, vibrating with the competing commands it was no doubt receiving.

Before Macella could open her mouth again, there was a blur of silver, and then the dagger was embedded in the monster's chest. She turned her head quickly enough to see Aithan lowering the hand he'd used to throw the dagger. He crouched to touch the ground, murmuring quickly in an unintelligible tongue. A line of crimson lightning shot across the floor and to the lamia, snaking up her body and binding her tightly.

The lamia screamed and hissed, but the sounds were weak, nothing like the ear-shattering wails from before. The Aegis gathered the end of the rope of lightning, winding it around his hand. He stood and yanked the rope. The lamia fell to the ground, still wailing weakly.

Aithan turned his flaming red eyes on Macella. *Come*, he thought.

CHAPTER SEVEN

M acella followed as he dragged the writing creature from the building and into the street. Unsurprisingly, a crowd had gathered a short distance away, no doubt drawn by the lamia's cries. The sheriff and several of his men were among them. Macella's guard sat on the ground behind the others.

"Here is your monster," Aithan snarled, jerking the lamia's body forward where everyone could see.

Several people screamed, and a few others made the sign of the evil eye. The sheriff, to his credit, did not back away.

"Who is it?" he asked, gesturing at the beast.

"Not the woman you imprisoned," retorted Aithan, nodding toward Macella, who had stopped several feet behind him.

"Who then?" Sheriff Pete demanded, his voice quavering.

Macella imagined this must have been an uncharacteristically challenging day for the weaselly lawman.

(15) The Aegis grunted contemptuously, then kneeled in front of the lamia. The fiery lasso of light faded. He murmured, holding his hand over the dagger embedded in the monster's flesh. Gradually, his hand took on a crimson glow. When it was as bright as his eyes, Aithan slammed the hand down onto the

dagger's hilt, driving it clean through the creature's heart and impaling it to the ground.

The lamia gave a final hiss before beginning to dissolve into thick, oozing smoke. As it did so, the scales began to evaporate, revealing the woman beneath. Once the Aegis had coaxed the smoke into a bottle and corked it, there was only the body of a regular woman lying prone on the hard earth.

It was, of course, Lilliana DuPree. The group of townsfolk seemed stunned into silence.

"After I sealed the rift, I sensed the creature moving toward your lockup. I came to evacuate your man and your prisoner, but the lamia arrived before I could get them to safety. The prisoner acquitted herself well in battle."

The Aegis paused and jerked his chin toward Macella's former guard. "He, on the other hand, nearly got us all killed and almost let this beast free to terrorize your streets."

Macella started to sway on her feet as the sheriff spluttered and stumbled over his words. She was suddenly utterly exhausted. She barely heard his panicked babbling—something about the viceroy, the estate, the loss of their most generous benefactress, and whatever other petty worries had awakened with Lilliana's crime and subsequent death.

Aithan scooped Macella into his arms, lifting her as if she weighed nothing. She was too tired to protest.

———※———

When she opened her eyes again, she was in her bed at the inn. Warm light filled the room. She still ached all over, but the rest had significantly improved her condition.

Macella shifted and felt someone in the bed beside her. Carefully, she rolled toward the familiar warmth. Aithan was watching her with his orange eyes, his head propped on one muscled arm.

"Good morning," he said, his voice a low rumble.

"Good morning," Macella whispered, her voice rusty.

"It's actually afternoon, I suppose," Aithan amended. "You slept in."

Macella furrowed her brow. "I slept all night and half the day?"

Aithan nodded. "You did not even wake when I cleaned you up."

Macella looked down at herself. She *was* clean, her wounds neatly bandaged. She was clad in a soft sleeping gown that she certainly did not own.

But what truly caught her eye was the gleaming silver charm hanging around her neck on a length of braided leather. It was shaped like an eight-pointed star.

"What is this?" Macella whispered, holding the charm up to catch the light. The silver surface glimmered.

"Since I cannot hide you among the stars like Callisto, I thought I could give you a star to carry with you for protection," Aithan answered. His eyes were serious, but soft.

"Thank you," Macella breathed. "It is beautiful."

"I owe you an apology, Macella," the Aegis said. "I should not have implied that you bore any blame for my not immediately discovering the rift. And I would be a fool to have any regrets about spending my night with you.

"This was all very new to me. And, honestly, I could not have managed it with anyone but you. You are like no one I have ever met." Aithan's voice caught. He took a breath. "You have evoked emotions I believed were impossible in an Aegis. I feel things that I thought had been removed during our transformations. I do not know what to make of it. But I know this for certain. Our Fates are intertwined, Macella of Shively. I was meant to wander into that brothel and to bring you on my journey. I was meant to stand at your side, to learn from and with you. I am yours, as I always have been and always will be. And I love you."

When Macella told Aithan of her plan, she was prepared for a skeptical grunt or an outright refusal. She had outlined several arguments in her mind before approaching him, making sure she had logic and reason on her side. Of course, she was completely unprepared for his response.

"Pardon?" Macella asked, unsure she'd heard him properly.

The Aegis chuckled. "I might not love this idea, but I have learned not to underestimate you, Macella of Shively. And I promised I would never stand in the way of your Fate. The pen calls to you as the fissures call to me. There is power in your words. If this is what you wish to do, I will not oppose you."

Macella smiled broadly, feeling an excited fluttering in her chest. This was her Fate. She could feel it. "Thank you, Aithan of Auburndale."

Aithan tried to look stern. "Keep your hopes reasonable, Scribe. I do not expect there will be much demand for such paltry entertainments."

He was wrong, of course. Apparently, Macella was far from the only person intrigued by the life of an Aegis. One of the kingdom's society papers responded less than a fortnight later. By the time the pair reached the location of Aithan's next mission, the story was already in print. Several copies and a small bag of silver awaited Macella at the post.

Soon enough, half the kingdom had read the tale of "The Aegis and the Lamia."

CHAPTER EIGHT

T he time passed peacefully for some time after Aithan of Auburndale slew
the lamia in Hurstbourne. They meandered through the countryside,
mostly staying on the fringes of towns, only occasionally resting in small villages.
It seemed that both the Aegis and the wanderer had had their fill of people for
a while.

(16) It was a wonderful time. Macella had begun to show real skill at wielding
her dagger. Aithan was a patient but relentless teacher. He never let her skip
a day of training, always pushing her to get a little stronger and a little faster.
Macella was surprised to discover that the muscles in her arms, legs, and core
had grown significantly firmer. She didn't tire as easily as she had at first, and she
could endure longer periods of walking without need of rest. Unlike for much
of her life, now Macella always had more than enough to eat. She felt healthier
than she ever had.

Most evenings, when the sun had set and they'd made camp, Macella would
tell Aithan stories—some old and some newly imagined. She tried to teach
him to braid, laughing at the clumsiness of his usually nimble fingers in her
mass of curls. Unused to learning new skills, Aithan took the lessons adorably
seriously. When he successfully manipulated her unruly mane into a braided

crown around her head, his eyes blazed so triumphantly that Macella couldn't help but kiss him, her delighted laughter muffled by their embrace.

The Aegis, in turn, would tell her of his many adventures, teaching her bits and pieces about his kind along the way. Each new revelation fascinated Macella. Afterward, they would make love, Macella finding that her fitness and increased stamina came in handy in many ways indeed.

While her body grew more confident, her mind and heart were uneasy. Aithan of Auburndale had proclaimed that he loved her. He did not ask anything in return, did not expect her to respond in kind. After that first declaration, he had not even mentioned it again. He seemed content to continue as they had.

Still, Macella struggled to parse her own emotions. She knew that she cared deeply for the Aegis. She had never felt this way before. But she had also never told anyone that she loved them—not a lover, not her family, no one. The idea terrified her. Love tied you to people and places. Love landed you with a pack of hungry children and a home too small to hold them all. Of course, unwanted children would not be a problem with the Aegis. But the deep-seated fear still whispered that she would lose something of herself by loving another.

Macella had never seen true love. Her parents seemed well-matched but showed no passion or even true preference for each other. They certainly didn't shower affection on their many children, especially Macella. She had always been a little different from the rest of the children, somehow slightly apart from the family unit. If her own blood had not loved her, how could Aithan? And how could she know if she loved him?

Macella imagined that Aithan could sense her inner turmoil. It was likely why he didn't press her or allow anything to change between them. They continued as they had begun. Macella loved every moment of their days—fighting, fucking, talking, or enjoying companionable silence, it all felt so right and so easy.

And that was even more frightening. What if she grew too attached, too accustomed to this life and then Aithan tired of it? Worse still, what if something horrible happened to the Aegis? Would she be able to return to her solitary life if she let him close and then lost him?

Whenever such thoughts threatened to overwhelm her, Macella pushed them away. There was plenty of novelty in their travels to distract her from her own thoughts. But Macella of Shively had long prided herself on knowing her own mind and trusting Fate. This new uncertainty felt uncharacteristic and unsettling.

⸺⳾⳾⳾⳾⳾⸺

As the planting season faded into the hot season in the western region of Kōsaten, Aithan of Auburndale sensed an impending fissure to the south. They traveled quickly, Macella finding that she'd become a better rider, as well as a stronger walker. In six days, the pair arrived in a midsized foresting village called Shelby Park.

This time, the Aegis insisted they enter the town together. "I think I would prefer they know you are under my protection. Before, I thought that the most dangerous thing would be their fear of me. Hurstbourne taught me otherwise," he said, his eyes darkening. "I learned they *should* be afraid of me. I learned there are much worse things than being feared."

Macella was not inclined to argue. She remembered how Aithan had looked when he'd found her bound, gagged, and beaten by Hurstbourne's sheriff and his men. She remembered how her face and ribs had ached for more than a fortnight afterward. She would rather be known to be his companion.

(17) Aithan immediately set out to hunt for the fissure, leaving Macella to the business of procuring lodging. Before she did, however, Macella visited the postmaster. There, she opened a parcel that included a letter, a few bank notes, and a copy of one of the kingdom's many society papers. Among the bits of kingdom news and happenings, Macella saw "The Aegis and the Lamia."

Vaguely, Macella heard a door open and then the postmaster chattering with someone else. It sounded very far away. Everything around her had faded, and there were only the words—*her words*—staring up at her from the pages of a society paper. A society paper that people all over the kingdom read. People were reading her words.

"I love that one!" the postmaster's cheerful voice cut into her reverie. "I never read a story about an Aegis before and that one was so exciting! I hope they print more like that."

Macella looked up, a little dazed. "I have not yet had the opportunity to read it," she heard herself say.

"It is riveting," said another voice. "The scribe truly has a way with words."

Macella turned her gaze to the speaker. It must have been the person the postmaster had been talking to while Macella was staring at the paper in her hands.

"I'm Zahra Shelby," the woman extended her hand to Macella. "Sheriff Zahra Shelby."

"Macella," Macella said automatically, shaking the sheriff's hand without truly seeing the woman. She turned to the postmaster. "Thank you for your help."

Still slightly dazed, Macella walked out of the building. The sky was just beginning to grow dark as the sun descended toward the horizon. Macella supposed she should find the inn and secure lodging, but she felt like she might just float away. She was holding a society paper that featured *her words*.

"Scribe," came a voice behind her.

Macella turned to see the sheriff standing a few paces away.

Sheriff Zahra Shelby was incredibly pretty, Macella noticed then. She was petite with a boyish frame, olive skin, and huge eyes. Her dark hair was pulled back in a single braid that hung to the middle of her back. She had a bow slung over one shoulder, a quiver of arrows on her back.

"What did you call me?" Macella asked, her voice an embarrassing squeak.

The sheriff walked closer to Macella, a mischievous smile on her face. "I called you Scribe. Because you are the Shield's Scribe, are you not?"

Macella's mouth fell open. She was not prepared for anything that had happened in the past quarter hour. "How...?"

"I watched your face when you saw the paper. You lit up." Zahra shrugged. "And I knew you had come into town today with an Aegis. So, I put the clues together. I'm good at that. Guess it's why I'm the sheriff."

Up close, Macella could see that the sheriff's huge eyes were mismatched: one was brown, the other green. Both were fringed by long, dark lashes. Macella realized she had been inaccurate when she'd thought that the sheriff was pretty. Sheriff Zahra Shelby was breathtaking.

"And you knew I was with the Aegis because...?" Macella raised an eyebrow. Unconsciously, she touched the star charm at her throat.

The sheriff grinned. "It's my job. This is my town, and I know everyone and everything that happens in it. Especially when there's possible danger."

Macella narrowed her eyes. She hoped the lovely Sheriff Zahra Shelby was not one of those closeminded fools who viewed Aithan as a threat. Macella stood taller, looking down at the sheriff. "Well, you are obviously good at your job, as is Aithan of Auburndale. He is off now, securing the area and eliminating any threats. And, if you will excuse me, I must procure our lodging and an evening meal. We have traveled hard and fast to come to your aid and thus require food and rest. Good evening, Sheriff Shelby."

Macella pivoted on her heels and began to walk away from the sheriff. She heard hurried footsteps and then Zahra Shelby was walking backward in front of her. The sheriff held her hands up in a placating gesture, widening her already large eyes further in appeal.

"That's why I sought you out," Zahra told her quickly. "I want to offer my services and ensure the Aegis has everything he needs to complete his work. And to offer food and accommodations at my own home. I meant no offense."

Macella slowed, processing the flood of words the woman had just released. "It's fine. Please stop walking like that before you twist an ankle or something."

The sheriff smiled broadly and fell into step beside Macella. "I know the Aegis is here to protect my town, and I intend to do whatever I can to assist."

Macella believed the sheriff was being sincere. She relaxed a little. "Are you sure you want to extend us the offer to lodge with you? We can afford accommodations at the inn."

Zahra waved Macella's comment away impatiently. "Of course, I'm sure. I don't do anything I'm not sure of. Ah, fuck."

The sheriff had a quick tongue and Macella had to concentrate to keep up with the flow of the conversation. Consequently, it took her a few moments to realize that there was a sour-looking fellow on the path ahead. Zahra had slowed almost imperceptibly. Her posture had grown stiffer.

Macella looked more carefully at the man. He was nondescript with a bland, ruddy face, blond hair, and what appeared to be a perpetual scowl.

"Evening, Vicereine Shelby," the man said too loudly and with an exaggerated bow.

"Evening, Lailoken," Zahra replied shortly, without slowing.

Lailoken stepped directly in front of the sheriff, forcing her to stop or barrel into him. Macella thought she would have liked it if Zahra had knocked him down. Lailoken was instantly repugnant to her. He looked like trouble.

"I heard there's an Aegis in town," Lailoken boomed, ensuring that anyone in the area would also hear the news. "Can you handle this with the viceroy away? Perhaps you should appoint some additional deputies to assist you."

"Thank you for your concern, Lailoken," Zahra replied with a tight smile that didn't reach her large, mismatched eyes. "The viceroy's absence doesn't put me at any disadvantage. Of course, the viceroy isn't charged with keeping the town safe. I am. Because *I'm* the sheriff."

Though Macella didn't think Zahra had said anything particularly harsh, Lailoken flinched and reddened. Zahra took the opportunity to walk past him and Macella followed quickly. Zahra Shelby did not look back when Lailoken called after her.

"Keep my offer in mind, *sheriff*." His voice was mocking.

"Prick," muttered Zahra.

"Prick, indeed," Macella said, when they'd put a fair amount of space between themselves and Lailoken. "What's his quarrel with you?"

Zahra sighed. She responded in a quick tumble of words, which Macella was beginning to understand was just her way of speaking. "He's an imbecile who thinks he should be in charge because he's large, loud, and stupid. He insinuates that I'm only sheriff because my father's the viceroy but overlooks the fact that I beat him at every test of speed, agility, and any weapon that requires more skill than brute force."

"Wow," Macella marveled. "Well, I want to hear everything about you defeating that big oaf in battle, but first—did you say that your father is the viceroy?"

"Yes," replied Zahra hesitantly, dragging out the single syllable.

Macella bowed hastily. "My lady."

"Don't do that," Zahra blurted, flapping an impatient hand at Macella. "I detest such formalities. Just call me Zahra. Or sheriff. Or dog face, even, but not *my lady.*"

Macella laughed. "Dog face? Who in their right mind would call you dog face?"

"Lailoken told everyone in our third year of primary school that I looked just like the new pug my father had gotten me for my birthday," Zahra answered as they resumed walking.

"Well, Lailoken is obviously both stupid *and* visually impaired," Macella replied seriously. "Either that, or your father gifted you the most beautiful pug that has ever lived."

(18) Zahra cast Macella a sidelong glance, her long lashes veiling her eyes. A smile tugged at her full lips. "Thank you?"

"You're welcome." Macella smiled back. "So, I am staying at a nobleman's home with his daughter the sheriff? This sounds like a storybook."

Zahra's eyes widened and she walked backward again so she could look at Macella. She bounced on the balls of her feet, her small frame practically vibrating with excitement. Macella could not help but laugh.

"Am I going to be in your next tale? Will you give me a fake name? Can you make me taller?"

Macella had to stop walking so she could catch her breath. Simultaneously following the swift turns in the conversation, laughing heartily, and keeping pace with the energetic sheriff was certainly a challenge. Zahra waited for Macella, large eyes dancing with glee. She reminded Macella of a mischievous sprite.

"I do not know why you insist upon believing that I am this so-called scribe, but I never said I am," Macella huffed. "And if I were, I would not tell the viceroy's daughter. I am sure the Aegis and scribe in question want to maintain some measure of anonymity."

Zahra winked and grinned widely. "Of course. I can be very discreet."

Macella guffawed, surprising herself. She was quickly growing enchanted with the impish sheriff. Zahra came back to Macella's side, taking her arm.

"Let's get you home. You must be in need of refreshment. We will have some chilled wine to cool ourselves! I'll send word to the inn to direct your Aegis to The Summit when he inquires about your lodging."

Macella felt a twinge in her chest at the idea of Aithan as *her* Aegis. She touched her star charm again. "Wine sounds wonderful."

CHAPTER NINE

Zahra led Macella to a structure that made Lilliana DuPree's house look quaint. The Summit was an actual castle. Macella had heard of castles but had no true concept of their nature. The warden of Shively did not merit a castle, and she hadn't visited any yet on their travels. This massive structure was built of polished stone in shades of brown and ivory. The outer gate was guarded by archers. Within the walls, people rushed around importantly, nodding deferentially to Zahra as she passed. Macella noticed how naturally Zahra took charge, emanating the authority of both the sheriff and lady of the manor. She might not like the formality of being vicereine, but she was a born leader.

Macella tried to keep her mouth from falling open as she looked about the courtyard, attempting to take it all in. She heard Zahra ordering servants to prepare a suite of rooms, sending for wine and vittles, and dispatching a messenger to the inn. A smiling servant took Macella's belongings, promising to place them in her rooms. Another took Zahra's bow and quiver of arrows, while a third appeared with a bowl of warm water. Macella followed Zahra's lead, washing her hands in the lavender-scented water. She trailed behind Zahra, trying to take in her lavish surroundings. The sheriff led her through an ornate archway and down a breezy passage.

"This is the best spot to take an evening meal," Zahra said, showing Macella into a lovely, screened lanai, draped with delicate silks. It overlooked a vast and sweeping valley, thick with blossoming trees glimmering faintly in the starlight.

"It is beautiful," Macella breathed, staring at the expansive night sky.

"Beautiful, indeed," Zahra agreed.

Something in her low voice drew Macella's attention. She turned her head to find that Zahra Shelby was looking at her, not the wondrous natural landscape. Macella felt her face grow hot and her pulse quicken. Zahra bit her lip.

A servant appeared, carrying a tray laden with cheese, bread, and fruit. Macella jumped a little, as if caught at some mischief. Zahra laughed throatily, lightly touching Macella's elbow to guide her toward a low, soft seat. Her touch sent a buzz of electricity down Macella's arm.

They sat comfortably on the low chairs, eating the fresh food, and drinking the cool, sweet wine. Whenever Macella's wine goblet threatened to empty, an unobtrusive servant would materialize and refill it. Soon, Macella found herself far more comfortable than she would have imagined she could be in such rich surroundings.

Zahra was easy to talk to. She talked fast and laughed loud, with a naughty wit that was just Macella's style. Soon, they had swapped basic background information and moved on to hopes and dreams. The sheriff was exceedingly easy to talk to.

"It would seem that I am already living the life I dreamed of," Macella told the sheriff, gesturing around her. "I am traveling the kingdom, visiting castles, and meeting fascinating people."

Sheriff Shelby's eyes twinkled as she reached out and brushed a strand of Macella's hair away from her face. Macella's heart sped up. Her cheeks grew warmer.

"Do not forget about writing famous stories," Zahra insisted. "I saw your face when you opened the society paper. It was undeniably the face of one realizing a dream has come true."

Macella could not help but smile. Stubbornly, she made a face at the sheriff. "I can neither confirm nor deny these allegations."

Zahra shrugged. "You don't have to. I know what you felt. I am certain it was akin to how I felt the day my father first pinned this badge to my chest."

"So, you have always dreamed of protecting your home?" Macella asked, shifting toward the other woman as a servant filled their goblets again.

Zahra nodded. "I always loved to fight and hunt. My mother encouraged it—said I'd always exhibited leadership skills. My father said I had a penchant for getting into mischief and for leading others into trouble with me. Neither of them was wrong."

Zahra smiled softly, her gaze wistful. Macella wondered if she was remembering childhood shenanigans or, perhaps, thinking of her mother. If Zahra Shelby held the title of vicereine in her mother's stead, it was likely that the woman had passed on from the mortal realm.

"I am certain she would be extremely proud of the woman you have become," Macella said quietly.

"Yeah," Zahra agreed. "She would be. As I am sure your parents must be proud of you, Scribe."

Macella looked away, her smile faltering. "Doubtful. But it is of no consequence. I am proud of myself."

"Here, here!" Zahra exclaimed, raising her goblet.

Macella clinked her chalice against it, feeling cheerfulness return. Not only was Zahra Shelby easy to talk to, but she also knew when not to speak and how to artfully shift a subject. Her good humor was contagious.

Zahra went on after drinking deeply from her goblet. "My parents never tried to force me into the mold of what a vicereine should be. They let me be who I am. To me, that is love. Love allows you to be your truest self."

Rather than thinking of her parents, Macella found herself thinking of Aithan of Auburndale. She knew that she had never been more herself than these last months with the Aegis. *Was* that love?

"I know that not everyone has my privileges," Zahra amended after a pause. Macella was grateful for the redirection.

"With our wealth and position in society, we could afford to do as pleased us. I am sure that when other parents try to shape their children in their own image, they believe it is for the children's good—for their survival. Perhaps that, too, is love."

Macella's parents had tried to teach her to survive in a hard world. Was that their way of showing love? Even if they could not understand that she needed more to survive than food and shelter? Even if they made her feel abnormal for having different dreams than those around her?

"Perhaps," Macella said aloud. "Perhaps that is a form of love. I suppose I still ended up exactly where I was meant to."

"Here, here!" Zahra exclaimed again, toasting Macella once more.

They drained their goblets before subsiding into a fit of giggles. Macella did not know why they were laughing, but it felt good. She was free and strong and following her Fate to new and exciting places. She had never dreamed she could feel this alive.

Macella yawned, realizing that they had been talking for well over an hour. They'd also eaten most of the food and drank copious amounts of wine.

"Oh, I'm a terrible host!" Zahra exclaimed. "You've been traveling, and here I am talking you to sleep and not allowing you to even freshen up. You must have been on the road for days. Taryn!"

Zahra jumped to her feet, comically smacking a hand against her forehead in distress. She pulled Macella up from her seat hurriedly. Macella, however, did not quite have her balance. She stumbled and Zahra steadied her, almost embracing her to keep her from falling. Their faces were inches apart. Macella could feel the sheriff's warm breath on her face, smelling sweetly of wine and citrus.

Zahra's huge eyes were heavy-lidded and smoldering. Macella couldn't look away. Zahra's eyes shifted slightly and then she pushed Macella firmly upright.

"Taryn will show you to the baths. Everything you need will be provided. Please ask if you desire anything else at all." Zahra paused, her breath catching. She smiled. "Any. Thing. At. All. I'll check on you in a little while to ensure you're comfortable."

Macella felt rather than saw the servant that must have been standing just behind her. A little dazed, she followed the tall, gaunt man into a nearby building and through a maze of corridors. At the end of a dimly lit corridor, the man directed her through another archway. He then bowed and excused himself.

Macella stepped through the archway into a warm, steamy room, lit by torches spaced along the walls. It was quiet, aside from the gentle trickle of water and the night sounds coming from the nearby garden. The room smelled of lavender and honey with just a hint of cinnamon.

Macella found robes and towels waiting for her next to a deep bath carved right into the sparkling stone of the floor. It was deep enough for her to completely submerge and spacious enough for a small party. The water's surface was generously strewn with petals of lavender and honeysuckle.

Macella laughed at the realization of where she was. She was about to take a luxurious bath in a bathing chamber larger than her birth family's entire house. She was doing this at the invitation of the Vicereine of Shelby Park, who she was quite sure was flirting with her.

Macella laughed aloud again, the sound echoing around the chamber merrily. The wine buzzed pleasantly through her veins. She saw her face reflected in a looking glass, her dimpled brown cheeks rosy from the wine, full lips stained red, her dark eyes bright and dancing. She undressed and started her ablutions at a standing basin, washing away the worst of the travel grit. The Shelbys' soap also carried that gentle lavender and honey scent. Macella used a pitcher to pour warm water over herself. She enjoyed the sensation of the warm rivulets sliding over her curves. It trickled away and into the drains at the perimeters of the room.

Once she'd rinsed clean, she stepped carefully down the carved stone steps into the sunken bath. The water was warm and inviting. Macella eased into the water, letting herself slip under entirely before emerging and resting against the tub's edge. She squeezed the excess water from her crown of braids and let herself slip deeper into the water. It lapped just below her collarbone.

(19) "I wasn't sure that I was going to enjoy staying at the viceroy's estate, but I take that back," a familiar gravelly voice said. "You should bathe every day that we remain here."

Macella opened her eyes slowly. "I don't believe it is very chivalrous to watch a woman undress without her knowledge, Aegis."

"But you knew I was here," Aithan replied, gazing at her unapologetically.

And somehow, Macella *had* known. She wasn't sure that she'd even consciously realized it, but she'd been expecting him—had sensed he was close. She smiled at him lazily.

"Well, it's only fair that you return the favor," Macella demanded imperiously, lifting a hand from the water to gesture impatiently at his clothing. "Go on, off with those garments!"

Aithan of Auburndale smiled a slow, sexy smile. "As you wish."

The Aegis must've already discarded his armor. Now he slipped his shirt over his head and dropped it to the floor. His silver hair fell around his shoulders, the crimson tips mingling with the silver hair on his chest. Macella watched as he unbuttoned his pants and let them fall to the floor beside his shirt.

She never grew tired of looking at him. The Aegis was a masterpiece of muscle and golden skin and scars. Broad chest and shoulders, tapered torso, each abdominal muscle defined—he was tall and muscular, but still svelte. And his cock was an absolute work of art. Macella watched him rinse away the day, the cascading water making his tawny skin glow.

Macella felt something flutter deep in her belly as he eased his way into the bath across from her. He grinned, either guessing or sensing exactly the effect he was having on her.

"There are so many things about my kind that I have not yet shared with you," Aithan said as he moved toward her, his gaze burning. "For example, did you know we can hold our breath for quite a long time."

The Aegis stopped before Macella, giving her a devilish smile. Without another word, he submerged himself in the bath. Macella wondered if she was supposed to keep count of how long he was underwater.

Then she felt his strong hands gently pushing her thighs apart and realized where this new revelation was headed. She had only a moment to brace herself before Aithan's tongue pressed against her clit. Macella arched her back and gasped as the Aegis took her clitoris between his lips and sucked gently.

The warm water lapped softly, agitated by Macella's movement. The Aegis gripped her ass with both hands, holding her still and applying a bit more pressure with his tongue. Macella tangled her hands into Aithan's hair, feeling him hum against her in response. She moaned.

"Do you need a hand with that?"

Macella's eyes snapped open at the sound of another voice. Zahra Shelby stood at the tub's edge, a thin satin robe covering her small frame. Out of its braid, her dark hair pooled around her shoulders luxuriously. It made her cupid's bow mouth particularly attractive and framed her two-toned eyes beautifully.

Macella had only a moment to deduce what she must look like to Zahra—her hands submerged while she squirmed and moaned—before Aithan surfaced and turned toward the sheriff.

"Sheriff," he said politely, inclining his head.

Zahra flushed, a comical variety of expressions flashing across her face. "I am so sorry—I beg your pardon...oh gods!"

Macella sat upright, eager to interrupt Zahra's stammering. "It's alright. I...hi. I guess you must have met Aithan of Auburndale prior to him joining me here."

"Fuck, I am so stupid!" Zahra exclaimed. Her eyes fell on Macella's breasts, and she turned even redder. She fixed her gaze on a spot above and behind Macella. "I thought we... I thought you were, um, attracted to—"

"I am!" Macella interrupted. "You're not stupid. That is, my attraction is not limited by gender."

Aithan coughed, which Macella suspected was actually an attempt to conceal laughter. He sat upright as well, an arm's length from Macella. Zahra pulled her attention away from Macella and flushed again when she met Aithan's gaze.

"I didn't know Aegises even, um, f..." Zahra broke off, sputtering wordlessly.

"We fuck," Aithan finished, trying not to smile.

"Oh gods, no!" Zahra cringed, her olive skin nearly the shade of the ends of Aithan's hair. "I was going to say, 'formed romantic attachments!' I didn't know Aegises formed relationships!"

"Oh, well, we typically don't," Aithan replied. "This is new."

Both Aithan and Zahra now looked at Macella, as if waiting for her to speak. Macella, for her part, was mortified. She had definitely flirted with the sheriff. Was that a violation of whatever she and Aithan had? Had she hurt him? What was he thinking? What was she supposed to do?

Breathe, Aithan said into her mind.

Macella took a deep breath. "I am incredibly attracted to you, Sheriff Shelby. I also am, well, um, attached to Aithan of Auburndale."

Zahra nodded. "I see. Well, I will bid you both good night, and perhaps we can all attribute tonight's missteps to too much wine. Let us all forget this little misunderstanding ever happened."

"Or," Aithan said, stopping Zahra before she could turn away. "I could bid you both good night and await Macella in our chambers whenever you've both...tired."

Macella's mouth dropped open. She stared hard into Aithan's eyes, trying to read his true feelings about this situation. He gazed back at her, smiling slightly.

"Macella, do you intend to abandon me tomorrow—with no chance of my ever regaining even a part of your heart—if you bed the lovely sheriff tonight?" Aithan asked, his voice so tender it made Macella's heart ache.

She shook her head no. Her heart fluttered against her ribs like a caged bird.

Aithan moved closer, reaching out and tracing his hand across her cheek. "Then I take no issue with you enjoying her company. Love and possession are not synonymous, Macella. Not with me—not with you. We are neither of us traditional; together we are downright unorthodox."

The Aegis gently took Macella's face in his large, strong hands. "We can make this whatever we choose. We only have to please ourselves. We decide."

Macella kissed him then, hard. He kissed her back, slipping his tongue into her mouth. He tasted like smoke and lavender and like her. She moaned.

The Aegis broke away, gasping for breath. "If you behave like that, you are going to make it difficult for me to excuse myself in good spirits."

Aithan stood abruptly, sending ripples through the bath. Macella saw Zahra's mouth drop open at the sight of Aithan's bare body, complete with a very erect penis.

"Well fuck!" Zahra exclaimed. "I wouldn't kick either of you out of bed."

The three exchanged glances and then broke into a fit of laughter. Again, Macella marveled at where she found herself. Could she and Aithan truly shape their world as they wished?

She was willing to try. Her Fate hadn't led her astray yet.

"Sheriff, would you mind escorting us to our rooms? I don't think we would be able to find our way without your assistance," Macella asked, standing to face Zahra.

Macella saw the sheriff's eyes drift over her full breasts and wide hips. Zahra bit her lip, glancing between Macella's body and Aithan's.

"This is fucking amazing," she said finally. "Leave your clothes; they'll be laundered and placed in your rooms. This way, please."

Grinning, Zahra spun on her heel and headed toward the door. Aithan helped Macella into a robe before donning one himself. As Macella started to follow the sheriff, Aithan gripped her hand, pulling her toward him.

"I truly am happy to leave you two to your own devices," Aithan said softly, his voice sincere. "Or to stay to merely observe. Or to stay and touch only you. That is to say, I want you to feel good about everything that happens this night."

Macella looked up into the Aegis's warm orange eyes. Her heart lurched, trying to tell her a truth she already knew. But she was not yet ready to hear it.

"Do you intend to abandon me tomorrow if you bed the lovely sheriff tonight?" she asked him with a teasing smile.

"Never," he replied, his gaze fiery, his voice low and firm.

Macella shivered, her heart stuttering in her chest. "Then I take no issue with you enjoying her company. But be careful—she is quite small."

Grinning, she squeezed his hand. Aithan smiled back at her, making her heart lurch once more. His smile was truly something to behold. It softened his intimidating features and made him look younger, more human. Entwining their fingers, Macella pulled him in the direction Zahra had gone.

CHAPTER TEN

Z ahra Shelby led them to a lovely set of rooms—a sitting room, several dressing chambers, and a bed chamber, all spacious and richly furnished. Macella would've marveled at the lushness of the accommodations, but with the Aegis at her side and the beautiful sheriff standing before her, she had no attention left for her surroundings. Zahra stood near the large bed, her small hands resting on the knot of her robe.

"Okay, so, I've lived in Shelby Park my entire life," Zahra blurted in her quick way. "I know everyone here, and they've all scrutinized my every embarrassing moment and awkward stage of development."

Zahra took a breath, trying—it seemed—to find the right words. Macella felt a twinge of empathy. She had not been rich or important, but she remembered how hard it was trying to grow into her true self while the people around her tried to bend her to their expectations.

"It is especially challenging to have casual dalliances," Zahra finished. "Everyone wants something from the sheriff. Or the vicereine, more likely."

Macella nodded, understanding dawning. "You need a good, uncomplicated fuck."

Zahra exhaled gratefully. "Exactly."

Aithan chuckled a low rumbling laugh. "This is fucking amazing."

They all laughed then, and any remaining tension seemed to melt away with the sound. Aithan squeezed Macella's hand and then gave her a small push toward the sheriff. It seemed Macella was to be in charge.

(20) She closed the space between her and Zahra, staring down into the woman's big, beautiful eyes. Zahra's plump pink lips parted, and Macella wanted to taste them, wanted to run her tongue along their curves. She lifted her hands, carefully running her fingers through Zahra's thick hair. It was silky soft and smelled of lavender.

Zahra stood on tiptoes and pressed her mouth to Macella's. Her mouth was soft and warm and sweet. Macella moaned with delight. Zahra made a pleased throaty sound, sighing against Macella's lips.

Macella slid her hands along the satin of Zahra's robe. She cupped the sheriff's small, pert breasts, running her thumbs lightly over the nipples, which stiffened under her touch.

Macella traced her hands down the sheriff's firm, flat stomach and found the belt of her robe. Stepping back, she pulled the belt loose and slid the robe from Zahra's shoulders. Macella dropped her own robe to the floor next to Zahra's.

Macella heard Aithan's humming approval. She smiled to herself, imagining how they must look together. The two women could not be more different. Macella was all curves, full breasts and butt, with a shape like an hourglass, and deep brown skin. Zahra was petite with narrow hips, perky little breasts, and glowing olive skin. It was a lovely combination.

Macella pushed Zahra gently toward the bed. She beckoned for Aithan to follow. The Aegis dropped his robe to the floor, and Macella watched Zahra taking him in again. The obvious desire on her face sent a flood of heat coursing through Macella's body. She felt a warm wetness gathering between her thighs.

Macella laid on her side beside Zahra. Aithan laid behind Macella, propped up on one elbow. He traced lazy pattens against her skin, contentedly humming some bit of an old song to himself. Fire followed his touch, crisscrossing Macella's skin with desire.

Macella found Zahra's mouth with hers again, sliding her tongue along those inviting lips. She ran her hand over Zahra's breasts, following her fingers with her tongue. As she took a pink nipple gently between her teeth, Macella slipped her hand through the soft hair between Zahra's thighs. Her fingers found the wet warmth and pressed, massaging gentle circles from Zahra's clit to her vagina and back again.

"Fuck, don't stop," Zahra demanded in her low, husky voice.

Macella felt it thrill through her body. As Zahra reacted to her touch, Macella felt an empathic pleasure of her own. She felt her excitement climbing, her own arousal rising to match Zahra's. Aithan breathed a sigh behind her, his touch a little more insistent against her skin.

It was all too much. A delicious tingling spread through Macella's belly. Her hips moved involuntarily, in rhythm with her hand. She could feel Aithan's cock pressing against her ass. Steadily, she flicked her tongue over one of Zahra's nipples.

Macella felt Zahra's orgasm building. The sheriff shuddered, gasping, and clutching at Macella's arm. Macella pressed a little more firmly, moving her hand and her tongue a little faster.

Zahra cried out, her voice throaty and hoarse and unbelievably sexy. Macella felt a tremor, her vagina clenching hard in response. She lifted her head, watching Zahra's face as she came. The woman was exquisite.

Macella pressed herself up, looking from the sheriff—panting, her eyes closed—to Aithan, whose eyes were open and burning. Macella shifted her weight, and Aithan, intuiting her intention, lifted her to straddle him.

Macella eased onto his cock with luxurious slowness. She wanted to savor every sensation as he filled her, to feel him pressing hard against her throbbing, aching need. Aithan groaned, clutching her hips, his nails digging into her skin.

Macella rolled her hips, coaxing him deeper. She threw her head back, her hands clenching her thighs, looking for something to hold on to before she plunged over the edge.

Instead, she felt a mouth on her right breast, an explosion of sensation. She opened her eyes and discovered a pair of mismatched eyes looking up at her. Without breaking eye contact, Zahra circled her tongue around the areola, grinning wickedly as she took Macella's nipple between her teeth.

"Fuck," Macella gasped, and then it was too much. Aithan moving beneath her, his hands gripping her waist, Zahra's mouth on her breasts, Zahra moaning as she sucked, no doubt responding to what Aithan's tongue must have been doing as she straddled his face. Macella felt a shimmering sensation, and then she was splitting into a million shards of light.

Distantly, Macella heard Zahra's throaty cry and Aithan's low growl as he came with her, his fingers digging into the flesh of her hips. Macella's mind receded as her body took over. Everywhere were clutching hands, searching mouths, and overwhelming, all-encompassing sensation.

When the world reformed into recognizable shapes and colors, Macella lay on top of Aithan, her face buried in the soft silver hair of his chest. She could feel one of the Aegis's arms draped across her back.

Macella pried an eye open. She followed the curve of her own arm and found that it was draped over Zahra, who lay on her back beside Aithan, one arm tossed over her head, her thick lashes fluttering against her cheeks, her hair an inky pool against the pale pillows.

Macella hated to move, but her hips wouldn't thank her tomorrow if she stayed in that position much longer. Carefully, she slipped off of Aithan and into the space on his other side. Aithan smiled at her but didn't open his eyes.

How do you feel? he asked in her mind.

I feel fucking incredible, she thought back immediately. *And you?*

I feel pretty fucking incredible myself. Aithan's mental voice was relaxed, content.

Macella loved the way it sounded. She would bet that his voice did not sound the same in anybody else's mind. That voice was a piece of Aithan he shared only with her. These little moments were theirs.

Macella closed her eyes, enjoying the pleasant heaviness in her limbs. She must have dozed off, because she awoke to a gentle warmth between her thighs. She opened her eyes to see Aithan carefully toweling her off. His orange eyes twinkled in the candlelight. Macella felt herself growing warm again, arousal blossoming deep in her belly.

"Let me," Zahra said, her throaty voice almost a purr. She slipped between Aithan and Macella, burying her face between Macella's legs.

Macella arched her back, crying out in pleasure and surprise. Her pussy throbbed, tender and swollen from her earlier orgasm. Zahra ran her tongue over its pulsing wetness, the pressure just light enough to tease Macella into an aching state of need.

Aithan stood behind Zahra, at the bed's edge. Macella watched his cock rise as he watched them, his eyes aflame with desire. Macella clenched at the pillow above her head with one hand, her other hand buried in Zahra's heavy tresses.

Be careful, she thought at Aithan. *She's quite small.*

Aithan smiled a half-smile and climbed deftly onto the bed behind Zahra. Effortlessly, he lifted her hips, positioning her on her knees. Zahra moaned her assent, the hum sending a jolt of pleasure through Macella's gut.

Slowly, Aithan eased his cock inside the sheriff, his eyes locked on Macella's. Macella felt Zahra's sharp intake of breath, the stutter in the rhythm of her tongue. Never looking away from Macella, Aithan eased back and forth, gradually deepening each thrust.

"Fuck me! Gods! Holy fuck!" Zahra cried out, giving up on her efforts to pleasure Macella and throwing her head back in ecstasy.

Macella slipped a hand between her legs, sliding two fingers into her own wetness, and massaging her clit with the heel of her palm. She kept her eyes on Aithan's, watching him watch her as the buzzing in her belly began to grow and spread.

"Oh gods, I'm going to cum!" Zahra moaned, clutching at Macella's thighs as her small body convulsed. Aithan thrusted faster, but Macella could see that he wasn't thrusting deeply, sparing the small sheriff the bulk of his girth.

Macella could almost feel the exquisite torture the Aegis must have been experiencing, her own need amplified by the want reflected in his eyes, the sheriff's gasps of pleasure. She moved her fingers in a firm circle, rocking her hips until she felt her vagina clenching hard around her fingers.

When Zahra's orgasm subsided, Aithan lay down beside Macella, sighing deeply and closing his eyes. He took Macella's hand in his, then brought it to his lips. Without opening his eyes, he slid his tongue over Macella's first two fingers, humming contentedly.

Zahra Shelby collapsed on her other side, breathing heavily. After a few moments, she flopped from her side onto her back, dramatically draping an arm across her face and sighing loudly.

"Today I learned that Aegises form romantic attachments, and they fuck," Zahra announced.

Macella burst into a fit of giggles. Zahra laughed her throaty laugh, and Aithan's low chuckle rumbled along. Macella felt very good about everything that had happened this night.

She must have fallen asleep again. Macella wasn't sure how much time had passed, but the sky beyond the windows indicated it was still far from dawn. Nevertheless, her bladder insisted that she get up.

Macella reluctantly climbed out of the bed, making her way to one of the dressing chambers to relieve and freshen herself after their exertions. When she returned to the bed chamber, she found Zahra slipping into her robe.

"There you are, Scribe," the sheriff smiled. "I must bid you goodnight. While I am sure the staff will be whispering about the vigorous nighttime activities between the Aegis and his companion, they will have no cause to suspect that you had any further company."

She grinned impishly at Macella and at Aithan, who was smiling with his eyes still closed. "I can move through this place without being seen. As I mentioned earlier, I know how to be discreet."

With a wink and an undeniably sexy smile, Zahra blew Macella a kiss and silently slipped from the room. Macella shook her head, laughing softly to herself. She crossed to the bed and sat beside the Aegis. Still smiling to herself, she used the damp towel she'd brought from the dressing room to clean Aithan up a bit.

(21) He laughed softly. "It is kind that when you wring every ounce of pleasure from my body, rendering me unable to move, you at least are kind enough not to leave me in a mess."

Macella laughed too. "You are a fraud and a cad, Aithan of Auburndale. You're just reveling in the moment. I have no doubt you are perfectly capable of motion. You could likely bed me again already if you had a mind to."

With his uncanny swiftness, Aithan sat up and whisked Macella into his arms. Quickly but carefully, he laid her down and rolled on top of her. Grabbing both of her wrists with one hand, he held her arms above her head. He kissed her deeply, slipping his other hand beneath her to grip her ass.

He pulled out of the kiss, leaving Macella gasping. Aithan ran his lips along her jawline, stopping just below her ear.

"Was that an invitation?" he whispered.

Macella felt heat flare, her pussy throbbing its hearty assent. She parted her legs as Aithan kissed her again.

He moved slowly, exploring her mouth, her throat and neck, her mouth again. While his mouth was patient, his cock was urgent. He thrust into Macella, deep and hard, and she cried out, the sound muffled in his kiss.

The pleasure was exquisitely painful. Aithan let himself release all he had been holding back with Zahra Shelby. The Aegis fucked her hard, each thrust pressing her into the soft bedding, pushing her closer to an inevitable climax. She was at his mercy, her arms secured above her head, his hand clutching her ass, holding her exactly where he wanted her.

She'd never felt him this intense, this deep. Filling her, stretching her, unrelenting. She could taste herself in his mouth, could taste Zahra Shelby, could taste his unique essence.

His fingernails dug into the flesh of her ass, another deliciously painful sensation. He seemed desperate for her, insatiable. Her own desire flared to match his. It was as if she had not had him in ages, the craving was all-consuming.

Macella surrendered to all of it, letting him take her as he wanted, letting the pressure build until she came hard, swearing and crying at the sheer magnitude of the sensations coursing through her body.

Aithan was not far behind her, speaking low in her ear and clutching her to him tightly as he climaxed. He rested with his face in the hollow of her neck for several long minutes, breathing heavily. Finally, he lifted himself onto his forearms and looked down at Macella.

"Are you okay?" he asked, a worried crease between his brows. "I usually try to be gentler. I try not to forget that your body is not as mine is. It is difficult not to lose myself with you."

Macella put on an expression of mock hurt. "I *was* okay, but now I learn that you've been holding out on me! For shame, Aithan of Auburndale!"

Aithan groaned, rolling off of her. "You are impossible, Macella."

"That I am," she agreed, yawning. "But you like a challenge."

"That I do," Aithan replied softly.

As Macella drifted into sleep, she felt Aithan carefully toweling her off again, wiping away the remnants of their lovemaking.

CHAPTER ELEVEN

I n the morning, Macella was unsurprised to find herself alone in the gigantic
bed. She'd known that Aithan would be extra vigilant in his efforts to locate
the fissure here after what had happened in Hurstbourne. He could not allow
anyone else to get hurt.

Macella touched her star charm, offering up a silent prayer for the dead child
and for Lilliana DuPree. She hoped they were together somewhere, and that
they were happy.

Macella thought about her own family—her parents and siblings and nib-
lings. Already, they were fading in her mind. That old life seemed imagined,
pantomimed. She had not truly begun to live until she'd left that charade
behind.

Macella stretched, feeling a delicious soreness between her legs. Gingerly,
she climbed out of bed and made her way to the dressing room, where she
found a basin of warm water awaiting her. Likewise, she found freshly laundered
clothes—her own supplemented with a few additional pieces, new and just her
size.

Rich people continued to amaze Macella. She found breakfast waiting in
their little sitting room: cheese, hardboiled eggs, soft warm bread, and an as-

sortment of fruit. She wondered how they'd managed to know exactly when she would awake so that the water and bread would still be warm when she reached them.

After she'd eaten her fill, the gaunt servant she had first seen the previous night appeared to clear away the table.

"Good morning, Taryn," Macella greeted him.

Taryn smiled thinly. "Good morning, miss. My lady wishes me to inform you that anything you wish is available upon request. We are all at your disposal."

"Thank you," Macella smiled. "I think I am just going to walk to the post."

Taryn looked a little scandalized. "We would happily send someone on your behalf. To the post or anywhere else for that matter. There is no need for you to take the trouble."

"It's no trouble," Macella assured him, moving toward the door. "I want the exercise and the opportunity to look about a bit more. I rather enjoy the novelty and beauty of new places."

"As you wish, miss." Taryn bowed. "Enjoy your sightseeing. My lady has requested that you and the Aegis join her for luncheon at half past."

Macella nodded and slipped from the room before she could do anything to further appall the staff. She wandered through endless corridors, occasionally running into someone who would point her in the right direction again.

Finally, she made her way out of the gate and set off on the path back into the village. The town was bustling with morning business. Macella was grateful that Shelby Park was larger than Hurstbourne. It was obvious that people here were more accustomed to strangers passing through; they did not gawk or attempt to force her into awkward conversation.

Macella's ruminations on her family had left her feeling strangely adrift. She knew that she had not been happy, had not been her true self back home. And yet, she wasn't allowing herself to fully embrace her new life. She was holding back from Aithan out of fear and doubt.

Macella didn't want to think on that more right now. Instead, she would remember where she'd come from and show her gratitude for what she'd learned on the path to the present moment. After scribbling a short note that she was well and had found work, Macella folded a few bank notes into the letter and addressed it to her family in Shively.

Feeling a bit better, Macella set off to explore the town. She hadn't seen much of it the previous day, aside from The Summit. The post was near the town's center, among a number of little shops. Macella enjoyed looking at the wares but didn't buy anything. She hadn't needed much since she'd begun traveling with the Aegis and what she did need had been acquired along the way in bits and pieces.

Macella wondered if she could draw portraits or teach art classes while she was here. Thanks to the money she had earned from her writing, she didn't particularly need to bother. She could focus on her next tale instead. The thought sent a thrill through her entire body. She couldn't believe she could earn real coin doing something she loved so much.

Macella's aimless wanderings soon led her to a bustling pier off of a small lake. She watched the fisherfolk pulling in nets and listened to the cries of birds and a few scattered children. She watched a plump, pretty woman in a purple cloak, with long red hair secured in a thick braid, haggling with a fishmonger. The small group of children seemed to be playing a game of hide-and-seek, one of them sitting near the lake with his eyes covered as the others ran away to conceal themselves. Pulling out her sketchbook, she found a spot to sit down and amuse herself by drawing the landscape.

(22) She was so immersed in her work that it took a few moments for her to recognize that the cries of workers and children had turned to screams.

Macella jumped to her feet. She saw people running away from the water's edge but could not distinguish the cause of their fear. Weaving through the bodies, she drew closer to the lake.

A child lay still near the water's edge. For a moment, the world grew hazy. Macella's vision blurred, and she was momentarily back in Lilliana DuPree's garden. This could not be happening again.

Then the child opened its mouth and screamed. Macella remembered to breathe. Her vision cleared and she saw that the child was very much alive, though paralyzed with fear.

Where is master? Master is calling. Must come. Must find master.

The voice in Macella's mind was unfamiliar. It was guttural—inhuman even. It made the hairs on Macella's arms stand up. She looked around frantically, but nobody was near enough to her to have spoken, and none of the other bystanders looked to have heard anything odd. The voice had truly been in her mind.

Must find master calling must find. Eat first? Maybe little eat. Just little.

Macella had only hesitated a few moments, but no one else had approached the child while she looked for the source of the voice. Collecting herself again, Macella remembered priorities. She ran toward the screaming child.

She fell to her knees, scanning the child for injuries. It immediately clung to her, terrified and crying. Macella could not make sense of what it was saying, but she followed its pointing hand.

At first, Macella could not process what she'd seen. Something had briefly emerged from the water's surface. Something person-sized but not human.

"Run home," Macella commanded, detaching the child from her, and standing it on its feet. "Run home now!"

The child turned and ran, apparently only needing a little push to snap out of its terror. Macella turned back to the water in time to wish she had taken the opportunity to run away herself.

Little food run away. No little food. Sad sad sad. Maybe big eat?

The creature climbing out of the water had a vaguely humanoid shape and characteristics, but only in the loosest sense. Its skin was slimy and greenish, its hands and feet webbed. It looked at Macella hungrily.

"I am not food!" Macella shouted, surprising herself and the creature.

It tilted its head, taking a few more hesitant steps toward her and onto land. Macella heard the other bystanders fleeing and screaming, but she didn't dare turn her head.

This not food? How not food? Master? No no no. Not master. Not calling. Maybe food. Maybe trick.

Now Macella was truly convinced that she was hearing the creature's thoughts. She did not know why or how, but she knew that it was hungry. She could feel the hunger in its mind.

"I am not food," Macella repeated slowly moving from her knees into a crouch. She took a wary step backward. The creature mirrored her movement, keeping the distance between them too close for comfort.

It trick. It food. So many food here. This good food place. The thing bared its teeth. They were brown, numerous, and sharp.

Macella!

"Macella, down!"

Two voices rang out: one in her mind and another out loud. Without a moment's hesitation, Macella dropped to the ground. An arrow whizzed over her head and lodged in the monster's chest with a wet *thunk*.

The monster screamed angrily, turning its attention from Macella to the archer. Macella looked as well, scrambling clumsily away from the distracted beast.

Sheriff Shelby was notching another arrow, preparing to shoot the monster again. Aithan of Auburndale was emerging from the nearby forest, running faster than Macella had ever seen anyone move. He spotted her, and she saw a look of relief pass over his face before his eyes found the creature.

There were now two arrows in the creature's chest; a third pierced its eye as Macella watched. The beast roared and charged toward the sheriff. It was awkward and clumsy on land, but it was still fast. Macella heard the wordless rage in its mind, the hunger barely contained.

To Macella's surprise, Sheriff Zahra Shelby didn't try to run. Instead, she pulled a large knife from her belt and widened her stance.

Just before the creature reached Zahra, the Aegis collided with it, knocking it off course. With surprising reflexes, the creature recovered, wrapping its slimy arms around the Aegis. For a moment, the two wrestled, the monster trying to lift the Aegis off his feet. Aithan was much larger than the beast, but Macella could see from Aithan's movements that the monster was stronger than it looked.

Aithan crouched, appearing to resist the creature's efforts to lift him. The creature strained, determined to pull him up and into a dangerous embrace. It snapped its teeth in frustration.

Suddenly, Aithan burst upward. The unexpected move threw the monster off balance, the force of its own efforts to pull the Aegis adding momentum. They fell to the ground, Aithan on top of the beast.

Macella sensed pain and fear coming from the creature now. She saw that there was a deep impression in the thing's head—almost a bowl. She saw water spill from the indention and sensed more pain.

Aithan pinned the creature with a knee on its chest. He grabbed the arrow in the creature's eye and yanked it free. Then he plunged it through the thing's skull.

Now Macella heard only silence in its mind. It did not move again.

Aithan stood, wiping slime from his face and skin. As Macella watched, the creature dissolved into oozing black smoke. The Aegis produced a glass vial, collecting the inky substance.

Macella made her way to Aithan and Zahra. She saw a crowd of onlookers keeping a safe distance. She wondered if they were afraid that something else might emerge from the lake or if they were wary of the Aegis.

"What the fuck was that?" Zahra demanded. Her throaty voice was even huskier than usual.

"Kappa," Aithan answered, frowning. "Water demon."

"Why the fuck didn't it die when I shot it in the head?" Zahra sounded personally offended that the kappa had not died at her hand.

Macella almost laughed at the woman's incredulous facial expression.

"It was too strong. It needed to be out of the water first. It is nearly impossible to kill a kappa in the water."

Macella and Zahra both opened their mouths to protest, but Aithan held up a hand.

"The head," he went on. "When on land, the kappa stores water in the divot on its head. It helps them retain their strength. I knocked it to the ground to spill the water and weaken it."

Macella remembered how she'd sensed pain and fear only after the creature had fallen over. Why had she been able to sense that? She needed to tell Aithan.

"Is your head just full of tidbits of information about all manner of monsters?" Zahra asked incredulously. "You just see these things and know how to defeat them?"

"That is what I am trained to do," Aithan replied simply. "Identify and assess the threat. If you had not already engaged it in battle, we might've been able to trick it into spilling its water. They are very polite, so sometimes you can get them to bow—"

"Enough." Zahra threw her hands up. "Get them out of water, empty their strange head bowls, and kill them like anything else. I don't need to know everything down to their favorite foods."

Aithan flashed a brief, wry smile. "They cannot resist cucumbers. Next to human blood, cucumbers are their favorite."

"Where the fuck did it come from?" Zahra asked. She retrieved her arrows from where they had fallen to the ground when the creature dissolved.

Aithan grunted, looking out over the lake. "I was coming this way because I sensed a rift. It must have come through it."

"Have you closed the rift?" Zahra looked around furtively, as if expecting to see more monsters appearing.

Aithan grunted again. "There is no rift."

Macella and Zahra looked at each other. Zahra raised an eyebrow. Macella shrugged.

"Is this a riddle?" Zahra huffed, her hands on her narrow hips.

The Aegis sighed. "Yes, but I don't have the answer. I sensed a rift. I started toward it, and then it was gone. Just gone. I could feel it no longer. I had a similar experience yesterday—the rift I had so clearly sensed on our journey here faded from my senses. I was going to discuss it with you last night, but I became...distracted."

Aithan glanced at both women, before turning his eyes back to the lake. For a brief moment, all three remembered how they had spent their night. Macella's heart hammered wildly, but no longer from fright. Zahra's face remained serious, but her eyes danced with mischief. Macella remembered those eyes looking up at her with that same expression, her mouth busy with other tasks. They had distracted themselves quite thoroughly indeed. Aithan cleared his throat.

"I sensed a rift not long ago somewhere in this vicinity," he went on, breaking the momentary steamy silence. "As I moved this way, however, it disappeared. I followed the screams to this location, where I find there was a demon, but no rift. Something is amiss."

Macella and Zahra looked at each other again. Macella saw her own worry reflected in the sheriff's wide eyes. Macella remembered another odd occurrence from their time in Hurstbourne. And then there was the voice in her head.

"Remember how the lamia behaved erratically," she said slowly, trying to find the connecting pieces in this strange puzzle. "I felt I could almost hear its inner turmoil—as if it had conflicting goals, incongruous demands. And, when the kappa emerged from the water, I heard—"

"Looks like I was right to be concerned," boomed an unpleasantly loud voice.

Macella whipped around to see Lailoken approaching, his face red.

"Not fucking now," Zahra groaned, her expression murderous.

The big man was making his way through the lingering crowd, pushing his way to the front. Macella noticed the pretty redheaded haggler from earlier nearly fall over as Lailoken elbowed past her. The woman caught herself, her braid swinging indignantly. She looked as if she would reproach Lailoken, but then Macella saw her stoop and pick something from the ground.

Zahra swore under her breath again, drawing Macella's attention. She followed Zahra's gaze and noticed that the onlookers seemed to be inching nearer, apparently emboldened by Lailoken's example. When Aithan looked their way, however, nobody moved any closer to their little huddle.

Macella saw that the redheaded woman seemed to have disappeared. She wished Lailoken would follow the woman's lead. Instead, he stopped a few paces away, eyeing the Aegis speculatively. Aithan did not acknowledge him, still gazing out over the water, lost in thought. Lailoken moved around the group, placing himself in Aithan's line of sight.

"You must be the Aegis," he boomed. "I'm glad you're here. I told the sheriff I'd be happy to help out."

Face perfectly blank, Aithan slowly looked Lailoken over. He said nothing.

Lailoken appeared a little unsure but barreled on. "Of course, our sheriff has many skills, but she can't help her sex and size. She's what she is and you're what you are. I'm somewhere between—a combination of the brains and the brawn. I have some thoughts on how to get this situation under control."

Aithan stared at Lailoken silently. The man shifted uncomfortably under the Aegis's cold stare. The moment stretched, nobody daring to speak.

(23) Then the Aegis's body went rigid, his orange eyes darkening. The pupils disappeared and the irises expanded, until his eyes were completely crimson.

A few people gasped or cried out. Macella knew what was happening, but she was the only one who did. Most people had very little interaction with Aegises. She could see how terrifying it was from a layperson's perspective.

Lailoken let out a very unseemly squeak and scuttled backward, almost falling over. Sheriff Shelby had repositioned her bow and notched an arrow before Lailoken had even completed his embarrassing reaction. She scanned the area for threats.

"What's happening?" she hissed, her voice low and even.

Macella stepped in front of Aithan, looking into his sightless red eyes intently. His eyes met hers, seeing her and simultaneously looking far beyond her. Macella concentrated.

She felt it then. Something hot and searing—a ripping sensation. She gasped.

Aithan's attention snapped to her then, his eyes clearing. He furrowed his brow, tilting his head and gazing into her eyes.

"What the fuck is going on?" Zahra repeated.

Aithan tore his attention from Macella. "We have got to move. There's another."

Without any further explanation, Aithan took off at a full sprint. Lailoken, too slow to get out of his path, truly fell over this time, as the Aegis brushed past him without slowing. Macella saw the man's fear, his wide-eyed surprise, and then his fury.

"Let's go," Zahra commanded, not even sparing Lailoken a look.

Macella followed the sheriff, who moved quickly through the parted crowd to a beautiful gray horse grazing nearby.

Zahra mounted the horse fluidly, reaching back to pull Macella onto the animal behind her. They took off at a gallop, following the Aegis's now-distant form. People scattered as they made their way closer to the center of town.

Wwwwhhhhooooooooo bbbbeeeeeccckkkkonnnsss uuuussssssss? Wwwhhhhoooooooo ccccoooooommmmmmmaaaannnnnndddssssss oooooouuuuuuurrrrrrr ssssssseeeeeerrrrrvvviiiicccccceeee?

Macella felt the hissing voice sliding icily down her spine. The Aegis was slowing, drawing his sword. Zahra reined in the horse, dismounting in another fluid movement. Macella followed less gracefully, scanning the area for the source of the cold hiss in her mind.

Then the screams began.

Immediately, the Aegis and sheriff were on the move. People scattered in every direction. Overturned carts and abandoned parcels littered the ground.

Macella began redirecting the crowd, physically pushing people away from the chilling voice. It wasn't hard to get the townsfolk moving in the right direction. When people were frightened, they wanted to be told what to do.

Macella heard a snarl that sounded eerily like the voice in her mind. She spun around to see a creature unlike any she'd ever imagined.

It stood near the center of the almost empty square, assessing the threats around it. On one side, Aithan of Auburndale's sword pulsed crimson light in time with his blazing eyes. On the other, Sheriff Zahra Shelby held an arrow at the ready, her mismatched eyes narrowed in concentration.

The creature itself was the size and shape of a wolf, hairless, and covered in sharp quills as long as Macella's forearm. Its terrifying teeth protruded in a grotesque underbite. Claws more like talons pawed at the ground.

Aaaaaaeeeeeeeeeegggiiissssssss. Eeeeennnnnnneeeeeeeemmmmmmmyyyyyyyyyy. Macella heard the creature recognize Aithan. The Aegis tensed, ready for an attack.

The monster shot forward, rolling itself into a tight ball. It bore down on the Aegis, a mass of deadly-looking quills. Macella stifled a scream.

Zahra loosed an arrow, which lodged itself among the monster's quills without slowing it in the least. Aithan dodged the beast at the last moment, leaping out of the way faster than the monster could change course.

The thing stopped, stood on all fours again, searching for the Aegis. Aithan was crouched low to the ground, his sword at the ready, his fiery eyes scanning his opponent.

Macella realized what the Aegis had to do, what he'd already been planning to do. Her heart leapt into her throat. Those quills could kill him, Macella knew.

This time when Aithan evaded the creature's charge, he immediately pivoted back toward it, getting low. The beast unrolled, standing on its feet. It turned in a circle, looking for the Aegis.

Aithan of Auburndale dove forward, turning in midair to land on his back. He slid several paces, skidding to a halt right beneath the beast's chest. The Aegis thrust his sword up and through the monster's exposed throat. Black blood poured from the wound, showering Aithan with muck.

The creature hissed loudly, the sound echoing inside Macella's head. Aithan slung it to one side, yanking his sword free as he climbed to his feet. The monster dissolved into the now-familiar oozing smoke. Aithan crouched to collect it, grunting thoughtfully as he did so.

"What the fuck is going on?" Zahra threw up her hands in exasperation.

"I do not know," Aithan said slowly. "A kappa and a brucha both appear after I sense a rift appear and disappear. They are both baser demons. Unintelligent. They do as they're commanded. They would never cross the barrier on their own."

Aithan turned to look at Zahra and Macella. His eyes had returned to orange, the whites and pupils back to normal. He turned his gaze on Macella.

"Something strange is happening," Aithan said. "And you can sense it as well, can you not, Macella?"

"Yes," Macella said quietly.

Zahra looked between them curiously, but Macella only looked at Aithan.

Don't say anything more right now. We do not know who to trust. Aithan's mental voice was calm, but Macella knew his mind must be racing.

"Okay." Aithan exhaled and turned to the sheriff. "You should have everyone take shelter until we resolve this. Nobody on the streets unless they wish to be considered a threat. They should not open their doors for any reason until we give the signal. All three of us. If they do not see all of us in the square ringing the bell, they stay inside. Am I clear?"

The sheriff tilted her head, shrewdly examining the Aegis. Finally, she sighed. "Yeah, okay. I'll send word around. Why don't you two head back to The Summit and get cleaned up? I'll join you for lunch, and you can tell me what the fuck is going on and what we're going to do about it."

Sheriff Shelby walked away, yelling at stragglers as she made her way to her horse. The Aegis and the wanderer watched her take off at a trot. Then Aithan took Macella's hand, and they made their way to The Summit together.

CHAPTER TWELVE

Macella used the walk to tell Aithan about how she'd heard thoughts from the kappa and the brucha, and even how she had sensed the rift opening when she'd looked into the Aegis's crimson eyes. Aithan listened without comment, his eyes scanning the horizon. When she finished, he looked at her carefully.

"Has anything like this ever happened before?" the Aegis asked.

Macella started to shake her head, but then thought better of it. "Not quite, but almost. When we were in the lockup with Lilliana—with the lamia. I felt like something was wrong. I did not know what I was sensing. But it's why I knew it was Lilliana and why I was sure I could reason with her. The creature felt divided, of two minds."

Macella had not realized it then, but she must have been sensing the lamia's thoughts without knowing it. How had she done that? Before Aithan of Auburndale, she'd never heard any thoughts aside from her own.

"But, this time, you heard much more clearly?" Aithan prompted. "You heard actual words, felt intent and emotion?"

Macella nodded. "It was as clear as if the beasts had spoken. Aithan, what is happening to me?"

Aithan stopped walking, turning to fully face Macella. She gazed at him, her eyes roaming the now-familiar features: silver hair against golden skin, high cheekbones, chiseled jaw. His orange eyes were always softer when he looked at her. Macella's heart lurched.

"I do not know," Aithan admitted. "I have never known a human to have such abilities—Aegises and master sorcerers can develop some such skills, but only after undergoing certain transformations. And, usually, only after years of training and practice."

Aithan studied her carefully, his eyes searching for clues in her face. Macella had nothing further to reveal. She did not understand what was happening.

"I have known that you are unique since I met you," Aithan said finally. "I believe now that neither of us knows just how unique. Whatever is in you appears to be growing stronger."

Macella took a deep breath trying to calm her racing heart. "Is there something wrong with me?"

Aithan's expression grew pained. He took her face in his big, rough hands, running a calloused thumb across her cheek. Macella leaned into his touch.

"Absolutely not," the Aegis answered, his voice full of certainty and devotion. "You are perfect. Do not be afraid of your true self. Accept all of yourself, as you accept all of me."

Macella felt his words washing over her, his admiration seeping into her skin. She had never had anyone speak to her this way, to see her as Aithan did. A dull ache throbbed in her chest, making her eyes sting with tears.

"We will figure this out, Macella," Aithan assured her, pulling her close. He kissed the top of her head, inhaling deeply before whispering into her hair. "I know who you are. I love all of you."

Macella inhaled sharply. He had not said those words since Hurstbourne. She knew he had to feel her muscles tense, sense her tumultuous thoughts. Macella felt guilty for her muddled reaction. She wrapped her arms around Aithan's waist, burying her face in his broad chest and squeezing him tightly.

Aithan held her for several long minutes before reluctantly prying himself free. "I've gotten kappa slime and brucha blood on you now. We had better hurry and get cleaned up. We have a lot to discuss with the sheriff."

Once they'd cleaned up, the pair reconvened in their sitting room. A generous lunch had been laid out: fresh fish, dressed greens, an assortment of seasonal fruits and vegetables, warm bread, thick hot soup. Macella's entire family could've feasted on this one lunch for days.

Zahra Shelby joined them, looking exhausted and effortlessly beautiful. She dropped heavily onto a soft cushion, not bothering with manners and politeness. Macella was again surprised by how quickly she had grown to like the woman.

"Everyone is inside and knows not to come back out," Zahra announced. "Most folks saw or heard enough about the demons loose today that it didn't require much convincing on my part."

She huffed, snatching a hunk of warm bread from the table before flopping back against the cushion. "Nobody injured today aside from a few scrapes and bruises from running and falling. No other creatures spotted. I've got my people positioned around town, ready to sound the alarm at the first sign of danger."

Zahra frowned deeper, savagely ripping into the chunk of bread with her teeth. She chewed furiously, devouring it in only a few bites. "Lailoken and a group of other concerned citizens are also standing ready if their services are needed."

The sheriff leaned forward, grabbing an apple from the table this time. A lock of her dark hair had escaped her thick braid. It fell across her face, covering her brown eye. Her bright green eye narrowed at Aithan.

"Now what the fuck is going on, Aegis?" Zahra demanded.

Aithan took a long drink from his chalice. When he spoke, his voice was low. "Excuse your servants please, Sheriff."

"Taryn, we won't be needing further assistance," Zahra called without hesitation, not looking away from the Aegis. "Everyone in this area is needed in the kitchens. I've given Kateryna instructions for all of you to help prepare The

Summit to house the townspeople if necessary. Nobody is to return to this area until I personally request it."

"Yes, my lady," Taryn replied with a slight inclination of his head.

They sat silently, listening to the soft shuffle of retreating footsteps. Zahra chewed her apple slowly, staring at Aithan with owl-like eyes.

Aithan sighed. "Here is what I know. Rifts do not close of their own accord. It is up to Aegises to close them, lest they grow and release hell upon the kingdom."

Aithan shifted, leaning forward to rest his elbows on his knees. "The rift in this area is somehow fluid, opening just long enough for a demon to be summoned, then closing before I can reach it."

Zahra leaned forward now, her apple forgotten. "Fuck."

"Someone is manipulating the rift?" Macella knew the answer even as she asked. "And they are summoning demons."

Aithan nodded, looking at Zahra. "Only a sorcerer could do this. Do any such reside in Shelby Park? Are there any strangers among you?"

"Just you two," Zahra replied. "I know everyone else here. Nobody has ever shown any magical tendencies in Shelby Park."

"Hmmmm," Aithan grunted. "Perhaps someone has slipped among you unnoticed. Regardless, this is why I have asked you to restrict the townspeople's movement. When I sense a rift, anyone in the area will be a suspect. We will not be able to stop this until we find the sorcerer."

Zahra nodded. "Okay, Aegis. So, you sense a rift, we haul ass to the source, apprehend anyone in the area."

"Essentially, yes," Aithan agreed. "But we need to do this quickly. If the first two demons are any indication, the hellions will only get more dangerous."

"Well, let's get moving," Zahra said, jumping to her feet.

Aithan stood up as well. Macella made to follow, but Aithan put out a hand.

"Macella, you should stay here," he said firmly. "Someone who knows the truth has to be safe in case tragedy befalls the sheriff and me."

Macella wanted to argue, but she knew it would do no good. There was some truth to what the Aegis said. Besides, she was more hindrance than help in a battle.

"Fine," she acquiesced. "But do not leave me here worrying alone for too long. I will imagine all manner of horrors."

Aithan stepped close to her. He touched a finger to the star charm at her throat. "You needn't worry. You will know if something has happened to me. You will sense it."

The Aegis kissed her before she could say anything more. Then he was gone, the sheriff right behind him. Zahra winked at Macella before they disappeared beyond the door.

Macella quickly realized she did not mind being left alone. She was exhausted by the day's adventures and eager to have some quiet time to put her thoughts on paper. Apparently following Zahra's command, not a single servant ventured into her rooms all afternoon. Macella nibbled on the lunch leftovers, scribbled in her journal, and ultimately fell into a light doze.

Find Aegis. Kill Aegis. Return to master. Find Aegis. Kill Aegis. Return to master.

When Macella startled awake, the sun was lower in the sky. She figured perhaps five hours had passed since the sheriff and the Aegis had departed. She wondered if they'd discovered any further crossers.

(24) *Smell Aegis here. Is here now? Find Aegis. Kill Aegis. Return to master.*

Macella sat bolt upright, looking around the darkening chamber. There, by the door, was a vaguely humanoid shape. Macella put a hand on her thigh.

"He is not here," she called to the figure. It stood in a shadowy corner near the door. It was not moving, wasn't even quite visible, but Macella sensed it there.

It not Aegis. It not master. It food?

Macella sighed in exasperation. "Gods, not again! I am not food. The Aegis is not here. Return to your master."

The creature stepped forward into the dim light. Macella saw that it was another of the slimy green-gray water demons—kappas, Aithan had called them. Macella stood, trying to glimpse the top of the thing's head.

It talk. It lie. It trick.

Macella thought fast. She bowed deeply. "My apologies. You do not trust me because I have not formally introduced myself. I am Macella of Shively."

Macella held her breath. She could feel the creature's mind buzzing with confusion. Finally, it bowed in return. Macella saw the indention on its head and waited for the water to spill over. Stealthily, she hitched her skirt a bit higher, sliding her hand toward the sheath on her thigh.

A ray of dwindling sunlight fell on the monster's head and Macella let her skirt fall. There was something on its head—some sort of top. The water did not spill over. Perhaps its master had learned from the previous encounter and provided additional protection.

Not Aegis. Not master. Not food?

Macella's mind spun for a backup plan. "Not food. I am the Aegis's lover."

Macella sensed the creature's confusion again. If she didn't give it a reason not to eat her, it would likely decide that she was a meal after all. Perhaps she could save herself and help the Aegis's mission as well.

"You should take me to your master," Macella told the kappa. "They will want to use me to get to the Aegis. Your master will be very pleased that you caught me."

Is trick? Master pleased? Tricky food maybe.

"Smell me!" Macella blurted desperately. "Smell me. You know that I am not the Aegis, but I have his scent on me. Your master will want me."

The slimy beast came forward awkwardly on its webbed feet. Macella stood extremely still. It stepped close to her, leaning in, and sniffing loudly. Macella tried to ignore the closeness of its jagged teeth.

It Aegis smell. It no trick.

"Follow," the kappa croaked, its voice so like the one in Macella's mind.

Macella let the creature lead her from the castle, slipping unseen through the corridors and out of an unguarded gate. Soon, she was being guided downhill through the trees of the valley beyond The Summit's walls.

Macella listened carefully to the kappa's mind, watchful for any sign it would turn on her before she could turn on it. She wanted the beast to lead her to its master. When she'd learned the sorcerer's location, she would kill the kappa and return to The Summit with the information.

It was very nearly dark when the creature slowed. Ahead, Macella could make out a small structure. The surrounding trees blocked the sky, making it harder to determine how late it actually was. She hoped she could make her way back to The Summit before night fell completely. She did not wish to navigate these woods and their inhabitants under the cover of night.

Master away. Take it inside. Tie it inside.

Macella stepped into the little cabin behind the kappa, reaching beneath her skirt as she closed the door behind them. It was more of a shack: small, consisting of a single room containing a cot, a messily strewn table, and a single chair. A door at the rear of the room led to what Macella assumed was a closet or privy.

The kappa placed the chair in front of Macella, gesturing at it with a webbed hand. "Sit."

Macella moved as if to take a seat but stumbled as she did so. As she recovered her balance, something fell out of her hand, tumbling to the ground at the kappa's feet.

The kappa looked down and its eyes grew wide. It crouched quickly, reaching greedily for the cucumber Macella had dropped. Macella whispered a prayer of gratitude for the luck that had ensured the servants had not cleared away the remnants of lunch. When she'd grabbed the vegetable and slipped it into her pocket, she had not known quite how she would use it but was sure it would serve its purpose.

Macella swung her arm in a sharp arc, bringing the hilt of her dagger down on the creature's skull. There was a sharp crack as the cover on the kappa's head broke into pieces. Surprised, the beast fell forward, spilling water onto Macella's boots. Macella did not let herself hesitate. She plunged her dagger into the creature's skull, falling forward to throw her weight behind the strike.

Covered in slime for the second time in one day, Macella struggled to her feet. She gagged as she pulled her dagger free. She held her breath, forcing herself not to vomit. She did not have time to vomit. She glanced at the various odds and ends scattered around the cabin, looking for something to hide the evidence of the kappa's demise.

Boots crunched on the gravel outside. Then on the wooden porch.

As Macella dove for the other door, the kappa dissolved into black smoke. Macella closed the door of the small closet just as the shack's front door opened.

Macella's heart pounded, her breathing sounding loud in her own head. She tried to slow her breath, pressing herself as far back in the tiny closet as possible. The door was poorly made, rough as the rest of the shabby cabin. Macella could see through gaps in the old wood. Someone was moving through the room.

They wore a cloak, their features impossible to make out in the dim cabin. Macella saw them stop at the swirling smoke.

"What happened to you?" Macella heard a familiar voice ask. "You were supposed to be killing the Aegis, instead you are dead, and he is following me."

The person stood, removing their hood to take a better look around the room. They scanned the space quickly with their mismatched eyes.

It was Zahra Shelby.

CHAPTER THIRTEEN

M acella gasped involuntarily. The sheriff's head snapped in her direction. She tilted her head and smiled cruelly.

"Of course," Zahra said. "You brought me something valuable. I should have known immediately. My senses are dulled in this form."

Macella watched Zahra collect the inky smoke. They both knew that Zahra knew Macella was in the closet and that there was no way Macella could escape. Zahra took her time.

"This is good. This is very good," Zahra said to the closet. "He will track me here soon, and I will have something that he wants."

The sheriff stopped before the door. Macella could not believe she had been so wrong about the woman. She has been so sure that the sheriff was good and true. Macella braced herself. She did not want to fight Zahra, but she could not let the sheriff use her against Aithan. Macella gripped her dagger as Zahra flung the door open.

But it was not Zahra. Macella dropped her dagger in surprise. As Macella watched, Zahra stretched, her features distorting as if she were made of mere clay. When the figure had reshaped itself, Macella was looking at a person she had never encountered.

They were tall with coal black skin, almond-shaped eyes, and long silver locs, tipped in jade. An Aegis.

An Aegis and a shapeshifter.

Macella gasped, shrinking back into the closet further. The Aegis's emerald eyes settled into orange as they solidified into their true form. Macella racked her brain for her newly acquired knowledge about the different Aegis guilds.

Green was the Guild of Apophis. Aithan had not yet told her of Apophis Aegis's special gifts. Unfortunately, she'd now learned firsthand.

"I do not have time for politeness, I am afraid," the Aegis told her in a husky rasp.

They whispered quickly in a language Macella did not know. The Aegis inhaled sharply and Macella felt her own breath burst from her lungs involuntarily. When she tried to speak, she found that she could not.

"I cannot have you interfering," the Apophis Aegis explained, as they tied her wrists together. They bound her ankles as well, and Macella found herself remembering Hurstbourne again. She was hoping not to make a habit of being bound and gagged in every town they visited.

"I am sorry about this." The Apophis Aegis smiled apologetically. The smile didn't reach their orange eyes.

Macella shivered.

The Aegis secured Macella's bound wrists to a hook in the closet wall. As they stepped back and closed the door, Macella saw their eyes blazing emerald as their face shifted into her own.

Macella watched in horror as her doppelgänger positioned herself in the single chair, which she'd dragged to sit in front of the closet. The false Macella tied a gag around her own mouth. Then she sat in the chair, holding her hands behind her back. Macella saw the glint of a long and wicked looking sai blade in one of the double's hands.

Macella heard the slightest crunch of gravel, a rustling on the wood of the porch.

False Macella emitted a series of muffled screams. Moments later, Aithan of Auburndale slipped into the cabin, his sword drawn. He scanned the room quickly, then focused on the seemingly bound Macella.

He sniffed and Macella realized that he would fall for this trick. Her scent was in the room, was coming from roughly the area where the doppelgänger sat. She opened her mouth uselessly, trying to call to him.

Aithan pushed the door shut with his foot, sword at the ready, then crossed the room swiftly.

"How did you get here?" Aithan demanded, and Macella realized the Apophis Aegis had not gagged her as completely as they'd intended.

(25) *Shifter Aegis!* Macella mentally screamed just as Aithan reached the pretender.

Aithan's head snapped up and he pivoted as the false Macella burst forward, sai extended. Because he'd moved at that last moment, the blade pierced the spot where Aithan of Auburndale's chest and shoulder met, rather than his heart. As he turned, Macella saw that the sai had pierced so deeply that the tip had emerged from his broad back. Blood spread rapidly across his thin shirt.

Macella's entire body convulsed in terror. She threw her body against the door, yanking her arms painfully but managing just enough force to knock the door open.

Macella saw Aithan stagger backward, his hand wrapped around the sai's hilt. Aithan had thrown her dark double aside, but she was climbing to her feet, eyes glowing emerald.

"Aithan of Auburndale," the Apophis Aegis said, settling into their true form again. "Son of Lucifer."

"Kiho of Russell," Aithan grunted, slowly pulling the blade from his flesh, and casting it aside. "Child of Apophis."

"Is there any possibility of you moving on, ignoring what you have seen here?" Kiho asked, pulling another sai from their belt.

"What are you doing here, Kiho?" Aithan asked, his voice pained. "Why are you doing this?"

Kiho laughed humorlessly, circling to Aithan's right. Aithan mirrored their movement, sword raised. Kiho extended a hand, whispered an incantation, and the discarded sai flew into their hand. The weapon dripped with Aithan's blood.

Macella felt sheer terror course through her veins. She'd never seen Aithan in a battle where he might be evenly matched. This Aegis might know how to truly harm him.

"Why aren't you helping us?" Kiho countered. "There are enough of us to fight back. If we all fight."

Aithan huffed an exasperated sigh. "What am I supposed to be fighting, Kiho? We've been given a job, and we do it. That is our fight."

Kiho shook their head. "You know you are not satisfied with this life. Leashed by entitled human despots desperate for power. Without us, they would lose their tenuous hold on this kingdom."

Aithan grunted. "And then what? We subjugate them and take the power for ourselves?"

"Perhaps," Kiho retorted in their raspy growl. "It is no worse than what they've done to us. The way they let only the very strongest of us survive, but not *too many* of us. Enough to keep them in power, too few to pose a threat."

"I do not wish for power," Aithan answered, grimacing as he moved his shoulder to lift his sword higher. The stain of blood was spreading across his shirt, making the fabric look bunched and sticky. "I wish for peace."

Kiho laughed darkly again. "You settle for scraps when you could feast. The problem is that, eventually, they will take even that. You think the Crown is going to let you keep your pet?"

Macella saw Aithan's muscles tense. The Apophis Aegis smiled grimly, gesturing to Macella with one sai. Macella's closet was nearly centered between the two Aegises. She whipped her head from side to side, trying to take in all of the deadly scene.

"She is none of your concern," Aithan said, his voice hard. "Why are you summoning these demons? How are you doing it?"

"If we can close rifts, it is only logical that we should be able to open them." Kiho shrugged. "With the assistance of sorcery and brimstone, I can exploit our natural connection to the Otherworlds."

Kiho gestured at a vial of the inky black smoke on their belt. Aithan growled, his expression furious.

"You are using brimstone? You know how dangerous that is. Your arrogance will be your death," Aithan thundered, his crimson eyes flaring.

"You think they have more right to it?" Kiho shot back.

Aithan's sword began to glow to match his eyes. His voice was low. "Last chance to stand down."

Kiho laughed, igniting their twin sais with emerald flames.

It was terrible. The two Aegises collided in a squeal of metal, moving faster than any two humans ever could. Macella yanked frantically at her bindings, struggling to pull free. She didn't know how she might help, but she could not stand silent and watch as Aithan fought for his life.

"I don't want to kill you, Son of Lucifer," Kiho rasped. "There are too few of us for us to destroy one another. Join us or stand aside, but do not try and hinder us."

"You know I cannot do that," Aithan replied, genuine sadness lacing his voice.

"I know, brother," Kiho agreed calmly. Deftly, they took both sais in one hand and used the freed hand to uncork one of the vials on their hip.

The smoke oozed out thickly. Kiho was speaking, quick and low, the smoke rushing into them through every visible orifice: eyes, nose, ears, and mouth. The emerald of their eyes and blade flared so brightly that Macella had to look away.

Aithan attempted to approach Kiho, but the smoke was swirling now, encircling Kiho's entire form. It appeared Aithan couldn't penetrate the cyclone, could not even draw too near it.

Macella did not know exactly what Kiho was planning but she knew it would be bad. She stood on tiptoe, then jumped. She did it again and again, though her arms ached, until her bound wrists slid off the hook holding her to the wall. She collapsed to the floor, just as something terrible began to happen.

Macella, run. Aithan's voice in her mind was urgent. Macella couldn't see a safe way around the swirling smoke, but even if she had she could have, she would not leave him now. He was still bleeding profusely, his skin growing ashen with the blood loss. An untold danger was unfolding. She could not leave him here to die.

In that moment, Macella realized that she could not bear to lose him. More than anyone else she had ever known, she needed Aithan at her side, she wanted him with her always.

She would not flee. Macella loved him far too much to leave him. She loved him with everything in her being. She loved this Aegis, *her* Aegis, Aithan of Auburndale.

Aithan's head snapped in her direction. Though his eyes were still bright pools of blazing crimson, his smile was even brighter.

Finally, he thought at her.

Macella could feel the joy in his mind. Her heart seemed to expand in her chest for a moment.

Then she felt a ripping sensation, a strange tearing that was inside her, but not truly happening within her being. Aithan's smile faded as they both turned their attention back to Kiho.

The smoke had cleared. Kiho's entire body seemed to be emitting an emerald glow. Behind them, the air began to shimmer. The shimmer pulsed and Macella could feel the gathering warmth emanating from that spot. The temperature in the cabin rose.

"Kiho, stop this!" Aithan roared, raising his sword, and beginning to advance.

Kiho turned their head toward him slowly, their jade eyes unseeing but aware. "We will not be stopped."

Kiho's voice had changed. Or, more accurately, had multiplied. It was as if there were several voices coming out of the Apophis Aegis's mouth.

The air behind Kiho split open. Macella had never yet seen an actual rift. It was beautiful and terrible. It was as if the air were suddenly on fire and the fire was hungry. It spread.

Macella heard more voices then—voices in her mind. Immediately, she knew she was hearing the monsters responding to Kiho's summons.

Aithan sprang forward suddenly, his blade arcing toward Kiho. Macella stifled a scream of alarm as the Aegis's sword stopped abruptly in the air in front of Kiho. The crimson of the blade met Kiho's emerald aura and could simply go no further.

Hungry. Master. Kill. Want. Eat. Freedom. Calling. Hungry. Hungry. Hungry.

Wwwhhhhhhooooooooo caaaallllllsssss ussssssssss?

The clamor of voices in Macella's head was becoming overwhelming. She wanted to cover her ears, but her bound hands wouldn't allow it. Not that the gesture would help. There was no way to muffle voices that existed inside your head.

Aithan's entire arm had reverberated with the force of his slash. Macella saw that the impact had been jarring enough to further increase the bleeding from the sai wound. She knew he could endure such punishment, but for how long?

"We are growing stronger," Kiho continued, their voice still multitudinous. "Thus far, I have only been able to summon lesser demons. But now, I can feel others awakening. Greater beings capable of greater things. Can you not hear them?"

Macella could hear them. Further, in the back of her mind, she could sense something stirring. Something dark and ancient.

"Kiho, stop!" Aithan roared. "This is folly! These creatures you summon cannot be controlled. If you wake them and release them, you'll doom us all!"

Kiho only smiled coldly, their emerald aura pulsating. Macella could hear more entities now. They were close.

Apparently, Aithan realized that reasoning with Kiho was futile. He pointed his glowing crimson sword at the rift. His eyes glowed scarlet as he began to whisper some incantation.

The edges of the fiery hole wavered, its spread slowing noticeably. Aithan grimaced in concentration. The rift stopped expanding. But it did not shrink.

"You are not strong enough, Aithan of Auburndale," Kiho taunted. "You cannot stop us. You cannot save them. You cannot even save her."

Kiho sneered in Macella's direction. Macella stared into their emerald eyes. An icy thrill ran up her spine. She sensed an all-encompassing need, a determined rage. Kiho would never stop. She could feel it.

Master calling. Hungry. Hungry. Kill. Eat.

Kkiiiilllllllllllll kkiiiiiiilllllllllll eaaaaaattttttttt

And further away, something stirred. Something that had been slumbering.

Macella saw Aithan sway a little. He was still concentrating on the rift, attempting to close it despite Kiho's taunts. It didn't budge.

Macella watched in horror as a creature began to emerge from the fissure. Sharp quills and snarling teeth. Another brucha.

The beast leapt free, charging toward Aithan, teeth bared. It began to fold as it ran, preparing to become a vicious ball of spikes as had the brucha in the town square.

Rather than letting it come to him, Aithan leapt at it. He beheaded it in one swift motion. His shirt was drenched in blood.

Macella saw a webbed hand reaching out of the rift. And another. While Aithan was distracted by the brucha, the rift began to expand again. Macella did not know what would come out if the hole grew large enough, but she didn't want to find out.

Meanwhile, Aithan was cutting down each creature that emerged. Macella knew he could not keep this up indefinitely. They had to close the fissure. They had to stop Kiho.

Do not be afraid of your true self. Accept all of yourself, as you accept all of me. That's what Aithan had said to her earlier when they'd discussed her strange new abilities. She had finally accepted him, accepted the truth of their love. Perhaps it was time for her to accept her own complexity.

Macella used her bound hands to pick up her dagger, then cut the ropes binding her feet. She didn't bother trying to free her wrists. She wouldn't need her hands.

Macella stood carefully, not wanting to draw the attention of the monsters emerging from the fiery tear. Instead, she walked toward Kiho.

"Macella, get back!" Aithan yelled.

By now, he was essentially one-handed, his injured shoulder not allowing for much arm movement. He drove his blade through a kappa's foot. When it leaned over to reach for the wound, Aithan slammed his elbow into its skull. The creature fell forward, spilling water on the dirty floor. Aithan freed his blade from the kappa's foot and drove it through the beast's back. Another brucha charged at him as he pulled his sword from the water demon's corpse.

Macella ignored him, walking until she was a few paces from Kiho. The Apophis Aegis turned their head to look at her, emerald eyes flickering in time with their aura. They grinned at Macella.

"And what will you do, human?" Kiho asked, voice laced with mockery. "What could you possibly do?"

Macella stared into their emerald eyes. She felt her own determination rising. This was why her Fate had led her to Aithan of Auburndale. She had work to do.

Stop. Macella pushed her own thoughts into Kiho's mind. She saw them recoil in shock and confusion.

Stop now! Macella commanded. Her head throbbed with the force of her effort to bend Kiho to her will.

Kiho's emerald aura dulled and flared suddenly. The fissure stopped spreading.

"What. Is. Happening?" Kiho growled, seemingly forcing the words through unwilling lips.

Macella did not reply. Her head felt like it might split in two. She could not keep this up for long.

Close the rift. Call off the demons. She could almost feel her own will spreading through Kiho's mind, trying to cloud their own intentions. The fissure shrunk slightly. Kiho's aura flared and dulled.

"No!" Kiho countered through gritted teeth. The fissure widened almost imperceptibly.

Macella could hear Aithan's battle with the demons continuing. Her star charm felt chilled against her throat. Neither she nor he could last much longer. Kiho was too strong. Hell itself was on their side, wanting to open into Kōsaten, wanting to consume the entire kingdom.

Macella could still hear the lesser demons clamoring from just beyond the rift, the others stirring in the distance. She had to do something more.

It trick. Master tricky. It trick to trap you. Eat master. Macella sent her frantic thoughts toward the demons, mimicking their own stunted speech.

The splitting of her awareness gave Kiho the upper hand again. Their emerald glow brightened. The fire in the air spread.

Macella trembled, sweat and tears running down her face. She pushed against Kiho's mind, but now there was more resistance. She was quickly losing ground. Her eyes watered from the pain in her head.

Suddenly, a brucha rolled toward them. Macella did not have the sense or energy to move out of the way. Luckily for her, the brucha was not aiming for her. It collided with Kiho's aura, bouncing back and shaking itself like a dog. It snarled at Kiho.

The brucha had not penetrated Kiho's protection, but it had distracted them. Macella felt confusion in their mind, felt them trying to refocus their summoning spell.

Tricky tricky food.

A kappa lunged toward Kiho. It, too, failed to pass Kiho's defenses, but they took a surprised step back, their emerald energy dulling perceptibly.

"Stop or you will die," Macella said aloud. Her mental energy was draining rapidly. She wiped tears from her face, not looking away from Kiho, and thus not noticing that her tears were bloody. She was using all she had left to push at Kiho's mind, trying to compel them to close the rift.

Macella could not break eye contact, but she no longer heard Aithan fighting demons. Instead, the remaining demons were closing in on Kiho. Shadowy hands reached from the fiery fissure.

Kiho stepped back again. "No!" they cried again, but now their voice was only theirs—no more otherworldly voices layered over their words.

Kiho stepped back again. Macella knew what she had to do.

Macella withdrew her mind from Kiho's, throwing all of her mental energy toward the minds of the monsters. *Kill them! Kill master!* She pushed her will into their minds, clouding their intentions with her own.

Kiho's aura brightened as she released her hold on their mind, but not for long. Their emerald aura touched the fissure, disappearing where the flames touched it.

Two bruchas and a kappa lunged at Kiho simultaneously. Kiho staggered backward, looking away from Macella and to the beasts. Before the Aegis could raise a weapon or resume their spell work, a shadowy hand seized the back of their cloak.

It was over in a moment. Kiho's eyes faded back to orange and their jade glow faded completely. They looked at Macella, hatred distorting their features.

"We will destroy you!" Kiho hissed.

Then the remaining demons charged, the shadowy hand yanked Kiho's cloak, and Kiho fell backward through the rift. The demons followed.

Aithan of Auburndale staggered to Macella's side, sword lifted in a trembling hand. The crimson glow of his eyes and blade flared. Macella watched as the fire caved in on itself before vanishing completely.

"Are you okay?" Aithan croaked.

Macella turned to him, saw his blood-soaked shirt, his ashen skin, his trembling arm. She wrapped her arms around him, ignoring the sticky blood. "I am fucking incredible."

"Good," Aithan replied. Then he collapsed.

Too weak to hold their combined weight, Macella crumpled to the ground with him. Using the last of her strength, she tore her underskirt and tied it as tightly as she could around his shoulder wound. Then she passed out with her head on his chest, the bloody tears from her face blending into his blood-soaked shirt.

Zahra Shelby insisted that Aithan and Macella stay at The Summit until they'd all made a full recovery. Lailoken had ignored the sheriff's instructions to stay inside and had formed a hunting party not long after Zahra returned to The Summit for her late lunch with Macella and the Aegis. Lailoken's people found the sheriff unconscious in the forest where Kiho had left her after ambushing her when she had wandered too far from Aithan during their hunt. The Apophis Aegis had taken Zahra's form before taking her place at Aithan's side. Eventually, the fake Zahra had slipped away, leaving an obvious trail for Aithan to follow.

It took a few hours more to find Macella and Aithan. Macella had been curled against the Aegis, fading in and out of consciousness, delirious from pain and worry. Somehow, they'd managed to pry a hysterical Macella away from Aithan and carried them both back to The Summit, going first to the town square to ring the all-clear bell.

(26) Macella refused to leave Aithan's side for the entire time he remained unconscious. She changed his bandages, carefully moistened his lips and tongue regularly, doggedly questioned the apothecary each time she visited, and watched Aithan intently for any sign of change. Nearly three full days passed. Macella lay in bed beside him, talking to him both aloud and in her mind. She told him stories about the places they had been and the things they had seen, weaving intricate fantasies about where they would go next. Aithan did not respond, but she knew he felt her with him.

Finally, she heard the familiar rumble of his voice. She had her head on his chest, dozing periodically and figuring out how to write her next story for the society papers. This one was not as straightforward as "The Aegis and the Lamia." She would have much to conceal.

"Good morning," Aithan said quietly, startling Macella out of her doze. "I had the most beautiful dreams."

Macella bolted upright, whipping her head around to look at him. His orange eyes were half open, a ghost of a smile on his lips.

Macella burst into tears.

Aithan held her silently while she sobbed into his chest. When she was able to pull herself together, she sat up again. She stared intently into his eyes.

"I love you, Aithan of Auburndale," Macella told him, with her mouth and her mind. She wanted him to feel the truth of her love, the surety.

The smile that spread across his face could have stopped the sun. Macella loved it. She loved him.

"And I love you, Macella of Shively," Aithan replied, running a gentle hand across her cheek. "Thank you for saving my life. Thank you for saving the kingdom."

"*We* saved the kingdom," Macella corrected him. "And, unfortunately, you can thank Lailoken for your life. He found us."

Aithan grimaced. "That is unfortunate indeed. Still, you deserve my gratitude. You saved us all."

Macella blushed, looking down at her hands. "I still do not understand how I did any of it. I could hear in Kiho's mind that a human compelling an Aegis was unthinkable. Impossible."

"But you did it," Aithan answered, lifting her chin with a gentle nudge. "You did the impossible. You embraced your gifts and did what could not be done. You are incredible."

Macella felt warmth spreading through her body. She smiled. "Well, you're welcome, I suppose."

Aithan pulled her down beside him, gathering her into his arms. He kissed the top of her head, burying his face in her hair.

"What happens now?" Macella asked quietly.

Aithan paused for a long moment. "I do not know. Trouble is coming. It will be bad. Our role in it will be precarious. It will not be easy."

They were both silent for a long moment. Macella listened to the rhythm of Aithan's breathing, her hand over his heart. His heartbeat was steady and strong.

"I realized something when we were in that cabin," Macella said slowly. "I realized that Fate led me to you because we were meant to be in this fight together. Our role in the coming conflict is just as destined as our love." Macella lifted her head to look at the Aegis. "It will not be easy, but we are capable of impossible things together."

Macella kissed Aithan softly, savoring the feel of his mouth against hers.

Pulling back, she whispered, "I will go with you, wherever Fate leads. Together, we shall do the impossible."

CHAPTER FOURTEEN

Aithan and Macella tarried several weeks in Shelby Park, safely ensconced at The Summit. Zahra made sure they were well taken care of, spoiling them to a degree neither of them was used to. Though Zahra pressed them to stay longer, they knew they had to move on. Whatever trouble was coming was well on its way; they needed to be on theirs if they were to have any chance at stopping it.

(27) "Where will you go?" Zahra asked, as they lay in bed on the night before their intended departure.

"We must discover how far this insurrection has spread," Aithan replied, sighing heavily. "There is only one place I can go to gather information such as this."

Her head on his chest, Macella felt Aithan heave another sigh. She'd known for weeks where they would travel next. She wasn't sure if Aithan had thought it at her or if she had sensed it some other way. Regardless, it was the only course of action.

"We will go to Smoketown," Aithan continued. "Then, I will cross the mountains and return to Duànzào. There, among my own kind, I will find the answers we seek."

"Perhaps you'll cross paths with my father on your journey," Zahra said. "He should be returning from court soon, traveling west as you journey east. Mayhap he'll have some bit of useful news from the Crown."

Aithan was silent for a moment. "I believe we will be giving the capital a wide berth. We are not yet prepared for the Crown to be made acquainted with the situation."

"Shit, of course," Zahra blurted in her quick way. "I, of course, won't speak of it, and none but we in this room know what truly happened that night. I vow it will remain so."

"We know," Macella assured her. "We trust you."

Aithan hummed his agreement. "If your father does have useful information, send word. We will check in with the post in each region."

"Of course, you will," Zahra said, her voice teasing. "The scribe has to quench the kingdom's thirst for her words! She must check with the post to peddle her wares and gather her riches!"

Zahra tickled the back of Macella's neck, sending a shiver down her spine. She let out a little squeak, making Aithan chuckle and Zahra cackle throatily.

"When do you next report to the Crown?" Zahra asked when they'd quieted. "Perhaps we shall meet again then, at court?"

"Not until the cold season, when hell slumbers," Aithan replied, his voice hardening slightly.

"It is a long journey to Smoketown," Zahra ventured. "You'll need to traverse nigh the entire length of the kingdom. Have you time enough to reach Duànzào and still return to court on schedule?"

"We will have time enough because we have no other choice," Aithan answered calmly.

"Then let my parting gift to you be a pair of fast horses," Zahra insisted, holding up her hands before either of the others could voice their protests. "It's already done. I chose them myself, and they're being readied for your journey even now."

Zahra sat up so that she could look at Macella and Aithan. Her mismatched eyes twinkled with mischief. "It's a selfish gift, really. I've named them Cinnamon and Jade. I thought that, thus christened, they might ensure you'll be unable to forget me."

Macella pulled Zahra down so that she could kiss the woman's bright brown eye, then her sparkling green one. "How could we possibly forget one such as you?"

Aithan reached a hand up to affectionately tug Zahra's braid. "You have been uncommonly kind. Aegises never forgets those who treat us well. You have my loyalty. Always."

"Always," Macella agreed.

Mere hours later, Zahra Shelby and a few servants bade them farewell as they mounted their new horses—already laden with ample supplies thanks to the sheriff's generosity. When she pulled Cinnamon's reins, turning the horse toward the rising sun, Macella wondered when they would see Zahra Shelby again. She hoped that, after they'd set the world right, she and Aithan might return to their wanderings, making The Summit a regular refuge.

(28) Aithan set a steady pace, allowing them both to get a feel for their mounts. The Aegis had immediately taken to Jade, a gorgeous black stallion whose coat glimmered iridescent green where it caught the sun. Aithan had helped Macella onto Cinnamon with a smirk, his mind radiating lasciviousness.

"What are you grinning about, Aegis?" Macella narrowed her eyes at Aithan as he adjusted her stirrups. "You are thinking something lewd. I can feel it."

Aithan smiled mischievously, sliding a hand up from the stirrup to caress her calf. "I was thinking that this particular steed seems a perfect fit for you. You will, ahem, *ride* it quite naturally."

Macella caught the implication in his mind. Cinnamon was a palomino: golden coat and white mane. Consequently, his coloring mirrored that of Aithan's own honey skin and silver hair.

Macella flushed and lifted an eyebrow. "Get on your horse, Aegis, or Cinnamon will be the only one of you getting ridden. We've got a great deal of land to traverse and no time to dally about."

"That is a truly cruel threat. And they say Aegises are heartless," Aithan replied, winking at her before swiftly mounting Jade.

Since then, they'd ridden mostly in companionable silence. The weather was at its hottest this time of year, so they rode late into the evenings and rose early to make progress before the sun reached its peak. During the day, they rested in taverns or inns if they were near a town, wherever they could find shade if not. Were he alone, the Aegis would've borne the heat and ridden all day, but Macella was grateful that he was thoughtful enough to spare her the types of exertions that Aegises could withstand.

Neither Macella nor Aithan had sensed any fissures in weeks. When Macella worried that the silence from hell was the calm before the storm, Aithan didn't disagree.

Instead, Aithan passed the time trying to test the limits of Macella's strange new abilities. They quickly learned that she, unlike Aithan, couldn't hear or direct the minds of ordinary humans. Without any hellspawn or other Aegises around, they couldn't fully explore her gift's obvious reliance on the Other-worlds.

Still, Aithan pushed her to try her powers on him. At first, Macella was reluctant. She didn't like attempting to read his thoughts without him intentionally sharing them, and she definitely didn't like exerting her will to compel him to do anything.

They'd decided to pass the day in a shady thicket of trees near a stream. Immediately, they'd stripped down to their undergarments and waded into the water to cool themselves. Now, Aithan and Macella lay side-by-side on a blanket in the grass, letting themselves dry slowly in the warmth of the afternoon air. It would be hours yet before the heat would break and they could be on their way.

"Macella, I am giving you my consent," Aithan insisted. "I trust you. You know that."

Macella tried to read the Aegis's thoughts. And immediately burst into a fit of blushing giggles.

Aithan smiled. "I suppose you heard that, then? It's true. All of this riding has further enhanced some of my favorite of your assets."

Aithan rolled onto his side and ran a hand along Macella's thigh. She shivered, hearing the lust in his mind. She wasn't completely sure if he was intentionally sending her his thoughts now or if she was detecting them of her own accord, but they were as clear as if he was speaking.

"You are going to ruin this entire experiment," Macella scolded him. "It cannot require much skill to detect the nature of your thoughts at present."

"Hmmm," Aithan murmured, sitting up. He shifted positions, leaning down to plant a kiss on Macella's thigh. "You might be right. How about we try something different? Compel me to stop."

Aithan trailed kisses up and down Macella's thigh, each pass of his lips moving closer inward. Macella shivered again. She had no desire to compel him to stop.

Aithan chuckled, apparently using his own telepathic skills. "It is a good test because we both know it's something I do not wish to do. Besides, the effect won't last long. You will release me to pursue my own wicked intentions."

Aithan resumed his kisses, pausing at the junction of her thighs. He inhaled deeply, then exhaled an appreciative hum. Macella gasped, her vagina throbbing in response.

"And since you don't want me to stop either, it should be an even greater challenge. Let us learn the true limits of your power." Aithan's low, velvety voice tugged at the throbbing between Macella's thighs.

"This is unfair," Macella growled. "But I pride myself on being strong-willed. These dirty tricks will not defeat me, you cheat."

Macella concentrated, determined to prove herself against the Aegis's little test. She pushed her thoughts into Aithan's mind. *Stop.*

"No," Aithan replied aloud. He pressed his face against her thighs, his mouth positioned exactly where he knew she wanted it.

Feather soft, he nuzzled against her mound. Macella's stomach clenched. She gasped and tried not to lift her hips. Determinedly, she reminded herself that the sooner she succeeded, the sooner the experiment would be over, and she could wrap her thighs around Aithan's head.

Macella pressed the force of her will hard into the Aegis's mind. *Stop!* she commanded.

Aithan stilled for a moment. A breath passed. Then Macella felt her awareness thrust away from him, her sense of his mind disappearing completely.

Before Macella could process what had happened, Aithan lifted his head and gave her a small smile. His orange eyes scrutinized her face.

"You did it," the Aegis said. "I felt the compulsion."

"What happened?" Macella panted. "It felt like my mind was bucked from a horse."

"I resisted," Aithan answered. "It is an instinctive response. I knew you would release me from your command, but still, my mind reacted on its own to defend itself."

Macella frowned. "Kiho tried to resist me as well, but they could not. Their attempts to push me out were so much weaker than what I just felt."

Aithan rested his chin lightly on one of Macella's thighs. "They could not resist you because they did not have the right gift. I am a Lucifer Aegis. My special abilities are similar to yours. They work defensively as well. We Aegises who can access the minds of others have to be able to protect our own."

Macella thought this over. "So, my abilities mimic yours, though yours work on humans as well, while mine do not. Do you think I can protect my mind as you do?"

"I believe you can learn to do so," Aithan said thoughtfully. Smiling, he added, "Would you mind if we saved that lesson for later? I was in the middle of something very important."

"This little test was your idea, Aegis," Macella retorted, rolling her eyes. "Now you want to move on? Mercurial."

(29) "Forgive me." Aithan's voice was apologetic, but his eyes were full of mirth. "Let me make it up to you."

Before Macella could respond, Aithan sat upright, grabbing her hips, and flipping her over in one swift motion. With Macella on her stomach, Aithan deftly loosed her underwear with one hand, tossing them aside. With his other hand, he palmed her ass, squeezing gently.

"Gods," Aithan sighed, kneading her with his strong hands. "You already had the most delectable ass I'd ever seen. And yet, somehow, all of this riding has only enhanced it. This just seems unfair. Excessive even."

Aithan leaned down and playfully bit Macella's butt, letting out a low growl. Macella giggled and squealed into the blanket. The Aegis massaged her deftly, moving his hands along the curve of her ass, his thumbs circling inward. Macella heard the wet kissing sound of her vagina's response to his attentions.

Aithan spread Macella's thighs and then she felt his breath against her skin, a moment before his tongue slid inside of her. Macella moaned, her voice muffled by the blanket. Aithan continued massaging her ass with his hands, holding her in place as his tongue massaged her pussy. He trailed his tongue in slow, lazy circles, exploring all of the sensitive flesh from her clit to her ass.

Macella moaned and gripped a handful of grass in one hand, a fistful of blanket in the other. Aithan's tongue did not relent, moving firmer and faster. Tremors spread from Macella's midsection, quaking outward through her entire body.

Aithan clutched her firmly as she came, his strong grip holding her bucking hips in place. Macella cried out, her voice breaking as the pleasure consumed her. It felt as if every part of her body was abuzz.

Macella arched her back as Aithan pushed her legs together and straddled the back of her thighs. She felt the hard press of his cock against her closed thighs, searching for her throbbing wetness. Macella tilted her hips back, and the Aegis slid into her, groaning at the tightness of the angle.

The friction and the depth of penetration sent a thousand new sensations through Macella's body. The buzzing sensation on her skin intensified, heat filling her belly. She thought she might explode into a million pieces.

Macella buried her face in the blanket, letting Aithan's rhythmic thrusts drive her into the soft ground. She arched her back more, reveling in the way the Aegis filled her, the way each movement reverberated throughout her entire being. She whimpered and moaned, letting the sounds of her pleasure echo through the peaceful woods.

Aithan lowered himself onto her, sliding his hands down her arms and finding her hands with his own. He intertwined their fingers, pressing his lips against the nape of her neck. Macella shuddered, loving the weight of him on top of her, the impossible closeness of their bodies. She buried her face in the blanket and grinded against him, desperately wanting more, wanting everything.

Macella felt the orgasm building, preparing to eclipse every sensation she'd felt so far. Aithan moaned against her neck, and she felt her pussy clench in response. She was shaking, clutching his hands tightly, his grip the only thing keeping her from falling over the edge.

"I love you," Aithan whispered against her skin, the flutter of his lips on the back of her ear setting her skin ablaze. "I love you. I love you. I love you, Macella."

It was the way he said her name, the way he held it in his mouth as if it were something precious, as if he would always keep it safe. Macella felt herself come apart.

Chapter Fifteen

Hours later, they rambled on through the countryside, Macella still prac-
ticing her new mind tricks. There was another reason Aithan was pushing Macella to better understand and control her emerging gift. As they rode on
in the relative cool of the evening, he explained.

"We cannot know how many hellspawn crossed into our realm during Kiho's
experimentation," Aithan sighed. "Though we acted quickly, they had ample
time to summon lower demons."

Macella shuddered, remembering the kappa's sharp teeth and the brucha's
vicious quills. "Lailoken and his group scoured the city and the wood while you
recovered. They found no other monsters."

Aithan nodded. "Yes, and they did a fine job. However, I am more concerned
about what we might have missed the very night we defeated Kiho. If they had
dispatched demons to complete other tasks..."

"They would likely have escaped," Macella finished, realization washing over
her in an icy rush. "When Kiho died, the monsters they'd summoned would be
masterless and thereby free to pursue their own base desires. We slew all demons
we encountered, but we must be on our guard against strays."

"You've a quick mind," Aithan said, a hint of pride tingeing his voice. "And natural instincts. You continue to impress me."

The chill that had engulfed Macella dispersed in a flush of warmth. She tried not to sound too pleased with herself. "I suppose this is why you have been encouraging me to explore my new gift. You would have me listen for otherworldly thoughts."

"There may be none or there may be scores," Aithan replied, confirming her words with a nod. "If we are both on our guard and attuned to any hellish disturbances, we will detect any demons along our path east."

Macella tried not to imagine the horrors that would commence if any of the creatures she'd met found their way into other parts of Kōsaten. The average citizen would not stand a chance. Macella prayed they had stopped Kiho early enough.

"Aithan," Macella said after a few minutes of contemplative silence, "do you think Kiho's actions have had other consequences?"

Aithan grunted, glancing behind them toward the setting sun. "It is very likely, but we cannot know. An inexperienced sorcerer experimenting with brimstone is a highly volatile situation."

Macella nodded. "I wonder if the lamia's odd behavior in Hurstbourne was an early sign of Kiho's misdeeds. I recall you saying that lamias typically would have fled, yet that one sought us out and attacked."

A look of momentary surprise passed over Aithan's face. "I had not considered the possibility. It all happened so quickly, and with your involvement, I figured the strangeness was accounted for. But you could be right. We have no idea how far this mess has spread."

They increased their pace, their new worries adding urgency to their journey. They traveled until it grew quite dark and then made camp. Afterward, Macella lay in Aithan's arms thinking over their earlier discussion. She had listened all day for unfamiliar thoughts but heard only Aithan. She worried that wayward crossers had scattered in many directions. If they did not happen upon them all on their journey east, would they ever be caught?

"Why do the seven shields not each cover a single region of the kingdom?" Macella asked Aithan. "Then we could be sure that there was always an Aegis in the vicinity of danger. We could be sure Kiho's escapees would be detected regardless of the direction they might've fled."

Aithan grunted thoughtfully, absently stroking her hair. "We are taught to move continually. Supposedly, this is to ensure that our unique gifts are equitably shared across the kingdom."

Macella heard the thinly veiled disdain in Aithan's tone. "But that is not the true reason?"

"I do not believe so, no." Aithan sighed heavily, pulling her closer. "As I told you on our first night, Aegises live a life free of attachment. Our loyalty, desire, and duty are devoted to the protection of the kingdom. By requiring us to live a nomadic lifestyle, the Crown ensures we will have difficulty forming other attachments. We are thus unlikely to grow comfortable, will not build community and relationships. We will always be outsiders."

Macella felt her jaw clench. She was struck anew by the injustices perpetrated against Aegiskind. Having long felt herself an outsider, she knew what a sad and lonely life they had been condemned to. Of course, she'd had a home, however indifferent.

Aithan pressed his lips to the top of her head. "I can feel righteous indignation radiating from your every pore. I thank you for your rage on my behalf. It is nice to be cared for. It is such a new sensation for me."

Macella pressed herself against her Aegis. "As long as I live, you will know this feeling. I defy their attempts to isolate you."

Aithan chuckled, the sound rumbling in his chest where Macella's head lay. "They never accounted for someone like you, that much is clear. Nor did I. But I am grateful that you chose to surprise us all."

"I am grateful to be an outsider with you," Macella replied truthfully. "I am certainly as surprised as you are, but none of us can thwart what Fate has decreed. Not even the Crown."

Aithan lifted Macella's chin until she was staring into his eyes. When he looked at her, his eyes appeared more warm amber than orange . He kissed her then, soft and slow, his hand cradling her cheek, his mind radiating love and gratitude. Macella let her own thoughts exude her joy, comfort, and surety as they drifted off in each other's arms.

They rose early, as the first hint of light pierced the night sky. The previous night's urgency had not abated, driving them forward at a rapid pace. They might have ridden all day without stopping, had it not been for all the blood.

The forest had thinned, offering glimpses of nearby farmland. Macella did not notice anything odd at first, but soon she caught Aithan's tension. His nostrils flared and his eyes searched the trees. Macella followed his gaze, uncertain what had caught his attention.

"Blood," Aithan murmured, keeping his voice low. "Lots of blood. But not human."

Macella heaved a sigh of relief, still searching the trees for any sign of disturbance. "Perhaps the farmers are slaughtering cattle today?"

Aithan shook his head. "There is nothing beyond these trees but open pasture and more woods. Anything slaughtered here did not meet its end at the hands of any human."

A chill prickled at Macella's skin. She exhaled slowly, opening her mind, and stretching her awareness as far as possible. At first, she heard nothing. Aithan slowed their pace, his dark eyes scanning the trees. Several long minutes passed.

Suddenly, a whisper of a growl brushed against Macella's consciousness. She stiffened, her head swiveling toward the sound. There was something in these woods that did not belong.

"What do you sense?" Aithan whispered, following the direction of her gaze.

"I do not know," Macella replied. "But it does not belong here."

Aithan brought Jade to a halt and Macella followed suit with Cinnamon. Quickly, Aithan tethered the horses, speaking to them in soothing murmurs before stepping off the road and unsheathing his sword. Macella grasped her dagger, following a few paces behind him as he crept into the trees.

They moved quietly, Macella trying her best to mimic the Aegis's silent footsteps. In her mind, the inhuman growl grew a bit louder, though still indistinct. After a quarter of an hour, she realized that she, too, could smell the coppery tinge of blood in the air. Her heart hammered in her chest. She reminded herself to take slow, steady breaths.

Gradually, the trees thinned, until they found themselves on the edge of a large pasture. In the early morning light, Macella saw the source of the smell. She swallowed hard against the bile rising in her throat.

The field was strewn with the bodies of dozens of dead sheep. Their ivory fur was streaked with blood, crimson gashes across their sides or tears in their throats. As Macella stared, it dawned on her that there was something terribly wrong about this attack.

It took her a few moments to realize exactly what was off about the massacre. It struck her suddenly: an entire flock of sheep had been brutally murdered and yet every carcass was intact. No limbs or hunks of flesh were missing. Whatever had killed the sheep had not attempted to eat them.

"This was not the work of any animal of our realm." Macella stated the obvious in a horrified gasp.

"No," Aithan agreed, moving toward the murdered flock. He crouched to examine the nearest sheep, then scanned the surrounding grass. "These sheep have been drained of blood."

Macella gasped again, though she had known their predator had been after something other than their flesh. Still, there had to be nearly fifty sheep in this pasture. What kind of monster could drain the blood of that many animals in a single attack?

"Chupacabra," Aithan replied aloud. He gestured to the ground around the sheep's carcass. "They do not leave tracks—even when they walk rather than fly."

Aithan stood, looking toward the distant trees. Macella moved to his side. She followed his gaze, sensing the otherworldly growl seething from that direction.

"How do we kill it?" Macella asked softly.

"When you encounter unfamiliar hellspawn, beheading is generally a safe wager." Aithan smiled. "I will find the chupacabra and remove its head, then I will collect you, and we can be on our way. I fear we have no time to waste. We must get to Duànzào and find answers."

Macella quirked an eyebrow at him. "You will 'collect' me after? And where will I be, exactly, if not with you?"

Aithan placed a gentle hand on her shoulder, gesturing with his head toward a cluster of trees near where they had initially entered the pasture. "I need you to take that young shepherd to the safety of her family and protect them until I eliminate the threat."

Macella saw her own surprise mirrored in the face that peered at them from a high branch. The shepherd had short, messy dark hair and a spattering of freckles that stood out against skin that had gone quite pale. It was clear that the shepherd had no more expected she'd been detected than Macella had expected the girl's presence.

"How?" Macella asked incredulously.

I can hear human minds, remember? Aithan thought with a smirk. *And I spotted her well before we reached the clearing.*

And you probably smelled her because all your senses are superior. I withdraw the question. Macella rolled her eyes petulantly.

"I will teach you to better hone your senses," Aithan whispered, still smirking. He lifted his voice to call to the treed shepherd. "We mean you no ill. We seek to destroy the beast that did this."

"I saw it," the girl called back in a high, clear voice. "Nobody can kill that...that monster."

Macella saw terror in the girl's face, in the way she clung to the tree. Whatever the young shepherd had seen, it had been horrifying. Macella wondered if the traumatized girl even realized what Aithan was.

"I watched him impale a beast the size of a bull and covered in spikes as long as my arms," Macella interjected, using the assertive but gentle tone she had used at home to keep the littles under control. "I have seen him slay a serpent monster twice his height. He is an Aegis. And you are very lucky that he happened to be in this region this morning."

The girl's eyes widened. "A real Aegis?"

Macella smiled, stepping nearer to the girl's tree. "If you come down and tell us what you saw, I promise he will kill your monster before it can cause further harm."

"Who are you?" the shepherd demanded, pulling her gaze away from Aithan to look more carefully at Macella.

"I am Macella of Shively, and this Aegis is my dear friend," Macella replied. "And you?"

The girl stared at Macella for a long moment before answering. "Tobiah."

"Tobiah, could you come down and tell us what happened here?"

After a little more coaxing and a few words of comfort, Tobiah was leaning into Macella's shoulder, relating her tale. It was soon clear why the poor girl had been so reluctant to leave the safety of the tree. She had witnessed the chupacabra's feeding frenzy.

Apparently, the farm was shorthanded at present, so Tobiah couldn't spend as much time with the sheep as she usually did. She'd left them under the care of her sheepdog while she tended to other tasks. When she returned to the pasture, there was no sign of the dog. Instead, there were dozens of sheep carcasses and an unbelievable creature finishing the remainder of the flock.

"I don't remember climbing the tree," Tobiah continued. "I saw this monster with blue-gray skin, enormous claws, and bones jutting from its back. It was hovering in the air—using wings like a giant bat—and it had a sheep in each of its four claws."

Tobiah stopped then, burying her face against Macella's shoulder. Macella patted the girl's back, exchanging a glance with Aithan. They clearly had no time to lose.

"Tobiah, can you show me—" Macella broke off, surprised by a sudden howl from the trees.

"Bo!" Tobiah yelled.

Before Macella could react, the girl had taken off in the direction of the howl.

Tobiah had only made it a few steps before Aithan caught her and pushed her back into Macella's arms. The girl struggled, but Macella held her firmly.

After realizing her struggles were pointless, Tobiah sagged against Macella. They watched as Aithan raised his sword and advanced toward the trees.

Just as he reached the forest's edge, a creature burst from the foliage. Aithan shifted out of its path, his attention still on the trees. A big ball of shaggy black fur barreled into Macella and Tobiah, almost knocking them flat.

"Bo!" the girl cried again.

Macella let Tobiah go so that the girl could embrace the sheepdog.

Down, Aithan commanded in her mind.

Macella dropped to the grass, pulling Tobiah with her. The big dog pressed against them, shaking, and whimpering pitifully. Gripping her dagger, Macella shifted so that she could get up quickly if necessary.

Suddenly, the stench of sulfur assaulted Macella's nose. Deceptively quiet, the chupacabra swooped into the clearing above Aithan's head. Its bulbous eyes glowed red to match the hideous tint of its massive fangs. Red spines lined a ridge down the beast's back. Focused on the sheepdog, the chupacabra flew over the Aegis without pausing. It was oddly graceful for such an awkward, lumbering beast.

Macella watched as Aithan leapt at the beast. He caught it by a hind leg, spiking it hard at the ground. Before it collided with the earth, the chupacabra beat its wings mightily, jerking free of Aithan and sharply changing direction.

Macella gasped, but Aithan was already bringing his sword around in a mighty arc. The blade cut cleanly through the chupacabra's neck. Its body flew several more paces before its wings stopped flapping, and the body crashed to the ground. It rolled end over end before settling in a twitching heap of gangly limbs.

"As promised," Macella said, smiling at Tobiah's awestruck expression.

Aithan made Tobiah promise to stay close to home over the next few days while he and Macella continued their journey and checked the area for other demons. He would not accept the girl's thanks or her invitation to stay for a meal, insisting that he and Macella had to make up for lost time by riding hard toward the next town. Macella pretended not to notice him slipping a pouch into Tobiah's pocket as he sent the girl on her way. She imagined the coin would go a long way toward making up for the loss of the sheep.

Cinnamon and Jade were rested and ready, so they responded quickly when Aithan coaxed them into a gallop. The wind on their faces countered the heat of the day enough to make the ride bearable, even for Macella. She let Cinnamon's steady hoofbeats lull her into a meditative state, focusing her awareness outward in search of otherworldly minds.

She was mentally exhausted by the time they made camp for the night. They'd detected no other crossers, but Macella knew they must stay vigilant. She tried not to think about the chupacabra's red fangs and the drained sheep. She was sure she would not be able to sleep, but then Aithan pulled her against his chest.

Her final thoughts before sleep took her weren't of vicious monsters, but of gentle hands stroking her hair and the steady, reassuring beat of Aithan's heart.

Chapter Sixteen

S oon enough, the journey took Macella and Aithan through another town. Eager for a good meal and cold ale, they decided to spend the hot afternoon hours in the local tavern. After entrusting Cinnamon and Jade to a stable hand, they entered the blissfully dim pub and, per the Aegis's usual custom, found a quiet corner to sit in. To their surprise, a barmaid appeared at their table almost immediately, a mug in each hand.

The woman smiled broadly as she placed the mugs on their table. "Welcome to Spring Mill. Would you care for some vittles as well? We have cold meats and cheese and fresh bread. No one wants anything hot this time of day."

"That sounds perfect," Macella replied, returning the woman's smile.

Aithan reached into his purse, extracting a few coins. When he held them out, the woman held up her hands and shook her head.

"You're an Aegis," the barmaid replied. "I can tell by your hair. Your money is no good here. We appreciate your service."

She turned on her heel and hurried away before they could respond. Macella raised an eyebrow at Aithan. The corner of his mouth quirked up in a smile.

"What am I missing?" Macella asked. "Did you catch something in her mind?"

Aithan's eyes twinkled. "I did. Try using your gift to find out for yourself."

Macella groaned in annoyance. For the first time, she wished her gift worked on ordinary humans. Before she could attempt to do as Aithan commanded, however, a man appeared beside the table.

"Pardon the interruption," the man began, holding his hat in his hands and grinning apologetically. "It's just—I never met an actual Aegis before, and I couldn't miss this chance to say hello. We're so happy you stopped here. My husband and I own this tavern, and Kaylee ran to tell us you were here. I just had to come out and welcome you."

Macella's mouth dropped open. She was used to common folk avoiding the Aegis or regarding him with suspicion and hostility. Instead, here were people actively seeking his acquaintance.

"If you need anything at all, please ask us," the man continued. "Thank you for protecting us."

Blushing furiously, the tavern owner retreated. Macella caught Aithan's gaze, using the eye contact to help her probe his mind more easily.

"Wait..." she began, but they were interrupted again.

A woman and a child had approached the table. The child peeked from behind the woman's skirts shyly.

"I'm sorry to interrupt," the woman began, "but my little one just wanted to meet you so badly. They've never seen an Aegis before."

The woman nudged the child forward. Its wide eyes were fixed on Aithan. It was clutching a piece of paper in one hand, a pen in the other.

"Go on," the woman coaxed. "Ask him."

"Will you sign my paper?" the child whispered, still gazing at Aithan raptly.

The child held out the paper and pen. As Aithan took it, Macella saw that it was a society paper. The bold letters at the top of the page read "The Aegis and the Lamia." Macella felt her jaw drop again.

Clearly suppressing a smile, Aithan scrawled his name across the bottom of the page and passed the paper back to the child. Aithan offered it his hand.

The child's hand was completely swallowed by the Aegis's massive grip. Macella thought they might swoon. The child couldn't take its eyes off of Aithan.

"I hope to be brave like you when I'm big," they whispered, clutching the signed souvenir to their chest.

"I am sure you will be," Aithan replied in his deep, rumbling voice. "In fact, I imagine you already are."

The rest of the afternoon passed similarly. Macella's surprise never waned as more and more people approached them and expressed their gratitude and awe. Word of their arrival had clearly spread quickly.

Eventually, the tavern owner intervened, insisting they move into a private room for their comfort. Macella felt Aithan's relief when the man closed the door behind him, leaving them blissfully alone. The room held two chairs and a small table laden with a pitcher of mead and a platter of fruit, bread, and cheese.

Macella poured them each a cup of mead, and they drank in silence for several minutes. Finally, Macella spoke. "I cannot believe this is because of my writing."

"I can," Aithan replied softly. "You exaggerate my merits and embellish my victories. You make me into a hero. People gravitate toward heroism; they hope to catch it like a virus."

"I embellish only enough to protect your identity. I record your heroism as truly as you live it," Macella countered. "This is how people should have always regarded you. I'm only sorry my stories have robbed you of your anonymity."

Aithan smiled at her affectionately. "It is no great loss. We'll manage. Do not worry for a moment about me. I am truly happy for you. You deserve to have your work valued."

"So do you," Macella retorted, leaning over the table to kiss the Aegis.

As their lips met, the door opened, and Kaylee the barmaid swept into the room, a pitcher in each hand. Macella sat back, smiling at the woman.

The barmaid blushed. "A couple of townsfolk wanted to show their gratitude by buying your drink."

She set the new pitchers on the table, then refilled their chalices from the half-full pitcher they'd already begun.

Aithan grinned at Macella. "This isn't completely terrible," he chuckled, taking a long drink.

Macella rolled her eyes. She noticed the barmaid was lingering, doing point-less little tasks as an excuse to stay in the room. She caught the woman's eye and smiled reassuringly.

Taking the encouragement, Kaylee spoke. "I suppose you're here 'cause of the demon? You already know that it's gone, of course. Do you think there might be another rift coming?"

Macella didn't have to be able to read human minds to feel the woman's anxiety, nor did she need to use her gift to catch Aithan's surprise at Kaylee's words. There had been no new rifts in the region since Kiho's death. Had one of their demons made it this far?

"I was not aware any of my kind had been in this region," Aithan said, his voice measured. "Who was it that dispatched the demon?"

"It wasn't an Aegis. It was a sorcerer of some kind," Kaylee explained. "The demon possessed a man, and this sorcerer came along and told it to get out. She did some kind of ritual, and the man was back to normal."

"Did you know the sorcerer? Is she still here?" Aithan's voice had a sharp edge to it now.

"No," Kaylee answered quickly, a flash of fear passing over her features. "She was a stranger, and she left after the man's family paid her."

Macella reached across the table, placing her hand on Aithan's. She knew how quickly human sentiments could change, and she didn't want Aithan's urgency to frighten the barmaid.

"It's lucky she was in the area." Macella smiled. "And a pity we missed her. How long ago did she leave?"

Kaylee frowned in concentration, counting on her fingers. "It was about four days ago, I think. You don't think there will be more demons, do you?"

"Certainly not," Macella assured her, gently pressing Aithan's hand.

"Definitely not," Aithan agreed, giving Kaylee a smile that made Macella's stomach flutter.

It must have had an effect on Kaylee as well, because the woman's anxiety seemed to vanish. She blushed and hurriedly gathered the empty pitcher and dishes.

"It is too bad we missed her," Aithan added. "I would have liked to talk to her about the demon she expelled."

"Oh, you could probably catch her if you had a mind to," Kaylee said breathily, still flushed. "I saw your horses. They look fast."

"Four days is quite a head start." Aithan sighed, holding Kaylee's gaze.

"She's magical, but she's not faster than a horse." Kaylee laughed. "She was on foot."

As the barmaid slipped from the room, Aithan and Macella's eyes met. Simultaneously, they began to gather their belongings and pack up the remaining bread and cheese.

"Pale skin, long ginger hair, gray eyes," Aithan listed as they prepared to leave. "Purple cloak. She was headed east."

Macella took a long drink of mead before smiling at Aithan. "Sounds like just my type. It is certainly convenient that we're already heading in the same direction. We'd better hurry."

Kaylee let the Aegis and his companion pass through the kitchens and out into the late afternoon air so they could avoid further attention or delay. Quickly, they mounted Jade and Cinnamon and turned their backs to the setting sun.

⚜

They rode hard over the next few days, stopping only to sleep and to question the people they passed in the small nameless villages along the way. Several people had seen the redheaded sorcerer heading east, though not many people had spoken to her.

That was, until they passed through the lands of a wealthy recluse. The servants and farmhands on the estate all told the Aegis the same tale: their master had fallen ill suddenly. Soon, he'd begun raving nonsense about cats. There was nothing anyone could do for him, until the sorcerer appeared. She'd explained that he was possessed by a demon and had offered to banish the evil spirit for a nominal fee. The wealthy man's steward had agreed, and the sorcerer exorcised the demon. The grateful landowner had paid her double the rate she'd asked for and gifted her a fine horse as well.

"You are sure your master's rants were about cats?" Aithan asked the third chatty servant they encountered. The Aegis's face was grave.

"Yes, sir. It was the strangest thing," the servant asserted. "The cats around here are pretty useful. They keep the vermin away. But while he was possessed, the master hated the poor creatures."

Aithan didn't bother talking to the landowner about his experience with demon possession. Macella could tell he already had a theory forming.

"We're not dealing with actual demons, are we?" she asked as they mounted their horses again.

"No, I do not believe we are," Aithan answered thoughtfully, his brow furrowed. "Not exactly. I will explain more later—if I am right. But we've got to keep moving if we are to have a chance of catching the sorcerer now that she is on horseback."

Macella didn't ask any more questions. She trusted Aithan implicitly and knew that he would tell her what she needed to know. She clicked her tongue and gave Cinnamon a gentle tap of her heels.

This time, Aithan pushed the horses into a sprint. Zahra Shelby had not exaggerated when she'd promised them the fastest horses she owned. Aithan's silver hair streamed behind him, the wind making the crimson tips flicker like flames. Macella reveled in the feel of the breeze cooling her warm skin, exhilaration thrilling through her as she leaned into the wind.

They slept only a few hours that night. Aithan explained that he hoped to overtake the sorcerer in the next large town.

"If the sorcerer is targeting the wealthy with her services, she will tarry a bit longer in Lyndon," the Aegis said as they made camp. "She cannot gamble on there always being wealthy landowners in the countryside. Towns are where she'll make her coin."

"How is she doing it?" Macella asked, settling herself against Aithan on the blanket. "How is she convincing people that they're possessed by demons?"

"With the right magical gifts, there are any number of possibilities." Aithan sighed, draping a muscled arm over her. "I cannot know for sure until we catch her."

(30) And so, they'd risen before the sun, packed up, and set off once more. They'd ridden fast, the countryside whipping past them in a blur of bright colors and rushing wind. In the pale light of the dawning day, Macella felt like she was flying. She felt a giddy laugh bubbling up in her throat.

Aithan looked at her swiftly, his eyes softening when he saw the expression on her face. Even as she kept her attention on the path, she could feel his gaze on her, sense the adoration resonating from his mind. She could feel a reciprocal sensation radiating from her own skin. Macella had never felt this kind of joy before.

She had never felt so free.

Beside her, Aithan guided Jade closer to Cinnamon. Macella felt him take Cinnamon's reins from her, bringing the two horses even closer. Macella turned her head and met the Aegis's burning gaze.

I love you, he thought, his eyes fixed on hers.

Macella's heart lurched. She could feel his love enveloping her like a warm embrace.

Aithan gathered both sets of reins in one hand, reaching for Macella with his free hand. He caught her arm, and then Macella was sliding off her saddle toward him. She cried out in surprise as Aithan caught her in the crook of his arm and covered her open mouth with his own. He kissed her hard, his tongue probing hers insistently.

In terrifying weightlessness, Macella kissed Aithan back. He tasted of sweetness and smoke, a flavor she had learned to crave as though it was some crucial vitamin that she'd lacked her entire life. She let Aithan support her, trusting his strength and superior senses. Cinnamon and Jade, just as intelligent as they were fast, held steady, ensuring Macella never slid entirely out of Cinnamon's saddle.

And, just as quickly, he righted her, returned Cinnamon's reins, threw her a sexy grin, and galloped ahead. Breathlessly, Macella urged the horse forward. The wind carried away her laughter as she strove to overtake him. All Macella could hear was rushing wind, pounding hooves, and all-encompassing love singing in her ears.

CHAPTER SEVENTEEN

They arrived in Lyndon just as the sun began to set. They gave their tired steeds over to a stable hand, with instructions to feed and water them, then wipe down their coats before guiding them to bed down in fresh hay for the night. Regardless of what transpired here today, they would have to rest the horses if they hoped to survive the long journey to Smoketown.

Macella watched Aithan hand the stable hand the reins, then rest his head against Jade's neck. She could hear the Aegis murmuring affectionately to the animal, who nickered in response. Macella smiled to herself and patted Cinnamon absently, thinking about how beautiful Aithan was in that moment.

Aithan lifted his head from Jade's neck and met her gaze. He gave Macella that smile that was only for her—the one that instantly melted her insides. The Aegis closed the space between them, pulling her close to him and leaning down to rest his forehead against hers.

"After we deal with this sorcerer, we are going to rest a full day and night, and I'm going to keep you all to myself in a locked room at the Lyndon Inn," he vowed, his voice low.

Macella shivered, her heart and vagina pulsing in unison. "Do you promise?"

Aithan kissed Macella's forehead then whispered into her hair, "I promise. And I would die before I would break a promise to you."

His voice was so sincere that it gave Macella a pang of love so intense it was almost painful. He planted a soft kiss on her lips, giving her another tight squeeze before releasing her.

He ran a calloused hand over her cheek and sighed deeply. "Let us clear up this business quickly so that I may prove to you I am a man of my word," Aithan murmured, his eyes twinkling. "These last days have been hectic, and I crave time alone with you. It is as if I never fully breathed before I met you, as if you contain some vital element I need to thrive. You are my air, Macella."

Macella recalled how much her own thoughts had mirrored Aithan's words—how she'd likened him to a crucial vitamin that she'd lacked her entire life. Before she could respond, Aithan kissed her lightly once more and strode off toward the nearest building, which looked to be a tavern. Macella jogged to keep up with him, her eyes scanning the streets for ginger hair or purple cloth. The few people milling about watched them pass in surprise, no doubt in awe of the Aegis.

They stepped inside the tavern, and Macella felt a chill douse the warmth of affection she'd been feeling for her Aegis. An atmosphere of tension permeated the tavern, putting Macella on high alert. She felt the same reaction flash through Aithan's mind.

Aithan made to inquire at the bar, but he hadn't made it two steps before a man eagerly approached him.

"An Aegis, just in time!" the man exclaimed, taking Aithan's hand, and shaking it furiously. "The sorcerer seems capable enough, but surely an Aegis can free our butcher from the demon."

"Where is this butcher?" Aithan demanded, extricating his hand, and pivoting toward the door.

"I'll show you," answered the man, scurrying to keep up with the Aegis's long strides.

"Let him rot," a woman's voice called from a table near the door.

Aithan and Macella looked toward the voice and saw a dark-haired woman scowling at their guide.

The man sniffed haughtily. "Some people aren't so quick to wish harm on their fellow man, Alameda."

"And some of us aren't willing to sell our souls in exchange for a chance at a miser's favor, Lucas," the woman shot back, her voice hard. "You think if you help him, he'll treat you a little better than he treats the rest of us poor folk? You think he'll sell you something other than the meat that's turning or too ruined with fat and gristle to be any good?"

The man called Lucas reddened. "I cannot just stand by and let something horrible happen to him."

Alameda rose, crossing to face Lucas in a few swift steps. Lucas flinched away when she stopped inches from his face. Her own face was set in a grimace, her eyes narrowed, her teeth bared.

"You cannot just stand by and let something horrible happen to him?" Alameda hissed through clenched teeth. "Like you've stood by and let horrible things happen to every hungry, desperate person who's ever gone to him for help?"

Lucas flinched again, harder this time, as if he'd been struck. Alameda turned her angry eyes on the Aegis. Macella saw her mouth quiver for just a moment before it straightened back into a hard line.

"The demon inside him is no worse than the beast he already was," Alameda said, never breaking eye contact with Aithan. "Let him rot."

Macella saw Aithan grimace. His eyes widened as he stared into Alameda's eyes. A sharp hiss escaped his lips, before his face hardened into the same angry mask Alameda wore. Whatever he'd seen in her mind had infuriated the Aegis.

"Take me to the butcher," Aithan commanded, his voice a low growl.

Lucas jumped and hurried to lead them from the tavern. Macella glimpsed Alameda's face one last time before the door closed behind them. The angry mask had crumpled, leaving in its place a look of pain so stark it made Macella's chest ache.

Lucas didn't say much as they walked, apparently sobered by Alameda's accusations. He led them swiftly to the center of town and one of the largest shops in the square. Lucas explained that it was the butcher's shop and that the possessed butcher lived in the rooms above it. A small crowd had gathered in front of the shop, whispering and wringing their hands. The crowd parted when they saw the Aegis.

Macella followed in Aithan's wake, the silence in the square revealing sounds she'd missed before. Somewhere inside the building, a man was yelling. Macella couldn't make out any words, but the agonized screaming made the hairs on the back of her neck stand up.

Lucas stayed outside as Aithan and Macella stepped into the butcher's shop. They found it empty, save for one woman sitting in a hardbacked chair, her tearstained face turning toward them as they entered. The screaming was much louder in here. Macella could hear the obscenities and nonsense now.

The woman stood up, her face hopeful. "You're an Aegis!"

"Where is the butcher?" Aithan asked, his voice soft.

Macella noticed how quickly his expressions could change, how compassionately he felt the emotions of those around him. How could anyone ever believe Aegises didn't feel?

"My brother is upstairs with the sorcerer," the woman replied, her voice faltering. "She told us to leave her alone with him. I'm sure she can help Kellen, but now that you're here, I don't have anything to worry about. Please save him!"

The butcher's sister paused, stepping closer to the Aegis. "He's...not always the man he should be, but he's the only family I have." The woman grabbed Aithan's hands imploringly, looking eagerly up into his face.

Aithan squeezed her hands reassuringly and then guided her back to her chair. "I will do my duty," the Aegis assured her. He motioned toward a door behind the woman's chair, his eyes directing Macella toward it.

(31) Macella opened the door and immediately flinched away from the butcher's booming voice. A narrow stairwell led to a dim landing. Aithan appeared at her back, his solid warmth reassuring. He slid past Macella, drawing

his sword. Macella noted that his eyes were orange; neither they nor his sword glowed crimson.

When they reached the landing, they found that a small sitting area led to a short hallway. The screams were coming from behind the door at the hall's end.

Stay back, Aithan thought at Macella as he treaded silently toward the door.

Macella gave him space but followed him. They both knew she wasn't going to leave his side if she didn't have to.

Aithan flung the door open, taking in the entire room and making his move before Macella even made it to the threshold. The butcher's shrieks echoed through the hall, louder than ever.

When Macella reached the doorway, she saw that this must be the butcher's bedroom. The screaming man—Kellen, his sister had called him—was writhing in the bed, his wrists bound to the bedposts.

At the foot of the bed stood a woman in a purple cloak. Her long red hair hung over her shoulder in a loose braid. Her gray eyes were wide, her mouth open in surprise.

Macella didn't know if she was startled by their sudden arrival or if she was reacting to the tip of Aithan's sword pressing against her pale throat. Likely, both. Macella crossed to stand at Aithan's side.

The woman's eerie light gray eyes slid to look at Macella. Macella felt a jolt of surprise as the woman's eyes passed over her. There was recognition in them. And fear. Macella could sense it. It wasn't distinct, but it was there. Something about the sorcerer made her mind almost accessible to Macella's gifts.

"Look at me!" Aithan snarled.

The woman's attention snapped back to the Aegis. Macella's sense of her mind dulled.

"P-Please," the sorcerer stammered.

"Release this man," Aithan growled, cutting off the woman's plea. "Do it now and I might let you live."

The sorcerer squeaked her agreement. Aithan lowered his sword slightly, jerking his head toward the bed. The woman scampered to Kellen's bedside. Macella watched as she produced a glass vial.

The sorcerer leaned over the man, whispering as she pressed the vial to his ear. Suddenly, his cries ceased. With a deep sigh, Kellen closed his eyes and was silent. The sudden quiet was unnerving after his constant screams.

The sorcerer corked the vial firmly before turning back toward the Aegis. Aithan narrowed his eyes. The sorcerer's shoulders drooped. She dragged her feet reluctantly as she walked back to the Aegis. She begrudgingly held out the vial.

The vial looked completely empty to Macella, but Aithan looked satisfied. He turned to Macella and held the vial up for her to see. She squinted. For a moment, Macella *almost* saw something, but then it was gone again. She shook her head at Aithan.

"Show yourself," Aithan commanded, shaking the vial sharply.

As Macella watched, the vial filled with translucent smoke. The smoke slowly solidified and darkened, settling into a deep green. And then she was looking at a strange little insectoid creature. It resembled a common grasshopper, but its head was pointed, its eyes red.

"A pelesit," Aithan explained. "Created from the tongue of a child's corpse, buried at a crossroads on a full moon."

Macella gasped and looked at the sorcerer in horror. Aithan glared at the sorcerer, his mouth curled into a sneer. The woman took a step back, her hands raised defensively.

"I didn't make it myself!" she insisted. "I found it! I was in Hurstbourne when you killed that kappa. There were all sorts of creatures around that should not have been there. I found the pelesit by the lake."

"You just happened to be in Hurstbourne when a rift was open and just happened to find a pelesit?" Aithan demanded skeptically.

The sorcerer nodded insistently. "I could never make one on my own. I am not that good at magic."

Suddenly, Macella was struck by an almost-forgotten memory. There *had* been a woman with a long red braid in the crowd by the lake. Lailoken had nearly knocked the woman over. And hadn't she seen the woman pluck something from the ground?

"I remember seeing you there," Macella said.

Aithan looked at Macella. Macella shrugged, raising an eyebrow. Aithan sighed heavily. He looked down at the vial in his hand. Abruptly, he closed his fist over the vial. A sharp crunch cut through the air.

His eyes took on that crimson glow for a moment. In a flash of flame, the remnants of the vial and pelesit disappeared, leaving Aithan empty-handed aside from a whiff of brimstone. The sorcerer clapped her hands over her mouth to smother her cry of surprise.

"Out," Aithan growled, pointing at the door.

Macella led the way, the sorcerer hurrying after her. When they reached the landing, Aithan gestured to a chair with his sword. The sorcerer sank into the seat, looking paler than ever.

"Macella, tell the butcher's sister that her brother is sleeping peacefully, and she will be able to see him shortly," Aithan directed.

Macella obeyed quickly. The butcher's sister wept copiously, throwing her arms around Macella. Then she ran to tell the waiting crowd the good news.

When Macella returned upstairs, Aithan was still standing before the sorcerer, sword in hand.

"Explain yourself," the Aegis instructed, expression grim.

"What's your name?" Macella interjected, stepping closer to Aithan.

"Aisling," whispered the sorcerer, her eyes on the floor.

"Aisling, why are you hurting people?" Macella asked gently.

Aisling's head popped up, and she met Macella's gaze with a frown. Her pale cheeks pinkened. "I have not hurt anyone."

"Wrong," Aithan spat, his tone venomous. "The longer a person is infested with a pelesit, the more likely they are to experience permanent damage to their minds. If infested for too long, they can develop paralysis or die."

Aisling cringed. "I always got it out before that. I didn't want to kill anyone."

"The man in the countryside was raving about cats," Aithan retorted. "When a host starts sharing the pelesit's fears, their mind is in grave danger."

Aisling bit her lip and looked away. "His people were quibbling over my fee! I'd meant to cure him sooner, but they were being miserly!"

"So, you set your pet monster on people and then charged them money to call it off?" Aithan snapped. "All while pretending to be ridding them of demons?"

"Aye," Aisling said defiantly. "But I wasn't hurting anybody! I chose people who could afford to pay!" The sorcerer glanced down the hall toward where Kellen slept. Her lip curled in disgust. "I chose people who deserved to pay."

Macella remembered the woman at the tavern—Alameda—and what she had said about the butcher's proclivities. Aithan shifted a little, obviously remembering the same thing. He lowered his sword.

"You deceived people and tricked them out of their money," Aithan said. "That is no honorable way to live."

"It is the only way I can live!" Aisling huffed angrily. "Not everyone is paid by the Crown, Aegis."

Aithan grunted dismissively. "You may not be good at practical magic, but I sense your gift. Why not use it honestly?"

To Macella's surprise, the sorcerer laughed. There was no humor in the sound. Macella wondered what Aisling could actually do.

"My gift is nothing but a curse," Aisling scoffed. "My gift is the entire reason I travel this life alone."

Aisling sagged back into her chair, looking defeated. Macella felt a stab of pity. She stepped forward and crouched in front of the other woman.

"I know what it is to travel this world alone," Macella told her. She gestured to Aithan. "We both do. We also know what it is like to have gifts that can be misconstrued as afflictions. Tell us about yours."

Aisling looked at Macella doubtfully. "I have the so-called gift of foresight. People gladly pay to know of their good fortune. Contrariwise, bearing news of misfortune is a fine way to get run out of town."

Aisling sighed and buried her face in her hands. Macella looked up at Aithan. The Aegis sighed and sheathed his sword.

(32) Macella reached out a hand to rest on the sorcerer's shoulder. When their skin touched, a jolt of sensation shot up her arm. Aisling's head snapped up. Her eyes were entirely white, staring sightlessly past Macella.

Macella winced and tried to pull away, but the sorcerer caught her by the wrist. Macella saw Aithan's hand cover the sorcerer's on her wrist, but then he froze, inhaling sharply. No one moved.

Aisling's mouth opened. The voice that came out was not the one they'd heard before. Instead, she spoke in a chilling, raspy falsetto that made the hairs stand up on Macella's arms.

"Impossible children, unbearable pain
Suppressed so long, love blooms again
Baptized in blood, forged in flame
Stars align, prophets proclaim
Love leads wanderers to their truth
Unknown power now unloosed
Darkness gathers, trouble brews
Predator or protector, one must choose
Fools fight for fortune, the peaceful court war
Not one prepared for that which is in store
A shield
A scribe
A sword
A pen
Against hell's fury
Against our end."

Aisling slumped in her chair. Macella fell back, scooting away on her butt until her back hit a wall. Aithan crossed swiftly to her side, wrapping his arms around her protectively. Macella clung to him, trying to calm her racing heart.

Aisling's eyes fluttered open. She frowned, struggling to sit upright. She looked around slowly, her eyes finally finding Macella and Aithan. Realization dawned on her face.

"What did I say?" Aisling asked, her voice trembling. "Usually, I am still in control when I have a vision. It is like I have two minds. But not this time. It's like...it's like my mind was ejected. I have no memory of what I saw."

Aithan helped Macella to her feet before responding. "The message was for us, not for you."

Aithan pulled Macella close. She wrapped her arms around him and felt him rest his chin on her head.

The sorcerer stared at them. "You are right, I believe," Aisling said. "I want to know nothing of this. Your Fate is not a safe one."

Aithan only grunted in response. He pulled a small purse from his pocket and tossed it to the sorcerer. She caught it, and her eyes widened, apparently surprised by the weight.

"Find an honorable way to live this life and the right people will find you," Aithan told her. "You will not always be alone."

Aithan kissed the top of Macella's head as the sorcerer retreated, clutching the purse tightly. He breathed in, then exhaled a humming sigh.

"The right people will find you," he repeated. "You will not always be alone."

After Aisling had gone, Aithan released Macella from his embrace but took her hand. To Macella's surprise, they walked back to the butcher's bedchamber. Aithan motioned for Macella to wait by the door.

In two quick strides, Aithan crossed to the bed, grabbed a glass of water from the bedside table, and threw it in the butcher's face. The man jerked awake, gasping, and sputtering in surprise. He tugged at his restraints as he looked frantically around the room. His eyes widened when he saw the Aegis looming over him.

"Wake up, butcher," Aithan growled. "We need to talk."

"Did you free me from the demon?" Kellen the butcher croaked.

"That remains to be seen," Aithan replied, his voice cold.

"W-What do you mean?" Kellen stammered. His eyes darted past the Aegis toward the door, landing on Macella.

"Look at *me*, butcher," Aithan hissed. "If I ever catch your eyes on her again, I will cheerfully remove them from your lecherous skull."

Kellen's eyes snapped back to Aithan. "What do you want from me? Payment? I can generously reward you for your service."

Aithan's lip curled in disgust. He pulled his sword from its holster and placed the point against the butcher's throat. Macella gasped. The butcher whimpered.

"Do not insult my honor, butcher," Aithan snapped. "I have done only my duty. Never before have I been so loath to do it. You do not deserve the second chance you have been given this day."

"I'm sorry," Kellen choked out, near tears. "Tell me what you want, and I will do it! Please!"

Aithan leaned over the butcher, placing his face mere inches from the other man's. Macella saw a tiny bead of blood forming where Aithan's sword rested against the butcher's pale throat. The butcher trembled, sweat rolling down his temples to join the water staining his pillows.

"I know what you do to the poor and desperate," Aithan hissed through clenched teeth. "That ends today. Henceforth, you will be a generous benefactor to all your neighbors. You will neither expect nor accept anything in return for your regular acts of kindness. And you will make what amends you can to those you have wronged. Starting with Alameda."

Somehow, the butcher had been growing even paler as Aithan spoke. At Alameda's name, he blanched whiter than his expensive bedsheets. He screwed his eyes shut, apparently unable to meet Aithan's accusing gaze. Aithan shifted his sword ever so slightly, applying a bit more pressure.

"Swear it," Aithan commanded sharply.

"I swear!" sobbed Kellen, tears streaming from his closed lids. "I swear I will make amends and be generous, and I will not surrender to my baser impulses."

Aithan stood, swinging his sword in an arc above the butcher's head. The butcher yelped, his eyes still tightly shut. He yelped again when his arms fell to his sides, the ropes tethering him now cut.

In a blink, Aithan sheathed his weapon again. "If I hear differently, I will return. And if I return, you will regret it more than you could possibly imagine."

The butcher did not open his eyes. He wept quietly as Aithan returned to Macella's side. Hand-in-hand they departed, leaving the butcher to his solitary reflections.

Macella composed her newest story in her mind as they rode on. She hoped the kingdom would enjoy the partially true tale of a sorcerer deceiving people and wielding a hellish menagerie of pelesits, kappas, chupacabra, and bruchas. In her story, the sorcerer was truly an oracle and predicted prosperity and safety for Kōsaten.

Aisling was right: people didn't want to know when their misfortunes were to fall upon them. Macella would leave them to their blissful ignorance.

"We have to get to Duànzào," Aithan had told Macella, holding her against him in bed.

They'd gone straight to the inn after sending the sorcerer on her way. Aithan had made good on his promise to keep her in the room for their entire stay. Macella relished every moment. She knew the next weeks would be hard traveling, if they hoped to get the answers they needed before it was too late.

"That prophecy was about us," Macella said. "The shield and the scribe. What does it all mean?"

"I don't know," Aithan had admitted. "But I know that Fate brought us together. And regardless of what comes with that, I am grateful. I am so grateful to share this life with you, Macella."

As Macella emerged from the inn in the warm glow of the morning sun, she thought over the Aegis's words from the previous night. He stood waiting for her, cooing at Jade and Cinnamon, who stamped impatiently, seemingly eager to run again.

I am grateful, Macella thought.

Aithan grinned widely at her, his orange eyes twinkling.

Macella trailed a hand up Aithan's arm as she passed him. He helped her onto Cinnamon, his hands lingering a beat longer than necessary. Macella smiled up at the sky as Aithan mounted Jade.

They turned their horses toward the rising sun, galloping toward their Fate.

Part 2
Stars Align, Prophets Proclaim

For thousands of years, Kōsaten was a desolate battleground. In this land of gods and monsters, humanity stood little chance of survival. When the first human mage, Khalid, was born, he devoted his life to making Kōsaten safe for human habitation. After much negotiation with the gods of both light and darkness, Khalid succeeded. The gods of light were weary of war, while the darker gods saw an opportunity for gain. In exchange for their power and favor, the death deities would receive the souls of all those mighty warriors recruited into the line of the Aegis. To keep those deities and their offspring in check, however, the gods of light created the Chosen—three beings of immense power and mystery, of whom we only hear whispers. And all of these great beings—Aegis and Chosen alike—are bound to the Crown.

The balance of life and death requires that exactly 13 Aegises remain active at all times. One, the strongest, is stationed at court to protect the Crown. Two, the newest, travel the kingdom gathering children to train as their eventual replacements. Three, the wisest, remain in Duànzào as teachers and trainers. Seven, the best and bravest, patrol the kingdom, sealing rifts and destroying demons. These 13 are a siblinghood of heroes, united to protect us, united under the Crown.

There are places in this kingdom that ordinary humans will never see. One such place is Duànzào. Like many of our words, the name of this sacred site comes from the ancient languages. Duànzào is the beginning for Aegiskind and befittingly translates to "The Forge." It is here where children enter, to re-emerge as fire-forged weapons. It takes years of training before a potential Aegis is able to attempt to cross the mountains of Smoketown and enter Duànzào. Only 1 in 10 returns as an Aegis—only those who can withstand hell's scrutiny.

While the Aegises protect us, Kōsaten's leaders also keep us safe. We owe the Crown our gratitude for centuries of peace. After Khalid's initial brokering, each successive monarch has undergone rigorous scrutiny from the gods of light. After all, Kōsaten's ruler is essentially the hand of the gods, implementing their will in our realm. Each new leader must be tried and deemed worthy before being bound to the Chosen, the Aegises, and all of Kōsaten. Though little is known about this testing and binding, we do know that the gods grant our ruler unique gifts, including long life, immaculate health, and certain other protections.

The balance of light and dark and countless lives—it is a heavy burden, carrying such immense responsibility. Only six have borne the weight of the crown since Kōsaten's inception: Khalid of Kōsaten, Orla of Bonnycastle, Maël of Beechmont, Omari of Audubon, Rhiannon of Wyandotte, and her grace King Khari of Butchertown. King Khari has endured the longest, ruling for nigh a century.

– From *The Epic of the Aegis and the Wanderer* by S.S. (The Shield's Scribe)

CHAPTER EIGHTEEN

The weeks faded into months as Aithan and Macella made their way across Kōsaten (33). Avoiding the capital, they took a longer route through the south of the kingdom. Macella was surprised by the variation in every new area: they'd left humid wetlands behind in the west and passed through lush green forests. Aithan warned that, as they reached the eastern region and began to move north, the land would change to a dry, arid plateau before becoming rocky and mountainous as they approached Smoketown.

Sleeping more often on the ground than in beds, they spent long days riding now that the weather had somewhat cooled. Occasionally, they gave their backsides a break and purchased a cart for Jade and Cinnamon to pull. Then, they'd sleep in shifts, traveling nearly around the clock. Whenever Aithan decided they were ready to travel quickly again, they'd sell their cart and mount up, letting Cinnamon and Jade run freely. The horses seemed to gallop even faster after days of being restricted by a cart.

In Glenview, the last large town in the south-central region of the kingdom, Macella ventured into town alone to visit the post and purchase supplies. Aithan camped on the town's outskirts, not wanting to be detained by well-meaning townsfolk. Macella felt a twinge of guilt at how her stories had changed his life.

A hefty purse awaited her at the post, along with copies of the kingdom's most popular society papers. "The Aegis and the Oracle" had been published as a three-part serial. The strategy of making their audience wait for each new issue had clearly paid off. With more paying readers than they'd boasted in some time, the editors encouraged her to send them more stories, promising to pay more for each tale she submitted.

Macella also had a letter from Zahra Shelby. She skimmed it with a smile, before adding a few additional lines to the letter she'd already written the sheriff. Macella sealed and sent her note and left payment and routing information for the postmages. Then she sent a note and a generous sum of money to her family in Shively. She hoped they were doing alright and that her earnings would last them a while. She knew that she and Aithan likely would not stop at another major post until they'd left Smoketown for the capital.

As she made her way back to Aithan, Macella read Zahra's letter more carefully. It was full of the sheriff's energetic humor and bits of news from Shelby Park. Macella laughed to herself when she read Zahra's account of officially deputizing Lailoken, who had been much less irritating since he'd seen the aftermath of a real battle with hellspawn.

When Macella reached camp, she read one of Zahra's passages aloud to Aithan:

It seems the scribe's writings have had unanticipated consequences. My father returned from court full of talk of Aegises. All the fine folk with too much time and money have been reading the society papers and now wish to rub elbows with the kingdom's heroes. Thus, the Crown has invited all of the wealthiest families to shelter at court with the Aegises for the cold season. It seems we will be reunited sooner than we'd hoped.

Aithan frowned, his orange eyes dark and grave. "The consequences could be disastrous if we do not broker peace before the cold season."

Macella caught the implications immediately. All of the Aegises would be sequestered together with all of the kingdom's most important citizens for many cold, dark months. If there were other Aegises of a mind with Kiho, the holiday could be catastrophic.

"Darkness gathers, trouble brews," Macella whispered the line from Aisling's now-familiar prophecy.

Aithan had remembered every word with uncanny exactness, and Macella had him recite it so she could record it in her journal. She studied it often, trying to make sense of its riddles. Unfortunately, she hadn't made much progress.

"Indeed," Aithan agreed with the ominous prediction. "We must make haste."

Macella learned to sleep in the saddle in front of Aithan, his arm around her waist, both bridles held in his other hand. Since the Aegis needed less sleep, this arrangement allowed them to travel a few additional hours each day.

To her surprise, however, Macella found her stamina increasing. She needed less sleep and fewer breaks throughout the day. Even after sleeping in the most uncomfortable arrangement, she somehow woke energized and refreshed. She was nearly as skilled as Aithan at handling the horses and had even almost beaten him in one of their many friendly races meant to pass the time.

When they needed to move their sore muscles, Aithan and Macella took breaks to spar. Macella had grown confident in wielding her dagger, so Aithan began to teach her to handle a sword. It was a short-lived attempt; his sword was far too heavy for her to manage. The Aegis promised to have one forged just for her when they reached the capital.

In the meantime, Macella acquired a holster for her other thigh, and Aithan trained her to wield her dagger with either hand. She mastered unsheathing it quickly from either holster, whether she wore them under her skirts or over her trousers. Soon, she wielded her dagger ambidextrously, as if she'd been doing so her entire life.

"You take to all of my teachings naturally," Aithan mused, watching her practice with her dagger. "It is as though you were born to do this."

Likewise, Macella's mental training went better than her sword fighting lessons. At first, Aithan easily pushed past the meager defenses she attempted to erect, but soon enough, she was able to keep him out of her thoughts. Repelling his attempts to compel her was more difficult, but she gradually learned to do even that.

Much sooner than she'd anticipated, Macella could see the hulking shadows of the Smoketown mountains in the distance. The harvesting season was well under way in this region of the kingdom, meaning their stay in Smoketown would likely give them an early sample of Kōsaten's dreary cold season.

"The tallest of those peaks will have snow on them soon," Aithan told her, pointing at the jagged mountain range. "The cold season is especially unpleasant in Smoketown."

Aithan's expression clouded over as he gazed at the mountains. Macella could sense a heavy sadness in his mind, an ache buried deep behind a wall of gritty determination.

To Macella's surprise, Aithan decided to stop with less than a day's ride left before they'd reach Smoketown. He insisted they tarry in the last large town before their destination, a trading post called Valley Station. Macella did not push the issue, sensing that he would be sharing a great deal of information with her soon.

As they neared the Valley Station Inn, Aithan indeed began to share. "I want us to rest here. The next part of our quest is treacherous. We should not embark upon it at anything less than our best condition."

Macella knew that they were probably more exhausted than they realized, considering how quickly they'd traveled in the last few months. It would be nice to sleep in a proper bed, with Aithan beside her. When he crossed the mountains into Duànzào, she would be alone with no way of knowing how he fared, no way to seek him out if he failed to return. The thought was more terrifying than she wished to admit.

As they made their way through town and settled into accommodations at the inn, Macella noticed the locals were more standoffish than any they'd encountered in a long time. No one approached them or tried to make conversation. Perhaps her tales had not traveled this far yet.

When she mentioned this to Aithan, he shook his head. "This close to Smoketown, people know more of the Aegis ways than the rest of the kingdom. They see and hear more of how we are made. They will not be swayed by pretty words. Many of them have even worked a while in Smoketown. Anyone who could stomach that cannot let themselves see us as human beings, let alone heroes. They would not be able to sleep at night."

Aithan's jaw was set, his lips pressed into a hard line. Macella saw that the closer they'd gotten to Smoketown, the more tense Aithan had become. More often than not, his expression was grim, and sometimes even sad. He didn't laugh anymore—hardly even smiled.

In their room, Macella watched Aithan gaze out of a window toward the mountains. She walked up behind him and wrapped her arms around his waist, laying her cheek against his broad back.

He sighed, lifting a hand to stroke her arm. "Aegises do not come back to Smoketown, unless they are on recruitment detail and are bringing in children," Aithan said softly. "And even then, they do not linger. It is a terrible place, full of terrible people. It is not a home."

Aithan turned toward her, pulling her into a full embrace. Macella could feel his heartbeat, steady and strong. He pressed his face into her curls.

"I wish you did not have to see this," Aithan murmured. "I wish I could spare you this knowledge."

"It is a burden I'm willing to help shoulder," Macella replied, squeezing him more tightly. "I would share all of your burdens."

(34) "Gods, I love you," Aithan half-growled into her hair. He placed a hand under her chin and lifted her face to his so he could kiss her.

Macella kissed him back, standing on her tiptoes to wrap her arms around his neck. The longer they kissed, the more urgent Aithan seemed to grow. His hands roamed over her body desperately. Macella pressed herself against him. She could feel his erection straining against the fabric of his pants.

Aithan gathered her skirts in his hands, lifting them until his hands found the skin of her thighs. He slid his hands under her ass and lifted her from the ground. Macella wrapped her legs around his waist.

She bent her head, kissing him hard as she felt his hands untying her undergarments. Groaning, Aithan broke the kiss to bury his face in her breasts. She felt one of his hands deftly undoing her blouse and corset. Macella lifted the garments over her head, letting them fall to the ground as she tangled her hands into Aithan's shimmering silver hair.

Aithan nuzzled Macella's freed breasts, running his lips lightly over each of her nipples before trailing his tongue around her areola in a slow circle. Macella gasped, her hands buried in his hair, her vagina throbbing against the bulge in his pants.

Frantically, Macella pulled a hand from Aithan's hair. She slid it over his firm chest and stomach. She reached between their bodies, feeling her own wetness on the back of her hand. She stroked the Aegis's erection through his pants, squeezing gently.

Aithan growled and took her nipple carefully into his mouth, sucking just hard enough to make her moan. Macella fumbled for the laces of Aithan's trousers.

The Aegis moved toward the low sofa. As Macella had managed to loosen his pants, Aithan let them fall to the floor before sitting down and sinking onto the chaise. Straddled across his lap, Macella helped pull his shirt over his head, kissing him hard as soon as his head was free of the fabric.

Aithan kissed her deeply. He cupped the back of her neck with one hand, the other reaching under her skirt. Gripping her ass firmly, he guided her onto his cock.

"Fuck," the Aegis whispered as Macella cried out in pleasure.

Slowly, she eased herself down until his throbbing manhood filled her entirely. Then, just as slowly, she rocked her hips, testing the depths of their union. Aithan moaned against her lips.

With the Aegis gripping her tightly, Macella rocked against him. She felt each movement echo deep in her belly, sending tendrils of pleasure throughout her entire torso.

When she thought she could not take a minute more of the exquisite torture, Aithan wrapped his arm around her waist, the hand on the back of her neck holding her firmly against him. The Aegis leaned back against the chaise's backrest, still holding Macella tightly.

Then, using the strength of his legs, the Aegis thrust upward, driving his cock deep inside her, his mouth against hers, smothering her sounds of pleasure. Again and again, he lifted his hips, each stroke hitting that place in her belly that made it feel as if she were suspended in midair.

Macella couldn't escape the agony of sensation, could not resist the desire consuming her. She felt herself bursting into twinkling shards of glass. Tears streamed down her cheeks as she came, convulsing against Aithan's strong embrace.

Aithan swiftly rolled them to the long end of the chaise, laying Macella on her back. He took both of her wrists in one of his hands, holding her arms above her head. Macella arched her back and closed her eyes as Aithan slid his other hand under her hips.

"Look at me, love," Aithan commanded.

Macella's opened her eyes and met the Aegis's burning gaze. Without breaking their eye contact, Aithan slowly eased back inside of her. Macella whimpered.

"Show me," Aithan whispered, and Macella understood.

Macella stared into Aithan's eyes, pushing her mind into his, letting the sensations consuming her flow freely. Aithan shuddered, and Macella felt the sensation in her mind and her body simultaneously.

Here was something yet new. Macella marveled at each discovery. Her gifts, his gifts, and theirs combined—they seemed perfectly matched by destiny. *Stars align. Prophets proclaim.*

Aithan held her gaze, moving slowly in and out of her quivering warmth. Macella's senses were all abuzz, pleasure permeating every inch of her mind and body. She felt herself beginning to quake.

In response, Aithan began to move faster, his strokes deeper, more insistent. Macella felt them both nearing the edge.

Her pussy clenched at Aithan's cock, the sensation a deliciously deep and ravenous yearning for more. Macella made a sound between a moan and a purr, straining against Aithan's grip on her wrists. The longing, the aching, the all-encompassing need rolled off of her skin like flames. Macella matched the Aegis's fiery gaze with her own, her eyes nearly black with insatiable hunger.

I love you, Aithan of Auburndale, Macella thought, as she let the orgasm take hold.

I will love you always, Macella of Shively, Aithan whispered into her mind, as he followed her over the edge.

Afterward, they fell into a comfortable doze, their bodies molded together on the chaise. It was a testament to their true exhaustion that they didn't even bother moving to the much larger—and undoubtedly more comfortable—bed.

It must have been a few hours later, if the darkening sky was any indication, when Aithan woke Macella with a kiss on her forehead.

"We need a hot meal," Aithan announced. His stomach rumbled loudly in agreement.

Macella laughed and stretched, her stomach adding its own opinion on the matter. "Okay, okay. I'm getting up."

While Macella washed herself with a basin of lukewarm water, Aithan ordered them a meal and a hot bath. By the time they'd both used the basins to wash away the remnants of the road and their romantic relations, a servant had arrived with their dinner. They lounged in their lodging's cozy, though sparse, sitting room, eating hot stew and fresh bread, while two servants passed in and out of the room with pails of steaming water. Their washroom held a large steel tub. They had their fill of supper long before the big tub was full.

When the servants had finished their work and departed, Aithan and Macella disrobed. Aithan got in first, his long legs stretching the length of the tub. He sighed contentedly.

Macella climbed in and settled herself between Aithan's legs, leaning back against his chest. The hot water felt good on her sore muscles, Aithan's warmth adding to her sense of rest and safety.

"This will be a tumultuous time in Smoketown and Duànzào. They will be holding trials day and night," Aithan said. He squeezed water from a sponge, letting it cascade over Macella's breasts.

"You believe they know of the coming conflict?" Macella exclaimed, twisting her head to look up at him. She was shocked that so many could be accomplices to Kiho's madness.

Aithan looked confused, then he smiled a little. "You seem to understand so much that I forget that you do not know all of our ways. There must always be thirteen Aegises. Kiho's loss has left a vacancy that must be filled. We can all sense the absence."

"Oh." Macella spoke softly, leaning her head back against Aithan's chest. She had killed Kiho, one of Aithan's siblings-in-arms. She wondered why their death had not haunted her. They'd been the first person she'd ever killed. She hoped theirs would be the only life she'd ever take.

Aithan smoothed her hair away from her face, stroking her curls fondly. He kissed her temple, murmuring against her skin. "Whatever is troubling you, I am certain it is not your fault."

"You know me too well," Macella sighed. "The issue is, I am not as troubled as I should be. I took a life, and it has not disturbed me. I think on it only as a tragic necessity. And now I venture among those who mourn them."

"Hmmm," Aithan of Auburndale grunted dismissively. "Aegises do not much mourn one another. We may be kin, but we are not family. We have been one another's greatest competitors, worst tormentors, witnesses to each other's most shameful secrets. We do not gather gladly."

Aithan lifted a cup of warm water from one of the pails the servants had left beside the tub. He poured the water over Macella's head, coaxing it through her curls with his strong hands. Macella relaxed against him as he followed another cup of water with soap.

"Surely some of you formed bonds," Macella protested, though her voice sounded less insistent than she had intended it to. The afternoon and evening of rest was relaxing muscles she had not even realized were taut. "You had to cling to each other, going through the things you did, right? You grew up together."

Aithan shrugged, still kneading her scalp. "Sometimes. Some of us have even briefly been lovers. It never endures. We don't suit each other well. Somehow, we do not quite trust each other enough to exhibit the vulnerability love requires. But, sometimes, among Aegises of the same guild, a closer kinship forms."

"So," Macella probed, "who will be grieving Kiho's loss?"

"Finley and Kai," Aithan conceded. "They are among the three Aegises stationed at Duànzào. Though we do not often return to Smoketown or The Forge, three of the eldest and wisest of us dwells in Duànzào to teach and train any new Aegis that survives the trials and conquers the mountain."

"And two of those three Aegises are Apophis Aegises, who will be grieving the loss of their sibling," Macella said doubtfully. "This venture is sounding increasingly unwise."

"They will not know how Kiho met their end," Aithan told her. "Besides, we Aegises know that our lives are tenuous and that violent deaths likely await us all. They will not be surprised, nor will they be thinking of vengeance."

"Still," Macella countered dubiously, "I hope that the third teacher is another Lucifer Aegis. You could use an ally."

"There are no other Lucifer Aegises," Aithan responded. "Diya is the third teacher. She is a Kali Aegis."

"No other Lucifer Aegises anywhere?" Macella asked. "You have no others in your guild?"

"I do not," Aithan answered, rinsing the soap from her hair. "I am of the only solo guild at present."

"Well, I am in your guild," Macella said. "Though I guess we're not exactly siblings. Your turn."

They repositioned themselves so that Aithan sat cross-legged in front of her. Macella stood on her knees to pour water over the Aegis's head, watching the silver and crimson darken to slate and ruby.

"Were you close to anyone in Smoketown or Duànzào?" Macella asked, working the soap into Aithan's long, wavy hair. She realized she had no inkling of who dwelled among the Aegis recruits. "There must be others around to look after the children."

Aithan grunted again, his jaw set. "There are others around. Their commitments to look after the children, I cannot vouch for."

Macella massaged Aithan's scalp, trying to soften the memories causing his muscles to tense. "You don't have to tell me more than what I need to know to prepare. I do not wish to make you recount painful memories."

She rinsed the soap from the Aegis's hair, trailing her fingers along his temples as she did so. Aithan sighed heavily, before turning around to face her. His orange eyes were unbearably sad.

"I cannot escape the memories," Aithan said quietly. "If I must relive them, at least sharing them with you serves an actual purpose."

Aithan took a deep breath. "There are only three types of people who reside full-time in Smoketown: child recruits, mages, and soldiers. None of them want to be there. The mages are assigned by the Crown to perform the transformations. Elder mages serve as caretakers. There was one such mage who was kinder than the others. His name was Anwansi. He is the only person in Smoketown I feel at all endeared to."

Aithan paused again, swallowing hard. Macella could feel a torrent of emotion boiling beneath the Aegis's stoic exterior.

"The soldiers serve as trainers." Aithan's voice was low and filled with venom. "Their job is to get the Aegis recruits in top physical condition."

Macella felt ill. She could sense the emotions emanating from Aithan's mind: fear, rage, shame, despair, fury.

"Being assigned to Smoketown means a soldier is either completely inept, unmanageable, or unstable," Aithan continued, his voice darkening further. "So, they stick them in a nowhere town with nothing to do but indulge their basest impulses."

Aithan was speaking through gritted teeth. Macella had never heard his voice so hard, had never seen such hate in his eyes. Her heart ached.

"Show me," she whispered, taking Aithan's hands in hers. "Let me help you carry it."

Aithan's tortured eyes met hers. He exhaled slowly.

A cane across his back. Again. Again. Again.

Exhausted, standing precariously balanced on a narrow post. Broken glass covers the ground below, the shards already slick with blood.

Shivering under a thin blanket, stomach growling, desperate to fall asleep and escape the hunger and cold.

Digging for hours until the trench grew large enough for him to roll the small bodies into it while the soldiers laughed and laughed.

The stench of the burning bodies thick in the air, permeating his hair and clothes no matter how much he washed.

The things in Aithan's mind grew unspeakable. Macella didn't realize how hard she was crying until Aithan's mind abruptly disappeared and he pulled her into his arms. She tried to blubber out an apology but couldn't seem to make her voice work.

"Shhhh," Aithan murmured. "It's okay, love. I'm okay."

Slowly, Macella regained her composure. She pulled back to look at Aithan's face. He seemed grim, but calm.

"And the Crown knows of these practices?" Macella's voice came out raspy with emotion.

"They know enough," Aithan replied. "More than enough."

Macella felt a black hot rage rip through her body. She suddenly wanted to destroy something, to watch it burn. She felt hot all over.

"It is no wonder Kiho wanted to bring down the Crown," Macella hissed. "How could they allow this barbarism?"

"Whoa," Aithan breathed, snapping Macella's attention back from the brink of all-encompassing fury. "Your eyes."

Anxiously, Macella reached up to touch her eyelids. "What happened? What's wrong with my eyes?"

"Your eyes are fine," Aithan assured her, pulling her hands away from her face. "For a moment, they looked darker than usual, that's all. I suppose I have never seen you so angry."

Aithan kissed Macella's forehead, then each eyelid, and finally her lips. She exhaled slowly, calming her racing heart. Aithan kissed her again.

"Let's get out of this water and into bed," Aithan suggested. "We need a good night's sleep."

Macella agreed wholeheartedly. She let Aithan help her from the tub. They toweled off and got into bed, despite the fairly early hour. Macella was exhausted, both physically and emotionally.

In bed, Aithan held her close against him. He ran one hand through her hair, the other tracing patterns against the skin of her arms, back, butt, and thighs. He breathed deeply, his face pressed to the crown of her head.

"You know that you cannot enter Duànzào with me," Aithan said quietly, pulling her even closer. "Only Aegises can cross through the veil that guards The Forge. I will make the journey as quickly as I can. I need you to keep yourself safe while I am gone."

Macella's heart stuttered. She'd known this plan already, but that was before she'd learned all she had about their destination. Now, she hated the idea of him in Duànzào and her in Smoketown, apart and without allies.

"We will get answers, we will leave this horrible place, and then we will hibernate in my quarters at court until the warm season returns," Aithan promised, his voice wistful.

"I do not care where we go next," Macella replied, burrowing nearer to her Aegis. "I just care that we go there together."

"Always," Aithan vowed. "Now sleep. We must be rested and prepared."

Macella closed her eyes and tried to clear her mind. If what she'd glimpsed in Aithan's memories was any indication, she was not prepared for what she would see in Smoketown. She would need her wits about her.

As it turned out, she was not at all prepared for what she saw. As they came upon the narrow road that was the only route in and out of Smoketown, Macella realized immediately that she could never have been prepared for what she was about to witness.

CHAPTER NINETEEN

"Look straight ahead," Aithan reminded Macella (35). He had warned her about this road before they'd departed the inn that morning. "Focus only on the road in front of you."

Macella tried, but her eyes refused to obey. She saw each of the dozen or so crudely hewn posts driven into the ground at haphazard angles. She saw the bodies, suspended by their necks, their hands bound.

Children of all ages, sizes, shades, and genders, in varying states of decay. Many were missing eyes, probably pecked out by birds. As Macella watched, a huge black crow landed atop one of the posts. She could not tell much about the child hanging from it; its features were so badly battered as to make it nigh unrecognizable. She was grateful for the child's shaggy hair, as its bangs at least obscured the empty eye sockets. The crow bent and pecked at the corpse's face. To Macella's horror, the child's feet twitched. It was not fully dead.

Macella look at me! Aithan's voice pressed into her mind along with a sense of pressure to comply. She did not have the energy to resist or protect her mind, even if she had wanted to. She was too overwhelmed. Macella felt her head turn until her gaze met Aithan's.

"Look at me, love," Aithan pleaded. "I am so sorry, Macella. Please, just look at me."

Macella felt the tears streaming down her face. She felt Aithan's will recede from her mind, but she kept her eyes locked on his.

"Who are they?" Macella whispered. "I mean...why?"

"It is a warning," Aithan replied, his mouth a grim line. "They are so-called deserters. Children who have tried to run away from their training. They line the road into camp so that they are the first thing new recruits see."

Macella swallowed down bile. She would not fall apart as she had the night before. She had told Aithan she would help bear his burdens. He had tried to warn her, tried to shield her, but she'd insisted. She would be strong.

Macella took a deep breath and looked forward again. She let her eyes glaze over and focused on the sounds of Cinnamon's hooves hitting the hard ground. She ignored the stench, did not think about the body so small it was barely more than a babe, refused to see the sets of still-twitching feet.

She did not look into the trenches beyond the posts, didn't imagine the children digging for hours until the trench grew large enough for them to roll the small bodies into while the soldiers laughed and laughed—

Macella, Aithan's pleading voice in her mind brought her back to herself again. She breathed in slowly, exhaled more slowly still. She felt the warmth and strength of Cinnamon through the rough fabric of her trousers, the weight of her dagger on her thigh, the supple leather of the reins in her hands. She looked straight ahead.

They passed acres of fields where thin, haggard children harvested vegetables under the watchful gaze of bored soldiers, before they came upon a series of buildings. Aithan pointed out the soldiers' barracks, a neat row of stone buildings. Nearby was a pleasure house, a tavern, and the canteen. There were soldiers scattered about the dirt roads between the buildings, but they gave the Aegis a wide berth. A tall, thin soldier with curly red hair actually blanched and ran inside of the barracks. Others simply busied themselves with tasks that required they move in the opposite direction of where the Aegis was headed. Aithan did not look at any of them, but Macella could feel him mentally noting every single one. She tried to follow his example, stifling the black rage that had been building within her since witnessing Aithan's memories of this place.

Farther along, past the training grounds, where Macella looked away from the frail bodies teetering from overexertion, Aithan showed her the mages' promontory and the children's quarters. The promontory looked the newest and best kept of all the structures they'd passed. The children's buildings, on the other hand, were the most dilapidated. There were gaps in the wood that surely let in the elements. The roof was clearly in need of repair. Macella felt a twinge of familiarity. It was like being back home in Shively.

They dismounted, tethering Cinnamon and Jade to posts Macella hoped were there to serve only that purpose. (She tried not to examine the ground for bloody shards of glass.) The building was quiet inside. There were a few very young children busy with battered books or scraps of fabric, all appearing mute and malnourished. Occasionally, they passed beds housing children obviously recovering from various ailments.

Silently, mages moved among these children, checking vitals, and administering draughts. They did not look up as she and Aithan passed. The children's eyes followed them, though. Or, more accurately, their eyes followed Aithan. One like him had brought them to this wretched place, sealing their Fates. One like them they were destined to become. If they survived.

Finally, Aithan stopped in a room holding a handful of rough-hewn cribs. There, among the orphaned infants, sat an elderly mage. He looked up when they entered, his lined face lighting up in a smile.

"Aithan of Auburndale," the mage exclaimed, standing to shake Aithan's hand. "It is a pleasure and a surprise to see you again in the land of the living."

"Anwansi," Aithan replied gruffly, returning the man's handshake, and clapping him on the shoulder. "This is Macella of Shively."

The mage turned his gray eyes on Macella and smiled. He took her hand warmly in both of his. He started a little, glancing down at Macella's hand in his and then back at her face intently.

"Well," Anwansi said softly. "You're something special, aren't you?"

Macella couldn't help but smile. "I have always thought so, yes. It is beginning to look like I'm right."

Anwansi laughed and turned back to Aithan. "I like this one. And I can see that you do as well. Very much, if I am not mistaken."

"You are not mistaken, you meddlesome old coot," Aithan said, his eyes twinkling despite his stern expression. "That is why I have come to ask for your help."

Anwansi sat down, eyeing Aithan warily. "What possible assistance can I offer you?"

"I need to go into Duànzào," Aithan replied. "I need you to keep Macella here with you, away from the soldiers. And I am sure she can help you with the little ones or let you bore her with stories of your youth."

"You aren't as much younger than me as you look, Aegis." Anwansi scowled. "That's one of the perks of being ageless."

"You do not age?" Macella choked out, her mind reeling.

Aithan turned to look at her, his face surprised, then remorseful. "We have never discussed this. I am so sorry, Macella."

Before Macella could reply, Anwansi interrupted. "It shouldn't matter to her. She no more ages properly than you do."

This time, Aithan and Macella both choked on their surprise. They looked at one another in bewilderment before turning back to Anwansi.

The elderly mage shrugged. "She is a bit younger than you at present, but the difference will become a mere nothing in a few decades."

Macella gaped at the older man. Her brain was still processing that Aithan had an abnormally long lifespan and now this man was saying she, too, had a form of agelessness.

"I age!" Macella exclaimed.

"Of course you do," Anwansi replied. "Just not at the normal rate. Much like mages and Aegises. How old are you now? Two score? Perhaps one and forty?"

"Three and thirty," Macella corrected, still reeling.

Aithan's mouth fell open. He looked at Macella in disbelief. "You don't look a day over twenty."

"I was a late bloomer. And I come from a strong bloodline," Macella said hollowly. "Or so I thought."

"You may not be wrong," Anwansi mused, tilting his head, and staring intently at her.

"How old are you?" Macella asked Aithan.

"Old enough to be your father, but not your grandfather as I had worried," Aithan answered, sounding bemused.

"He is young for an Aegis," Anwansi interjected. "But he's not getting any younger, so he'd better be on his way. I sense your business in Duànzào cannot wait."

"I see your gift has not faded completely," Aithan said, shaking his head ruefully.

"Not quite yet," Anwansi agreed. "So, I will keep your lover here with me until you return. And if you are not back here in, say, three days, I should get her out of town right away?"

"You haven't lost a step." Aithan smiled. He turned back to Macella, his eyes growing serious. "You know we have no time to waste. I will go and see what I can learn. You stay out of trouble. I will return in no more than three days."

Macella's star charm went cold against the skin of her throat for a moment. Or perhaps she just imagined it did. Either way, she was still trembling as she kissed Aithan goodbye and watched him take up the reins and turn Jade toward the mountains.

"If he doesn't return in three days," came Anwansi's voice from behind her, "there's no chance I'll be able to convince you to leave Smoketown, is there?"

"Not even the slightest chance," Macella answered, watching Aithan's broad back growing smaller as he and Jade galloped toward the mountain pass into The Forge.

"As I expected," the old mage sighed. "In that case, we'd better get started. We have much to do."

CHAPTER TWENTY

The older man led Macella back inside, taking her into a room behind the one that held the infants. Macella did not want to look at them, knowing what they would have to endure. How could someone send a baby to a place like this? She clenched her teeth tightly, barely suppressing the rage she'd been fighting all day.

"It does not have to be this way," she told Anwansi when she followed him into the smaller room behind the nursery.

The room held a bed, a simple desk, and a chair. Shelves lined the walls. Every available surface was covered in books and bottles.

Anwansi gestured toward the chair and lowered himself to sit on the bed. "What doesn't have to be this way?"

Macella carefully shifted a stack of books and sat down. She looked at Anwansi appraisingly. She got the impression that he knew precisely what she meant.

Macella frowned. "This place," she replied. "These children do not have to be treated this way to become Aegises. This is needless cruelty."

Again, Macella felt herself growing hot with anger. Anwansi and the other mages had watched and not intervened to deter the soldiers' behavior. Though she had not seen any blatant abuse perpetrated by the mages in Aithan's memories, they were not especially kind to the children. And, worse, they stood silently by for decades while adults hurt children every day.

"You are right, and you are right to be angry," Anwansi said quietly. "I have had many, many years to reflect on the flaws in this system. But this is the way it has always been, for as long as Kōsaten has employed Aegises."

"That does not mean that this is the way it should be, nor does it mean this is the way it must stay!" Macella snapped, standing up again to pace the length of the tiny room.

"How long have your abilities been growing?" Anwansi asked abruptly, surprising Macella so much that she stopped pacing.

She started to ask what he meant or how he knew she had special abilities but realized the answers did not matter. "Since I began traveling with Aithan of Auburndale."

Anwansi nodded. "And I imagine they have grown stronger the closer you've come to Duànzào."

Macella gaped at him. She *had* noticed her increased stamina, as well as how quickly she'd learned to wield her dagger and protect her mind. She had not connected it with their proximity to The Forge, but Anwansi could be right.

The old mage nodded again. "As I thought. Well, I do not know what you are, my dear, but I know if you are going to try to enter Duànzào, you will have to be prepared. We will have to gather some things."

Macella didn't know how to reply to this, so she just sat back down and stared at the old man. He was agreeing to help her, so she decided to try holding her tongue and listening for a while.

"You are well past the optimal age for transformation, so we can't risk that," Anwansi continued, staring at Macella thoughtfully. "But you'll need some protection to get you through the veil."

The old mage stood and began rummaging around the room, pulling books from all manner of places, and tossing them just as quickly aside. Macella stayed out of his way.

"What was Aithan like as a child?" Macella ventured, worriedly following the old mage with her eyes as he stood on tiptoe to retrieve a book from a high shelf.

"Much the same," Anwansi answered absently. "Or, that is, much the same as the man he was before he met you. He seems different now."

Macella tilted her head quizzically. "How so?"

Anwansi shrugged, managing to pull the book from the high shelf. "He was always quiet. His mind was sharp, but he didn't speak unless he had to. He never laughed, almost never even smiled."

"I do not imagine the children here have much to smile about," Macella interrupted, unable to keep the sneer out of her voice.

Ignoring her outburst, Anwansi carried the book over and set it on the desk in front of Macella. "Actually, the only time I remember him smiling is the day he bade me goodbye," the old mage continued quietly. "Now he looks as if he's grown accustomed to having reason to smile. I saw it the moment you arrived. He loves you and he is better for it. If anyone in this world deserves to find love, it is those who have survived this place. Could you recognize this if you saw it in the wild?"

Anwansi changed the subject abruptly, pointing to a drawing in the book. Macella studied it carefully. The bloom was pinkish and slightly bell-shaped. Its leaves were long with jagged edges.

"Helleborus," Macella read the caption below the drawing. "Yes, I believe I could identify it."

"Good," Anwansi said, snapping the book shut. "Let's go. I will need time to prepare the mixture and it has to stew under the night sky. If it steeps tonight, we might have just enough time to prime you for a full day before your journey."

Macella followed Anwansi from the room, her head full of questions. The old mage took a walking stick from beside the door before stepping out into the afternoon sun. Macella watched him make his careful way down the steps and onto the dirt path leading toward the mages' promontory.

Macella matched the man's careful pace. "Are you sure you are fit for all of this activity?"

Anwansi laughed. "I've allowed myself to age finally, but I'm not yet decrepit. I've held onto some of my magic. I never knew why I was tarrying so long, but now I think I do. It was for this. I could not leave this world before I did something to atone for all the evil I have tolerated."

Anwansi stopped walking and looked at her sadly. "I don't need to have Aithan's gift of telepathy to know how disgusted you are with me. You spoke rightly before when you said it doesn't have to stay this way. But it has because people like me have stood by and done nothing."

Macella looked away. She thought about the reprehensible things she'd seen in Aithan's memories. Anwansi had let those awful things happen to him. She couldn't absolve this man of his guilt.

"How will helping me get into Duànzào help you atone?" Macella retorted. "You do not even know the purpose of our journey."

"I don't need to," Anwansi replied. "I see in your spirit that it is the *right* purpose. You are Fated to change everything. I can sense it. I will do my part to ensure you have a chance to do what we mages have been too weak and spineless to do."

With that, the old mage started determinedly toward the promontory again. Macella followed, a begrudging smile tugging at the corner of her mouth. She would never cease to be amazed by the complexity of the human experience.

When they reached the promontory gate, Anwansi turned to her again. "I will gather what we need inside. You go around to the garden and gather a few handfuls of Helleborus. I will meet you back at the children's quarters."

Macella rounded the building and found a large garden overflowing with all manner of plants and herbs. She wandered up and down the well-worn paths until she spotted a patch of Helleborus. She gathered a few handfuls before starting back toward the children's quarters.

(36) When she reached the main path again, Macella paused. Dozens of children were rushing toward what Macella assumed must be the dining hall, since it was nearing mealtime. Very few of the children looked at her; they were focused on their destination. Macella, on the other hand, scrutinized every child. What she saw made her blood boil.

Not one among them was clean or healthy-looking. Instead, they all looked haggard, bruised, and thinner than they should be. As she watched, an older child pushed several others to the ground in an attempt to get into the food line ahead of them. A nearby soldier laughed and clapped the older child on the back.

At the door of the dining hall, Macella saw a mage administering draughts to each child before allowing them to proceed. The children obediently downed the mixtures, grimacing and sometimes gagging before pushing on toward the food line. The mage looked on dispassionately as a child vomited violently. When the child had finished retching, the mage handed them another dose of the same draught.

Macella felt that hot, black rage rising again. She took several deep breaths and forced her feet to move toward the children's sleeping quarters. Before she got there, however, she noticed two soldiers and a child lingering outside of the dining hall.

The child was clearly distressed, but the soldiers didn't seem to notice or care. They were too busy arguing. Almost involuntarily, Macella moved toward them. She recognized one of the men—the one she'd seen earlier with the curly red hair. His companion was shorter than him and much wider, with a shaved head and stocky frame.

"Fine, I'll bet the little shit can hold them for three minutes," the stocky man was saying. "He's been in training long enough to do twice that."

The redheaded soldier laughed. "Look at his arms! You may as well just give me your money right now."

They didn't even notice Macella as they handed the boy two pails of rocks. To her horror, the boy held his arms out like a T. He shook with the effort of holding the pails steady. The stocky man glanced intently between the boy and a watch he held out for the other soldier to see. The boy gritted his teeth, his arms trembling.

"Hold on, damn you!" the stocky soldier yelled, glaring at his watch. "Don't you dare lower your fucking arms!"

The other soldier laughed raucously. "It's only been a minute and he's already shaking like a leaf! You're going to lose, Grizzle."

The redheaded soldier was right. The boy made a valiant effort, but a few seconds later he collapsed. The buckets hit the ground loudly, their contents spilling. The boy knelt beside them, his chest heaving. Macella could see the way his thin arms locked, the muscles spasming.

"Ha! Pay up!" yelled the redheaded soldier as the man he called Grizzle swore in frustration.

Macella involuntarily moved closer as she watched Grizzle resentfully count out a few coins.

"You cost me my drinking money, you little fuck," Grizzle growled, kicking the boy in the side. "Now I'll have to entertain myself by kicking the shit out of you."

"I'm sorry, sir," the boy answered, with tears in his voice despite his carefully blank expression. "I would've done better after something to eat. I just feel a bit tired from the work this morning."

"Damn your excuses!" Grizzle exclaimed, kicking the boy again.

This time, Macella saw tears forming in the boy's eyes.

Grizzle drew back his arm, preparing to swing a meaty fist at the boy.

Without thinking, Macella ran forward. She pulled the boy out of the path of the blow, leaving Grizzle confused. He turned and looked at her dazedly, then frowned.

"Who the fuck do you think you are, woman?" Grizzle demanded, looking as if he was considering hitting her next.

"Go inside and eat," Macella commanded, pushing the child toward the dining hall.

He was obviously just as confused as Grizzle but chose to obey her rather than wait for whatever might happen next.

"Drinking money be damned. I can find much better ways to entertain myself with you," Grizzle said, looking Macella over. His leer lingered on her breasts before he met her gaze again with a smirk.

Macella was hot with fury. In one fluid movement, she spun toward the soldier, unsheathed her dagger, and held it to his throat. His eyes bulged in surprise.

"You will not touch me, nor will you touch that child again," Macella hissed, pressing the point of her blade against his skin.

"Are you fucking crazy, woman?" Grizzle demanded. "Soldiers are the law in Smoketown. You cut me and you'll have a score of brawlers to deal with. And the Crown as well! Do something, Torch!"

Macella slid her eyes toward the other soldier without turning her head. "Do something, Torch, and I will slit you open from neck to navel."

Torch went pale and took a step back. "Something's not right about this one, Grizzle. I saw her come in with that Aegis. I think we should go."

"Yes, why don't you do that?" came another voice.

Macella hadn't heard the old man approach, but she recognized Anwansi's grandfatherly intonation. She saw Grizzle narrow his eyes at the mage.

"You don't give me orders, old timer," Grizzle spat. "And neither does some mongrelfucker bitch."

Macella felt hot all over. It was as if she might burst into flame at any moment. She pressed the blade harder against Grizzle's throat, drawing a bright drop of blood. She smiled viciously at the sight.

"I think everyone could use some lunch," Anwansi said, putting a hand on Macella's arm. "Come, Macella. Let me show you the dining hall."

There was both a warning and a plea in the old mage's voice. Macella took a long breath. Finally, she lowered her blade.

Grizzle immediately pressed his hand to his throat. "This isn't over, bitch," he said as Torch pulled him away.

"Damn right," Macella replied. "That's just a taste of what I'll do if I catch you bullying another child."

Anwansi's hand tightened on her arm. She let him guide her toward the dining hall, even though what she wanted to do was to see how many times she could stab Grizzle before he bled out. Instead, she stepped into the dining hall with Anwansi.

About four dozen children of various ages sat eating at long wooden tables. The room was silent aside from the sounds of spoons and forks scraping against plates and bowls. Macella saw several children licking what appeared to be empty plates. As she watched, an older girl snatched a hunk of bread from a smaller child and shoved it into her mouth.

"If you are trying to calm me down, this is not the way to do it," Macella grumbled, shaking Anwansi's hand off of her arm. "These children are half-starved."

"I am simply giving Grizzle and Torch time to clear the area before we pick up the Helleborus you dropped and return to my room." Anwansi sighed.

"Why are they not better fed?" Macella demanded, watching a little boy crawl under a table in a fruitless search for fallen scraps. "I saw vast fields of crops on my way into town."

"The soldiers control the rations," Anwansi replied hesitatingly. "They say it is a part of the children's training. Their bodies and minds are being prepared to withstand hardships worse than hunger. The soldiers sell the excess crops in the surrounding towns."

Macella turned to him in disbelief. "So, they starve the children in order to make more money off of the crops—the crops that the children plant and harvest?"

Anwansi eyed her warily. "Let's not discuss this now. Your eyes were just returning to normal, but you're getting worked up, and now they are changing again."

Instinctively, Macella touched her eyelids. That was the second time in as many days that someone had commented on her eyes when she was angry. What did they see?

"Come," Anwansi instructed, moving toward the door again. "We haven't much time."

Outside, they gathered the fallen Helleborus. There was no sign of the soldiers, aside from the overturned pails. Macella realized it was her first day in Smoketown, and she'd already failed at Aithan's request for her to keep away from the soldiers and stay safe.

Anwansi hurried her inside, as if worried she might do something rash. Something *else* rash, that was. Macella had always been passionate, but she'd also been fairly levelheaded with a long fuse. In Smoketown, she felt like she could explode at any moment.

"Aithan might well end up needing you—more than he already does, I mean," Anwansi scolded her when they reached his room. "If he doesn't come back from Duànzào, there's no one but you to go after him. Try not to start a war with the entire regiment before you see this other impossible task through first."

Macella felt a little ashamed of herself. "You are right. I apologize, mage. I will hold my temper."

Anwansi nodded sharply. "Good. I knew you were a bright one the moment we met. Pluck the petals of those Helleborus and collect them in that bowl."

For the rest of the afternoon, Macella plucked and ground and shredded and measured and every other chore Anwansi tasked her with. She could not complain. The old mage was working as diligently as she was. Macella realized that there was someone else in the kingdom who cared for Aithan of Auburndale's wellbeing. She softened a little more toward the elderly mage.

A child brought them a meal and they ate while they worked. By the time the light began to fade from the sky, Macella was exhausted. Finally, Anwansi declared the mixture ready. Macella helped him place it on a stone hearth behind the sleeping quarters.

(37) "Stand there," Anwansi commanded, gesturing for Macella to stand over the hearth. "Breathe deeply."

Macella obeyed. At first, there was nothing. But as Anwansi started a fire and blew a puff of crimson powder into it, the air Macella was inhaling began to change. Anwansi whispered in a language Macella didn't know. His outstretched arms shook, and beads of sweat began to sprout on his forehead. The air thickened with the sweet smell of rotting fruit.

Macella knew she had to keep breathing for the spell to work, so she ignored the sickeningly sweet smell and inhaled more deeply. Her head began to swim, and tears pricked at her eyes. Suddenly, she felt very sad and very alone.

Finally, Anwansi lowered his arms. Immediately, the smoke evaporated, and the air cleared. Macella looked around dazedly. She had no idea how much time had passed. It had grown quite dark. It must've been late because the night had grown cold, all traces of the day's warmth gone. Macella found herself shivering, her fingers and toes gone numb.

"I think we should have a cup of tea to warm ourselves, and then we should retire. We both need to rest," Anwansi pronounced, taking Macella by the elbow and steering her back inside. Behind them, the mixture sat warming in the reeds, emitting no smoke and no trace of the sickly-sweet stench.

They drank their tea among the sleeping infants. In the dying firelight, Macella could see the exhaustion in Anwansi's wrinkled visage. She wondered when he'd last used his magic to this extent.

Macella soon retired to the room that had been prepared for her—another small and unadorned space, empty save a hard bed, desk and chair, and her belongings. Macella was too exhausted to care. She crawled into the bed, expecting sleep to find her quickly.

Instead, she lay awake, missing Aithan. The room was brutally cold. The building was so poorly insulated from the elements that she might as well have slept outside. There was no fire in her room, nor were there any in the children's rooms she'd passed. She knew this place must be frigid in the cold season.

Macella rose and retrieved a heavy fur from her pack. She spread it over the thin blanket she'd been given. When she crawled underneath, she felt much warmer, though she missed the solid, reassuring heat of Aithan at her side.

Macella touched the star charm at her throat. It was cool, despite being against her skin. It had been cool to the touch since Aithan had left for Duànzào. She was sure of it.

She thought of Aithan's warm, bronze skin, his sweet smoky scent, his strong hands. If he were here, he would breathe in her curls and hum some quiet tune as she drifted into sleep. He would reassure her that she was not standing alone against insurmountable cruelty and centuries of tradition.

Macella had not felt this isolated since she'd left Shively. Things were happening to her that she could not understand or explain. Apparently, she didn't age like a normal human, and something strange happened to her eyes when she grew angry. She'd only recently learned of and accepted her ability to see into and manipulate minds. Yet the new revelations just kept coming.

The world seemed so much bleaker than it had mere days ago. It was as if this wretched place was draining the joy from her body and replacing it with hopelessness and rage. How was she supposed to help Aithan, help these children, and help the kingdom? She was one woman—just a scribbler and a wanderer, not a warrior or a hero. This was all too much.

Macella squeezed her eyes shut against the tears threatening to escape. She worried that if she cried, she'd have to face the severity of the situation and, if she did that, she would become too overwhelmed to function. She had to keep this terror small and contained.

Macella exhaled slowly. A few tears trickled onto the thin pillow. Determinedly, she remembered a trick she'd overheard her mother whispering to the little ones many years ago.

Count your blessings, her mother had said. *It's better than counting clouds or sheep because it will help you fall asleep, and it will give you pleasant dreams.*

One, Macella thought. *Aithan of Auburndale.*

CHAPTER TWENTY-ONE

S he woke suddenly a few hours later, instinctively reaching for her dagger. She sensed that she wasn't alone in the tiny room. Dagger in hand, she grabbed the stump of candle beside the bed and lifted it high to illuminate the small space.

A child sat hunched on the floor near her door. He had his thin arms wrapped around his knees. His shaggy hair fell over his face, his bright hazel-green eyes peering at her curiously from beneath his bangs.

"Hello," Macella said softly. "What are you doing in here?"

The child shrugged his bony shoulders. "You helped Noah."

Macella frowned, sheathing her dagger. She rubbed her eyes and sat upright, looking more closely at the boy. He looked vaguely familiar. He must've been one of the children who had passed her in the rush to the dining hall. Macella assumed that Noah was the boy Grizzle and Torch had been tormenting.

"Are you friends with Noah?" Macella asked gently, wondering why this child had wandered into her room in the dead of night.

"Nobody is friends," the boy replied. "Aegises do not have friends."

"That's not true," Macella corrected. "Aithan of Auburndale is my friend, and he is an Aegis."

The boy gazed at her with his bright greenish eyes. "I saw you come in with him. He rode a black horse."

"Yes, you're right." Macella yawned and rested her chin in her hand. "The black horse is named Jade. The palomino is Cinnamon. And I am Macella. What is your name?"

"Tuwile," whispered the boy. "Aithan of Auburndale will not return. You must help him."

Macella looked up sharply. "What did you say?"

Tuwile ignored her question. "Are you going to help us all? Anwansi thinks you will."

Macella felt a pang in her chest. "I am going to try. I just have not yet figured out quite how."

Tuwile nodded thoughtfully. "Nobody ever tries to help us. They just let us die. They do not care about what happens to us. Nobody listens to us."

Macella slid from the bed to sit cross-legged on the floor facing the child, struck by a sudden idea. In her anger, she'd only been able to imagine violence. But here, in this meager room with this fragile child, she remembered the small, hungry girl she used to be. She remembered who she was and who she would always be.

(38) Macella pulled her journal from her pack. "I am listening. Tell me about what has happened to you."

The boy told his story. Macella recorded the horrors in dry-eyed anguish. She would not, could not fall apart this time. It was her duty to witness. She would not allow these children to be silenced, would not suffer them to carry this burden of trauma alone.

After Tuwile slipped away, Macella continued writing, processing all she'd seen and learned about life in Smoketown. By the time she'd finished, she'd formed the ghost of a plan.

This time, Macella of Shively fell into a deep sleep immediately. In her dreams, Aisling's eyes glowed white and her ginger hair burned like flames as she chanted at Macella about shields and swords, predators and protectors. When Macella woke, she knew exactly what she had to do.

Immediately after they broke their fast, Anwansi directed Macella back to the hearth behind the building. They repeated the process from the previous night. Macella took over the care of the babies afterward so that Anwansi could lie down. He looked even more tired than he had the night before. This use of his magic was clearly draining.

After all the babies had gone down for a nap, Macella slipped from the nursery. Passing quietly through the hall, she looked around her with focused attention. Now that she had decided to bear witness, she was determined to see it all.

The first room that she peeked into was the building's makeshift infirmary. The children placed here were not ill enough for the true infirmary in the mages' promontory, but not well enough to resume their training. Macella ignored the surprised look of the attending mage, walking through the room with her attention on each occupied bed.

A girl of about ten shivered beneath a thin blanket, her dark hair stuck to her sweaty forehead. A boy in his early teens stared listlessly at the ceiling, stiffly bound and gauze-wrapped arms resting at his side. A child of five or six clutched at their stomach, whimpering quietly.

"What ails these children?" Macella asked the mage in a voice that made it clear she expected to be answered truthfully.

The mage was youthful, though Macella could not be sure of his age, of course. He might be her own age or as old as Anwansi for all she knew. He considered her carefully with wide gray eyes.

"A fever," he said finally, gesturing to the shivering girl. He indicated the others with a wave of his hand. "That one's arms are each broken in several places. This one is not responding well to their latest transformative tincture."

His voice was carefully neutral. He might've been reciting a list of items to buy at the market. Macella noted the way he looked past the children as he described their ailments. He could not see them, nor could he acknowledge their humanity.

She remembered what Aithan had said of the townspeople in Valley Station—those who knew of Smoketown's horrors. *Anyone who could stomach that cannot let themselves see us as human beings, let alone heroes. They would not be able to sleep at night.*

Macella took a final look at each child before leaving the infirmary. Most of the other rooms were occupied only by empty beds. One held children too old for the nursery but too young to train. A bored mage sat reading a leatherbound tome while the younglings occupied themselves with a paltry supply of worn toys.

In a sparse classroom, a group of children sat silently as a mage lectured and scribbled on a large board. Macella noticed phrases like *impervious to fire* and *eats the liver of drowned victims*. The children pored over drawings in huge books, some making careful notes or labeling diagrams.

Macella wandered out of the children's quarters and along the path toward the training fields. She knew she should not venture too close to the soldiers, but she was curious about the trials. When she reached the building nearest the training grounds, she found a spot in its shade where she could watch without being observed herself.

The oldest, strongest, and fastest among the children were pitted in a series of tests and obstacles the likes of which Macella had never seen. The soldiers berated them as they attempted everything from traversing a series of increasingly slender posts embedded in hot coals, to battling their peers in brutal hand-to-hand combat. No matter how well a child performed, the soldiers never appeared satisfied. Those who lost their sparring matches were immediately made to complete some grueling physical task, such as supporting pails of stones while standing one-legged on a narrow post. Macella watched for nearly an hour, and the children were never given a break, never allowed a moment to rest or take a sip of water.

She knew that the best of these children would be sent to cross the mountain into Duànzào. On the path there, they'd face hell itself and if they survived, emerge in Duànzào. They would undergo even more training with the wisest Aegises, before taking their place among their ranks. But looking at them now, Macella saw only frightened, battered children, not warriors.

She walked back to the nursery with a heavy heart, but greater conviction. She would see her plan through. She would handle the consequences as they came.

Anwansi and the babies slept most of the late morning away. Macella used those quiet hours to write and worry. Aithan of Auburndale did not return that day, though Macella watched the mountains hopefully whenever she had a few moments to spare. Anwansi met Macella at the hearth twice more, napping after every session.

"Stay close," Anwansi instructed before taking to his bed. "Grizzle is too prideful to tell the others he was bested by a woman, but that doesn't mean you are safe. There are many more like Grizzle, and worse yet, that I would have you steer clear of."

Macella did not tell him of her morning outing. To pass the time, she busied herself around the children's quarters, seeing where she could make small improvements. Though some of the mages looked at her curiously, nobody interfered. She stuffed straw in the cracks and crevices of the walls, cleaned every surface she could, mended blankets and clothes, and generally channeled her anxiety into mindless tasks.

Sitting with Anwansi that evening, she thought over her plan. "How long has Tuwile been in Smoketown?"

Anwansi turned to her in surprise. "Tuwile? He came to us as an infant. I tended to him in this very room. How did you know him? I thought this was your first visit to Smoketown."

"I did not know him before last night," Macella replied. "He found his way to my room somehow. We talked for some time."

Anwansi stared at her, his expression alarmed. He let out a shaky breath. "What did he say to you?"

"He meant no harm," Macella answered reassuringly, meaning to ease Anwansi's obvious distress. "He asked me was I going to help them—the children.
And he told me about the terrible things he has endured here."

"Is that all?" Anwansi pressed. "Did he say nothing else?"

Macella paused, remembering. "He told me that Aithan would not return.
He said I must go and help him."

"We're out of time," Anwansi whispered. "You have to go after him. You'll
leave at first light."

Macella felt cold. "Why? What has happened?"

Anwansi looked at her carefully, before taking her hands in his. "Tuwile ran
away a few days before you and Aithan arrived. They caught him on the very
morning you entered the encampment. His body is probably still hanging on a
post lining the road into Smoketown."

Macella's heart plummeted. She remembered the bird picking at the battered
face of a child whose feet twitched as she watched. His bangs had fallen over his
pecked-out eyes. She could not have known how those eyes had been a bright,
curious hazel-green. Tuwile had looked familiar because she'd seen him in his
last moments of life.

Macella shuddered, staring wide-eyed at the old mage.

"He came to warn you," Anwansi explained. "We must heed the warning."

Macella immediately prepared Cinnamon for their journey. Lying in bed
that night, she thought over Anwansi's instructions. There was only one path
through the mountains into Duànzào. She was to stay on that path until she
reached the veil. There, the death deities would judge her and either allow her
to pass or condemn her to death. If she survived, she would have to stand against
three experienced Aegises to liberate Aithan. If Aithan was still alive.

Macella closed her eyes, her hand over her star charm. She whispered a prayer
to Fate and another to Aithan. "Hold on, love. I'm coming."

"No matter what happens, you post this as soon as possible," Macella said, pressing the parcel into Anwansi's hands.

"If it requires my very last breath, it will be done," Anwansi promised, his voice breaking. "It is odd how, now that I know I'm nearing the end of my purpose, I'm feeling sentimental. I regret that I won't be able to see the new world you and Aithan will create."

"Thank you for your help, Anwansi," Macella said, swallowing a lump in her throat. She had not expected to feel attachment to the old mage, but now she had to blink back tears.

"Thank you for giving me the chance to regain some of my honor before I leave this life," Anwansi countered. "Now go. You'll want as much daylight as you can get."

Macella turned toward the mountain. She inhaled the crisp morning air, felt the morning dew settling on her skin. Then she clicked her tongue at Cinnamon and headed off to find her love.

If the Crown was aware of the reprehensible behavior of those they have entrusted with the care of our most treasured heroes, their retribution would be swift and merciless. The citizens of Kōsaten would settle for nothing less. Thus, it is this scribe's duty to relate to my royal readers exactly what liberties their soldiers have been taking with the Crown's benevolence. I caution my readers of delicate constitution to read no further. The contents of this account are shockingly heinous.

— From "The Aegis and the Journey Home" by S.S.

CHAPTER TWENTY-TWO

"How do the transformations work?" Macella asked, gathering the strands of Aithan's silky silver hair between her fingers.

(39) Aithan sat on the floor, his head between Macella's thighs as she sat in a hardback chair, her sleeping gown hiked up and gathered around the Aegis's bare shoulders. She had decided to braid his tresses away from his face and use the temporary stillness to learn more about his life in Smoketown.

Aithan leaned his head back against her pelvis, looking up at her with his fathomless orange eyes. Macella leaned down to kiss his forehead, then his lips, before sitting up and nudging his head upright.

"Stop moving about and let me work," she scolded him, starting again on the braid he'd just ruined. "Tell me about this strange world I am about to enter."

"Hmmmm," Aithan grunted, sounding resigned. "There is not much to tell. The transformations are the easiest part of an extremely difficult process. They are not pleasant, and they are often deadly, but the training and the trials are far worse."

Macella gathered another handful of Aithan's hair. "The transformations are first?"

Aithan nodded, grinning apologetically when his hair slipped from Macella's grasp and the braid she'd begun quickly unraveled. The Aegis made a big show of planting himself and sitting perfectly still before speaking again.

"The transformations begin almost immediately," Aithan explained, keeping his head completely immobile. "As soon as a child is recruited, the Aegis responsible begins administering the various tinctures and mixtures prepared by the mages for that purpose."

Aithan's voice took on a faraway quality. "From that point on, the recruits imbibe a daily regimen of potions designed to make their bodies stronger and more efficient, to make their minds sharper, their senses keener. Many do not survive the process. Those who do, begin training and consume an increasing amount of the mages' concoctions over the years, until they are ready to climb the mountain and face the trials."

"Do you remember what it felt like?" Macella asked, her voice hardly a whisper.

"Lonely," Aithan answered immediately. "Physically, it was quite painful, but the emotional toll was worse. It felt utterly and devastatingly lonely. I was becoming something different, something other. From the point of being placed in the Aegis's cart and taking the first doses of the mages' amalgams, until the day I met you, nobody looked at me as human anymore.

"For all those years, I seldom heard a kind word, rarely a gentle touch," Aithan went on, his voice wistful. "There were brothels, of course, but purchased kindness is no substitute for genuine connection."

Macella felt an empathetic pang. Finding genuine connection with other people had always been a challenge for Macella as well. That was, until she'd met Aithan. It seemed they had both been searching for a life where they would be truly seen.

Aithan leaned his head against Macella's inner thigh, pressing his lips against her skin. She could feel him smiling. Her heart stuttered.

"And then along came a miracle," Aithan murmured, tracing his lips in a slow line along her inner thigh as far as his head would turn and then back again. "I walk into the same kind of place I frequented in every identical town, and I hear a group of pros taunting a new woman mercilessly. She is bothered by their words, but not showing it, and gods is she lovely. When she passes by me, I catch her scent, and it is like the first sip of cool water in the morning."

Aithan turned his head to trace his lips along Macella's other thigh. She felt an involuntary clench deep in her belly. Her breath caught in her throat.

"I have to speak to her," Aithan continued, his breath warm on Macella's skin. "I can't stand to have her think of me the way other people do. The passing sense of her mind that I glimpse is sincere, determined, and hopeful. I want to know more. I want her to have the chance to judge me for herself. I cannot have those intelligent brown eyes looking at me in disgust."

Aithan lithely shifted his body to face Macella, his long legs over hers on either side of the chair. Carefully, he rested his chin on the small patch of chair available between her thighs. Macella closed her eyes, her heart speeding up when Aithan inhaled deeply, before letting out a pleased hum.

"I have never gotten over your incredible scent, have never gotten used to you seeing me as I am and choosing to link your Fate to mine," Aithan breathed. "Every moment with you—every look, every touch, every kiss—is a miracle to me. The years of loneliness...they fade away more and more each day I spend with you."

Aithan leaned forward, planting a kiss on Macella's clitoris through the soft cotton of her undergarments. A jolt of electricity shot through her. Aithan kept his lips where they were, slipping his hands beneath her gown to cradle her butt.

"I never even thought to wish for this," Aithan murmured against her, each movement of his lips and each breath sending thrills of pleasure through her body. "I do not possess enough imagination to conjure up feelings this wonderful."

Aithan's fingers fluttered against her skin as he untied the laces of her panties. Macella fought the urge to press her thighs closed around his head. Her fingers flexed, still tangled in his half-done hair.

"You are miraculous," the Aegis whispered, pushing the fabric aside to plant a kiss against Macella's clit. She gasped and felt his smile. "Your love has transformed me in ways no magic ever could."

"I thought I was supposed to be the one with the gift for crafting pretty words," Macella said breathily.

Aithan slid his tongue between the folds of her labia, deftly tracing the length of her slit before replying. "The truth happens to be beautiful in this instance. I mean it, Macella. No matter what you see in Smoketown, know that you have saved me from it. Whatever suffering I endured, I have been rewarded tenfold with you."

(40) Macella moaned and clamped her thighs against Aithan's ears as he took her clitoris in his mouth and gave it a gentle suck. Humming, Aithan pulled her closer, his hands kneading her ass as his tongue worked her clit. Macella gave up on salvaging his hair, tangling her hands in the silky strands, and tugging gently. Aithan growled in encouragement, eliciting a moan and shiver from Macella.

"You are only telling half the story, Aegis," Macella moaned, arching her back. "You seem to be omitting crucial information."

Aithan kissed her clit again before lifting his head to look at her. The way his eyes shined as he smiled at her made her heart lurch yet again. She could not imagine looking at Aithan of Auburndale and seeing anything aside from his immense beauty and goodness.

"What information have I forgotten?" he murmured, pressing his lips against her inner thigh.

Macella tugged his hair again, pulling him upward. Obediently, he climbed to his knees, and Macella leaned to kiss him. She loved the warmth of his mouth, the taste of her essence mixing with his own smoky sweetness. Breaking the kiss, she slid her hand into his waistband, motioning for him to stand.

Aithan stood. Macella ran a hand over his bare chest, sliding her fingers through the soft silver hair. She looked up into his eyes as she loosened his trousers. His cock was hard and waiting. Macella wrapped her hand around its shaft. Still holding eye contact, she ran her tongue along one side, before taking the tip in her mouth a moment and then licking the other side. Aithan groaned.

"You are forgetting that your love is also a gift," Macella told him, continuing the path of her tongue between words. "You have always been exactly who you are, and that is enough. No matter what others saw, you were always who you are meant to be, Aithan of Auburndale. You are good and brave and true, and I love you exactly as you are."

Macella took him into her mouth as far as she could, using her hand to cover the length of shaft she could not reach. Aithan's breath quickened as she worked her hand and mouth. She felt the Aegis's hands resting lightly on her head, his fingers twitching against her curls.

Your love is miraculous. You are miraculous. You deserve to be loved as you are, Macella thought at her Aegis as she moved her mouth faster, sucking harder.

"Fuck, Macella, *fuck*," Aithan growled, backing away.

Macella looked up in surprise, still holding his cock in her hand. "What's wrong? Was that too much pressure?"

Aithan took her hand and pulled her to her feet. She opened her mouth to protest, and he crushed his mouth against hers. His hands roamed greedily over her body. He slid his hands beneath her gown and lifted it over her head, before kissing her again, hard.

Aithan held Macella tight against him, the throbbing hardness of his erection straining against her belly. Macella's pussy throbbed in response, the wetness spreading, dripping down her thighs.

"If you keep that up, I am going to cum in your mouth," Aithan whispered against her lips. Macella thought that sounded just fine, but before she could voice the thought, Aithan was already responding. "I want to cum inside of you."

Macella shuddered, her body obviously agreeing with that sentiment. Aithan spun her so that her back was pressed against his chest. He trailed his lips up her neck until he reached her ear. Macella shivered.

"I want to cum inside you," Aithan whispered again.

With one hand, he cupped her breast, squeezing her nipple between his fingers. He slid the fingers of his other hand through the soft hair between her legs until he found the waiting wetness. Macella whimpered.

"I want to feel your pussy clench. I want to hear you saying my name," Aithan murmured against her ear, his fingers rubbing against her sex, teasing at her nipples. "I want to feel you cum. Will you cum for me?"

Aithan moved his fingers faster, pressing more firmly. Macella arched her back and cried out, reaching up to grip the back of Aithan's neck. He bit her ear gently, his fingers working small miracles between her legs.

"Will you cum for me, my love?" Aithan asked again, his fingers moving even faster, right where the sensation was most intense.

Macella's body shook as Aithan held her tight against him, ensuring she couldn't flee his agile fingers.

"Y-yes," Macella stammered, and then she was climaxing, calling out his name, clenching and shaking and falling apart.

Even as the tremors were still racking her frame, Aithan was bending Macella forward over the chair. She braced her hands against it, her back arching as he plunged into her. The sensation was sudden and deep, and Macella had only moments before she felt her excitement climbing once again.

Aithan held her hips tightly, his thrusts hard, fast, and uninhibited. Macella heard his moans underneath her cries, the sound of his pleasure sending ripples through her. He came inside her, so deep that Macella thought she might implode. The world disappeared and there was nothing but sensation and Aithan and Aithan and Aithan and Aithan...

CHAPTER TWENTY-THREE

W hen she came to, Macella was not in a nondescript room at the Valley Station Inn, tangled in Aithan of Auburndale's arms. Their time together there was only a pleasant memory. She was not in a room at all. She was not with Aithan.

Macella looked around her, gasping for breath. Nothing looked familiar. Her mind was utterly blank. What had happened?

Macella fought for focus. Her mind felt fuzzy and distant. She tried to remember how she'd gotten here.

She didn't know how it had happened, but she found herself lying on the hard ground. She struggled to her hands and knees. The air felt thick as if she were breathing smoke. Coughs racked her frame until she was forced to vomit phlegm and the remnants of the little she'd eaten prior to her early departure.

When she'd expelled all that she could, Macella climbed unsteadily to her feet. The mountain looked different than it had before—colors seemed inverted and muted now and, rather than being covered in a light dusting of snow, the terrain looked dry and arid.

The memories of the morning began to come back to Macella. She and Cinnamon had left Smoketown, following the mountain pass toward Duànzào.

The air had grown cooler as they'd ascended, until they reached a point where it was cold enough for the snow to stick to the ground and trees. Then...

Then there was nothing. Her memory refused to go any further. She'd been marveling at the snow one moment, then she'd gotten lost in a memory of Aithan, and the next moment she woke up in this desert, struggling to breathe. The heat was surprising after her chilly ride up the mountain. Macella's skin felt like it was on fire. The only part of her that felt cool was the spot on her throat where her star charm lay. Aithan. She had to get to Aithan.

She blinked several times, trying to clear her field of vision. Macella's eyes and throat burned badly. She fought off another coughing fit, forcing herself to take deep, slow breaths. The burning didn't abate. Instead, it spread, moving from her throat down through her chest. As if the spread had distilled it somewhat, the burning sensation subsided enough for Macella to regain her bearings a bit.

"That's it. If you stop fighting it, it gets easier," said a deep voice.

Macella stifled a scream, spinning to look for the source of the voice. Instinctively, she reached for her dagger, but it wasn't there. Her pack and supplies were also missing, along with Cinnamon, but she didn't have time to think about that.

(41) Instead, she looked at the person who had spoken to her. He was tall like Aithan, with a muscular build and dark brown skin. His curly silver hair was tipped with onyx. His orange eyes, full of deep sadness, searched her face. Macella relaxed. She could sense that the man was no threat. Strangely, she felt like she *almost* recognized him. Like someone she'd had a pleasant passing conversation with long ago.

"Who are you?" Macella croaked, her voice hoarse from coughing.

The man stepped nearer. Macella studied his face and saw that the shape of his eyes was familiar. He smiled sadly, revealing deep dimples in his cheek. His mind emanated a complex set of emotions that she couldn't parse—shame, guilt, joy, despair, and hope.

Macella's heart began to gallop in her chest. Suddenly, she couldn't breathe again. Her heart and her extra senses were trying to tell her something impossible. Here was the crux of another truth she had known all along and never faced. Here was another missing piece of the puzzle of who she was.

The man saw the recognition dawning on her face. His sad smile wavered as he spoke. "I am called Matthias."

His voice was low and warm and familiar. Macella felt tears pricking her eyes, adding to the burning sensation she'd begun to grow used to in the few minutes since she'd awoken in this desolate wasteland. She blinked rapidly against the unbidden emotion.

"You are dead, aren't you?" Macella asked Matthias, instead of the true question looming in the space between them.

"I am," Matthias agreed.

"You are an Aegis," Macella said, still stalling for time. She couldn't let either of them utter the truth just yet. "Is this Duànzào?"

"No," Matthias replied, his eyes never leaving her face. "You cannot enter Duànzào until you pass through this place where the veil is thinnest. A place where you will be tested and deemed worthy or unworthy. If you are worthy, you will be allowed to proceed. If you are found otherwise, you will never leave this place alive."

Macella swallowed hard. She'd known this to be true—Anwansi had warned her—but it was still a shock. She knew that she would die trying to get to Aithan if that was what was required, but the possibility felt much closer than it had before. Now that she stood in this wasteland, breathing fire, it was all too real. It was beyond real, now that she was past the veil and talking to her father.

The pull of his voice, the look in his eyes, the emotions flooding his mind—they were all telling Macella the same thing. He was her father. She'd known almost immediately. And suddenly, so many things made sense: how she'd always felt different and distant from her family, how little they'd cared for her or her for them. She'd never been fully theirs.

"How?" Macella asked, her voice breaking. "I cannot refute that you are my father, but how? How can this be?"

Matthias drew in a sharp breath, his expression crumbling. He looked so utterly heartbroken that Macella almost reached out to comfort him. Instead, she crossed her arms tightly, trying to hold herself together.

"I never wanted this for you," Matthias whispered. "I tried to keep you hidden away."

Macella felt the world spinning. He hadn't denied it. Somehow this Aegis had truly fathered her.

"You left me with my mother and her husband to hide me?" Macella replied, her voice coming out flat and lifeless, as if she'd been wrung out. "They raised your bastard so that no one would know an Aegis had somehow fathered a child?"

Matthias's expression was suddenly fierce, though his orange eyes still shone with tears. "You are no bastard! We haven't much time. Though in the world outside this place it will be as though but a few minutes have passed, for you it will be far longer. Still, you must begin your journey soon. The gods are not known for their patience."

"Please tell me what you can," Macella begged, suddenly desperate. She could not let her only chance at learning the truth slip away. "Just a few minutes. Please."

Matthias heaved a heavy sigh. "I will tell you what I can about your history, but I am mostly here to prepare you for what comes next."

Macella leaned forward eagerly. Despite everything—her terror and anger, her fear for Aithan's safety, her aching muscles and burning throat—she craved this information. She had been following Fate for years, trying to discover who she was and why she was here. Her life with Aithan had revealed some of those answers. And now, impossibly, she was face-to-face with someone who could tell her more.

Matthias sighed before stubbornly repeating his earlier assertion. "You are no bastard. You have never known your mother. She...she died in childbirth."

Matthias's voice broke. Macella had thought he couldn't possibly look more heartbroken, but his expression now proved her wrong. He passed a hand over his face, obviously trying to wipe away the painful memories. He took a few deep breaths to compose himself before continuing.

"It was my fault," Matthias confessed. "I knew better. I knew the risks. We loved each other so much, and she so desperately wanted us to have a child. We had heard that there were ways—dangerous, magical ways."

Macella felt her world reorienting around her, the puzzle pieces shuffling to reveal a new picture. Her life had been a lie. She had never known her mother or father. She had never truly been a part of the family that raised her.

"There was an exiled mage, powerful and elusive," Matthias continued. "She was called Maia. We searched for her for years. We'd heard whispered stories that she had once fallen in love with an Aegis and that, with her skill and her immense magical ability, they'd managed to conceive a child.

"We had almost given up when Maia found us. She'd known we were searching for her, of course. And she tried earnestly to dissuade us." Matthias sighed, his head bent with guilt. "She told us what had happened to her family.

"They'd sent six Aegises to apprehend them. Her partner fought hard—they both did—but it was no use. Her Aegis was killed. Thanks to her magical gifts, Maia managed to conceal herself, though she was gravely wounded."

Macella shuddered, squeezing her arms even tighter around her ribs. "What about their child?"

Matthias lifted his head, turning his tortured expression on Macella. "No one knows for sure. Some stories say they killed him. Others say they took him to the Crown and imprisoned him. Or that they studied and experimented on him for many years and then killed him."

Macella swallowed hard. "So, you knew they would come for us, but you did it anyway?"

Her father looked at the ground again. His broad shoulders sagged. He ran his hands through his curls in a gesture that felt somehow familiar to Macella.

"Lenora was the only person to ever look at me without fear, distrust, or disgust," Matthias said, his voice raw. "She was the only person who ever looked at me with love. Until you."

From the point of being placed in the Aegis's cart and taking the first doses of the mages' amalgams, until the day I met you, nobody looked at me as a human anymore, Aithan had told her. *Every moment with you—every look, every touch, every kiss—is a miracle to me. The years of loneliness...they fade away more and more each day I spend with you.*

Like Aithan, her father had been othered for most of his life. How could she not understand? He'd found what she had found in Aithan with his Lenora.

Macella's heart lurched. Her mother's name had been Lenora. Lenora had been an ordinary human who had looked at an Aegis and seen something beautiful. Just as Macella had.

But Macella was no ordinary human. She was the offspring of an Aegis. An Aegis that Macella might have loved once, though she had no memory of their relationship.

"Can I see her?" Macella heard herself asking. Her heart ached with a longing she'd never felt before. She wanted to see the other half of the union that had created her. She wanted to look for glimpses of herself in her mother's features, just as she'd been unconsciously searching Matthias's face throughout their conversation.

"I'm sorry, Macella," Matthias sighed. "She is not in this realm. It is not typical for those who pass through this place to see their loved ones. Though I hoped this time would never come—I hoped that you would never see this place—but I bargained with Hades for the privilege of seeing you if you did have the misfortune of finding yourself here. Your mother cannot visit this place."

Macella's heart pounded. "That is not what I meant. I have a gift. I can see into the minds of those like us."

Matthias's eyes widened in surprise. Macella knew his shock was a reaction to learning of her gift, but she'd surprised herself as well. She'd said *those like us.* For the first time in her memory, she had thought of herself as belonging to a group.

"When you were young, I thought that sometimes you knew things you couldn't possibly have known, things I'd never said aloud. But I had no idea that you truly had such a gift as this. We know so little about the nature of Aegis offspring," Matthias marveled, gazing raptly into her face.

Macella thought her heart might burst. This man—her father—had memories of her. Memories that made him smile and look at her with love and pride. He remembered a life that they had shared. He knew things about her that she did not know about herself. Macella swallowed hard against the lump forming in her throat. She felt the burn of tears building again, forcing her to blink rapidly against the sting.

But they were on borrowed time. Macella took Matthias's hand in hers, not attempting to hide the desperation in her plea. "Please think of my mother."

Matthias smiled his sad smile and exhaled a deep breath. Macella gazed into her father's eyes and concentrated, probing for his mind. It felt both familiar and foreign to her. She was not used to any mind but Aithan's, but still, her father's thoughts felt familiar. Perhaps it was because she'd frequented his mind as a girl.

A face filled Matthias's mind. Skin the rich brown color of freshly turned earth. Almond-shaped eyes that crinkled merrily at the corners. A wide smile with the slightest gap between the front teeth. Dark hair piled atop her head in a coif of intricate braids.

Lenora sat next to a window, the sunlight streaming in making her skin glow. She held a leatherbound journal in her lap, a pen in her hand. Macella's mother looked up thoughtfully and then scribbled in the journal. She smiled softly to herself, pausing periodically to glance out of the window. Macella then watched her mother stand up and turn toward her—toward Matthias in his memory—and shyly ask if he wanted to hear a poem.

Matthias thought of standing with her mother beneath a canopy of trees. Lenora's mass of braids was interwoven with an array of white and purple flowers. A smiling woman spoke to each of them, they each spoke in return, and they exchanged silver rings. They beamed at each other in the memory, and Macella was struck by the obvious magnitude of their love for one another. This was the love that had led to her life.

Then her mother was squatting, sweating, and panting, Matthias supporting her as she clung to his arm. A beautiful woman with auburn hair and golden skin knelt before Lenora, urging her to push and whispering incantations. The woman struck Macella as familiar, but she didn't have enough attention to spare for that train of thought. She was enraptured, watching her own birth.

Light pulsed from the woman's palms, the glow engulfing Lenora's lower body. Matthias remembered the trill of Macella's first cry. He lowered Lenora onto a pile of furs and kissed her sweaty brow, tears streaming down his face. The mage—Maia—laid a crying infant on Lenora's chest. Lenora held the baby against her body, crying and laughing simultaneously.

Lenora's laughter weakened, but even as she struggled to breathe, she continued to smile with her eyes on Macella. Blood soaked Lenora's gown and stained the pile of furs. Maia worked frantically, chanting and enveloping Lenora in warm light. Matthias held his wife, begging her to stay with him.

"She is perfect," Lenora whispered. "Like you. Make sure neither of you ever forgets it. Remember how much I love you and how unbelievably happy you have made me."

Macella felt tears streaming down her cheeks. She watched as, day after day, Matthias took her infant self to a patch of earth covered in white and purple flowers. Eventually, toddler and then child Macella helped him pick fresh blossoms to replace any withered buds.

Matthias held her close and told her stories. He picked her up and soothed her when she fell down. He taught her to sword fight with sticks and how to write and read. He smiled sadly at her when she read him little stories and poems that she'd written in a half-full leatherbound journal. He tossed her high into the air and caught her again and again as she squealed with glee, her wild curls blowing in the breeze just as his did.

"How long were we together?" Macella whispered, afraid to break the tenuous thread of memory.

"Not long enough," her father replied sadly. "For an Aegis, it was hardly a blink of the eye. Only ten short years had passed when I gave you to Shamira. She had been one of the Aegises that came for Maia and her family. She was wounded early in the fray, though as a Kali Aegis, she was known to be our fiercest combatant.

"The Crown thought that perhaps Shamira had not fought her hardest, so she was punished. She was demoted to recruitment duty," Matthias explained.

An image flashed through Macella's mind—a woman with a blue-tipped bob. She gasped, "The Aegis with the sharp, uneven haircut! I remember her!"

No wonder the memory of the Kali Aegis had been unsettling back when she'd told Aithan about it during their time in Hurstbourne. The terrifying woman had been the one to take her away from her father.

"I gave her all I had in payment," Matthias went on. "She, in turn, paid a family to take you in. They never knew what you were or from whence you'd come. To them, you would've appeared to be no more than about four years old."

Macella quickly calculated the years. Anwansi had been right about her delayed aging and had accurately guessed her true current age. She was at least forty, perhaps a year or so older depending on what her foster parents had thought.

"She made sure to find a large family with many young children so that you would blend more easily," Matthias continued. "I imagine it was not difficult. The Crown ensures Aegises are taught where to find the poorest and most fruitful citizens in the kingdom. They are the best places to purchase child recruits.

"I never knew where she took you—I didn't want to know, could not trust myself to know—so I cannot tell you any further details about the arrangement. They might have pretended you were a distant relation they'd agreed to care for until eventually everyone forgot you hadn't always been there. The neighbors probably whispered you were your false father's bastard.

"They would never know that, in this one instance, an Aegis had paid a family to keep a child rather than to give one up. An Aegis was giving a family a child, rather than stealing them away," Matthias finished heavily. He seemed suddenly exhausted, as if sharing his memories had caused him to relive them.

Macella felt sick. Not only had her parents not been her parents, but they'd also been paid to take her in. She had ridden in one of those desolate carts with the discarded and stolen children of those too poor to care for them. This was too much pain and loss. Too many unfortunate children.

"Why do I not remember any of this?" Macella demanded, shaking her head. "Why can I not recall the first ten years of my own life?"

Matthias bowed his head. "That was a parting gift to keep you safe. To give you a fresh beginning. I asked a favor of the goddess Meng Po."

The implications hit Macella hard. She placed her hands on her knees and took several deep, slow breaths. Her head was spinning. She'd had no idea how much had been taken from her.

"Even Shamira cannot remember all—I had your name and every particular of your location and new family wiped from her mind. I wanted to keep you safe," Matthias insisted. "It killed me to have to give you up, but I believed it was the only way to give you a chance at a life. It completely ripped me apart. It was worse than losing Lenora all over again. I almost didn't care when they came for me."

Macella no longer bothered to stifle her tears. She wept openly, noticing that tears were streaming down her father's face as well. The air was thick with ash and the smell of brimstone. Matthias's tears left tracks in the ash coating his face. Macella imagined her face must look much the same.

"I'd known I would not be able to keep you with me forever, but when Maia was captured and killed, I knew our time was up," Matthias pushed on, his tone urgent. Now that he had related most of the story, he seemed eager to finish. "A mage in hiding cannot sustain their magic indefinitely. They do not have access to the powders and potions they need. Thus, their magic begins to fade, and as the magic fades, so does their life force."

Macella thought about Anwansi and how he'd once been one of the mages that oversaw the Aegis transformations. He had overseen Aithan's own conversion. Now, Anwansi was aged, his magic far too weak to allow for more than his caretaking duties.

She thought of the woman with the auburn hair in Matthias's memory—the mage that had helped her parents conceive her, the woman that had fallen in love with an Aegis and conceived her own child.

"Often, elder mages let their magic wane when they are ready," Matthias continued. "I suspected Maia let herself be found. She'd lived a long life and seen so much grief. She probably had little energy for hiding anymore. She did not have a reason to keep hiding."

Maia had watched her lover die—had watched her child be taken, likely to his death. She'd been hunted for decades, coming out of hiding only once to grant another star-crossed pair their wish of progeny. She'd seen Macella born, seen Macella's mother die. After so much loss, she had to have been utterly exhausted with life.

Anwansi had seemed exhausted as well. Perhaps his many years of service had caught up to him, or perhaps he was worn down from years of witnessing cruelty and abuse. Macella wondered how much of his magic Anwansi had used on her and, consequently, how much of his life force she had drained.

"Once they executed Maia, it was only a matter of time before they found me. I couldn't bear to leave your mother's grave behind. There was no fleeing for me. I was bound to that place," Matthias continued. "When they questioned me, I swore that you and your mother had both died in childbirth. I assume they believed me, since they gave me to the Chosen for execution instead of torturing me for more information."

Macella felt a wave of grief wash over her. Her family had been torn apart so senselessly. Her father had died to protect her, but he hadn't been able to ensure her a safe, simple life.

"Thank you," Macella said finally. She had so many conflicting emotions vying for dominance, but she knew that, regardless of the way things had happened, it was clear her father had loved her. That was something to be grateful for.

"I wish I could've saved you from ever seeing this place. Though I prepared for the chance of meeting you here, I'd hoped it was a needless precaution. I never wanted this for you," Matthias lamented.

"It was my Fate," Macella replied, her belief in her own words calming her slightly, bringing her back to her sense of self. "It was my choice."

Matthias looked baffled. "Why would you choose this? Why would you risk near-certain death?"

"The same reason you did," Macella retorted. "The same reason my mother did. For love."

Matthias's face softened. He sighed. "You have fallen in love with an Aegis? Of all the people in the kingdom, you've somehow fallen for one such as us. I hope you've chosen well, my child. I hope this person deserves your love."

"He is the person I was meant to love for all my days," Macella proclaimed, lifting her chin defiantly.

"You are your mother's mirror image in this moment," Matthias marveled, his voice wistful. "I have seen that look of love and determination many times. This Aegis is very fortunate."

"Fortune has smiled upon us both," Macella corrected smilingly. "I am fortunate to be loved by Aithan of Auburndale."

"Impossible!" her father cried suddenly, making her start in surprise. "Aithan of Auburndale? No. No, this can't be."

Matthias looked as if he might collapse. If the dead could die again, he might have expired right that moment. Macella stepped closer to her father, extending her hand to touch his arm. Despite the heat of their surroundings, his skin was cool.

"What is it, Matthias? What is wrong?" Macella implored, staring into his orange eyes, and feeling the panic and disbelief emanating from his mind.

Just as Macella caught a hint of what was upsetting Matthias, a flash of lightning ripped through the suddenly darkened sky.

"There's no more time! I bargained for the chance to speak with you if you ever crossed the veil, but I was only granted a limited portion of time," Matthias exclaimed, running his hands through his wild curls in distress.

"The other deities must be growing impatient. If they decide you're worthy of examination, one will consider you for their favor. Then you must pass their trials. It will not be painless. And the cost is immense, daughter!" Matthias reached out and gently touched Macella's cheek.

Macella suddenly felt cold. This was too soon. She had so many more questions for her father. There were so many more things she wanted to know about
him, about her mother, and about herself.

But she could sense his desperation. They were out of time. Pushing down
all of her longing, she nodded at Matthias to go on.

"They do not grant their favor for free, child," Matthias explained. "Your
soul will belong to them, as mine does. As does Aithan of Auburndale's." Her
father shook his head at Aithan's name, disbelief flooding his mind once more.
"Impossible."

Impossible children, unbearable pain. Suppressed so long, love blooms again.
The first lines of the prophecy popped unbidden into Macella's mind. Maia and
her partner, Matthias and Lenora—they'd lost their impossible children and
endured unbearable pain.

Then, somehow, decades later, love bloomed unexpectedly between two
wandering, impossible children: Aithan of Auburndale and Macella of Shively.
Son of Maia and her Aegis. Daughter of Matthias and Lenora.

A clap of thunder reverberated around them. Macella felt its vibrations in
her feet. Her heart raced, whether from this latest revelation or the fear of what
would follow that thunder, she did not know.

"What will I have to do?" Macella asked, her heart in her throat. "What are
the trials like?"

Matthias shook his head sadly. "I wish I could tell you, my child. No Aegis
remembers the trials except in glimpses and dreams. All of the death deities take
part in different ways, but Meng Po always uses her gift of forgetfulness. It is a
mercy. I believe the memories would drive us mad otherwise."

Macella thought about how her father had given her the same "gift" so that
she wouldn't remember her early years, could not remember his face or his love.
She had felt that absence her entire life, even if she hadn't been able to name
it. She wasn't sure she believed that having your memories stolen—even the
terrible ones—was a mercy.

"They will decide any moment," Matthias blurted hurriedly. "I've never heard tale of the child of an Aegis going through the trials and transformations, because no such children have ever existed in recorded memory."

"Except for us. Except for me and Aithan of Auburndale," Macella whispered. *Impossible children.*

Without warning, Matthias's body went rigid. Thunder boomed again. A long and pregnant pause followed. Macella didn't move. She dared not even breathe.

CHAPTER TWENTY-FOUR

H er father's orange eyes went black, the irises expanding until the whites disappeared (42). His mouth opened and a flood of light made Macella raise an arm to cover her eyes. The light went from white to cerulean, cerulean to crimson, crimson to violet, and on and on, the colors flashing with increasing speed.

A chorus of chilling whispers filled Macella's mind.

Too old.

Amalgamation.

Untrained.

Abomination!

Untried.

Unprepared.

Unpredictable.

Crossbreed.

Dangerous!

Untamed.

The voices swirled around her or swirled through her mind—she could not be sure. They grew louder and faster and less intelligible as the light from

Matthias's mouth flickered through an assortment of colors so vast Macella had no name for many of them.

Mine.

The light extinguished as suddenly as it had appeared. Macella's father looked at her, his eyes unseeing. Macella felt dizzy. She forced herself to take a breath. All was quiet and perfectly still. Even the ash in the air seemed suspended.

Had they decided she was not even worthy of examination? Was she about to be struck dead? Or maybe she would be trapped in this pocket of hell forever.

Matthias's body began to rise. His muscles went limp. The sky behind him grew darker as he rose. Macella watched, eventually having to turn her face nearly completely upward. Finally, he stopped. His body tilted forward and for a horrible moment Macella thought he would plummet to the ground.

Instead, his head slowly turned toward her. His mouth opened in a horrible approximation of a smile.

"Macella of Shively, born of Matthias and Lenora, Magic and suffering. Macella, orphan abomination, blood of Hades."

Macella forced herself not to look away from the grotesque puppet show. She knew that she could not betray the depth of her fear. This was why she had come.

She had noticed the black ends of Matthias's silver hair and had mentally noted that he must have been a Hades Aegis. She hadn't had time to ask what gifts the deity bestowed. She supposed if she survived this, she would learn.

"Child of both worlds, life and death in your blood. My gifts already flow through your veins."

Macella gasped. Of course. The strange things she could do hadn't ever manifested before she'd encountered hellspawn, rifts, brimstone, and an Aegis. Suppressed once she'd left her father, her gifts must've been dormant, waiting to be unleashed.

The Matthias puppet nodded, his terrible grin widening. *"My children can commune with those who have passed through the shadow of the valley of death. My children can cloak themselves in shadow and flame."*

Macella didn't know about shadows and flame, but she did have other gifts. Her ability to access minds didn't work on ordinary humans, but she could hear the minds of Aegises and demons. And, of course, Tuwile had come to her after his death. "You are why I can speak to the dead and touch the minds of those connected to the Otherworlds?"

Matthias's head tilted. *"My children can commune with those who have passed through the shadow of the valley of death. My children do not manipulate minds."*

Macella frowned, perplexed. "But I can."

Matthias's head tilted in the other direction. *"Curious little crossbreed. It is no wonder the others refuse to try you. Too old, too unbroken, too unpredictable. Perhaps we should not allow you to leave this place."*

Macella felt a stab of panic. She had not come this far to fail. She had learned so much in this horrible place. She had so much left to do. So much to fight for. So much love had led her here. She had to live.

Macella bared her teeth at the deity puppeteering her father's body. "My Fate did not lead me here to die, Hades, god of the underworld. Try me and let me pass."

Her voice sounded steadier than she expected. She was sure she'd be struck down any moment, but she would go out the way she had lived—sure of her Fate and standing by her decisions, for better or worse.

The death deity was silent. Macella counted her breaths, forcing herself to inhale and exhale slowly. She would not die a coward.

Finally, Hades spoke again. *"You know the price, child of my blood? You choose to pledge me your soul?"*

Macella swallowed hard. "My mind is my own. My heart belongs to Aithan of Auburndale. My life belongs to Fate. You can take whatever's left."

Hades laughed, a terrible sound like dirt hitting a coffin lid. Macella's skin crawled.

"Foolish girl. So be it. Let your trial begin."

And thus began the pain.

When Macella came back to herself, she had no idea how much time had passed. She had only hazy half-memories of what had happened after she pledged herself to Hades. What she knew immediately was that she had changed in some deep and fundamental way that made her more herself than she had ever been.

She stood up expecting to feel pain (her last memory was of a searing, impossible pain), but she did not. She felt better than she ever had before. She was not tired, hungry, hot, or cold. It was a strange sense of her every physical need being met.

Macella could tell that it was quite chilly on the mountain, but the cold was ancillary. She could ignore it. She looked around, noticing how the mountain had returned to its normal state. There was no trace of ash or angry deities or her father. It was an ordinary snow-frosted mountain again.

Macella felt a new pang in her chest, a new sense of longing. She missed a life she could not remember, a father she didn't know, and a mother she'd never met. Yet with that yearning there was a new sense of self, a sense of belonging she'd never known.

Macella looked down at her thigh holsters and was surprised to see that each now held a dagger. She unsheathed and examined them. Her original dagger was almost the same, but now the hilt held three onyx jewels. The other dagger was pure silver and featured the same jewels in its hilt.

Despite one being iron and the other silver, their weights were somehow equal. Glad she'd learned to wield with both hands, Macella gave the daggers a careful twirl. She could tell that with a little practice, she would be able to wield them simultaneously with ease. She felt a smile spread across her face. The daggers felt warm in her hands.

Macella inhaled harshly as a memory flashed through her mind, sharp and sudden. *She was surrounded by flames, bleeding and sweating, her chest heaving. The daggers were warm in her hands. Behind her, a roar. She swiveled and threw her silver dagger, eliciting a satisfying wet thump when it connected with fur and muscle. But, as she turned, her iron dagger slipped from her other hand, slick with sweat. Immediately, pain shot through her entire body, bringing her gasping to her knees.*

"Again, crossbreed."

Macella snapped back to herself, her skin prickling with goosebumps. She knew with perfect certainty that the memory was but a glimpse of her time with Hades. She knew that she had already practiced wielding her daggers simultaneously. She had practiced extensively, as a matter of fact.

Though in the world outside this place it will be as though but a few minutes have passed, for you it will be far longer. That's what Matthias had told her. Macella could feel that he was right. She had spent a very long time with Hades and the inhabitants of Underworld.

Macella exhaled and twirled her daggers again. Then, without thinking, she moved through a series of drills Aithan had taught her. Though she'd only been wielding one dagger at the time of those lessons, she was able to maneuver both now, improvising easily. She did not move quite as smoothly and quickly as Aithan of Auburndale, but it seemed her own natural abilities were adequate enough without any of the mages' transformations or the soldiers' overzealous training.

Would the mages' attentions have increased her natural gifts? Macella wondered how she might've turned out if she had gone through the transformations and full Aegis training. She wondered what Aithan would've been like if he hadn't.

Aithan. She had to get to Aithan.

Macella's pack was on the ground nearby. She checked it carefully, relieved to find that Anwansi's parting gift was intact inside. Macella carefully rewrapped the glass vial and tucked it among her other supplies. She put on her cloak and shouldered the pack. It felt light, its weight negligible on her back.

Macella realized that the world looked clearer than it ever had before. The colors were crisper, objects in the distance more distinct. She could even hear water trickling nearby and smell the familiar scent of horse mixed with nature's many other aromas.

Macella took a few moments to catalog the changes in her body. It was remarkable. She wondered again how her natural makeup had impacted her change into...whatever she was now, and how her body would've fared if she'd had her genetic inheritance supplemented by the mages' potions. She supposed she'd be like Aithan of Auburndale. Had the mages' input enhanced his natural gifts?

A lapping sound reached her ears over the steady trickle of water. Following the sound, Macella came to a small stream. Cinnamon stood drinking the cool water, his big black eyes watching her approach. Macella stroked his mane. Curiously, she peered into the water.

At first glance, her reflection seemed almost the same as it always had. Rich brown skin, wild curls, full lips. As she looked closer, though, she began to notice small differences.

Her eyes were darker. The irises, formerly deep brown, were nearly black now. Similarly, her hair had darkened from a dusty black to true onyx, except for a few shiny silver curls scattered throughout.

Macella smiled, revealing dimpled cheeks—cheeks that she had inherited from her father, Matthias. Matthias had loved her. Her mother, Lenora, had loved them both. Just as Maia and her Aegis partner had loved Aithan. Just as Macella loved Aithan.

"Impossible children, unbearable pain
Suppressed so long, love blooms again
Baptized in blood, forged in flame
Stars align, Prophets proclaim"

Macella knew exactly who she was and why she was here. With one last look at her reflection, she mounted Cinnamon and turned toward Duànzào and her Fate.

CHAPTER TWENTY-FIVE

M acella did not ride far before what could only be The Forge came into view in the distance. She tethered Cinnamon and shouldered her pack. She assumed the Aegises stationed in Duànzào had some way of sensing when anyone passed through the veil, but she should still attempt some measure of stealth. She would continue on foot.

After another quarter hour's journey, Macella approached a large clearing. She could see several structures, as well as a massive training ground. She detected no movement on the grounds. Everyone must have been inside—unless they were holding very, very still and luring her into a trap.

To the right of the training grounds, several long stone buildings and a row of neat wood cabins backed against the surrounding forest. Farther ahead, another row of neat cabins edged the far end of the field. Several buildings lined the side of the clearing where Macella stood. No firelight flickered in any of the windows, no smoke curled into the night sky. All was silent.

Macella waited several long minutes, scanning the clearing for any activity, listening for footsteps or breathing, and even searching for scents on the wind. Nothing.

The nearest structure was a barn. Macella could smell the hay and the pungent aroma of animal dung. She crept toward the building, keeping to the shadows. She slipped inside, noticing the slight increase in temperature from the body heat of the animals. There were several horses, a few goats and cows, and a family of hogs, all in pens and stalls.

Macella saw Jade almost immediately. Aithan's black steed stood in a stall near the rear of the barn, shaking his head and stamping restlessly. Macella crossed to him, making low soothing sounds.

"Shhh, it's me," she whispered, stroking the horse's nose. Jade snorted and nuzzled her hand. "I know. I want to get out of here too. I've just got to find Aithan first."

Jade watched her as she searched around his stall. She found Aithan's pack and supplies tossed carelessly aside. As quickly as she could, she resaddled him, repacked the saddlebags and strapped Aithan's belongings onto Jade's back.

"Quiet," Macella commanded Jade, leading him from the stall. She silently pleaded with the other animals to obey as well.

When she and Jade emerged from the barn, the clearing still appeared empty. Macella quickly drew Jade into the trees. She tethered him loosely, sure that they would be mounting up in a hurry.

"Be ready," Macella ordered, patting Jade's side. "Aithan and I will be back soon."

Macella left the horse among the trees and slipped back into the shadow of the barn, trying to determine what to do next. Aithan could be anywhere. It would take her all night to search all of these buildings, and she'd surely be caught in the attempt. Macella fidgeted with her star charm anxiously.

An idea struck her. Macella closed her eyes and focused her attention. She searched her surroundings for the mind she knew best. At first, she heard nothing. For the first time, she realized that she did not know the range of her telepathic abilities. How close did she have to be to "hear" someone?

Just when Macella considered giving up, she felt a familiar whisper in her mind. It was distant and indistinct, but it had to be him. Macella opened her eyes and looked in the direction her mind had indicated.

There was a massive obstacle course and at least a hundred yards of open clearing between her and the part of the settlement where Aithan of Auburndale must be. She would be open and exposed for a dangerous amount of time. Surely, she'd be detected.

"My children can cloak themselves in shadow and flame."

Macella heard the terrible voice of Hades in her memory. Then another memory, unbidden, seared through her.

Burning alive. She was engulfed in flames, screaming as her flesh melted and blackened.

Just as quickly as the memory had come it was gone, leaving Macella with a racing heart and phantom flames on her skin. Macella looked down at her arms and stifled a scream. Black flames flickered against her flesh, spreading over her clothes, and finally engulfing her body.

Macella's mind and body screamed opposing commands. Her mind insisted she save herself from burning to death, but her body was calm. She was warm, but unharmed. The fire was not consuming her, it was coming from *inside* of her.

Sighing, Macella relaxed and listened to her instincts. She had ignited for a reason. She just had to determine why. Then she could figure out the purpose of this particular gift.

She looked across the dangerous expanse of the encampment. Her last thought before the invasive memory was of how she would be seen and caught if she ventured out there. Macella remembered Hades's words again.

Epanofório. The word materialized in Macella's mind. She whispered it aloud, the syllables unfamiliar on her tongue. The black fire immediately took on a hazy quality. Macella's body was now cloaked in shimmery air. She unsheathed her silver dagger and held it near her face.

Her reflection did not appear in the shiny blade.

Macella almost laughed aloud. She was torn between slightly mortified disbelief and sheer amazement. She could see the translucent flames dancing over her arm, but the dagger reflected only the shadowy building behind her.

Macella refocused on the task before her, telling herself she could examine her feelings about her new gifts later, when Aithan was safe. She wasn't sure of the limitations of her apparent invisibility. She could not waste time if the illusion was only temporary or contingent on some other precise aspect of this moment. Macella took a deep breath, then burst into a sprint. Again, she noted her increased speed which, though still not nearly as remarkable as Aithan's, surpassed anything she'd ever exhibited before. Rather than losing precious seconds going around the obstacle course, she opted to run through it.

She was able to avoid most of the obstacles, but not all. Without hesitation or forethought, Macella leapt over a chasm full of sharpened wooden spikes. She caught the dangling rope suspended over the pit and used her momentum to carry her across. She nearly even landed on her feet but had to put a hand down at the last moment to steady herself.

This time, Macella let herself laugh softly. She was barely winded, her breathing measured and even. She resumed her sprint immediately, covering the open field in the length of a few breaths. She slowed, slipping into the shadows of another cluster of buildings: a row of small log cabins. Silently and slowly, she made her way around the nearest cabin and into the unseen landscape beyond.

And then she saw him.

(43) Aithan sat perfectly still, his head lowered, his hair a silver and crimson curtain concealing his face. A heavy iron collar hung around his neck, its chain anchored to a spike driven into the hard ground. Iron shackles bound his wrists. His clothes were torn and bloody, his breathing so slow it was almost imperceptible.

Macella felt rage course through her, making her skin burn. She ran to him, arriving at his side almost before she realized she was moving. She barely had a moment to marvel again at her enhanced speed before Aithan lifted his head and the rage threatened to consume her.

His beautiful face was battered and bruised, his lip split, a blood-caked gash on one cheek. One of his beautiful orange eyes was swollen shut. The other looked like it had only just healed.

Macella exhaled slowly, willing the flames to first reappear and then recede into her skin. Aithan watched her materialize, his brow furrowed. He didn't seem surprised to see her. He gazed at her with his good eye, a smile playing around his dry, cracked lips.

"This is my favorite dream," her Aegis murmured, his voice scratchy and hoarse. "But you look different this time."

Macella dropped to her knees and took his face in her hands. His skin felt feverishly warm. She ran a finger over his cut cheek, and he winced.

Aithan's eyes widened. He inhaled sharply. "Macella, no! How are you here? You have to go *now!*"

"Hush," Macella replied, pressing her waterskin to his lips. "Drink."

Aithan obeyed, his intact eye searching her face. When she pulled the canteen away, he immediately spoke again. "Macella, you have to go. I am conserving energy. It will be days yet before I will suffer from the lack of food and water. But if they find you, they will break me much more quickly than that."

"They are not breaking anyone," Macella hissed, pulling the cloth-wrapped vial from her pack. "We are walking out of here the same way we will walk through the rest of this life. Together."

Macella felt fiercely sure of this truth as she stared into Aithan's bruised face, drinking in the sight of him. Even in his current state, he was the single most beautiful thing she'd ever seen. She felt a rush of emotions radiating from his mind—not just surprise, but confusion and bewilderment. Macella focused her attention, letting herself see what Aithan saw.

He studied her face intently. Macella watched as he retraced the last few moments in his mind, certain now that he had not been dreaming. Macella saw herself appear before him, her skin coated in black flames. As the fire faded, Macella saw her face clearly for the first time since she'd crossed the veil.

Her brown skin glowed, healthy and vibrant. Her raven curls were lustrous, the silver highlights gleaming starkly beautiful in contrast. Macella gasped at the sight of her eyes. As she materialized in Aithan's memory, the whites of her eyes had disappeared.

Her eyes shone entirely black.

As the flames vanished, Macella saw the blackness shrink and the whites of her eyes return. The only people she'd ever seen with eyes that changed like that were Aithan and Kiho. Aegises. Aithan's mind felt hushed, awestruck.

"How?" he whispered.

For the first time, she felt Aithan probing her mind for answers. She did not resist. She opened to him, letting herself remember the past two tumultuous days.

Macella thought of the rage that had threatened to consume her when she'd confronted Grizzle. She remembered the terrible loneliness that had plagued her after she'd breathed the smoke from the Helleborus mixture, how she'd lain in bed trying not to be overcome with despair. She saw Tuwile in the corner of her room, warning her that Aithan of Auburndale would not return without her help. As Tuwile shared his story in her mind's eye, Macella juxtaposed the tousle-headed child who came to her in the night against the image of the pummeled child on the post with the twitching feet.

Macella felt Aithan's shock as he took her hand, strengthening the connection between their minds. She showed him her departure from Smoketown, how she'd woken up beyond the veil. She swallowed hard.

Macella thought of Matthias, replaying the images she'd seen in her father's mind. She showed Aithan the memory of her mother, of her father's grief, and of the Kali Aegis who'd taken her to her false family. She showed him the love in her father's eyes when he looked at her—eyes that were the same orange hue as Aithan's.

Aithan gasped, his mouth falling open in such an exaggerated expression of surprise that it would be comical if the situation were less serious. Suddenly, Macella felt another first—the fear that Aithan might not be able to love her anymore. She hadn't thought of how he might react to her parentage; she'd thought only of getting to him. He'd told her plainly that Aegises did not do well in romantic affairs with their own kind.

She was not even of his guild. Surprised she hadn't noted it before, Macella realized she was a Hades Aegis—the only living Hades Aegis. Aithan, in turn, was the only living child of Lucifer. They were of separate, solitary guilds. Would he still feel the bond they'd shared?

Aithan snapped his mouth shut and lifted his shackled hands to her face. Gazing steadily into her eyes, he ran a hand over her cheek. "I will love you always, Macella," he vowed. "In every form and phase, come what may."

Macella felt a wave of relief. She turned her head to kiss the hand cupping her face. "I will love you always, Aithan. Come what may."

Macella leaned forward and kissed Aithan's bruised lips, tasting his familiar smoky sweetness. The touch of his lips warmed her skin in ways her new black flames could never rival. She broke the kiss, leaning her forehead against his and breathing in the moment. She'd found him. Her Aegis was alive.

Macella forced the moment to a close, remembering that she and Aithan of Auburndale had a bond unlike any other, but he did not yet know it. She had to show him right away. Macella pulled back, her eyes searching his face.

"I learned something of you as well," Macella said gently, holding Aithan's gaze. "I am going to show you now, love. Brace yourself."

Macella recalled the mage in Matthias's memory. She lingered on the image of the woman with magic pulsating from her hands, her golden skin and auburn hair, looking as enchanted as the spell she cast. Macella let Matthias's words reverberate through her mind.

There was an exiled mage, powerful and elusive...she was called Maia. We searched for her for years. We'd heard whispered stories that she had once fallen in love with an Aegis and that, with her immense magical ability, they'd managed to conceive a child.

As quickly and as delicately as she could manage, Macella replayed Maia's story—Aithan's story. She felt realization dawning in his mind even as she shared how the Crown had sent Aegises to execute his family. By the time she showed him Matthias's shocked expression when she'd spoken his name, Aithan had already deduced the truth. Macella saw the image of Maia reflected back at her from Aithan's mind.

She heard Aisling's prophecy whispering from Aithan's memory. *Impossible children, unbearable pain. Suppressed so long, love blooms again. Baptized in blood, forged in flame. Stars align, prophets proclaim.*

"Impossible children," Aithan exhaled. "We are the impossible children."

Macella nodded. "I was baptized in my dying mother's blood; you came here to be forged in flame."

Aithan's eyes widened. "And you crossed into Duànzào. That means you are our thirteenth. You are Kiho's replacement."

Macella felt her eyes widen. She had not thought of the implications of her journey through the veil in this light. She'd simply done what she had to do to get to Aithan of Auburndale.

"But my eyes aren't orange, and my hair did not turn entirely silver," she protested. "Has there ever been an Aegis without those characteristic markers?"

Aithan shook his head. "Not to my knowledge, but you are different than any other Aegis in history. You are a crossbreed, you were already fully grown when you faced the trials, and you did not endure the mages' potions and procedures. You did not undergo the same transformations during your formative years."

Macella had to admit his logic was sound. She'd had but a few days of Anwansi's ministrations to prepare for her crossing. How different might she be if she'd spent her youth being shaped by magic?

"If that is so and crossing the veil has made me into my truest self..." Macella trailed off, replaying the prophecy in her mind before speaking the lines aloud. "*Love leads wanderers to their truth, unknown power now unloosed.*"

Aithan shook his head in disbelief. "It looks like you have unloosed your power, indeed. We have learned far more than I anticipated we would by coming here."

"Yes, well, we must escape this place if all this newfound knowledge is going to do us any good," Macella declared. "I've brought you a gift from Anwansi."

Macella opened her hand to show Aithan the little bundle she held. She unwrapped and uncorked the vial, then held it near Aithan's face. Thick, inky red smoke rose from it. Aithan whispered a low incantation, his eyes deepening to crimson, the whites disappearing. The smoke streamed into his nose, mouth, ears, and eyes.

As Macella watched, the bruises on his face began to fade slightly, his swollen eye opening and shrinking to its normal size. His skin took on a healthier hue. Even his cracked lips began to heal, despite the dehydration he'd endured.

"He must have used a great deal of magic on that," Aithan said as his eyes returned to their normal orange color. "We routinely use potions to expedite our healing, but I've seen none act so quickly as this one."

"I am afraid he's overexerted himself since we arrived," Macella replied with a grimace. "His efforts helped me survive beyond the veil. He was clearly exhausted when I departed."

"We will thank him when we get back to Smoketown," Aithan replied, snapping Macella back to the urgency of the moment. His eyes were suddenly bright and alert. Macella felt the hairs on her arms stand on end. "We should make haste."

"Stay a little longer, won't you?" called a voice from somewhere beyond the cluster of buildings. "We haven't yet had an opportunity to get acquainted with our newest sibling."

Chapter Twenty-Six

M acella spun toward the sound, her daggers in her hands before she'd even completed the movement (44). Aithan drew himself up as far as his chains would allow. Macella shifted her weight slightly, ready to shield him. She wouldn't leave him exposed and unable to defend himself.

"Perhaps another time, Finley," Aithan growled. "We really need to be on our way."

A figure emerged from the shadows, stepping into view but not approaching beyond that. Their graceful build and delicate features matched their velvety voice. With their porcelain skin and silver hair, they possessed a striking, ethereal beauty.

"I think your friend might like to hear what we have to say," Finley countered, spreading their hands imploringly. "Perhaps she can talk some sense into you."

"Or perhaps she can help us persuade you in other ways," hissed another voice from the shadows on their other side.

Macella shifted again, her attention now divided between Finley and the newcomer. She peered into the trees and saw a figure drop to the ground from a high branch. He emerged from the shadows, glaring at Macella with almond-shaped orange eyes. Aithan growled low in his throat.

"Now, Kai," chided Finley. "There's no need for that. You are obviously still miffed that Aithan bested you, but that is no excuse for incivility."

Kai tossed his head, flipping his sleek silver bangs out of his eyes to better glare at Macella. The tips of his thick, tousled tresses were emerald, like the ends of Finley's lustrous locks. His left eye was heavily bruised and there was a half-healed wound across one of his high cheekbones.

"When Kiho wrote us last before their untimely death, they mentioned this woman would be Aithan of Auburndale's weakness," Kai snarled, never taking his eyes from Macella's face. "They suggested that if they couldn't persuade Aithan to our side, she would make a useful bargaining chip. We should not squander their parting advice."

"I will slay you where you stand if you so much as muss her hair," Aithan snarled back, his eyes deepening to crimson.

"Bold words for an unarmed Aegis," Kai mocked. He unsheathed the sword at his hip and Macella saw that it was Aithan's.

"Clearly, I did not need my weapon to defeat you the first time. Remove my chains and see how you fare now that I am starved and dehydrated. Perhaps you'll have a ghost of a chance," Aithan taunted in return, his eyes gleaming dangerously.

"Dear brothers, let us try to discuss this like adults before we resort to violence again." Finley sighed. They looked as if they found the entire display distasteful. "Sheathe your daggers, sister. We won't attack without warning."

The third and final Aegis in Duànzào joined them. She was tall and broad-shouldered with reddish brown skin, short, straight hair falling over her right eye, the ends cerulean, the sides of her hair cut low.

"I am Diya of Park Hill," she told Macella. "This is Finley of Fairdale, and that sour fellow is Kai of Clarksdale. We need to talk."

"I am sure it would be much more comfortable having this conversation with Aithan of Auburndale unshackled," Macella retorted, making no move to sheath her weapons.

Diya sighed heavily and crossed her thickly muscled arms. "There is no need or point to releasing him before we've had our say. Besides, I am of the Guild of

Kali. I can make you feel as if your body is being pierced with a thousand knives at once. It makes no difference if we free Aithan or not. I can easily subdue him again."

"We have a code of honor," Aithan interjected, a warning note in his voice. "We do not use our gifts against one another. A code Kiho violated, I remind you."

Kai bristled. "Whatever you say Kiho did, they were doing what they had to do, knowing you would betray us."

Macella watched the verbal sparring, noticing how each Aegis present shared so much, yet were all so different. Kai was tense and simmering with rage, his mind radiating resentment. Finley was lovely and aloof, almost bored with the entire exchange. Diya was no-nonsense and impatient, uninterested in the petty back and forth.

And Aithan was composed, his face stoic. The only indication that he was at all concerned with the situation was in the tightness of his clenched jaw.

"Enough, Kai," Diya snapped. "We all mourn Kiho. I know that you two had developed a closer relationship of late and that your heart is especially heavy. But Aithan and his partner are not our enemies. They were the last of us to see Kiho alive. Do you not think that they might have questions about Kiho's actions? Perhaps if we explain Kiho's motivations to them, they can be won over to our way of thinking."

"What is there to explain?" Kai demanded, throwing his free hand up in frustration. "Kiho realized it is time to stand against the systems that push us to the margins of society. We all see the necessity of the fight, except Aithan of Auburndale and his pet."

Macella felt her skin grow hot. Her lips curled into a sneer as she narrowed her eyes at Kai. "My name is Macella of Shively and the next insult that rolls off your tongue will be followed by the taste of blood."

Kai opened his mouth to respond, but he was interrupted by a surprisingly loud guffaw from Finley. They were looking at Macella with renewed interest. "Oh, I like this one, Aithan. She's fiery."

"She is," agreed Diya. "Which makes me believe she might be drawn to our cause."

Macella gave Kai a last warning glare, before shifting her attention to Diya. Relaxing only slightly, she nodded at the Kali Aegis. "Speak your piece. I'm listening."

Diya regarded Macella carefully before speaking. "If you have entered Duànzào, then you've at least passed through Smoketown. You have seen the atrocities perpetrated upon the children there, yes?"

Immediately, an image of Tuwile's mutilated body flashed through Macella's mind. She thought of Noah on the ground, Grizzle kicking and cursing him. She saw the small child crawling beneath the table in the dining hall searching for scraps. The boy with the broken arms. The exhausted children battling one another on the training grounds.

Diya saw the confirmation in Macella's face and continued without further prompting. "The Crown has allowed—nay, *encouraged*—these practices for hundreds of years. They have benefited from having our protection, while enforcing our oppression. We are valuable to them as long as they can control our power, as long as they can keep us contained."

"Kiho believed the Crown's lies exceed our knowledge of their treachery," Kai interrupted, his teeth clenched. "Kiho believed that even our most basic beliefs are rooted in lies—that we *could* number more than thirteen, but the Crown fears allowing us to grow beyond their control."

Macella heard the surprise in Aithan's mind as he considered this possibility. His face, however, registered no change.

"They steal or buy us, only to devour us," Finley intoned, their melodic voice heavy with melancholy. "Whether we survive the trials, training, and transformations, or if we die as children, our lives are over from the day we're loaded into one of those wretched carts."

Macella remembered the forgotten life she'd seen in her father's memories. How many of the children in Smoketown were taken from loving, if poor, homes? Matthias had confirmed the unspoken understanding that Aegises were "recruited" from the poorest communities in Kōsaten. Macella had always known how the Crown preyed on desperation, offering coin in exchange for relieving impoverished parents of a few mouths to feed. She knew there were people who happily relinquished their children without pay, just to be freed of the burden of caring for another or dealing with difficult personalities. But she'd also heard about the more nefarious recruitment practices—like deeming certain parents unfit and removing the children into Aegis training "for their own safety."

"We have allowed it for too long," Diya declared. "How many more children have to suffer and die before we act? We can no longer just stand by and do nothing."

"What of the Crown's might? We cannot stand against an army," Aithan said, his tone even.

"We can also gather an army," Kai replied, his eyes alight with bloodlust. "An army that only we can control."

"It is madness to believe that we could control an army of hellspawn," Aithan said incredulously.

"It is madness to live our lives in chains!" Diya roared, her patience finally snapping. "We have survived on scraps for centuries. We have sacrificed our lives to protect humans who would gladly watch us burn. Enough is enough! It is time we fight back!"

The prophecy echoed again in Macella's mind. *Fools fight for fortune, the peaceful court war. Not one prepared for that which is in store.*

"People will die," Macella said quietly. "A war between the living and the demonic will claim many innocent lives."

"Doing nothing has already claimed many innocent lives," Kai shot back. "Do not our lives have equal value?"

Macella looked at Kai. He was practically vibrating with barely contained rage. His orange eyes flickered jade. Macella looked at Finley. They'd found a post to lean indifferently against while watching Macella with a careful, measured calm. Macella looked at Diya. Her irritation was plain on her face. It was clear that these three of Aithan's siblings had chosen a side. They would not be easily persuaded to another course of action.

They were angry, and rightfully so. Macella had only lately learned of the plight of Aegiskind, and she had already only narrowly avoided lashing out. Diya, Finley, and Kai had lived much longer than she had and had endured the horrors she'd only glimpsed in Aithan's memories. They lived in the shadow of the Smoketown mountains, unable to escape its misery. They were the ones who trained Smoketown's survivors, preparing them for their solitary, damned lives.

Still, when she thought of the creatures she'd seen—the kappas, bruchas, lamia, and chupacabra—she could not imagine unleashing demons upon the kingdom. They would wreak havoc on soldiers and civilians alike. Macella had heard their minds and glimpsed the insatiable desires that fueled them. And, when Kiho had opened their final rift, the ancient minds that stirred at their summons had been far worse. No, those monsters would not be controlled.

"We cannot let you open the doorways of hell," Aithan intoned, his voice sorrowful.

Macella knew he had followed her thoughts to this inevitable conclusion.

"You can," Finley insisted, their voice imploring despite their casual stance. "If you do not wish to stand with us, so be it. Just do not hinder us."

"Just stand aside," Diya agreed. "Our quarrel is not with you."

"Stand by and do nothing, as you have done while our kind have been systematically destroyed," Kai added, voice dripping with disgust.

Aithan turned his attention to the Apophis Aegis, his eyes hot with anger. "Careful, Kai of Clarksdale. You are coming dangerously close to impugning my honor."

Kai grinned viciously at Aithan. He tossed Aithan's sword carelessly to the ground, reaching over his shoulders, and unsheathing his own weapons: a pair of gleaming sickles with wickedly sharp blades.

Macella shifted toward Kai, her skin growing hot, a ghost of black flame flickering over her arms.

"You are quicker to shed our blood than to stand against them?" Diya demanded, her hand twitching toward the battle-axe strapped to her back.

"There is no us and them," Aithan insisted, his voice exasperated. "We are also human. Our quarrel is with the Crown, not with humanity. There has to be a way to enact change that does not require further loss of life."

Kai laughed mockingly. "You truly think they consider you human? They do not. You're a glorified guard dog. No, they treat their dogs better than us. You are a beast to be used and discarded. Less than a whore."

"We are clearly not going to come to agreement," Diya interrupted, unstrapping her battle-axe. "Aithan of Auburndale and Macella of Shively, do you stand with us or are you against us?"

Macella exchanged a look with Aithan. "There has to be another way."

Kai scoffed. "As I said from the beginning, they will stand with the humans like good little lapdogs."

"Do not conflate compassion with obeisance," Macella snapped, her skin flaring hotter. "Anyone who would, without hesitation, resign scores of innocents to brutal deaths is indeed the beast they think us."

Kai laughed a bitter, humorless laugh. "They would not so much as bat an eye were every Aegis to perish this moment. Do you think your *compassion* makes you any less beastly? Adorning your collar with flowers does not change the fact that you are leashed."

Macella's black flames grew brighter. She took a breath to calm them before replying. "You seem to view compassion as a liability. You think that our humanity is weakness when it is, in fact, our greatest strength. Do you not wonder how I crossed through the veil unharmed, despite never going through your transformations?"

Careful, Macella, Aithan whispered into her mind. *They cannot be trusted.*

Macella ignored him, her eyes on his siblings. Her question seemed to take all three of the other Aegises by surprise. They clearly had been too preoccupied to consider this mystery. Diya tilted her head, examining Macella shrewdly.

"I am born of a true union between Aegis and human," Macella said, drawing herself up to her full height. "I am proof that we can not only coexist but thrive and evolve together."

Macella watched her meaning dawn on each of their faces. The myriad of emotions that passed over them were varied, but there was a familiar and common thread that filled Macella with resignation: fear.

(45) "This is a threat we cannot allow," Diya grimaced, her hand tightening on her weapon. "Aithan of Auburndale, will you join us, or will you die here with this crossbreed?"

Macella's skin blazed black flames, her daggers glowing onyx. Aithan's eyes darkened to crimson as he strained against his shackles.

"Do not do this," Aithan roared, yanking his chains viciously.

Macella saw Finley turn away, their eyes fixed on a distant point. On her other side, Kai's eyes were jade pools, his sickles glowing emerald. Macella's stomach sank as Diya's intention leapt from the Kali Aegis's enraged thoughts.

"Diya, no. Please," Aithan begged.

Then Macella was on the ground, writhing in absolute agony. It was as if she was being dragged across a bed of broken glass. Far away, someone was screaming. Was it Aithan? Was it her?

She did not know, but she wished they would be quiet so she could pass out and escape the sensation of her flesh ripping at a thousand points simultaneously. The pain blotted out everything, engulfing her senses, blocking her ability to see or hear or even breathe.

It blocked everything, that was, except a hazy memory. A memory of burning flesh and haunting laughter. Pain.

Macella was well-acquainted with pain.

Her mind stepped away from the suffering in her body. She searched for the source of the glass shards, the place from which the pain originated.

Stop. Macella pushed her will into the cerulean source of the sharpness. *I can make you turn the pain on yourself, and I will do so, unless you stop now.*

For a moment, Diya resisted. Macella's mind fought to push through her agony long enough to demonstrate her fortitude to her attacker. *Drop your axe.*

Distantly, Macella heard a clang as Diya's axe hit the hard ground. Macella pushed a final thought at the Kali Aegis, her mind moments from being reclaimed by the pain searing her every nerve.

Last warning, Macella threatened.

Macella's body sagged in relief as the pain abruptly withdrew. She lay still on the ground, stunned. The screaming stopped.

"Macella! Macella!" Aithan's anguished voice cut through the haze around her brain.

Macella inhaled sharply, forcing herself to her hands and knees. She lifted her head and found Diya staring at her in horror. Kai and Finley eyed Diya anxiously, awaiting her next command.

"She was in my head," Diya growled. "Kill them both. Now."

Diya picked up her axe as Kai and Finley immediately moved to obey. Kai started straightaway for Aithan, his jade eyes filled with bloodlust. Finley approached Macella, their beautiful face blank and distant. Macella pivoted, preparing to shield Aithan from Kai's descending sickles.

"Stop," Aithan commanded, grimacing. His eyes glowed crimson and Macella could feel the strain of his mind against the will of the two Aegises.

Diya's eyes glowed cerulean, her mouth twisted into a sneer. Her bloodthirsty rage rose to nearly match Kai's. Her knuckles around the axe handle had gone white.

"You would use your gift against your own?" Diya shouted. "You would protect the humans because of this crossbreed?"

Macella climbed to her feet, feeling her strength returning as translucent ebony flames flickered over her body. She gripped her daggers tightly. She could feel Aithan's hold on Kai and Finley slipping.

"We are your family, Aithan of Auburndale!" Diya screamed. "They took everything we ever had and yet you would turn against *us*? Are you such a coward?"

Again, Aisling whispered in Macella's mind. *Darkness gathers, trouble brews. Predator or protector, one must choose.*

Aithan turned his head and met Macella's eyes. She could see herself reflected in his mind—her eyes completely black, her flesh aflame, unburnt. He smiled.

Love leads wanderers to their truth. Unknown power now unloosed. Aithan thought the lines of the prophecy at her. Macella could feel something new growing in his mind.

"I am Aithan of Auburndale, born of an Aegis and a human mage," Aithan said, turning back to Diya. "I am Aegis, I am human, and I am a protector. And that is the last time one of you besmirches my or Macella's name."

Aithan released his hold on the Apophis Aegises, but as they lunged with Diya merely steps behind, surprise halted them midstride.

(46) Aithan's body erupted in crimson flames. Like Macella's, Aithan's flames appeared to come from within, covering his skin and clothing without burning him. With a roar, he burst to his feet, the chain around his neck ripping from the ground in a torrent of screeching metal. He swung the chain in a wide arc toward his siblings. Finley evaded it gracefully, but the chain wrapped around Kai's ankles. Aithan jerked the chain sharply, sending Kai crashing to the ground.

Even as he took down Kai, Aithan reached one shackled hand up to grab the collar around his neck. The metal took on his crimson flames until, with another roar, Aithan twisted his wrist and snapped the collar in two.

That's new, Macella heard him think, and then Diya's axe was swooping toward him. Aithan threw up his shackled hands, the chain between them stopping Diya's axe from reaching him. Aithan twisted, wrapping the chain around the axe, and ripping it from Diya's grasp. Diya stumbled forward, but recovered quickly, grabbing Aithan, and delivering a vicious head butt.

Kai was back on his feet, advancing toward Aithan. Macella sprung at him, daggers at the ready. Kai pivoted toward her, meeting her blades with his sickles.

And then everyone was fighting.

Macella spun away from Kai and immediately bent backward to avoid the graceful swing of Finley's emerald spear. She dropped low and swiped Finley across the thigh with one dagger, then pivoted to throw her other dagger at Kai's advancing form.

Kai knocked the dagger away with a sickle, then brought the other blade down toward Macella. She parried with her remaining dagger, punching him in the stomach with her other hand. Then Finley's spear stopped inches from her face, caught in Aithan's wrist chains. Deftly, Finley danced away, freeing their spear with acrobatic dexterity. Macella rolled to where her other dagger lay, grabbing it as she climbed to her feet.

Macella and Aithan stood almost back-to-back. Macella held a dagger in each hand; Aithan was empty-handed, wrists shackled. Around them, the other Aegises were also repositioning themselves or recovering lost weapons.

"We need not do this," Macella said, her chest heaving. "Let us find another way."

"This *is* the way," Kai hissed, charging at Aithan.

And then the battle began in earnest.

Aithan dodged Kai's attack, wrapping his hands around his wrist shackles, and sidestepping another swift pass from Kai as crimson flames spread to the metal cuffs. As the restraints fell from his wrists, Aithan caught Finley's spear mid-swing and used the Apophis Aegis's momentum to throw them at Kai.

Macella avoided Diya's axe, using her agility to her advantage against the much larger woman. "I suppose when you can subdue your opponent with your gift, you don't actually have to be skilled with a weapon."

Diya lunged at Macella, incensed by her goading. Macella dropped to a knee and pivoted away, delivering a series of quick slices to Diya's thigh and then to her calf as she stumbled forward. Diya stumbled to one knee, crying out in rage. She glared at Macella. Macella grinned back.

I guess you were right about me being a threat, Macella taunted in Diya's mind.

"You fucking mutt," Diya snarled. "Stay out of my head."

"I am not ashamed of what I am," Macella shot back. "Perhaps you should reflect on why my parentage would offend someone who prides herself on standing for the marginalized? You use the same insults against me that have been used to insult Aegises for centuries."

"Shut up and fight!" Diya growled, climbing back to her feet, and charging at Macella again.

Aithan's sword lay several yards away, where Kai had tossed it. Kai and Finley were advancing on him, Finley limping noticeably from the cut Macella had left across their thigh. Macella braced herself for impact but, just as Diya reached her, Aithan's sword flew past them, knocking Diya off course. The tip of Diya's axe grazed Macella's temple, less than a finger's breadth from her eye.

Macella whipped her head toward Aithan, her mouth falling open. Aithan smiled and shrugged, his sword now firmly in hand. *That's new*, she thought at him. *I suppose I am not the only one unloosing unknown power.* She heard Aithan chuckle low in his throat.

Macella took a moment to feel a joy incompatible with the situation. She was fighting for her life, after all. Yet, she was fighting beside the love of her life. She knew who she was and where she'd come from. There were worse ways to die.

Kai advanced on Aithan, brandishing his sickles. Aithan raised his sword.

Finley and Diya came at Macella from either side, the point of Finley's spear aimed at her torso as Diya's axe arced toward her from above.

"Epanofório," Macella whispered.

Invisible, Macella stepped out of the path of their attack. Were it not for Finley's superior gracefulness, they would've run Diya through and likely been brained in the process. As it was, their spear grazed the big woman's side, leaving a bloody gash.

That's new, Aithan mimicked her earlier words, finding her mind though he could not see her body.

Macella stifled a laugh and threw both of her daggers in quick succession. In the minds around her, Macella saw that, to them, her daggers appeared in midair, apparently only regaining visibility after she released them. The first struck Diya in her already bloodied calf muscle. The other embedded itself in Finley's uninjured thigh. Both Aegises went down.

Aithan's sword scraped against the inner side of one of Kai's sickles. Aithan twisted his wrist sharply and the sickle flew from Kai's grasp, skidding across the ground. Before Kai could lift the other sickle, it flew from his hand in a sudden jerk, landing on the ground near its mate. Aithan spun to stand between Kai and his fallen weapons, pressing the blade of his sword against Kai's throat.

A little help please, Macella thought at Aithan.

Macella let her flames darken until she reappeared. She looked pointedly at Aithan and gestured to her daggers. The one in Finley's thigh was buried halfway up the blade. Both of Finley's thighs were now bleeding heavily. Diya could not seem to decide whether to pull Macella's other dagger from her calf, or to apply pressure to the spear wound on her side.

Macella extended her hands. Aithan smiled at her indulgently, then glanced at her daggers. The daggers jerked free and flew into her hands, their blades slick with blood. Finley gasped and clutched at the wound. Diya grunted, dragging herself toward a nearby boulder so she could prop herself against it.

Macella pointed one blade at Diya, keeping the other trained on Finley. "Yield. We will let you live and you, in turn, will grant us time."

"Time for what?" Kai demanded, a bright line of blood trickling from where Aithan's blade pressed against his throat.

"Time to try to change things without unnecessary bloodshed," Macella answered, eyeing each of the three Aegises carefully. "Vow to delay your plans until we've had a chance to try things our way."

"And how long will that be? We will not be delayed indefinitely," Finley asked, their voice bored and indifferent once again.

"Until after the cold season," Aithan replied. "Let us spend our sojourn at court in our efforts. When we depart from Pleasure Ridge Park, you will have assurance of our success or failure and can govern yourselves accordingly."

"How do we know you won't simply tell the Crown of our treasonous intentions?" Kai demanded, his eyes narrowed in suspicion.

"The same way we know you won't betray our true parentage," Macella retorted. "Lives were sacrificed to keep my lineage a secret to the Crown, and I would have it stay that way. The Crown certainly knows Aithan's origin, but they cannot know that he knows, nor the extent of his power now that he does."

Diya looked from Finley to Kai. Finley sighed. Kai scowled.

"The Crown would be rather keen to gain control of her peculiar skill set," Finley drawled, shrugging their shoulders delicately. "And they would surely execute Aithan to keep him from becoming a threat."

"Agreed," Diya said. "I swear to delay our plans until after the cold season, and to keep your secrets."

"Finley," Aithan prompted.

Finley waved a hand impatiently. "Yes, I vow the same—wait until the warm season, keep the secrets, and so on. Can we get on with it? I'd like to get inside and have some healing elixir and a strong drink."

"Kai," Macella said, raising an eyebrow at the Apophis Aegis.

Kai's eyes glowed emerald, and then Macella was looking at herself. She had nearly forgotten that Apophis Aegises could change their shape. Kiho had also taken on her form once. She scowled. Her doppelgänger scowled back.

In an exaggerated nasal voice, Kai mimicked Macella, drawing out the single syllable. "Kaaaaaaaaaiiiiiiiii."

Aithan snorted a laugh and quickly attempted to hide it in a cough. Finley huffed an annoyed sigh, tossing their shimmering silver hair over their shoulder. Kai returned to his normal form.

"I swear to wait until after the cold season before I slaughter everyone standing in my way," Kai grumbled. "And I swear to keep the secret of Macella's parentage and Aithan's self-discovery until I'm forced to reveal it by your inevitable betrayal."

"I suppose that will have to do," Aithan said, lowering his sword. He stepped nearer to Macella, his warmth steady and reassuring.

Kai gathered and sheathed his sickles, wiping blood from his throat. He ignored Aithan and Macella as he passed them. Without glancing back, he scooped Finley from the ground, carrying them toward one of the distant buildings.

"This is so undignified," Finley complained. They winked at Macella over Kai's shoulder, before dramatically draping an arm across their face.

Aithan reached out a hand to help Diya to her feet, but she knocked it away and struggled upright on her own. She used her battle-axe to steady herself as she scowled at Aithan and Macella.

"Do not make us regret this," Diya warned, her voice low and seething with anger.

"Do not make *us* regret sparing *you*, Diya of Park Hill," Macella retorted, unconsciously twirling her daggers as she glared up at the Kali Aegis.

"I hope you will come to think differently, sister," Aithan said quietly, looking away from Diya, toward Smoketown. "I believe that we can find a better way forward."

Diya sniffed and turned away without answering. She made her slow way in the same direction Kai and Finley had gone. Behind her, a trail of blood splatters painted the rocky ground.

When she was nearly out of earshot, Diya spoke again, as if to herself. "We were never going to kill you."

Aithan silently watched Diya limp away. Macella wiped her daggers against her trousers, then returned them to her thigh holsters. She suddenly realized what an incredibly long day it had been.

"They despise me," Macella said, a little sadly. "I thought my own kind would be more accepting."

"They'll come around," Aithan answered, taking her hand, though still looking at Diya's now-distant form. "They are not used to being bested, nor are they generally good with people. We learned a lot about survival growing up in Smoketown, but not much about interpersonal relationships."

"I hope we can make things right." Macella sighed.

"I believe that we will," Aithan stated, turning his gaze on her. "I believe that we can do anything together. You have certainly proven that you're a force to be reckoned with."

Then she was in Aithan's arms, his face buried in her hair, planting kisses in her curls. She wrapped her arms around him, pressing herself against him. The adrenaline coursing through her veins in wake of the battle, and the thrill of being with Aithan again, made for a heady mixture. Macella felt warm all over.

"Gods, I have missed you," Aithan told her, holding her close. "It feels like an eternity. I was not sure I would ever see you again."

Macella felt as if she could not get close enough to him. She squeezed him tightly. For this man, she had literally crossed through hell and battled the strongest fighters in the kingdom. And she would do it all again without hesitation if she had to.

"I was afraid as well," Macella answered, lifting a hand to touch her star charm, now warm against her skin.

"You were amazing," Aithan murmured into her hair. "You fought as though you have been training your entire life. I am in awe of you."

Macella felt herself glowing with pride. "It felt natural. Exhilarating, even. Is that strange?"

A low laugh rumbled in Aithan's chest. "Battle is usually exhilarating to our kind. And you were fighting for us, for love. It was brave and righteous. Arousing, even. Is that strange?"

Macella's breath caught in her throat. Maybe it was the heat of the battle, her gratitude and relief at finding him alive, or just that they were together again despite all the odds against them, but she suddenly felt a different excitement spreading.

"I do not think that is strange at all," Macella replied. "You certainly looked very appealing breaking free of those chains."

(47) Aithan lifted her face and pressed his mouth against hers hungrily, his hands moving from her hair to her neck, down her back and to her waist. Macella stood on tiptoe, sliding her tongue against his, and squirming against the answering stiffness of his erection. She felt a frantic need, an almost painful desperation to christen their reunion.

Aithan lifted Macella from the ground, beginning to walk toward the nearby buildings. *I crave you this moment. We can rest the night here safely, unless you object.*

In reply, Macella wrapped her legs around Aithan's waist, her tongue more insistent in his mouth. She rolled her hips, grinding against the hard bulge of his cock. Aithan growled, carrying her swiftly to one of the small log cabins. He pressed her against the door, kissing her harder while he unbuttoned his trousers with one hand, the other hand clutching her ass.

Macella moaned against his mouth, her pussy throbbing against the rigid press of Aithan's erection. Her nipples strained against the fabric of her binder, sensitive and yearning for Aithan's touch. She was unused to being so confined. She'd only worn the restrictive undergarment for the support it would provide during battle, but now it was in the way. Aithan intuited her desire, taking his hand from his unbuttoned pants to slip it under her shirt. He brushed his thumb lightly over one stiff nipple, groaning when Macella responded by biting his lip and grinding harder against him.

The door opened and Aithan stepped inside, kicking the door closed behind them. Macella broke the kiss to look around them briefly, catching her breath as she took in the narrow bed, small table, and single chair that furnished the cabin. Aithan tossed her onto the bed, immediately stepping out of his boots and trousers, and pulling his torn shirt over his head. Macella felt around in the semidarkness until she found the table, along with the matches and candle she'd spotted atop it.

She lit the candle and took Aithan in, wanting to retrace all the familiar planes of his body with her new eyes and all the new knowledge she'd acquired during their short time apart. Aithan of Auburndale was as beautiful as he'd been since the moment she'd first walked into his rented room and saw him reflected in the mirror, his orange eyes boring into her and igniting little fires on her skin even then.

Aithan's eyes were full of longing as he looked at her now. He bent to remove her boots as she pulled off her blouse and unlaced her binder. Every touch of his hands against her skin sent electricity coursing through her body. Her newly heightened senses made each smell, sight, and sound sharper, more arousing.

Aithan growled again, yanking her pants over her hips, and sliding them off. "Your mind, your feelings—they're even clearer to me than before. And you are driving me absolutely fucking wild right now."

In response, Macella sat up and grabbed Aithan's arm, pulling him down on top of her and wrapping her arms around him. She kissed him hard, her heart pounding, her skin hot. In the back of her mind, she wondered what would happen if her skin erupted in black flames with Aithan this close to her.

Aithan chuckled, taking his mouth from hers to move it to her breast. *It won't hurt me,* Aithan thought, circling her nipple with his tongue. *Hellfire*

cannot harm an Aegis. Besides, anything that you touch will be protected from your
flames. We're going to have to expedite your training if we—

Shut up, Macella thought back. She reached down and took his cock in her
hand, guiding him into her eager, throbbing wetness. Aithan groaned and bit
her nipple, gently but firmly, as he thrust into her. Macella cried out, tilting her
hips up to force him deeper.

Aithan gripped her hips, plunging into her again and again, running his lips
along the skin of her neck, his warm breath sending jolts of sensation through
her core. Macella shuddered, her pussy clenching, throbbing, pulsing as Aithan
thrust into her again and again, in a deliciously agonizing cadence.

Macella clamped her legs tightly against Aithan's hips, shifting her weight
and lifting herself off the bed. Aithan let her roll them over, his hands gripping
her hips to preserve their union. Macella straddled the Aegis, grinding against
him, and reveling in the slippery friction against her clit.

Macella ran her hands over Aithan's muscled arms, guiding them up until she
could hold them above his head. She kissed him again, her tongue searching his
mouth, every atom in her body vibrating. She rolled her hips, easing Aithan's
cock incrementally in and out of her pussy, increasing the pressure against her
clit more and more as her body began to shake.

Macella could feel Aithan fighting not to take control, letting her restrain
him, enjoying the exquisite frustration of her slow grind. She could feel his need,
the way he wanted to flip her over and fuck her hard from behind, releasing the
last of the post-battle adrenaline in a burst of carnal pleasure.

That thought unraveled her, and then Macella was panting Aithan's name
as she came in a series of spasms and quakes. As soon as her shudders began to
slow, Aithan flipped her onto her stomach, then roughly jerked her hips up as he
positioned himself behind her. Macella arched her back as he entered her again,
eager and unembarrassed. He came minutes later, Macella burying her cries in
the bedding as he gave a final deep thrust and collapsed onto her with a satisfied
sigh.

Aithan rolled onto the narrow bed beside Macella and pulled her tight against
him. He wrapped his arms around her and kissed the top of her head.

"I love you so much, Macella," he whispered. "You disregarded everything I told you to do when we parted, and I cannot do anything but marvel at your bravery and devotion. Thank you for coming after me, you hardheaded, brilliant, awe-inspiring creature, you."

"It is Fate, you foolish man," Macella replied, yawning and reveling in the feel of Aithan's skin against hers. "Besides, I have no idea what in my character would lead you to believe I'd actually leave without you."

"Self-delusion, I suppose," Aithan admitted, stroking her curls. "It was the only way I could convince myself to leave you behind—the belief that, if I did not return, at least you would be safe."

"I do not wish to be safe," Macella told him, craning her neck to look into his face. "I wish to be with you, whether in peril or protection."

"I know, my love." Aithan kissed her lightly on the lips. "I swear it is not a lesson I'll need to learn a second time. I shall not part from you again."

"Good," Macella said, snuggling against him once more. "I'm glad that's settled."

"Now onto bigger challenges." Aithan sighed. "How are we going to prevent the coming war?"

"I have the shell of a plan." Macella yawned again. "But I will enlighten you tomorrow, if you will allow it. It has been an exceedingly long and eventful day."

"Indeed, it has," Aithan agreed. He flicked a hand at the candle, extinguishing the flame with his newfound gift. "Rest, love. You have honored Matthias and Lenora with your bravery this day."

Aithan of Auburndale held her close, his face buried in her curls. His hands traced patterns over her skin, the comfort of his touch melting away any remaining tension in her body. Macella fell asleep to the sound of him humming the refrain of an old ballad.

CHAPTER TWENTY-SEVEN

They rose early to find a parcel of bread, cheese, cold meats, and hardboiled eggs, along with a carafe of spiced wine, awaiting them on the doorstep of the little cabin. *Finley*, Aithan thought as he showed Macella the bundle's contents. They gathered Macella's discarded pack and ate as they walked to the place where Macella had tethered Jade, passing the carafe of wine between them in amicable silence. They were surprised again when they found that someone had unburdened Jade during the night, laid him a bed of hay, and apparently fed and watered him as well. Jade lowered his head and nickered at Aithan, who patted him affectionately in return.

"Finley, again," Aithan guessed. "They prefer to roam at night and are prone to kind deeds when properly drunk. They probably felt a bit guilty about some of Diya and Kai's behavior toward you."

Aithan looked toward the cluster of buildings his siblings had vanished into the previous night. "They've always hidden a compassionate streak under all that aloofness."

Macella felt the conflicting emotions in Aithan's mind. She reached out and squeezed his hand, then handed him the last of the wine.

"Of all the living Aegises I have met thus far, I'd say Finley is my second favorite," Macella said with a smile.

As they made the short ride to where Cinnamon waited, Macella told Aithan what steps she'd already taken toward their goal of stopping the war. When she relayed the contents of the scribe's latest tale, Aithan shook his head in disbelief.

"It is a smart and dangerous move," he murmured, looking back toward Smoketown. "The Crown will have to take some action to appease the people, but they will be displeased by the power play. I suppose we'll find out how displeased when we arrive at court."

"We will make it easy for them," Macella replied, an angry smile spreading across her face. "We will begin the changes now, and they will get the credit."

They found Cinnamon similarly cared for, obviously by the same secretly compassionate sibling. Macella decided that she quite liked the beautiful Apophis Aegis. She patted Cinnamon amid the nickers and nuzzles of his reunion with Aithan and Jade, then mounted up.

She was relieved to learn that their path back to Smoketown, despite being identical to the route to Duànzào, did not require them to pass again through the veil. Instead, Macella was able to enjoy the crisp mountain air and the changing colors of the leaves, as she explained to Aithan the next steps of her smart and dangerous plan.

With Aithan's refinements, the plan gradually became smarter, if no less dangerous. When they reached the foot of the mountain, they left a note for Diya and the others in the trunk placed there for their supplies and correspondence. Soon after, they were leaving Jade and Cinnamon with a stable hand and making their way into the Smoketown children's quarters.

They found Anwansi, not in his room, but removed to the infirmary in the mages' promontory. The old man looked ancient now, diminished and depleted. Still, his eyes brightened when he saw Macella and Aithan enter the room.

"It is good to see you again in the land of the living, Aithan of Auburndale," Anwansi greeted in a papery thin voice.

Aithan took Anwansi's withered hand in his. "It is good to see you as well, old friend. Thank you for taking care of Macella."

Anwansi smiled at Macella as she approached his bedside. "She was quite a handful, I hope you know. She's fiery."

"So everyone keeps telling me," Aithan replied, his eyes twinkling as he looked at Macella fondly. "I find that she is pretty tractable when you stay out of her way."

Macella laughed and took Anwansi's other hand. Anwansi started in surprise, glancing at her hand and then more carefully at her face. The old mage's grin widened, adding even more wrinkles to his lined face.

"Well, you have stepped into your truth beautifully." He beamed, giving Macella's hand a weak squeeze. "I am so glad to have met you."

"And I you." Macella squeezed his hand in return.

"Thank you, Macella," Anwansi said earnestly, his face growing serious. "Thank you for giving me the chance to atone."

Instead of answering, Macella simply squeezed his hand again. She thought she would cry if she spoke at that moment. But she had plenty to thank him for as well.

"Thank you for sending her after me," Aithan interjected gruffly. "Neither of you can be trusted to follow directions, but I suppose that worked out in my favor."

Anwansi nodded, his grin returning. "You have been saved for a purpose. Much lies before you. Much is at stake. Now it truly begins."

"What begins?" Aithan asked quietly, his eyes on the old mage's face.

"Everything," Anwansi stated simply.

Macella leaned down to place a kiss on the old man's cheek. She grinned at him, then looked at Aithan. Her Aegis nodded, a smile tugging at the corner of his mouth.

A shield, a scribe, a sword, a pen. Against hell's fury. Against our end.

(48) "Well, let us not keep Fate waiting," Macella agreed, letting her eyes shift into glowing onyx.

An hour later, the children of Smoketown were gathered in the warm dining hall, enjoying an early and plentiful lunch of thick soup, hot bread, and cold milk. Despite their obvious confusion, the children ate heartily, eyeing the adults as if afraid they were setting some elaborate trap. The adults attending them looked equally confused but followed the orders they'd been given—refilling empty glasses and supplying second helpings of food.

Every mage and soldier not directly attending to the children in the dining hall or caring for the sick, gathered in the large meeting hall of the soldiers' barracks. Macella stood at the front of the room, the other adults seated in rows of benches before her. Roughly forty soldiers and twenty mages stared at her in shocked silence. Aithan leaned against the wall behind her, his arms crossed, his eyes slowly scanning the crowd.

As Macella finished detailing the immediate changes taking place in Smoketown, she was greeted with a dazed hush. The mages looked mostly confused and a bit skeptical, while the soldiers ranged from amused to enraged. Macella waited.

She was unsurprised when Grizzle stood up, red-faced, and shouted, "You are out of your fucking mind! We're not taking orders from you, even if you are with an Aegis. We are the law in Smoketown!"

Macella kept her face carefully blank as she turned her attention to the beefy soldier. "I am sure you will receive formal orders from the Crown very soon; however, the new protocols are effective immediately. As for the law, this is your opportunity to atone for the many crimes you've perpetrated against the kingdom's most precious children. You should be grateful that you are receiving mercy rather than vengeance."

At these words, most of the soldiers erupted in angry outbursts. Macella watched their mouths move, noticed their hands inching toward their belts, waiting to see who would become the cautionary tale. She was almost certain she had wagered correctly, but there was always a chance that things could go differently.

Grizzle broke free of the crowd, his eyes on Macella.

She grinned. *I told you*, she thought at Aithan.

Nobody likes a sore winner, Aithan thought back, mentally rolling his eyes, though his face remained stoic.

Grizzle charged at her, and Macella couldn't believe how slow and clumsy he seemed in comparison to Kai, Diya, and Finley. She effortlessly avoided his lunge, drawing her dagger and slashing at his side as she spun away.

Grizzle stumbled, clutching his side. Macella kicked him hard in the back of the knee and watched him go down. She yanked him upright by the collar of his shirt, pressing her dagger to his throat.

Several other soldiers moved as if to come to Grizzle's aid. Aithan pushed himself off the wall and stepped forward. The men, apparently deciding that Grizzle could handle himself against a mere woman, sat back down. The room grew quiet again.

"The Crown and the citizens of Kōsaten will no longer tolerate the mistreatment of Aegis neophytes," Macella declared, her voice ringing throughout the hall. "You all have been offered mercy, a mercy that you have never extended to the children entrusted to your care. It is a mercy you do not deserve and yet you reject it so callously."

"Do something!" Grizzle yelled at the other soldiers. "Get this crazy bitch off of me!"

A murmur ran through the crowd, but no one moved. Macella let her gaze move slowly over the assembly, making sure to look unblinkingly into the eyes of anyone willing to make eye contact. The silence returned.

"For your crimes against the children of Smoketown, by the power bestowed upon me by Aithan of Auburndale and under the authority of the Crown, I hereby sentence you to death," Macella announced, slitting Grizzle's throat.

The pause before the uproar seemed to drag on for a long while. Macella watched as the onlookers' faces went from angry to shocked, then back to anger as they processed her actions. Then there was noise and scuffling and a few bloody lips and blackened eyes, before Aithan drew his sword and the room filled with crimson light before falling silent again.

Once everyone had settled back into their seats, the outrage palpable in the air, Aithan let his crimson glow fade. He did not, however, sheathe his weapon. Macella let Grizzle's body fall to the floor.

"We understand that this transition might feel sudden and may cause you some discomfort," Macella continued, wiping her blade clean on Grizzle's sleeve, and standing up. "However, given the magnitude of your atrocities, we think that a little discomfort is a much gentler punishment than you deserve. If you disagree, I have no problem delivering the retribution you are owed, as I have done for your comrade, Grizzle."

Macella and Aithan tarried another fortnight in Smoketown to help secure the transition. A few more examples had to be made before everyone seemed to accept the situation in which they found themselves, but soon enough, the new order began to take root.

The children were given a few days' holiday to rest and let their bodies adjust to the sensations of having enough food and sleep. When their daily life resumed, it was on a new schedule Macella had devised—one in which lessons and training sessions were balanced with breaks for rest and even recreation. She knew, of course, that their training was of utmost importance to Kōsaten's safety, but she believed they could be allowed to behave as children, rather than soldiers, for a few minutes each day.

Macella also assisted Aithan in improving the children's physical training. She couldn't help but feel pride watching him work patiently with the children, teaching them to fight in the same way he had taught her. He pushed them hard, as he had done her, but without any of the cruelty the children were accustomed to. Soldiers and students alike watched awestruck whenever he demonstrated his own skills, especially if he indulged them and fought with his eyes and sword glowing crimson.

When Macella and Aithan departed, oversight in Smoketown passed to Diya, Finley, and Kai, who would monitor the encampment until they, too, left for their sojourn at court. If things went as planned, new, proper commanders would arrive in Smoketown before the cold season.

"I knew you were something special," Anwansi whispered to Macella, as she and Aithan sat with him on the night before they were to leave Smoketown.

"Thank you," Macella answered, tears pricking her eyes. "Thank you for helping us."

Anwansi smiled and turned his head to look at Aithan. "I always knew you were special too. I'm so glad I stayed around long enough to see just how right I was."

Aithan's big hand swallowed the mage's frail one as he leaned over his old friend. Aithan kissed Anwansi's forehead. "Only you could compliment someone and make it sound like you're complimenting yourself."

Anwansi wheezed with laughter.

He died that night as he slept.

As Macella and Aithan rode out of Smoketown, down a road no longer lined with bodies, Macella looked back at the mountains. So much had happened in the short time they'd tarried here, and there was so much yet to come. She knew that the fight was not yet won.

Macella saw movement at the side of the road. Anwansi stood there, smiling widely at her. Macella waved, and the old mage waved back.

She turned forward and caught Aithan watching her. He glanced between her and the general area where Anwansi stood, then raised an eyebrow at her.

"Anwansi is seeing us off," Macella explained, taking a last look at the old mage before he disappeared. "He wants us to remember that we are not alone."

Aithan looked back at the spot where Macella had seen Anwansi. He smiled. Macella thought about how differently they'd both felt when they'd last traversed this road.

"There are others who seek a better way," Aithan agreed. "We are far from alone."

Together, they rode away from the mountains and toward an uncertain future.

Citizens of the kingdom can rejoice at the swift justice the Crown exacts upon those who commit acts that offend the ideals of our great nation. The Crown has already dispatched several of its best commanders to oversee the restructuring of the Aegis training. These generals carry with them much-needed warm clothing, shoes, rations, and other supplies previously squandered or sold by wayward soldiers.

While several exceptionally immoral individuals were justly executed for their crimes, most have been allowed the mercy of working toward atonement. Among these reformed servicepersons are many who have zealously embraced the changes. Of their own volition, these soldiers have moved the children into much more suitable accommodations in the formerly unused sections of the soldiers' barracks. They have also begun work on transforming the former children's quarters into a proper schoolhouse, per the Crown's command."

– From "The Aegis and The Forge" by S.S.

CHAPTER TWENTY-EIGHT

Though relatively short, their tarry in Smoketown proved longer than either of them had wished (49). By the time Macella waved goodbye to Anwansi, she was more than ready to be far away from the town. She sensed the same wanderlust in Aithan's mind. With all that had happened, she felt as though she had aged several years in a matter of weeks. Macella knew their visit had been serendipitous and that she and Aithan had taken action that would impact the very fabric of Kōsaten's society. They had done the right thing—what they'd been meant to do. Still, she felt a sense of relief as they galloped west with the wind in their hair and the mountains behind them.

As the weeks passed, the air grew cooler and cooler, announcing the imminent arrival of the cold season. Because of the changes to Macella's body, traveling became an easier and faster affair. She no longer needed more rest than Aithan, no longer suffered much from the harshness of the elements or the discomforts caused by long hours on horseback. Consequently, they were able to travel quickly enough that, when they did take breaks, they could rest themselves for as long as they pleased.

Every day seemed to bring new discoveries. Macella's training became more intense, testing the limits of her endurance, skill, and strength. She quickly realized how much Aithan had been holding back before. She had known, of course, that he was incredibly strong and fast, but facing off against him unrestrained revealed the extent of his might.

Aithan pushed her hard, sometimes pairing physical attacks with mental compulsions or prodding her mind for her next move. She soon learned to defend herself against both types of attacks, occasionally even mimicking Aithan's tactics. While she couldn't match his physical strength, her telepathic abilities rivaled his. Consequently, she was sometimes able to eke out a victory or a draw with a bit of mind manipulation and invisibility.

Of course, Aithan also had new abilities. Macella learned to keep a tight grip on her daggers to keep Aithan from disarming her with his telekinetic gift. Likewise, she had to be mindful of her surroundings, since the Aegis could use much of it against her. She only had to be struck from behind with a stray branch or clipped with a few stones before she learned to avoid Aithan's projectiles and sword simultaneously.

Usually, their sparring sessions ended with Aithan helping her up from the ground or stopping with the point of his blade against her throat. Still, Macella was improving. She lasted longer against him, occasionally scoring narrow victories. At night, when she cleaned their wounds and Aithan massaged her sore muscles, Macella felt that she could pass the rest of her days this way.

Her gifts began to feel natural, taking on an automaticity that allowed her to use them more quickly and easily. She could silently call her flames at will and extinguish them just as quickly. She slipped in and out of visibility seamlessly, taking to the ability just as quickly as she had taken to telepathy and compulsion. Macella had never felt so alive.

Yet there was also a darkness ahead. In a mirror of their journey to Smoketown, Aithan grew increasingly tense as they neared the capital. Though he did not seem sad as he had then, it was clear that Pleasure Ridge Park was also not a place of fond memories.

"The city is a place of decadence and despair," Aithan told Macella as they traveled at an easy trot.

They were nearing a large town, the last before the capital. Macella knew they would find a room and tarry a few days, resting and preparing for the trials ahead. She had never imagined she would see the capital city, let alone the palace itself. Now, she would spend an entire season ensconced in its opulence.

"Anything you desire, you can find in Pleasure Ridge Park," Aithan continued. "And, for the right price, you can have it. Of course, there are many who cannot afford food. My first time in the capital was eye-opening. Never before had I seen such wealth and such want."

Macella pressed her mouth into a hard line as she watched the memories Aithan shared with her. Thin, gaunt beggars ignored by lords in grand carriages. Brothels serving every proclivity, the basest acts performed by those in the most dire need of the coin they earned. Members of the nobility taking only bites from course after course of the finest foods, while elsewhere, the poor died of starvation in the street.

"It is like no other place in the kingdom," Aithan continued gravely. "Our strength is of no use there. We can rely only on intellect and cunning. The Crown is always listening, always planning. Many a seemingly minor misstep has ended up costing a life. We must tread carefully."

Macella grimaced. Shelby Park had been her first and only brush with nobility; it was her introduction to wealth and luxury. Yet the images of Kōsaten Keep in Aithan's memory were as far above that as Shelby Park had been over her home in Shively. Macella was going to be completely out of her depth.

A burst of color fluttered into Macella's line of sight. Laughing, Macella plucked the floating pink camellia blossom from the air and tucked it into her hair. She turned her head and met Aithan's smiling gaze.

"You will fit in beautifully," Aithan assured her warmly. "Well, perhaps I am being too hopeful—you'll very likely stand out more than we wish. There are none in Pleasure Ridge Park so lovely as you."

Macella's cheeks felt warm. She shook her head, a few curls falling from her bun into her eyes. Obviously, Aithan's love obscured his vision, but she didn't mind. At least he had distracted her from her anxieties about navigating high society.

"Will the Crown object to you bringing a guest?" Macella asked, wondering why she hadn't thought to worry about this before.

"I do not know," Aithan replied honestly. "The situation has never arisen. But I suspect that, given all of the extra guests joining us this cold season, your presence will be less remarkable."

Macella nodded, thinking how the scribe had once again aided them in their efforts. Were it not for the popularity of those tales, all of the kingdom's wealthiest citizens wouldn't be falling over themselves to acquaint themselves with the Aegises. Under these circumstances, perhaps it would be understood that the heroes would accumulate friends and hangers-on.

"How do you expect this cold season in the capital to compare to your usual holiday?" Macella asked, guiding Cinnamon nearer to Aithan and Jade.

Aithan stared thoughtfully at the horizon. "Hmm. Well, Aegises generally pass the season mundanely. We relinquish our harvests of brimstone to the royal mages. We are examined and often administered various new or rare tinctures and treatments the royal mages have concocted since the prior season. We train and exhibit before the Crown and the rest of the court. We report on our activities through the year and receive new edicts from the Crown."

"That sounds...surprisingly dull," Macella admitted.

Aithan laughed. "Our entertainment is certainly not the Crown's priority. However, even in a typical season, there are important and wealthy guests at court. We are given the opportunity to observe and partake of the frequent revelries, though we have heretofore tended to remain on the periphery."

Macella quirked an eyebrow and gave Aithan a wry smile. "So, you sit by yourselves and drink and watch the fancy folk grow inebriated, and fuck a few when you are bored?"

"More like when they're bored." Aithan shrugged. "It used to be almost a fetish—a thrilling tryst with an Aegis was fodder to regale your friends with in private. Rich fools slumming it for the novelty of it all. However, thanks to the scribe, the public opinion of Aegises has drastically changed. We will see how it manifests at court this season."

Macella watched her Aegis from the corner of her eye. "Do you have any paramours at court? Anyone anxiously awaiting the cold season to reunite with their intermittent fling?"

"I have luckily avoided such entanglements. I've only rarely found myself solicited," Aithan replied with a knowing half-smile. "Others of our kind enjoy the sport of it, so those of us who are less inclined can often remain unbothered. Cassian and Cressida find it amusing to compete with one another, wagering on who can bed the most nobles. And Finley is quite a favorite among the entitled and indolent. They shower Finley with gifts and, in turn, Finley torments them—stringing them along with just enough attention. It's fascinating to observe."

Macella could easily imagine beautiful, aloof Finley with hordes of desperate admirers vying for their attention. Yet, as undeniably gorgeous as Finley was, Aithan was uncommonly attractive as well. How many glamorous, sophisticated pursuers had courted his favor? Would he be embarrassed by her unrefined manners when contrasting them with the fine folk at court?

"You are telling me that the gentry are not falling over you as well?" Macella said skeptically. "I find that hard to believe."

"You are adorable when you feign jealousy," Aithan told her, reaching out to take her hand. He leaned to kiss it, then let go and righted himself in his saddle. "I have no patience for the wealthy and their games. I have never had any more than transactional trysts and the briefest of romances across my solitary life before you. I assume that I was unknowingly awaiting our moment."

Warmth spread through Macella's chest. She smiled at Aithan lovingly. "It is not your affection I'm jealous of. I know they cannot usurp my place in your heart. It is their manners, experience, and etiquette that concern me. I would not have you embarrassed by my ignorance of high society."

Aithan gently tugged on Jade's reins, bringing the horse to a halt. Macella drew up close beside him, opening her mouth to ask why they had stopped. Before she could speak, Aithan had taken her face in both of his hands and covered her mouth with his. He kissed her long and slow. When he finally pulled back, he wore an incredulous smile.

Still cradling her face in his hands, he murmured, "You are the most ridiculous of creatures. As if I could ever be embarrassed by you."

Macella's heart stammered. "I know, but—"

Aithan kissed her again, cutting her off. His tongue probed her mouth with sensuous patience, until she felt a pool of warmth spreading through her belly. She gasped when he pulled away, her breathing shallow.

"I could *never* be embarrassed by you," Aithan repeated, his voice raw and gravelly. "I will teach you the etiquette, but exactly as you are this moment, you are far more elegant than anyone I have ever encountered."

Macella stared into his amber orange eyes. She saw in them such a mix of love, devotion, and gratitude that she nearly wept. She smiled instead.

"I love you," Macella whispered.

"I know," Aithan replied, kissing her quickly once more. "Let us hasten to Clifton so that we may spend a few days expressing that love."

Aithan grinned at Macella as he leaned forward and urged Jade into a gallop. Laughing, Macella squeezed Cinnamon's ribcage with her thighs and clucked her tongue. The horse readily galloped after Jade.

They rode hard, racing one another for as long as Jade and Cinnamon had the energy. In the end, Macella begrudgingly accepted the match as a draw. By then, they found themselves on the outskirts of Clifton. Its proximity to the capital made it a wealthy trading town; the modern buildings and fashionable attire of its inhabitants marked it as such.

They chose a smaller inn that appeared less frequented than several others in town. The proprietor and everyone else they encountered were kind to the point of officiousness. Macella saw in their treatment of Aithan the fetishization he had mentioned. Her words had made Aegises more acceptable to the masses, but to the wealthy, it appeared that association with their kind was something to collect—something to amass to increase their own importance. Though it peeved her, Macella was glad she had the opportunity to observe such behavior before arriving in Pleasure Ridge Park. She would now know what to expect of the nobility at court.

Aithan, for his part, appeared perfectly indifferent to their attentions. He was stoic as ever, though polite, and easily rebuffed unwanted advances. Macella could see now how he had avoided romantic entanglements at court.

Soon enough, they were settled in a comfortable room, having eaten a late meal and washed themselves, before gladly climbing naked into bed. Macella rested her head on Aithan's chest, draping an arm across him, and enjoying his familiar warmth. Aithan kissed the top of her head, inhaling deeply, and exhaling a contented hum.

"Tell me about the Crown," Macella said, running her fingers through the soft silver hair on his chest. "I understand that King Khari has ruled for longer than any monarch before her, but I know so little aside from what I learned in school or the occasional secondhand society paper I managed to acquire."

Aithan ran a hand along her arm as he gathered his thoughts. Her skin warmed under his touch. Macella never grew tired of being close to him, of feeling his hands against her skin. She pressed her lips against his chest, planting several kisses before resting her ear against his heart once more.

"King Khari has ruled for so long because she knows how to unite the kingdom," Aithan explained. "After Khalid's reign, commonfolk began to forget how the world had been before he'd brokered peace between the gods. They forgot that they needed a ruler at all. Eventually, the favor and protection of the gods was not enough to keep Kōsaten's citizens united under the control of a single ruler. Different provinces began to declare sovereignty and a desire to govern themselves."

"Yes, I remember learning that Queen Rhiannon's reign was tumultuous," Macella replied, searching her brain for the fuzzy details she'd learned in primary school. "The kingdom was practically on the brink of civil war, if I recall correctly."

"Indeed, it was," Aithan agreed. "King Khari of Butchertown saw all of this and began her rule with several breaks from tradition. She took a spouse from each region of the kingdom, sharing her power superficially across what she hailed as 'the Crown.' Whenever one of her partners desires to age and eventually depart, the king takes a new young spouse."

"Wait," Macella interrupted. "The Crown does not age?"

"They are much like us and the mages in that respect," Aithan explained. "The supreme sovereign—presently King Khari—is endowed with the gift of timelessness after completing the necessary trials. She has chosen to share that gift with her spouses throughout her reign."

Macella processed this, realizing that the Crown was far more formidable than she'd realized. Most commonfolk knew that King Khari had ruled for longer than the average person's lifespan, but Macella had never thought about how this was so. She doubted most people even considered it, given how little the average person had to do with Aegises, mages, and the like. An entirely new world had seemingly opened to her since meeting Aithan of Auburndale.

Aithan continued the history lesson. "King Khari left the upper eastern region to rule and has reigned for nearly a century. Presently, she rules alongside three other monarchs. Queen Annika of Edgewood is the newest and youngest, joining the Crown only a few years ago after the previous sovereign from the west departed. Monarch Meztli of Park Duvalle has defended southern Kōsaten's interests for several decades. And Queen Awa of Highview has represented the northern territories for King Khari's entire rule."

Macella felt a surprising pang of sadness for the Crown. "So, the king's marriages are simply business arrangements? Is there no consideration of affection in these alliances?"

Aithan shrugged, kissing her head, and squeezing her more tightly against him. "I cannot say unilaterally, but love is certainly not prioritized. I believe that they might fall in love after the business is arranged. Though I was not yet living at the time of the king's marriage to Queen Awa, I have heard that they were initially enamored with one another. But that had long cooled by the time I was presented to the Crown for service. Now they hold one another in contempt and vie for power."

"That is tragic," Macella murmured against Aithan's chest. "I pity them."

"You won't for long," Aithan assured her. "There are few innocents in Kōsaten Keep. Every member of the Crown swindled and sacrificed to be exactly where they are, no matter how unpleasant their situation may seem."

"This sounds far more dangerous than battling hellspawn." Macella sighed. "It sounds like we are willingly walking into a nest of vipers."

Aithan chuckled dryly. "I'd prefer the vipers."

"That is very reassuring," Macella replied, rolling her eyes, and thumping him lightly on the chest.

Aithan took her hand from his chest and pressed it to his lips. "It will be more dangerous even than I am prepared for. Before now, I have done only the Crown's bidding. I have never defied them nor provoked their ire. I learned how to navigate the politics. But, knowing what I know now—knowing who and what I truly am—everything has changed. It is worth the risk to do what is right."

Macella ran her hand down Aithan's chest and across the taut ridges of his abdomen. "It sounds as though I turned your life upside down."

Aithan pulled her on top of him, holding her against his chest. Macella lifted her head to look into his face. He was smiling, his eyes crinkling at the corners in that way that sent butterflies to her stomach.

"I think you turned it right side up," Aithan corrected, kissing her lightly on the tip of her nose. "You made it into a life, instead of just an existence. For the first time in my life, I am not alone. I have someone to fight beside me, something to fight for."

Macella's heart seemed to swell in her chest. Would she ever get used to the joy of loving this man and of being loved by him?

"Remember that I was also alone," she told him. "I was always on the outside, searching for meaning and purpose. Finding you, finding out who I am, finding something to fight for—it has indeed changed everything."

(50) Aithan kissed her then, slowly, holding her tight against him. Macella opened her mouth, surrendering to him completely, wanting nothing more than to be here, in this moment. She leaned into the kiss, feeling the heat of their skin touching.

The kiss deepened, the heat spreading through Macella's body, radiating from the pool of warmth in her belly. Between the press of their bodies, Macella felt Aithan's manhood swelling. He tangled a hand into her curls, the other trailing down her back, then cupping her ass.

Macella moaned, repositioning herself so that her clit lay against his hard shaft. Aithan's hand gripped her ass, pressing her against him. She felt his breath catch in his throat as she moved against him, achingly slowly. Her escaping wetness allowed her to glide up and down the length of his cock. The friction and pressure on her clit was excruciatingly pleasurable.

Aithan took his hand from her hair to grip her waist. Urgently, he guided her up and down, again and again. Macella felt a glittery, buzzing sensation growing deep in her pelvis. Aithan held her steady, his mouth still on hers as he moved her against him, up and down, again and again.

The buzzing sensation exploded into a shower of sparks. Macella's hips bucked involuntarily, and she cried out against Aithan's lips. He groaned, his hands tightening on her ass, not letting her escape, keeping the pressure on her clit. Her orgasm intensified and she broke the kiss to press her face into his neck and let herself moan and whimper and gasp for breath. Her face and his neck were wet from tears she hadn't realized she'd wept.

When the sensations subsided a bit, Macella pressed her mouth against Aithan's neck, biting gently. She reached between them and positioned his cock against her sex. She felt herself quivering, anticipating the exquisite pleasure of penetration. Aithan gasped as she bit his neck a little harder, burying him deep inside her wet warmth.

She lifted herself onto her elbows, grinding against him and finding their rhythm, as she kissed him once again. Aithan lifted his hips, simultaneously pushing her hips down, plunging as deeply as the position would allow. Macella felt the pressure deep in her belly, the spot already abuzz from her previous orgasm. Aithan lowered his hips and thrust upward again, pressing her hips down to meet him. The third time sent tremors through Macella's entire frame. She cried out, lifting herself to an upright position.

Aithan sat up, holding her tight against him and taking control. With one arm around her waist, the other hand clutching the back of her neck, he again guided her up and down, each stroke sending tremors through her body. Macella tangled her hands into the silky strands of his hair. Her pussy clenched, encircling him tightly as he plunged into her over and over. His tongue traced along the sensitive skin of her neck, making her shudder.

"More," Macella gasped, tugging Aithan's hair. "More. More. Please."

Aithan growled, shifting his weight to roll her onto her back. Hooking his arms behind her knees, he thrusted deeper. Macella moaned, loving the weight of his body on top of hers. His face in her neck, Aithan drove into her, giving her every bit of the more she had been begging for.

Macella clutched at Aithan's back, her nails digging into his skin. Releasing one of her legs, Aithan propped himself up. He circled one nipple with his tongue, then took it into his mouth, sucking gently. Macella arched her back, her thighs clamped tightly around Aithan's waist. She met each thrust eagerly, feeling tendrils of flame threatening to escape her skin.

Aithan lifted his mouth from her breast and looked at her. His eyes were dark with desire, but his mouth quirked in a wry smile. As usual, they were more in tune with one another during lovemaking than almost any other time.

"Do not singe the sheets," he warned, before lowering his head to take her other nipple between his teeth.

Laughing and moaning simultaneously, Macella fought to contain her inner fire. Aithan's tongue flicked over her stiff nipple, sending tendrils of pleasure throughout her body. The threads reached to the core of her being, exploding deep in her belly where Aithan's cock probed her depths. She felt an overpowering, indescribable euphoria as she came apart.

"I love you. I love you. I love you," Aithan whispered as he came, gripping her tightly and burying his face in her neck.

The next few days were a haze of the same. They stayed in bed, having meals delivered to their room, and ignoring the outside world. They made love repeatedly, sometimes slowly and gently, other time ravenously and with reckless abandon.

When they were not expressing their love physically, Macella would read to Aithan from her journal, or he would tell her stories of his previous sojourns at court. Often, they simply lay in companionable silence, drifting in and out of sleep and enjoying being close to one another. It was a sad day when Aithan announced that it was time for them to move along and get to Pleasure Ridge Park.

CHAPTER TWENTY-NINE

T hey rode hard and arrived in the capital in a matter of days. As they entered the city, Macella's senses were immediately overwhelmed. She had never seen so many people, had never heard so much noise. The air was thick with a million different scents—unwashed bodies, baking bread, horse dung, perfume, smoke, and on and on. The press of buildings and bustling bodies made Macella feel claustrophobic.

Breathe, Aithan whispered in her mind. *Shut out what does not matter. It will get easier over time.*

Macella inhaled, trying to ignore some of the scents on the wind. She focused her attention ahead, on the road to Kōsaten Keep. The castle loomed over the city, growing larger and more imposing every moment. It sat majestically atop a hill, gleaming in the afternoon sun. The keep was built of helmipietra, a pearl-colored precious stone that glittered like jewels. Garnet and gold banners hung from the parapets, waving in the breeze.

Every step toward the castle brought more novelties, more sights, smells, and sounds. Macella kept her attention primarily on Kōsaten Keep, allowing only her periphery to explore her surroundings. Still, she was struck by the variety of people and businesses along the main road. She felt like it would be suffocating to live in such a place. She already missed the space and freedom of their nomadic life.

They passed a square bustling with jeering people. Macella's attention was caught by their gleeful anger. Looking more closely, she saw that the subject of the people's scorn was a single man. His head and hands were encased in a wooden contraption that made him unable to move from the kneeling position he was bound into. He was bloodied and filthy, and as Macella watched, several people spat on him or threw projectiles.

"Public punishment is common here," Aithan told her grimly. "He likely was caught stealing. This is one of the gentler disciplinary measures the capital's soldiers utilize."

Macella looked away, swallowing hard. If the man's gaunt frame was any indication, he probably had been stealing to survive. And if this was a gentle punishment, she did not want to see a harsh one.

Soon enough, they had passed through the outer walls of the keep, and the surroundings became less overwhelming. Workers and soldiers moved about in bustling importance. Macella gazed awestruck at the massive scale of everything around her. The walls seemed impossibly high, the turrets practically reaching the realm of the sun.

Finally, they reached the castle's entrance, dismounted, and handed Cinnamon and Jade off to waiting stable hands. Macella took a deep breath as she stared up at Kōsaten Keep's grand façade. Anxiety flooded her veins.

Then, Aithan of Auburndale was beside her, offering her his arm. Macella looked up into his smiling amber eyes.

"My lady," Aithan said, inclining his head.

Macella smiled. Her heart slowed a bit. She took Aithan's arm and let him lead her inside.

Nothing could have prepared Macella for the opulence of Kōsaten Keep. She hardly knew where to look, as Aithan led her through a foyer the size of an inn. Aithan was smirking, amused by the awestruck tenor of her thoughts. He guided Macella toward an eastward-leading passage.

"Pardon me, sir," came a voice from behind them.

Macella turned to see a pale, gaunt man in the attire of a high-ranking servant. Aithan lifted an eyebrow at him without speaking. The man bowed deferentially.

"The Aegis quarters are in the west wing of the keep," he stated, gesturing toward the opposite passage. "Allow me to escort you."

"The servants' wing is this way," Aithan replied, his eyes narrowed at the man. The man bowed in agreement. "Yes, sir. However, the Crown has prepared updated accommodations for our protectors this season. I am sure you will find them superior to your previous lodgings."

Aithan nodded curtly, his mouth set in a grim line. His jaw tightened when two more servants appeared to take their packs, a third trailing behind, bringing the belongings that had been strapped to their horses. The servants led them down halls decorated with beautiful tapestries and paintings of past royals. Macella wasn't sure she would be able to navigate this massive structure; already she had lost track of the twists and turns the servants had taken.

"You are among the first to arrive. This entire section has been designated exclusively for Aegises," the high-ranking servant explained. He looked at Macella and added, "And their guests. This includes the courtyard, west garden, the west dining hall, and the newly fitted training grounds past the hedgerow."

The doors along the corridor were all a deep mahogany, intricately carved with shields. On the first, bearing a shield adorned with green painted ivy, hung a wreath of flowers wrapped in black mourning ribbons.

Macella noticed that each of the doors they passed bore a shield adorned with flora that was either green, blue, purple, or gold. The lead servant stopped before a door on which the shield nestled amongst scarlet devil's orchids. He took out a key and opened the door, waving them inside. They stepped into a large and richly furnished sitting room. The other servants scurried into inner rooms to put away Macella and Aithan's things.

"The Crown does ask that you restrict yourselves to the Aegis area until you are presented to the nobility at a welcome dinner the Crown has arranged in a fortnight," the servant continued. "It will mark the official start of our cold-season event."

Aithan only grunted, gazing around the immaculate room. Macella could tell he was suddenly uneasy. She wanted the servants to go away so she could ask what was plaguing him.

"You will also find that any of your belongings left in your previous rooms have been transferred here, along with some additional new wardrobe items. Courtesy of the Crown, of course." The man bowed again.

"Of course," Aithan agreed, his voice dry with sarcasm.

The man looked at Macella and frowned. "We had not anticipated that you would have company. I will send up some girls immediately to make the rooms more suitable for a lady and to have you measured for some proper attire."

Macella's mouth popped open in surprise. "Oh, no. I couldn't possibly trouble you. This is lovely. And I could not impose on the Crown to outfit me for court. I will go into the city—"

The man held up a hand, interrupting her. "No, please. We insist."

Macella looked helplessly at Aithan. He was watching the servant with coldly assessing eyes. The man began to back out of the room. His three assistants reappeared, slipping quickly out the door ahead of him.

"I will also have someone bring up some refreshments and to fill your tub. I am sure you are weary from your travels." The man backed out of the door, leaving the room key on a small table before disappearing.

Aithan stepped behind Macella and wrapped his arms around her waist. She relaxed against him. His breath was warm against her ear.

"We must be very careful," he breathed. "We are usually treated as servants and soldiers, but never with this level of officiousness. It is clear that we will be show ponies this season." *That means they will be watching us even more closely than we expected*, Aithan finished in her mind.

Macella nodded her understanding, leaning into his warmth. She already felt overwhelmed by their surroundings and the tension of the environment.

There was a light knock on the door. At Aithan's acknowledgment, the door opened, and three new servants entered. The first was a girl carrying a basin of water and two towels. She set the basin on the table near the door and slipped from the room. The second servant, a nondescript younger man, was carrying a tray laden with a selection of cold meats, cheese, bread, and fruit, as well as water and a carafe of wine. He put the tray on a table and silently withdrew.

The other servant was obviously much older, though her face was barely lined. She was plump and matronly, with rigid posture, deep brown skin, a neat afro, and stern expression. She looked at Macella shrewdly.

"It's you that'll be needing new clothes, then?" the woman asked in a brisk voice. She had none of the carefully polite manners everyone else had exhibited thus far. Macella liked her immediately.

"So I've been told," Macella replied dryly. "I am Macella."

Macella thought she caught the woman's mouth quirk up in a smile, but just as quickly the matron schooled her face into its stern expression again. She pulled a length of string from her bag and approached Macella. Aithan kissed Macella's head and moved away, going to the basin to wash his hands and face.

"I am called Lynn. Let me have a look at you," the woman demanded. "I have to get started right away. You'll need something to wear when you're presented to the Crown tomorrow."

Macella felt a stab of anxiety. Aithan had explained that guests were presented to the Crown the day after their arrival. It was an opportunity to pay one's respects for the hospitality. Macella was not looking forward to her first brush with royalty.

For the next few minutes, Lynn measured the various parts of Macella's body with lengths of string that she tied off, cut, and slipped into her bag. Macella obediently lifted her arms, turning this way and that as directed.

Finally, the woman stepped back and scrutinized Macella's face. "I have just the fabric to complement your lovely skin," she said matter-of-factly.

Macella blushed. She sensed that this was not a woman who frequently doled out compliments. Before she could properly thank her, Lynn walked briskly from the room, her swishing skirts the only sound in her silent wake.

Aithan chuckled. "I told you that you were going to stand out. You are just too beautiful."

Macella rolled her eyes, crossing to the basin to wash her hands and face. The water was warm and smelled of lavender. As she dried her hands, Macella was struck by the softness of the towel. Again, she marveled at the extent of luxury afforded to the nobility.

Of course, the food was delicious. Macella and Aithan ate and drank until they felt full and content. Macella thought that the extravagance at least somewhat compensated for the stress of their stay.

As they finished their meal, a procession of servants came in and out of the room with pails of steaming water. In all of the activity, Macella had yet to explore their quarters beyond the sitting room. Now she peeked through the door where the servants had disappeared to see a lavishly tiled bathing chamber. The centerpiece of the room was a massive iron clawfoot tub, now filled with lavender-scented water.

Macella tried another door. Through it she found a huge bedroom, occupied by an ornate fireplace and an enormous four-poster bed covered in rich silks and furs. A mahogany wardrobe stood open, revealing several Aithan-sized ensembles hanging inside. A chest of drawers held additional, less formal clothing and undergarments. The clothes and supplies they had brought with them were all neatly tucked away as well. Beside the chest, another door led to a dressing room furnished with a large painted screen, a massive-looking glass, and tables bearing various grooming items.

While Macella watched, a second chest was carried into the bedroom and placed on the opposite side of the bed. A dark-haired girl followed the chest, her arms full of fabric. Macella soon saw that these items were for her—tunics, undergarments, and other informal articles of clothing that looked to be near her size.

(51) Together, Macella and Aithan took a long, lazy bath in the ornate tub. Macella melted into the water as her Aegis washed her hair, kneading her scalp with his strong hands. Once she had dried herself with another absurdly soft towel and moisturized with a rich, sweet-smelling cream she found in a cupboard, Macella felt like a royal herself.

While Aithan lingered a little longer in the tub, Macella found her way back to their bedroom. The afternoon was fading, and soon they would likely be summoned to the Aegis dining hall for dinner, but there was time for a brief respite. Macella climbed into the huge bed.

She stretched herself like a cat, reveling in the luxury of the bedclothes. She had never felt a bed so soft, nor blankets so sumptuous. The rich fabrics felt lush against her bare skin. A little moan of pleasure escaped her lips.

"You are a goddess," Aithan's low baritone rumbled from nearby.

Macella opened her eyes and saw that her Aegis stood at the end of the four-poster bed. He was as completely naked as she was, his hair still wet from the bath. Macella smothered a gasp as she looked at him—his golden skin aglow, firm chest and rippled abs glistening with oil, and his penis growing stiff as she watched.

"I feel unworthy to touch you," Aithan continued, not looking away from her as he took his thick cock in one of his big hands. "I just want to watch you, worship you."

An insistent throbbing had begun between her legs. Macella caught Aithan's intentions from his look and the tenor of his mind. As usual, he consumed her senses. She felt the muscles in her stomach clench involuntarily.

"Touch yourself for me," Aithan commanded, his voice low and insistent. He stroked his cock slowly, his burning gaze roaming over her body.

Exhaling a jagged breath, Macella slipped a hand between her legs. She ran her fingers through the soft hair until she found the sensitive flesh of her clitoris. She thought of Aithan's tongue pressing the same spot and stifled a moan. Butterfly-soft, she caressed her clit, imagining Aithan's breath against her skin, the scratch of his stubbly cheek against her thigh.

She heard Aithan's breath hitch, his hand moving slightly faster on his throbbing cock. Macella's skin buzzed, her excitement building as she watched him watching her.

"Good girl," Aithan murmured, his words sending a shiver through Macella's body. "Show me."

Macella pushed her thoughts toward him, showing him their imagined tryst. She arched her back, slipping two fingers into the waiting wet warmth of her sex. She bit her lip hard, pressing her fingers as deep as they could reach, simultaneously rubbing her clit with her thumb. Aithan groaned.

She imagined Aithan's orange eyes gazing into hers as he kissed his way up her torso, over her breasts and neck to her lips, before thrusting inside her. Gasping, she moved her hips in time with her fingers, working herself toward an inevitable climax.

"Fuck," Aithan rasped, clearly aroused by the dual vision of her on the bed and the scene in her mind. "Cum for me, Macella."

Turning her head to smother her moans in the pillow, Macella came, her pussy clenching around her fingers. She writhed against the blankets, letting the convulsions die down before removing her slick fingers from between her thighs. She panted, her chest heaving.

Aithan slipped into the bed swiftly, reaching her before she stopped trembling and immediately igniting her desire again. Taking her hand, he placed her fingers in his mouth, humming appreciatively as he sucked her wetness from them. Then he was inside her, thrusting deep into her welcoming warmth, just as she had imagined. No, it was infinitely better than she imagined. The way they fit together, the way her body responded to him and his to hers—it was something she couldn't do justice to in her meager fantasies. Together, they were pure magic.

Macella felt herself climbing toward another climax. She turned her head to one side, trying to muffle her cries in the plump pillows. Aithan planted kisses along her throat and neck, stopping with his mouth against her ear.

"This is the one thing we need not be careful about in the palace," he whispered. "There is no need to be quiet. Let them hear you. Make our presence known."

Aithan moved faster, thrusting hard, driving her against the soft bed. Macella let herself go, her moans throaty and hoarse. She came hard, calling Aithan's name.

Afterward, they lounged in the bed until forced to leave it by a dinner summons. Macella knew they were among the first to arrive, but she was curious about who else she would soon meet. Her interactions with Aegises so far had been quite varied and unpredictable. Aithan, and even Finley, had been remarkably kind, but Kiho, Diya, and Kai had been challenging. What would Aithan's remaining siblings be like?

Additionally, Macella had not forgotten that her stay at court would inevitably bring her face-to-face with the Aegis who had participated in the slaughter of Aithan's family, as well as Macella's separation from her father. She knew that some of Shamira's memories had been purged as her own had been. The woman did not know her name or remember where she had left the Aegisborn child, but would Shamira recognize Macella? If so, how would she react—would she tell the Crown or keep quiet so as not to risk the discovery of her involvement in Macella's concealment?

Macella dressed in tights and a gorgeous pale blue tunic embroidered with golden daffodils. Delicate lace accentuated her neckline and hem. The fabric felt like a cloud against her skin. She slid her feet into a pair of lace-up ghillie flats that also fit her perfectly, seemingly designed with her feet in mind.

After she finished dressing, Macella found Aithan waiting for her in the sitting room. She laughed aloud when she saw him. He wore a golden tunic embroidered with crimson orchids, along with trousers and leather boots.

Aithan smiled. "Clearly, we both value comfort and simplicity over fashion. We should enjoy these clothes over the next fortnight. Once the Crown begins parading us out to entertain their fine guests, we will be expected to dress more formally."

"This is the nicest clothing I have ever touched, and yet it is considered informal here," Macella mused, shaking her head. "I am profoundly out of my league."

Aithan took her hand and kissed it. He twirled her in a circle, examining her from all angles. He hummed appreciatively as he took her in.

"You are a goddess," he told her again. "You look very much like royalty. Would that I could keep you tucked away in this room and away from the unworthy nobles."

"You want to keep me locked up like your secret mistress, do you?" Macella teased, intertwining their fingers.

"That doesn't sound so terrible, does it?" Aithan grinned, cupping her face with his free hand. He leaned down to kiss her tenderly on the lips.

"I suppose not," Macella agreed when Aithan pulled away. In his mind, she added, *But I do not recall any mention in the prophecy of us saving the world from the comfort of your bed.*

A servant led them to their designated dining hall, pointing out the corridors to the courtyard, west garden, and training grounds. Macella caught glimpses of the lush lawn through enormous arched windows. The setting sun cast the carefully cultivated greenery in a warm glow. The view at sunset from the courtyard would be stunning. They could probably see most of the city from atop this hill.

Macella knew that the Aegis dining hall was a smaller, less extravagant space than where they would dine once the nobility arrived, but she still was not prepared for its lavishness. The room could have seated three times as many Aegises as it would be serving. It boasted a high ceiling, beautiful stained-glass windows, and was lit by jeweled chandeliers on pulley systems around the room's perimeter. Long tables were covered in garnet and gold cloths. Elaborate candle centerpieces added ambience.

Only one of the long tables was occupied, and it only held two Aegises. They looked up as Macella and Aithan entered. When they saw Aithan, they both stood to greet him.

"Aithan of Auburndale, son of Lucifer!" bellowed one of them.

"Valen of Valley Station, son of Mictlāntēcutli," Aithan replied, crossing the room to meet him.

The two men clasped forearms in a hardy handshake, sharing an easy smile. Macella stood next to Aithan, looking up at Valen. Everyone was looking up at Valen, actually, due to his incredible size. He towered even over Aithan—Macella looked like a child in comparison. The sides of his head were cut close, while the rest hung in two long, gold-tipped cornrows down his back. His long silver beard was gathered into three braids.

"Son of Lucifer." The second Aegis had a low, sultry voice. She held out her hand to Aithan, her manner much colder than Valen's.

Aithan turned to the woman and shook her hand briefly. "Cressida of Crescent Hill, daughter of Mictlāntēcutli."

Macella watched the exchange curiously. These were the first Mictlāntēcutli Aegises she'd encountered. Aithan had told Macella they could drain you of energy with their touch. Perhaps that was why Aithan avoided prolonged contact with Cressida, though he had not been uncomfortable with Valen. It must be the woman herself, not the guild.

Cressida was lovely—tall and voluptuous with fair skin and shiny hair that fell to her waist in silky ringlets. She had a heart-shaped face dominated by large eyes framed with long lashes. Macella could see why she was a favorite among the nobility. Aithan had said she and another Aegis, Cassian, liked to compete to bed the most nobles. Now, seeing Cressida for herself, Macella couldn't imagine Cassian being able to match Cressida's attractions.

"Who is this gorgeous creature and how did you trick her into being here with you?" Valen demanded, laughing heartily at his own joke.

Aithan smiled, proudly resting a hand on the small of Macella's back. "Cressida, Valen, this is Macella of Shively."

"It is lovely to meet you," Macella told them with a smile.

The next moment, her arm was engulfed in Valen's large hands. He shook heartily. Macella's entire body moved.

"Pleasure is all mine," the giant Aegis thundered. "I am Aithan's much younger, much better-looking brother of sorts."

Macella and Aithan laughed.

Cressida only rolled her eyes. "Charmed," she said, turning back to their table. "Let's get back to the meal, shall we?"

On Macella's running mental tally, she added Cressida to the list of Aegises who were unfriendly or outright hostile toward her. At least she could add Valen to the nice list with Aithan and Finley.

For the next few hours, Macella listened to Valen's wild stories, including many meant to embarrass Aithan. For his part, Aithan was more talkative than she had ever seen him. He corrected many of Valen's facts and details, adding a more rational perspective to the outlandish events being related. Between the delicious food, fine wine, and hilarious conversation, Macella could ignore Cressida's coldness.

Macella learned that Cressida and Valen were some of the newest Aegises and thus were on conscription detail. They had delivered their last groups of recruits to Smoketown only a week before Macella and Aithan had arrived there. Given the time of year, they had decided against attempting another tour, instead deciding to head to the capital together. They had already been at the keep for a fortnight.

Finally noticing the lateness of the hour, the four Aegises decided to retire to their chambers. Macella declined Valen's hearty invitation to discard Aithan and come share his room. She could hear his booming laughter echoing through the corridor as they parted.

Just as Macella and Aithan reached their room, they saw one more Aegis. She appeared behind them, a parcel of food in her hands. She must have slipped into the dining hall from some other entrance after they'd departed.

"Shamira of Beechmont, daughter of Kali," Aithan greeted her gravely.

Macella's breath caught in her throat. This was the moment she had dreaded. She locked eyes with Shamira and felt a shiver travel the length of her spine. They were the same terrifying orange eyes she remembered. The sharp, asymmetrical bob haircut with cerulean tips had not changed.

Shamira looked away from Macella and met Aithan's gaze. "Aithan of Auburndale, son of Lucifer."

Macella knew Aithan was thinking of his parents, the parents Shamira had helped murder and maim. She slipped her hand into his, squeezing Aithan's hand to remind him that he was not alone. He squeezed back.

Shamira looked at Macella again. Her eyes narrowed. Something flickered in her orange eyes. Macella clenched her teeth.

"Macella of Shively, this is Shamira of Beechmont, Protector of the Crown," Aithan introduced the two women.

Macella wondered if Shamira had any inkling that they had met before. She inclined her head slightly in greeting. Shamira nodded back curtly, then stepped past them and continued down the hall.

"Enjoy your night," Shamira called over her shoulder.

CHAPTER THIRTY

The following morning, they broke their fast early to allow themselves ample time to prepare for their audience with the Crown. Macella bathed again and tried on her fancy new undergarments and silk stockings. She couldn't fathom the point of such fine fabrics for clothing that hardly anyone would see. Still, it felt wonderful against her skin.

Just as she began to wonder what she was supposed to wear over her skivvies, Lynn bustled into the room, followed by three teenage girls. Lynn's arms were full of something rust-colored. The girls behind her held all manner of items Macella was unfamiliar with.

"Good, you're bathed and oiled. That will save us time," Lynn said briskly, snapping her fingers at the servant girls and pointing. "Into the dressing room. Is the Aegis in there? He can dress in the bathroom. He doesn't need the space."

Luckily for Aithan, he had already dressed and left on some errand elsewhere in the castle. Lynn hustled her into the dressing room. The servant girls were arranging their wares on a table.

Knowing there was no resisting, Macella surrendered to Lynn's ministrations. An hour later, she stared dumbfounded into the looking glass. She was utterly speechless.

Her gown was a rich velvet the color of harvest leaves. The wide neckline left her bosom and shoulders bare, but her arms were covered in long sleeves that hung nearly to the floor. The cinched waist highlighted her curves. The gown's narrow skirt pooled onto the floor behind her. Her gold slippers peeked from beneath the hem.

Her curls had been gathered atop her head, a few tendrils falling to frame her face. One of the girls had traced her eyes with kohl and painted her lips a deep burgundy. Her cheeks were dusted with something shimmery and gold. They had let her wear her own familiar star charm necklace; it rested reassuringly against her throat.

Lynn smiled, her eyes twinkling. "This will do for today. Your gown for the welcome feast will be better."

With that, she snapped her fingers at her assistants. They scurried from the room ahead of her, passing Aithan as he reentered. Macella emerged from the dressing room, meeting him at the door to the sitting room.

Aithan stopped, almost starting in surprise. Macella stared silently back at him, waiting for him to speak. She had already enjoyed the sight of him in his formal black trousers and boots, topped with a scarlet tunic and a high-collared scarlet coat accentuated with black lace orchids.

Aithan's mouth opened and closed several times. He came forward, circling her to take her in from all angles. Finally, he stopped in front of her and looked into her face.

"Every time I think that you could not possibly be more stunning, you prove me wrong again," he said, his voice gruff.

Macella beamed. "Thank you, my love. I like it too."

Aithan offered her his arm. She took it and he led her from the room. Macella wasn't sure how he navigated the corridors to the throne room with his eyes on her, but he hardly seemed to look away until they reached a huge pair of ornate wooden doors. He spoke briefly to the doorman and then resumed staring at Macella. She blushed.

(52) When they entered the throne room, Macella struggled to keep her mouth from falling open. She had never seen a room so large, and certainly not

one so lavishly decorated as this. Soldiers stood along walls covered in beautiful and intricately woven tapestries in shades of garnet and gold. The floor was polished so that it shone, reflecting the many candles and torches in their gilded holders throughout the room. Macella felt grateful for her luxurious new attire. She would not have dared enter this room in her own clothes.

Though there was much to attract the eye in the room's décor, Macella's eyes were still immediately drawn to the dais, on which sat four thrones. Aithan had told Macella that King Khari allowed each new spouse to design their throne as they wished. She wondered what each seat revealed about its royal occupant.

As they approached the Crown, Macella studied each monarch. King Khari's throne was first, a massive construction of iron and wood, interlaced with vines of gold. The king herself was smaller than Macella had expected, only about as tall as Macella. That was where any similarities between them ended, however. Far less curvy than Macella, the king looked strong and fit for battle. Even with her surcoat and furs obscuring her frame, it was evident that she was well-muscled. She was strikingly beautiful with golden skin, which her closely cropped white-blond hair complemented nicely. Her hazel eyes were shrewd and calculating.

Seated beside the king was her first wife, Queen Awa. She sat on a throne of pristine ivory, delicately inlaid with obsidian gems. Her elaborate white and silver gown reflected the same immaculate style as her throne. Queen Awa was tall and thin, with the darkest skin Macella had seen—black with a hint of blue beneath. She had a smooth, teardrop-shaped face completely devoid of expression. Her downturned black eyes were cold.

Next, Monarch Meztli sat atop a seat of dark, intricately carved stone, decorated with patterns of geometric shapes, faces, and animals. The designs were traced in gold and accented with turquoise and amethyst. Monarch Meztli was nearly as tall as Queen Awa, with broad shoulders and a rectangular frame. Their deep purple silk tunic brought out the reddish undertones of their sandy brown skin. Monarch Meztli's sleek, straight black hair hung loose, falling nearly to their waist. They had a finely chiseled face with high cheekbones and dark, fathomless eyes.

Finally, there was the young Queen Annika. Her throne was carved of beautiful driftwood, interlaid with blue gemstones. The queen was round, with plump cheeks and an ample bosom spilling from the low neckline of her burgundy velvet gown. Her flaxen hair hung in shimmering golden waves around her shoulders. Queen Annika's porcelain skin stood in stark contrast to her bright, cobalt blue eyes.

"I present to you, Aithan of Auburndale, one of the seven shields of Kōsaten, newly arrived at the palace, your graces," announced the herald, before stepping back into his place against a nearby wall.

Aithan stepped forward, dropping to one knee before the dais. Though her head was respectfully lowered, Macella peeked up through her lashes to watch the faces of the Crown as Aithan genuflected. While Queen Awa and Monarch Meztli looked on with indifference, Queen Annika's dancing blue eyes were on Macella instead. Something about the young queen's gaze made Macella uneasy. Her senses told her to be watchful of the innocent-looking new sovereign.

"Aithan of Auburndale, son of Lucifer." King Khari greeted Aithan in a rich, velvety voice. "The Crown thanks you for another year of service. You may rise."

Aithan stood, bowing his head to each of the rulers in turn. "Thank you, your grace. And you, Queen Awa, Monarch Meztli, and Queen Annika. It is my honor to serve the kingdom."

"You've brought a guest?" Queen Annika asked, her voice high, clear, and melodious.

Though they looked surprised Queen Annika had spoken, the other three monarchs turned their attention to Macella, who felt her cheeks go hot as her heart raced. Macella didn't raise her head, anxiously running through the formal introduction customs in her mind. Aithan extended a hand to her, and she took it gratefully, stepping to his side.

"Allow me to introduce my companion, Macella of Shively," Aithan said as Macella carefully gathered the skirts of her new gown and dropped to one knee.

"Well," said the king in a politely bland voice. "How unexpected. Rise, Macella of Shively, and let us have a look at you."

Macella did as she was commanded, lifting her face, while keeping her eyes lowered. "The Crown has my deepest gratitude for allowing me the honor of residing among you for the cold season."

To Macella's great surprise, King Khari stood, her furs brushing the ground as she descended the steps of the dais. She stopped directly in front of Macella, reaching out a hand. Tentatively, Macella took the proffered hand. King Khari brought Macella's hand to her lips and kissed it.

"My, but she is lovely," King Khari told Aithan, her ochre eyes studying Macella. In her periphery, Macella thought she saw Queen Annika frown.

"She is, indeed. Thank you, your grace," Aithan answered.

The king turned her attention back to Macella. "You are young to have so much silver in your fine raven hair."

Macella's heart stuttered. "A birthmark, your grace. I suppose I was born elderly."

The king surprised Macella by laughing loudly. She released Macella's hand and turned away. She took her throne once again, smirking at her guests.

"I believe she will be a fine addition to our party," King Khari concluded. "I look forward to talking with you both further once the season is underway. You're dismissed."

⁂

Over the next fortnight, Macella grew familiar with the castle's amenities. She explored the west garden and practiced on the training grounds, restricting the latter to the most basic of activities, and limiting her training to the least busy times of day in order to keep the knowledge of her abilities from becoming generally known. She found that she enjoyed watching the sun set over the city. From the hill on which sat the keep, the view was breathtaking. The buildings of the city softened in the pink glow of the sunset, making it appear tranquil and pristine.

While Diya, Finley, and Kai were the last of the Aegises to arrive, Macella met all of Aithan's other siblings over the following days. Unsurprisingly, she found most of them to be more like Cressida than Valen, though they were all, for the most part, quiet and self-contained like Aithan.

Together, however, they seemed a bit more garrulous. Macella learned the most about the various Aegises when in the dining hall. After the mead had flowed a while, and with Valen's encouragement, most took their turn sharing or countering each other's stories. Cressida was often charming during these exchanges, especially after Cassian arrived. It turned out Cassian, also a Mictlāntēcutli Aegis, was Cressida's twin brother. His shorter ringlets and big, bright eyes were exact replicas of Cressida's. Macella was forced to revise her earlier opinion: Cassian might just be a match for Cressida in the quest for suitors.

Elsewhere in the castle, the members of Kōsaten's nobility were also arriving and settling into their quarters. Macella wondered when Zahra and her father would arrive. The Crown's sequestering of the Aegises meant that she and Aithan would not see Zahra until the welcome dinner, and who knew how long it would be before they had the chance to speak in private.

Luckily, Macella had underestimated Zahra's cunning. One morning, Macella lay on the sitting room chaise in Aithan's arms, reading him a passage from her journal. They didn't look up when a servant slipped into the room to clear the dishes from the morning meal.

Then Aithan stirred a little, sniffing audibly. Before Macella could catch the scent, the servant plopped onto the chaise near Macella's feet. Macella's surprise turned to laughter as she took in the woman's face.

Zahra Shelby had somehow managed to acquire royal servant's garb, avoid detection by members of the staff, and find her way to their apartment. Now she sat grinning at them, her eyes twinkling mischievously.

"Alright, we admit we're impressed," Aithan allowed, with a rueful smile.

Macella jumped up and embraced the smaller woman, who squealed in delight. After a few moments of hugs and exclamations, they sat down to speak properly.

"I haven't got much time," Zahra told them in her hurried way. "I am borrowing this attire and have only a small window before I need to return it to its rightful wearer, or we shall both be found out. Tell me everything. Are we at war yet?"

As succinctly as possible, Aithan and Macella related what they had learned in Duànzào and what they, with the scribe's help, had done in Smoketown. By unspoken agreement, they did not share what they had learned about their own origins. They would not put Zahra at risk by making her privy to such dangerous information.

"Well, shit," Zahra breathed as they finished. "You two do not waste time."

"Let us hope our efforts have not been in vain," Aithan replied. "We need the Crown's backing to fully enact our plans."

"How can I help?" Zahra asked immediately, tucking a strand of dark hair back into her servant's cap.

Macella felt a surge of affection for the sheriff. She took her hand and squeezed it. Zahra grinned, her mismatched eyes full of determination.

"Spread the scribe's cause," Macella instructed. "Repeat her rhetoric. Get the nobility invested in the welfare of the Aegises and the young recruits. Guide them to praise the Crown's efforts to reform Smoketown."

Zahra nodded rapidly, clearly already beginning to internally strategize. Again, Macella felt a burst of adoration. It was amazing having someone like Zahra on their side.

"Consider it done," Zahra promised, hopping to her feet. "I am out of time, I'm afraid. I'll see you at the welcome dinner. Hopefully, after that, they won't keep you all so isolated. It was almost a challenge finding you out."

Aithan and Macella walked her to the door, embracing her again. Zahra kissed them each on the lips lightly, then paused, looking intently into Macella's face.

"There's something different about you," Zahra asserted, tilting her head quizzically. "I like it. And I love the hair."

And then she was gone, as quickly as she'd come. Minutes later, an actual servant arrived to clear their dishes. Macella and Aithan couldn't stop themselves from laughing, finally processing the sheer absurdity of Zahra's espionage.

———◦⨷∽◦⨷∽◦———

A few days more found the castle buzzing with energy. The frost covering the grounds, announced the true arrival of the cold season. A few stragglers might yet arrive, having been waylaid by some setback or another, but nearly all of the expected guests had settled into their quarters and were preparing for the welcome dinner that evening.

Again, Lynn and her assistants came to dress Macella. When Macella saw her reflection this time, she nearly wept. Without thinking, she turned to Lynn and pulled the woman into a tight hug.

"Thank you for doing this for me," Macella whispered, her voice thick with emotion. "You are amazing. You've made me look as if I belong here."

"You *do* belong here," Lynn whispered back with fierce intensity.

At those words, Macella had to blink quickly to push back the tears threatening to escape and ruin her makeup. Lynn patted Macella's back awkwardly, then stepped away. She was actually smiling, though trying to suppress it. Smoothing her dress, she snapped her fingers impatiently at the servant girls, who were staring openmouthed at Macella and Lynn.

"Gather these things up immediately! We have other guests to attend to," Lynn commanded sharply.

The girls jumped and quickly began to gather up their various tools and such. Macella turned back to her reflection as the other women left the room. She heard Aithan, who had been dressing himself in the bathing chamber, approaching the dressing room. He gasped when he reached the door.

Macella wore an elegant gown with a high collar and long sleeves. Though it covered most of her body, the dress hugged her curves like a second skin until it reached mid-thigh and flared slightly, pooling on the floor around her silver slippers. The gown was formed of fine silver silk, overlaid in crimson lace embroidered with orchids. A split in the skirt opened mid-thigh, revealing a layer of crimson tulle. Laced along her spine, thick crimson ribbon secured her bodice.

Macella's jet-black curls were free and smoothed, falling around her face, its silver strands a perfect match with her dress. Curls fell over her left eye; one of the girls had pinned back the other side with a ruby-encrusted silver clip. Her eyelids and cheeks had been lightly dusted with a sweet-smelling shimmery powder. Her lips were painted crimson.

"Gods," Aithan murmured, his eyes moving over her face and body again and again. "You are breathtaking."

Macella turned to face him, her own breath catching in her throat. Aithan looked stunning. Moreover, Lynn had clearly considered his ensemble when planning Macella's.

Aithan wore a silver silk tunic over black trousers. The tunic's neckline and hem had been embellished with a lovely pattern of crimson stitching. He wore his crimson surcoat, which was accented with silver buttons and overlaid with black lace orchids. His sword was sheathed in a beautiful new crimson holster.

"I cannot take my eyes off of you," Aithan said, shaking his head slowly and sighing deeply. "Gods. You were meant to live as royalty."

Macella crossed to him, reaching up to touch his cheek. "I was meant to live with you."

Aithan caught her hand and brought it to his lips. "I could not ask for anything more than this life with you."

As they passed through the sitting room, Aithan stopped Macella again. A box sat atop one of the room's tables. Aithan lifted the lid to show her its contents.

"A gift to complete your ensemble," he said, smiling.

The box held Macella's daggers sheathed in two new thigh holsters. She could smell the rich leather. Kneeling before her, Aithan ran his hands beneath the layers of tulle that filled the slit in Macella's dress. His hands lingered on her thighs as he fastened the new holsters in place. The supple leather felt reassuring against her skin.

"Now we are ready." Aithan smiled up at her, his hands still beneath her skirts. "Unless..."

His eyes gleamed mischievously up at her. Macella felt a familiar thrill shoot through her. She laughed and swatted him away.

"If we are late, the Crown will be furious," she scolded, adjusting her dress so that her silhouette was smooth, and her weapons concealed beneath the tulle.

Grinning, Aithan offered her his arm. Together, they made their way to the massive doors of the formal dining hall. High-ranking servants were arranging the Aegises into a procession. Each of the Aegises was finely dressed, their weapons polished and sheathed in new, custom holsters. A servant approached Aithan and Macella, inquiring their names and checking a list.

"I'm sorry," they said. "The Aegises will all be formally presented to the nobility and seated at the high table with the Crown. I am not sure where their guests are to be seated."

"Never mind, Bailey." The gaunt fellow who had greeted them upon their arrival appeared beside them. "Show Aithan of Auburndale to his position. I will escort Macella of Shively to her seat."

Macella pressed Aithan's hand and then let the man lead her away from the grand doors to the dining hall. She could feel Aithan watching as she followed the man down a nearby corridor. Macella assumed that she'd be discreetly guided through some other entrance and seated at a table far from the high table, with the lesser nobility. Perhaps there would be a vacant seat near Zahra.

Finally, they did reach a door. The servant knocked lightly, and the door opened slightly. A soldier appeared, looking stern. Macella could hear the low hum of voices and the clink of glasses. This was certainly the grand dining hall.

"Macella of Shively, at King Khari's request," the servant informed him.

Macella balked. She opened her mouth to protest, but the servant was already handing her off to the soldier and turning away. The soldier inclined his head to her as he took her hand and steered her into the room.

CHAPTER THIRTY-ONE

M
acella only had a moment to take in the room's grandeur before she
realized she had stepped through the door onto a dais elevated slightly
above the rest of the room (53). An endlessly long table stretched the length
of the dais. At its center, their backs to the entrance Macella came through,
sat the Crown. King Khari was at the exact center of the table. Queen Annika
sat immediately to her left, with Monarch Meztli beside her and Queen Awa
farthest from the king.

Macella hazily heard her name announced, and then the soldier passed her
hand to King Khari. The king smilingly kissed Macella's hand and offered the
seat immediately to her right. Macella bowed to the Crown and sank gratefully
into the proffered chair. She could hear the increased buzz of voices. Undoubtedly, the other guests were trying to determine who was this person so honored
with the king's attention. Macella's cheeks were hot.

"You look stunning, my dear," the king said in a low voice, her hazel eyes
somehow cold even as she smiled at Macella. "Even if you had not been invited
to the high table by dint of your relationship to dear Aithan of Auburndale, I
would have demanded you join me the moment I laid eyes on you. You look as
though you belong at my side."

Macella swallowed hard, hazarding a timid smile. She could feel Queen An-nika simmering, listening intently from the king's other side. How many other eyes and ears were trained on Macella at that moment?

"You are too kind, your grace," Macella replied carefully. "I am honored by the invitation."

Queen Annika sniffed. "I would like to take my dinner sometime before I expire of hunger." The young queen's voice was petulant, but not explicitly directed at anyone.

Macella saw Monarch Meztli and Queen Awa glance briefly at one another. King Khari's smile tightened as she sat back in her chair. Without addressing Queen Annika, the king gestured to the herald.

The gentry sat at long tables arranged in a rectangle, with the raised, high table completing the shape. The center of the room was vacant, obviously serving as a space for dancing. Macella hoped she would not have to dance. Her legs felt rubbery with nerves.

The herald silenced the room with a note from his horn. All eyes turned to the high table. King Khari smiled broadly, motioning for the herald to begin.

"King Khari, Queen Awa, Monarch Meztli, and Queen Annika welcome you to Kōsaten Keep for the cold season," the herald said grandly. "Before we begin dinner, the Crown wishes to introduce our guests of honor, the Thirteen."

The grand double doors were pushed open. The nobles turned their atten-tion to the entrance, craning their necks in attempts to catch a glimpse of the Aegises. A man appeared at Macella's elbow, offering her a heavy crystal glass of wine. Macella took it gratefully.

"Shamira of Beechmont, Protector of the Crown," the herald announced.

Shamira entered, dressed similarly to Aithan but in cerulean and silver. She knelt before the dais, then sat one chair to Macella's right, leaving an empty space between them.

"Three wise and experienced Aegises commit themselves to training the next generation of protectors," the herald boomed as Shamira took her seat.

He then introduced Diya, Finley, and Kai in succession. Each wore silver tunics, black trousers, and boots. Diya's surcoat and tunic stitching were cerulean like Shamira's, while Finley and Kai's were a beautiful, rich jade.

The herald continued the presentations, reminding the guests that the newest Aegises scoured the kingdom for recruits. Macella watched the nobles' eyes go wide when Valen entered, his massive frame clad in the apparent Aegis uniform for the evening. His golden surcoat strained across his broad shoulders as he knelt before the Crown. Macella realized that she was shorter even than Valen on his knees.

The guests' eyes popped again when Cressida entered, but for obviously different reasons. The cut of her gold surcoat and the cinched waist of her tunic accentuated her curves. She'd left her long ringlets down, the gold-tipped silver locks beautifully complementing her ensemble.

"Finally, our bravest fighters roam the kingdom, seeking and eliminating the dangers that threaten our people," the herald announced. "The seven shields tirelessly defend us against hellish foes."

Macella leaned forward, eager to have Aithan near her again. The herald cleared his throat. The room waited.

"The shields risk their lives every day," the herald said solemnly. "This year, one shield made the ultimate sacrifice. The Crown wishes to offer their gratitude to Kiho of Russell for giving their life to protect Kōsaten."

Macella glanced down the table. Kai sat rigid, his face set in a sneer. Beside him, Finley looked disinterested, but Macella saw them slip a hand under the table to rest on Kai's knee. The herald bowed his head in respect; the other guests followed suit. After a moment, the herald lifted his head again and began to announce the remaining shields.

Bellona of Glenview's cerulean surcoat looked icy against her creamy, freckled skin. Her thick, woolly silver braid fell over her shoulder when she knelt to the Crown. Bellona took a seat beside Shamira and Diya.

Cassian of Crescent Hill received the same amorous looks his twin had elicited. His gold-tipped silver ringlets fell into his wide eyes, giving him a boyish charm. A great many eyes followed him to his seat between his sister and Valen.

Kenji of Butchertown's strong, svelte frame was resplendent in his violet surcoat. His straight silver hair was parted down the middle, falling to his broad shoulders to frame his face, his expression brooding. The violet tips of his hair brushed the high collar of his surcoat when he lowered his head to kneel before the Crown, obscuring his almond-shaped eyes.

Loi of Hillview soon sat beside Kenji. They had a similar build to Kenji, though they were shorter and moved with a lightness that Kenji did not possess. Their sleek hair was cut close on the sides with longer, spiky, violet-tipped hair on top. Loi's eyes kissed at the corners, fringed by thick lashes.

Belatedly, Macella realized that not only were the Aegises dressed according to guild, but they also seated themselves with others of the same death deity. Suddenly, she wanted to hug Lynn again. The woman had dressed Macella so as to make sure that Aithan of Auburndale wouldn't be alone in his crimson attire.

Vespera of Valley Station's dark skin looked beautiful against her violet surcoat. She was nearly as dark as Queen Awa but had closely cropped silver and violet coils and a heavy, voluptuous frame. She, too, seated herself with her guildmates.

"Aithan of Auburndale," the herald announced finally.

Macella's heart sped up as she watched Aithan enter, cross the polished parquet floor, and kneel before the dais. When he rose, he met her gaze immediately, looking relieved. Aithan took the seat between Macella and Shamira. He found her hand under the table and gave it a squeeze. Macella squeezed back, exhaling a long sigh.

Soon, a parade of servants entered the room, carrying platters of delicious-smelling food. The tables were then covered in dishes bearing all manner of delicacies, some of which Macella could not even identify. For over an hour, everyone was occupied with filling their bellies with food and wine. Macella began to feel pleasantly drowsy.

Then the king turned toward Macella.

(54) "I know who you truly are," King Khari said, her voice low and cold despite her smile. "I should have Shamira rip out your throat."

Macella froze, snapping out of her contented stupor. Beside her, Aithan stiffened. His hand twitched involuntarily toward his sword.

Macella forced herself to exhale slowly. "I beg your pardon, your grace. I know not what you mean."

"Do you take me for a fool?" the king hissed icily, her face still blandly pleasant. "I am not one of the filthy, uneducated yokels you grew up amongst. Though your competence may have appeared as genius to them, I am not so easily confounded."

Again, Aithan's hand inched toward his weapon. *Steady*, Macella thought at him. She held King Khari's gaze, not daring to look away.

How could the Crown have learned of her parentage? She'd only just learned of it herself. Had Shamira recognized and betrayed her? Had one of the Aegises from Duànzào broken their vow?

"Your grace, I meant no offense," Macella blurted, floundering for some way of appeasing the king. "I have the utmost respect for the Crown."

"Is this how you show respect?" King Khari snarled, reaching into her coat, and producing a piece of parchment. She slid it toward Macella.

Macella warily took her eyes from King Khari's face to look at the parchment. It was a society paper featuring "The Aegis and the Journey Home." Macella's confusion gave way to relief and then a jolt of terror.

The Crown did not know of her parentage. They knew that she was the Shield's Scribe. The impossible, forbidden truth of her existence was not yet revealed to her most dangerous adversaries.

Unfortunately, that did not mean that Macella was safe—far from it. It was quite clear that the Crown was severely displeased with her description of the atrocities in Smoketown. Surely, they would be even less pleased with the other steps she and Aithan had taken. Macella would need to appease them quickly and garner some good will before "The Aegis and The Forge" reached the capital.

"Your grace, I can explain," Macella began.

Faster than a snake's strike, King Khari produced a small blade and stabbed the place where Macella's hand lay on the table. It sunk into the sliver of wood between Macella's second and third finger.

"Your pretty words will not sway me, Scribe," King Khari hissed through her teeth. "I have no use for scribblers and storytellers."

The activity should have drawn the attention of the other guests, but at the same moment, something much more striking occurred. Apparently, King Khari was not the only person who had drawn a weapon. Aithan of Auburndale's sword and Shamira of Beechmont's halberd were locked, each Aegis glaring at the other, neither giving an inch. The room fell silent, everyone seemingly waiting to be told how to react to what they were seeing.

We can rely only on intellect and cunning. That is what Aithan had told her about surviving in Pleasure Ridge Park. His sword wasn't going to get them out of this terrible mess. Perhaps her pen could.

Aisling's haunting voice whispered in Macella's memory. *A shield. A scribe. A sword. A pen. Against hell's fury. Against our end.*

She would convince the Crown that a scribbler and storyteller could, in fact, prove useful. Macella smiled widely, covering King Khari's hand with her own. She closed the king's fingers around the hilt of the small knife, tugging to free it from the table, before gently pushing the king's hands toward her lap.

Macella laughed loudly and stood to her feet. "King Khari has prepared the most wonderful surprise!"

Her exclamation drew the attention of nearly everyone in the room. Only Aithan and Shamira kept their eyes on each other. King Khari sat back in her chair, her eyes cold as she smiled blandly back at Macella. Macella forced her voice to hold steady, to be melodic and enchanting, as when she would tell stories to the littles to keep them entertained.

A wry smile caught Macella's attention from a table across the room. She met Zahra Shelby's gaze. The sheriff winked at Macella. The encouragement helped Macella steel herself to continue.

"You have gathered here this cold season to celebrate the heroes who protect our kingdom." Macella gestured to the Aegises seated along the high table. "You have read of their brave deeds and heard of their immense strength and skill. But your king wants you to understand, to see with your own eyes the talents of these servants of the Crown."

What are you doing? Aithan's mental voice was strained.

Trying to keep us alive, Macella thought back. *Trust me.*

Always, Aithan replied, his mind immediately growing calmer.

Macella turned slowly toward Aithan and Shamira, every eye in the room following her movements. She then looked back at the Crown. King Khari narrowed her eyes, leaning forward slightly. Monarch Meztli looked almost interested, their black eyes finally on something other than their wine glass. Queen Annika's bright blue eyes followed Macella. Queen Awa's face remained impassive. Macella turned back to the crowd.

"When you return to your provinces for the planting season, you will be able to assure your people that the Crown's might is unrivaled, that King Khari is a powerful protector and a most formidable leader."

Macella turned to King Khari and gave a low bow. A few people clapped tentatively. A few others raised their glasses toward the king in salute. Macella turned back to the crowd.

"King Khari, Queen Annika, Queen Awa, and Monarch Meztli would like to present this exhibition of their mightiest warriors," Macella announced. "Aithan of Auburndale, one of the seven shields of the kingdom, versus Shamira of Beechmont, Protector of the Crown."

Several people gasped, others clapped, and many cheered or called out their hearty approval. Macella had gambled that the revelers would be easily won, and she'd been correct. Of course, King Khari's reaction was the most important. Macella held her breath; she could feel Aithan's tension, his body coiled and ready to attack. If the Crown refused to play along, he would obviously die fighting.

Macella prayed that her words would render such a conclusion unnecessary. She would, of course, die fighting at his side if the time came. But not today. Not if she could save them.

Macella turned her head to smile at the Crown, her arms still outstretched toward the waiting crowd. King Khari glanced at her partners. Queen Annika was grinning, clearly enjoying the entertainment. Monarch Meztli raised an eyebrow and took another sip of their wine.

Queen Awa lifted her chin even higher, her posture as rigid as ever. Her face remained smooth and expressionless, her dark eyes fixed on Macella. Almost imperceptibly, she nodded.

King Khari clapped once, adjusting her crown to sit at a rakish angle atop her shorn blond head. "Let the exhibition begin."

Macella exhaled slowly, relieved. Aithan and Shamira moved to the center of the polished floor, their weapons raised. Macella took her seat beside the king.

Win, Macella thought at Aithan. *We must demonstrate our value to the Crown.*

Aithan shifted slightly, and Macella knew he had heard her. His face was set in grim determination. He would not be defeated.

(55) Shamira attacked first. Leading with the point of her halberd, she feinted toward him, then spun away, bringing her halberd around in an arc as she did so. Aithan did not react to the false move, easily blocking her blade and getting close enough to throw a punch, which Shamira only barely dodged. Quickly, she lifted her weapon again.

A series of advances and deflections now began, each Aegis demonstrating their distinct skill with their weapons. Neither could gain the upper hand, both well-trained in wielding blades. Macella saw that the nobility were entranced, watching the swordplay. The Crown, however, seemed more restless.

"This is a bit dull, isn't it." Queen Annika leaned toward King Khari, her breasts threatening to spill from her bodice. Sure of the king's attention, however momentary, she added breathily, "Shamira is the strongest of the Aegises, is not she? That's why she protects *us*. She seems evenly matched here."

King Khari raised her eyes from Queen Annika's ample bosom, narrowing her eyes at the fighters. "That is concerning indeed, my queen. It is my duty to ensure your safety above all else."

Macella saw Queen Annika's blue eyes dancing with mischievous glee. She'd suspected that the seemingly harmless youngest queen would be trouble, but she may have underestimated just how much trouble. Monarch Meztli gave Queen Annika a withering look before calling for their goblet to be refilled.

Meanwhile, Aithan and Shamira continued their deadly dance. Queen Annika hadn't been wrong in her assessment: the two were evenly matched thus far. It was evident from the exclamations of the watching nobility that both Aegises were faster and more graceful than any fighters they'd ever seen. And they were holding nothing back, delivering strikes that would easily have destroyed a human adversary. Still, there would be no clear winner. Macella could see that now.

"Perhaps they need additional motivation," Queen Annika suggested.

"Perhaps some of us should learn patience," Queen Awa countered. Her voice was rich, deep, and, based on the rapt attention of everyone in the vicinity, obviously rarely heard.

King Khari drew herself up, glaring at her eldest spouse. The king kept her gaze on Queen Awa as she turned back to Queen Annika. She took her young queen's hand.

The king's voice dripped with venom as she replied. "Your wish is my command, my love."

Macella felt a chill creep along her spine. There were obviously variables here that she had not accounted for. With so many around her locked in complex power plays, how were she and Aithan to stay in favor with anyone?

King Khari gestured for an attendant. The man scurried to her side, leaning into the space between Macella and the king. The king motioned the man closer, catching Macella's eye as she did so. Making sure that Macella heard, the king stage whispered into the man's ear.

"Summon the Chosen."

Macella stiffened. She'd heard enough about the Chosen to know that their presence meant imminent doom. She had not factored this turn of events into her hasty plan.

It seemed as though a chill spread along the table. Macella quickly realized that every Aegis at the table had heard King Khari's command. The tension was palpable. Though the Aegises kept their faces passive, Macella felt the same emotion in every one of their minds—abject terror.

King Khari let out a whistle, as if cheering along with the rest of the onlookers. Shamira's attention snapped to the king, even as she evaded Aithan's sword. From the corner of her eye, Macella saw the king's hand move in some gesture too discreet for her to make out. From the answering look on Shamira's face, it was nothing good.

The Kali Aegis advanced with renewed energy, grunting each time their blades met as Aithan deflected her attacks. Baring her teeth, Shamira lunged, the point of her halberd trained on Aithan's midsection.

As Aithan prepared to block her attack, Shamira suddenly pivoted, swinging her halberd in a low arc, and sweeping Aithan's feet. Recovering quicky, Aithan hit the ground and used his momentum to propel him into a backward roll and then into a low crouch, his sword extended at his side.

Shamira did not relent for a moment. By the time Aithan had landed his crouch, she was already bringing her blade down again. Aithan lifted his sword in the nick of time, their blades meeting with a deafening clang.

The two Aegises grimaced at each other, Shamira throwing her weight forward to press their blades closer to Aithan's face. Macella could feel the desperation emanating from Shamira's mind. Whatever the king had signaled to the Kali Aegis had increased her resolve. She was determined to defeat Aithan at any cost.

But Aithan of Auburndale was not to be underestimated. Macella had told him to win—that their lives might depend on it. He would not disappoint her. He would never fail her.

Slowly, Aithan began to stand. The muscles in his arms stood out as he pushed against Shamira's halberd. The Kali Aegis tried to use gravity to her advantage, but to no avail. Inch by inch, Aithan rose, their crossed blades still inches from his face.

Shamira seemed to realize that her efforts were in vain. Her eyes narrowed and her lip curled. Macella felt a sudden, intense feeling of foreboding.

It happened fast. So fast that anyone who wasn't an Aegis likely missed it. For just a moment, Shamira's irises expanded, glowing cerulean. At the same moment, she shifted her weight off of her halberd, leaping backward and kicking Aithan in the stomach. Aithan fell back, unable to catch himself this time. He hit the floor hard.

Macella felt her skin growing hot, rage coursing through her veins. Shamira's kick had not taken Aithan down. Macella had felt it in Aithan's mind. As Shamira kicked him, she had also used her biokinetic gift to momentarily inflict excruciating pain.

And she was about to do it again.

Time slowed down for Macella. It was as if she was watching each terrible moment unfold underwater. Aithan was struggling to his feet. Shamira was advancing, her blade swinging hard toward Aithan's neck. Beside Macella, King Khari was leaning forward, one hand curled in a tight fist, the other clutching her goblet.

Shamira's orange eyes began to take on a darker hue. Her halberd hurtled toward Aithan, her aim true. Aithan was raising his sword, but not quickly enough. Shamira's eyes glowed cerulean for a split second. Aithan stumbled, catching himself with his sword. He was completely exposed. Shamira's blade was a hand's breadth from the spot where Aithan's neck and shoulder met.

Stop! Macella commanded, her gaze locked on Shamira.

Shamira faltered, a look of surprise crossing her face. Her head snapped up. She met Macella's furious glare. Shamira's face darkened.

Then she was jerked forward, her eyes widening in surprise. Aithan held the shaft of her halberd. Anyone without particular knowledge and Aegis vision could not have noticed that, though Aithan's hand had shot up quickly, the halberd was already moving toward him when he grabbed it. They certainly did not see his eyes glow crimson for the briefest moment.

Macella let out a shaky breath as time seemed to resume its normal cadence. King Khari crossed her arms, sitting back in her chair. Beneath the king's placid expression, Macella could feel a barely contained rage simmering.

On the floor, Aithan shot to his feet, tossing the halberd aside and viciously headbutting Shamira as he rose. Instead of letting her stagger back, Aithan jerked the woman forward. Before she could even attempt to counter, the point of Aithan's sword was beneath her chin.

The watching nobility erupted in cheers. Queen Annika clapped enthusiastically, but none of the other monarchs moved. King Khari stood, lifting her goblet. The crowd quieted.

"Well done, Aithan of Auburndale," she called, smiling widely.

Another round of applause followed her words. Aithan released Shamira, stepping away from the other Aegis. Shamira paced farther away from him, turning her back to the onlookers, her shoulders heaving. Aithan turned to face the king. He bowed, his eyes on her face.

"As dear Macella explained, we wished to show you some of the great skill you have read of in the society papers," King Khari continued.

Macella felt a shiver along her spine as the king turned toward her. She felt the menace beneath the king's words. This was a woman who could smile in your face while peeling the skin off of your body. King Khari was not to be trifled with.

Macella prayed she had gambled wisely. She hoped King Khari could see that Aithan's skill, and Macella's words, could be useful to her—or at least that they were worth keeping alive. But perhaps the king would consider the opportunity to exhibit her own power more important.

Macella felt the fire building under her skin, ready to be unleashed if needed. She rested her hands on her thighs, feeling for the reassuring presence of her daggers.

"That was truly a magnificent exhibition," King Khari boomed, turning her smile back toward her guests. "It has actually shown more than we expected."

The king's words were laced with menace. Macella saw Shamira stiffen before turning back to face the Crown, her fists clenched at her side. It was clear that the moment of truth had come.

"Shamira of Beechmont, you were one of the seven shields for Queen Rhiannon of Wyandotte before me and have protected the Crown through the entirety of my reign. You have served Kōsaten well," King Khari proclaimed, lifting her goblet toward the Kali Aegis.

Again, people applauded. The king waited for the applause to subside before continuing.

She lowered her goblet and looked introspective. "However, it is your duty to be the strongest." King Khari's voice was solemn now, her smile gone. "You have failed the Crown today."

A murmur ran through the room. Zahra caught Macella's attention again, her large eyes wide with concern. Several people shifted uncomfortably. The raucous mood of revelry was quickly growing apprehensive. Macella felt cold.

"Fortunately for you, you will now have the opportunity to make up for your shortcomings," King Khari continued. "You will redeem yourself through another exhibition of the Crown's might. You will help show our guests that, although we have the mightiest of heroes protecting the kingdom, there is none mightier than your king."

(56) In the absolute silence that followed the king's words, Macella heard a whispering sound that made the hairs on her arms stand on end. The Aegises around her went rigid, their senses no doubt alert to the same approaching danger.

Try not to react like the others, Aithan thought frantically. *Only Aegises will feel the true weight of their presence.*

Macella didn't have time to respond. She did not need to ask who he meant. The Chosen were coming. They would arrive at any moment.

The door behind the high table opened and the room filled with light. Around her, Macella saw that the monarchs were shielding their eyes—all except King Khari. Every human in the room was reacting the same way. Macella quickly lifted her hands to her face. She watched from between her fingers as the other Aegises stared, transfixed, at the doors. Macella noticed that the whites had disappeared from the Aegis's eyes, replaced with jade, cerulean, violet, or gold. She squinted, willing her eyes to remain as they were.

After a moment, she saw that the light seemed to originate from three cloaked figures. They were tall and slender, completely shrouded in pristine white robes. They glided into the room and bowed to King Khari. Macella wondered how much the squinting humans around the room could see. Several veiled servants had come forward, holding small screens and fans to shield the eyes of the other monarchs.

When the Chosen stood again, their light dimmed slightly, allowing the watching guests to better see the huge figures. Every Aegis in the room dropped to one knee. Macella felt a slight compulsion to do the same.

Don't, Aithan warned again in her mind.

Macella looked toward the parquet where Aithan and Shamira knelt. Macella saw that Shamira was shivering. Actually, *all* of the Aegises seemed to be shivering. Except Aithan. And Macella.

I feel it, but I can resist, Macella thought back at him. *And I think you can too. You should be shivering, and your eyes should have changed.*

Macella felt Aithan's surprise. He must not have realized that he, like Macella, seemed to have some inherent resistance to the power of the Chosen. Perhaps it was their hybrid nature as Aegisborn. Aithan began to tremble, but Macella knew it was a mere pretense. He felt the same chill she did, but not the icy touch engulfing the other Aegises.

"You are bearing witness to a rare occurrence," King Khari told her guests. "So few people in our history can say that they have been in the presence of Kōsaten's mightiest beings. The Chosen and the Aegises, both endowed by the gods, both bound to *me.*"

King Khari's voice was nearly as cold as the energy of the Chosen. She surveyed the room, starting with her spouses—her gaze resting the longest on Queen Awa—and then eyeing the nobles and, lastly, the Aegises. Macella kept her eyes averted and shielded, not wanting to meet the king's gaze.

"Bound to me because I am the mightiest," King Khari bellowed, her voice like the crack of a whip. "Bound to me because I claimed victory from the gods and now enact their will. The Chosen and Aegises serve *me*."

After a pause, the king began again, her voice sweet and reassuring. "And I, of course, serve Kōsaten. I keep you all safe. I keep my sovereigns safe."

King Khari stepped behind her spouses' chairs. She rested a hand on Queen Annika's shoulder, the other on the back of Monarch Meztli's seat. Queen Annika beamed up at the king. Monarch Meztli stared into their goblet.

"Anything that threatens that safety, however minutely, must be quelled," King Khari asserted, her hand shaking in its tight grip on Monarch Meztli's chairback. "And today, you, Shamira of Beechmont, have become such a threat. You have demonstrated that you are not strong enough to protect my beloveds and myself."

Shamira had gone extremely pale, her skin shimmering with sweat even as she shivered. None of the other Aegises lifted their heads. Through her fingers, Macella locked eyes with Shamira. A jolt of emotion—anger, panic, regret, despair, relief—rushed through Macella's mind.

"I hereby sentence you to death," King Khari declared.

Chapter Thirty-Two

Macella blinked, and the Chosen were across the room, encircling Shamira. Each of the three figures extended a hand toward the Kali Aegis. Macella could see that their hands looked human, though with completely flawless, almost marble skin—one hand amber, another porcelain, and the third onyx. The hands glowed, emitting an even brighter light than the Chosen had been exuding since they entered the room. Macella felt the air in the room grow colder. The kneeling Aegises clenched their chattering teeth, their muscles tensed.

Shamira was on her knees, her head lifted, and her eyes glowing cerulean. A network of veins surfaced on her skin, crisscrossing her face and neck with jagged blue lines. She began to cough and gag, her body contorting painfully as she choked. Her back arched so sharply that Macella heard the crack of her spine. Macella smothered a scream as several shocked cries echoed around the room.

Macella looked on in horror as Shamira spat an inky black goo that dripped down her chin before taking on a smoky form and disappearing into the light of the Chosen's hands. Soon, the same liquid smoke began to drip from Shamira's eyes, tracing black tears down her cheeks. It seeped from her ears and her nose as her veins blackened. The cerulean glow faded from her eyes, leaving them entirely blank—no iris, no pupil, only white nothingness.

Macella felt a sharp stab of pain in her chest that left a dull ache behind. Around her, she could sense the other Aegises experiencing the same feeling. Luckily for Macella, the general expressions of surprise throughout the room masked her reaction. She fought to regain her composure.

The Chosen lowered their hands. Shamira's body fell limply to the polished floor. A few people cried out or gasped in surprise as the Chosen vanished, reappearing again behind the high table. They bowed to the king.

"You are dismissed," King Khari informed them, waving them away.

In perfect unison, the Chosen turned and glided from the room. The rustle of their robes against the floor made Macella's skin prickle. She was not the only person who breathed a sigh of relief when the door closed behind them and their cold light faded away.

Two soldiers lifted Shamira's body and carried it from the room. The kneeling Aegises remained still. A heavy silence hung in the air as the guests blinked and rubbed their eyes. Everyone seemed to be holding a collective breath.

"Aithan of Auburndale," King Khari's voice broke the silence. She sounded almost jovial now that she was clearly back in control of the situation. "You have greatly impressed your king."

Aithan bowed his head in acknowledgment from where he knelt, mere meters from the spot where Shamira's corpse had lain. Macella saw her lover's clenched fists and the grim set of his jaw. She wanted them to be back in their chambers, wrapped in soft blankets. Better yet, she wanted them far away from Kōsaten Keep, in some nondescript inn, leagues away from King Khari's calculating gaze.

The king rounded the high table and crossed the parquet to where Aithan knelt. A servant hurried forward, extending a piece of clothing. Macella felt bile at the back of her throat. It was Shamira's surcoat.

King Khari removed a pin from the coat. She held it in her palm, studying it for a long moment. When she looked up, the smile on her face filled Macella's veins with ice.

"Aithan of Auburndale, son of Lucifer, you have proven yourself the strongest of your kind. In recognition of your skill and as a reward for your loyalty, I hereby name you Protector of the Crown," King Khari declared. "May the gods prolong your days, that you may serve your kingdom well. Rise."

Macella's jaw dropped. Zahra Shelby gasped. The room erupted in applause as Aithan stood. His face was carefully blank, as only years of silent suffering could teach. King Khari affixed the pin to Aithan's lapel. Macella could see that it was a silver shield, engraved with the Crown's insignia.

"Aegises of Kōsaten, take heed," King Khari said, turning from Aithan to look at the high table. "Laziness is punished. Loyalty is rewarded. You will grieve the loss of Shamira and of Kiho by training harder, growing stronger. It is your duty.

"With the improvements in training and education our Aegis neophytes will receive henceforth, I am certain your fallen siblings will be soon replaced. Already, several of our finest generals have arrived in Smoketown, along with schoolmasters, medical mages, and additional supplies," King Khari said solemnly, nodding slightly at Macella. A smirk tugged at the king's lips, vanishing before Macella could be sure she'd seen the expression at all.

The king smiled, clapping her hands once. "We will discuss strategies and reassignments tomorrow. Tonight, we celebrate! You may all rise. Musicians, a lively tune please. Servers, more wine and ale!"

Macella forced a smile that felt more like a grimace as the other Aegises resumed their seats. She felt numb. Bound to the capital, unable to travel or pursue their own interests, living under the watchful eyes of the Crown. It would be miserable. Moreover, it would be exceedingly dangerous. Tonight's proceedings had demonstrated just how dangerous. Now, they would have to navigate these tense political intrigues indefinitely.

Her fake smile faltered as she thought of an additional problem. Shamira had served the Crown for King Khari's entire reign of nearly a century. If Macella remained in Pleasure Ridge Park with Aithan for too long, the Crown would notice that she did not age properly. Only Aegises, the Chosen, the Crown, and mages lived such long lives. They would know that Macella was not human.

Perhaps she could learn to be a mage. Or perhaps she could find a mage who could endow her with the illusion of age. Maybe she could live discreetly on the outskirts of the city, where Aithan could steal away to visit her without the Crown's knowledge. Macella's mind spun through solutions, each more impossible than the next.

Macella felt a warm hand on hers beneath the table. Aithan had rejoined the high table along with King Khari. Exhaling, Macella gripped Aithan's hand gratefully. Her heart grew steadier, her smile more sincere.

The king turned to Macella once more, her ochre eyes dancing with triumph. "You will, of course, live here at the castle with dear Aithan. I know that you would not wish to be separated. Nor would I wish to lose you. Your presence has greatly added to the palace's pleasures."

On the king's other side, Queen Annika tried to hide her scowl. Macella could tell that Monarch Meztli and Queen Awa were listening as well. She gave the king what she hoped was a genuine-looking smile.

"Your grace, you are too generous," Macella said, inclining her head. "We are both so grateful for your thoughtfulness."

Satisfied, the king turned away. Macella met Queen Annika's gaze and was shocked by the naked hatred she saw in the woman's bright blue eyes. As soon as the king turned to her, however, Annika's face contorted into an expression of convincing sweetness and devotion.

The evening wore on as servants continued to pour drinks and the guests relaxed back into their revelries. Macella grew exhausted from feigning enjoyment. She wanted to be alone with Aithan, out of her fancy clothes and makeup, and free to be her true self. Though Aithan and the other Aegises were allowed to look stoic, Macella knew Aithan was as ready to be done with the charade as she was.

Finally, the king announced that she and her spouses were retiring. She encouraged the guests to remain as long as they wished, then offered Queen Annika her arm. Monarch Meztli and Queen Awa followed them from the room.

Immediately, it was as if a weight had lifted from the guests' collective shoulders. Macella realized that even these wealthy, titled nobles were acting a part before the Crown. She wondered if anyone could ever be truly at ease in the presence of the monarchy. If the escalating energy in the room was any indication, the answer was no.

Now that the formality of the evening was alleviated, people began to move around the room freely, conversing merrily with associates and enemies. The most daring—or perhaps the most foolish—among the gathered gentry approached the high table to engage the Aegises in conversation. They quickly learned who were the most amenable to the attentions and focused their efforts where they anticipated the most gain.

Macella and Aithan took the opportunity to escape, slipping through the door behind the high table. Before they did so, Macella saw Zahra look in their direction with sympathy and concern in her mismatched eyes. She would likely find her way back to their chambers on the morrow. Macella was a little comforted by the thought.

Aithan and Macella walked back to their quarters in silence. As terrible as things were, Macella felt far better leaning on her Aegis's strong, warm arm. His steadiness reminded her what was real: their story, their love, their Fate.

Macella could hardly wait to get into their room and fall into his arms. She had no desire to talk to anyone else. Macella's only thought was that she did not want to see another living soul that night.

She soon realized that she should have been more specific in her mental phrasing.

As Aithan closed the door behind him, Macella felt an internal alarm go off. The hairs on her neck stood up, and she grabbed Aithan's arm. There was someone in their room.

Intuiting Macella's alarm, Aithan drew his sword, stepping in front of Macella and scanning the room for threats. Macella saw a figure just beyond the glow of the candle a servant had lit. She waited for Aithan to subdue the intruder.

What is it? Aithan asked in her mind. He had not moved toward the figure.

"Who are you and why are you in our chambers?" Macella demanded.

"You can see me. I somehow knew you would be able to. It is why I waited here for you," said the woman, in a voice Macella thought she recognized.

"Macella, who are you talking to?" Aithan asked, bewildered.

The woman stepped into the candlelight. She looked as resplendent in her silver tunic and cerulean surcoat as she had earlier that night. Before she died.

It was Shamira of Beechmont.

"Tell your beau that I have had quite enough of his sword for one night," Shamira told Macella, scowling at Aithan.

"You can sheathe your sword, love." Macella touched Aithan's arm. "It's Shamira."

Aithan looked at Macella sharply. Realization dawned on his face. He sheathed his sword and followed Macella's gaze, focusing on the general area where Shamira stood.

Aithan swallowed hard. "Tell her that I had no notion that the king would—" He broke off, his expression miserable.

Shamira sighed and waved the apology away. She began to pace the length of the room in apparent agitation. Macella wondered if the dead felt emotions in the same ways as the living.

"Tell him I can hear him and to say no more," Shamira commanded gruffly. "Few people understand the king's capacity for cruelty as I do. And even I could not have predicted the sequence of events tonight."

Macella relayed Shamira's words to Aithan mentally. She took his arm again. She felt that they could both use the support.

"I assume I will begin to understand more very soon," Aithan said gravely. "As I will be assuming your former duties."

Shamira looked shocked. "Can he hear me?"

Macella frowned in confusion for a moment before she understood the source of Shamira's misconception. "No, but he can hear my mind, as you know. I have grown accustomed to utilizing his gift."

Shamira looked between Aithan and Macella, shaking her head. "You must truly love each other. You seem so...attuned to one another."

Aithan smiled sadly when Macella relayed Shamira's words. "This is a rare and marvelous gift, and one that has been too long denied to our kind."

"Your parents had it," Shamira replied, a pained expression clouding her face. "Both of you had parents that experienced love. And I helped take that away."

Macella drew in a sharp breath. Shakily, she communicated Shamira's words to Aithan.

His expression also grew pained. "You knew," Aithan said. "You knew all this time."

"You recognized me too?" Macella asked. "How?"

Shamira sighed heavily. "I did not know you when I was alive. Those memories must have returned when I departed the realm of the living. But I knew of Aithan of Auburndale's parentage."

Even as Macella shared the other woman's words with Aithan, she was blurting out another question. "Why? Why would you keep that from him for all of these years?"

"To stay alive," Aithan interrupted before Shamira could answer. "I know that you kept that secret, and any others, so that you could survive. I only wish that you could tell me about them—Maia and my other parent."

"I did not know them," Shamira said. "I was young and eager to prove myself when I was sent on a mission to kill a deserter and anyone that harbored them. I was not given any further information.

"I did not so much as make it through the door. The mage had lain quite the maze of traps. I was incapacitated before the fighting even began." Shamira looked sadly at Aithan. "I never saw your parents. When I awoke, I was in a cart with a covered and bound body and a crying child. I was young, but not a fool. I soon figured out what it meant."

"You were punished," Macella added, remembering Matthias's tale. "That is why you were assigned to recruitment. And that is how you met me."

Shamira looked down at her hands as Macella filled Aithan in. Aithan exhaled a heavy breath, clearly processing these new details of his early life. Macella leaned into him.

"When Matthias came to me, I'd had many years to wallow in remorse," Shamira continued. "I thought that I was being given the opportunity to redeem myself. Besides, I would not even remember exactly what I had done, so I was at no risk of revealing my treason on my own, and I had no fear of Matthias betraying the secret.

"The secret I did have, however, was that I knew of Aithan's parentage," Shamira continued. "King Khari courted me during her rise to power, gradually gaining my trust. I was no one then, still on recruitment detail, only visiting the castle for the cold season. I had been physically and mentally disciplined for my failure. Khari knew that my allegiance to Queen Rhiannon was tenuous and promised that, when she was crowned, I would have a role at her side."

Shamira paused, allowing Macella time to communicate with Aithan or, perhaps, gathering her thoughts. Then she continued, "I shared the secret with her, giving her fuel to defeat Queen Rhiannon. Information is one of the only currencies that are valued in Pleasure Ridge Park. Information and power."

"King Khari knows," Macella gasped aloud. "She knows what Aithan is."

Shamira nodded. "She believes, however, that *he* does not know. Now that I am dead, no other person lives who knows the truth. The other Aegises who survived the attack on Aithan's family all died in the line of duty early in King Khari's reign."

Macella watched Aithan's face harden as she relayed these latest horrors. She was suddenly extremely tired. This was going to be her life now. Secrets, lies, and bids for power. And the threat of death always uncomfortably close.

"Thank you for coming to us," Aithan said, clearly exhausted as well. "Few people could have given us back these pieces of our past."

"Or the information about the king," Macella added.

"Those are not the only reasons I came," Shamira said. "I am determined to remain in this realm for as long as I can so that I may help you."

"Help us how?" Macella asked.

Shamira's eyes took on a vicious gleam. "I am going to help you destroy King Khari."

The cold season passed in a flurry of activity. There were dinners and dances and drinks galore. Macella was surprised by how truly she enjoyed the society of the other Aegises and even a few of the gentry. Finley and Valen ensured that Macella felt included while they spent long evenings laughing and sharing stories or having heated over-long disputes. Zahra's wealthy friends were extremely well-educated, and Macella often found herself immersed in stimulating intellectual conversation. It amazed her how far she had come from her old, sheltered life.

Unfortunately, many of Macella and Aithan's hours were spent walking a delicate line as they spent an increasing amount of time in the Crown's company. Aithan, of course, was occupied with his new role as Protector of the Crown. He often rose well before the sun, only to return to their quarters long after nightfall.

Macella was nearly as busy as Aithan. Allowing her to earn her keep, the Crown had employed Macella as Royal Scribe and tasked her with drafting the official bulletins released to the kingdom each month. They required that she study Kōsaten's history and become familiar with the Crown's views. Furthermore, King Khari insisted that, since she was to remain prominent at court, Macella take lessons in manners, elocution, and combat—only one of which gave Macella any pleasure. She was glad to be given an excuse to keep fit, even though she had to carefully mask her true skills to avoid suspicion.

She was still permitted to write for the society papers, but under the unspoken threat of severe penalty should she displease the Crown. Macella had never worked so hard in her life, both emotionally and mentally. Though she knew that she was remaining true to her Fate, she longed for the freedom to wander again.

Fortunately, when the first green buds appeared to herald the planting season, Macella and Aithan could claim at least temporary victory in their quest to avoid outright war. Kai, Finley, and Diya admitted that the Crown's recent concessions were a step toward the reparations due to Aegiskind. To compensate for the deaths and Aithan's reassignment, the Crown appointed Cressida and Valen to the seven shields, leaving their two recruitment roles vacant. Diya, Finley, and Kai would head home to await the emergence of two new Aegises to train so that they might fill the holes in their ranks.

"You realize that, if we truly find *two* new siblings, our suspicions of the Crown will be substantiated," Kai said in their farewell conversation. "We know that there is but one spot to fill, otherwise we exceed thirteen."

"And if they have lied about that, we know there is more treachery yet to discover," Diya agreed grimly.

Shamira's story flashed through Macella's memory. Indeed, there remained a great deal of deceit left to uncover. And they would uncover it, but they were not yet prepared to take on the Crown. They had to bide their time, using their positions at court to obtain information and resources.

"Let us fight that battle when it is upon us," Aithan suggested placatingly.

The castle was much quieter as the guests slowly departed, leaving only the keep's year-round inhabitants. Macella stood in their cold-season quarters, staring morosely at their empty wardrobes. Aithan joined her, standing behind her and wrapping his arms around her waist.

"Do not look so melancholy," he murmured into her hair. "Our permanent quarters are twice as luxurious as these. You've directed the apartment's fitting up perfectly. We will be quite comfortable."

Macella sighed, leaning back against his chest. "We will also be much closer to the watchful eyes of the Crown."

Naturally, as Protector of the Crown, Aithan needed to be able to reach them at a moment's notice, day and night. Consequently, his and Macella's new accommodations were nearly adjacent to the Crown's suite of apartments. There was even a hidden passageway through which Aithan could travel from their rooms directly to those of King Khari, Queen Awa, Monarch Meztli, and Queen Annika.

A passage that the monarchs, theoretically, could travel to reach Macella and Aithan's chambers. Passages Queen Annika could hide in to listen to their private conversations. Passages King Khari could slip through in the night to murder them in their bed.

"We will fulfill our Fates," Aithan assured her, holding her tightly. "We are where we are meant to be."

"And you are not alone," added Shamira, appearing before the empty wardrobe.

Even as a startled Macella began to alert Aithan to Shamira's presence, she sensed another person entering the sitting room. Macella and Aithan spun around in unison, slipping reflexively into defensive postures.

To their surprise, Queen Awa glided toward them, striking as always with her statuesque frame draped in a white gown that stood in stark contrast to her smooth black skin. She moved past them, stopping to stand beside Shamira. Macella mentally showed Aithan the image of the two women standing close to one another, looking into each other's eyes.

"Shamira has assured me that you can be trusted," Queen Awa explained in her sonorous tenor. "You will help me dethrone the king."

Macella looked up into Aithan's face. He met her gaze, his face smoothing into the peaceful expression he saved just for her. Macella's heart jolted, reminding her of what was real, what was true.

Stars align, prophets proclaim, she thought fleetingly. Aithan nodded, kissing the top of her head. They intertwined their hands and turned back to Queen Awa and Shamira of Beechmont.

Aithan looked toward the door of their chambers, which Queen Awa had left slightly ajar. His eyes glowed crimson. The door swung shut, the key turning in the lock with a click.

"Let us begin," Macella said, her eyes glowing onyx.

It is easy to forget that Aegises have been vital to Kōsaten for as long as the kingdom has been inhabitable. From the moment Khalid brokered peace between the gods, the Aegises were a necessity—our first line of defense against the creatures that would prey on our inherent weaknesses. It is odd, then, that we have deceived ourselves for so many years believing that Aegises lack human emotion. How could that be so when their commitment and sacrifice are so clearly indicative of a deep love for humanity? How many of us would be willing to give up our own comfort, stability, relationships, even our lives, for thankless strangers? Dear reader, if you have learned nothing else from my writings, remember this: Aegises are the most human of us all. They are the very best of what humanity has to offer. And if you should ever have the privilege of knowing and loving an Aegis, never, ever let them go.

– From *The Epic of the Aegis and the Wanderer* by S.S. (The Shield's Scribe

GLOSSARY OF PROPER NOUNS

Aegis (ē-jis): (from Merriam-Webster)

(in classical art and mythology) an attribute of Zeus and Athena (or their Roman counterparts Jupiter and Minerva) usually represented as a goatskin shield.

Aegis has Greek and Latin Roots. We borrowed *aegis* from Latin, but the word ultimately derives from the Greek noun *aigis*, which means "goatskin." In ancient Greek mythology, an aegis was something that offered physical protection, and it has been depicted in various ways, including as a magical protective cloak made from the skin of the goat that suckled Zeus as an infant and as a shield fashioned by that bore the severed head of the Medusa. The word first entered English in the 15th century as a noun referring to the shield or protective garment associated with Zeus or Athena. It later took on a more general sense of "protection" and, by the late-19th century, it had acquired the extended senses of "auspices" and "sponsorship."

Pronunciations include dictionary style and the author's attempt at phonetic spelling.

Aisling [ash-liŋ; ash-ling]: (Irish) a dream or vision

Aithan [ā-than; a-than]: (Greek) firm, strong

Annika [an-ik-ə; an-ick-uh]: (Swedish) grace

Anwansi [än-vän-sē; on-von-see]: (Igbo) uncanny, magic

Awa [ä-wə; ah-wuh]: (Arabic) beautiful angel, night

Bellona [bə-lō-nə; bell-o-nuh]: (Roman) to fight

Cassian [kas-sē-in; kas-see-in]: (Latin) hollow

Cressida [kres-ə-də; kres-uh-duh]: (Greek) gold

Diya [dē-ə; dee-uh]: (Sanskrit, Arabic) light, glow

Duànzào [dü-in-zaú; doo-in-zow]: (Chinese) the forge

Epanofório [ā-pän-ō-fòr-ē-ō; a-pon-o-for-ee-o]: (Greek) cloak

Finley [fin-lē; fin-lee]: (Irish, Celtic, Gaelic) a hero or battle warrior with fair
skin

Kai [kī; kye]: (Hawaiian, Japanese) of the sea; keeper of the keys

Kellen [kel-in]: (German) swamp

Kenji [kin-jē; kin-jee]: (Japanese) vigorous, intelligent second son

Khalid [kä-lēd; kah-leed]: (Arabic) immortal, eternal

Khari [kä-rē; kar-ee]: (West African) kingly

Kōsaten [kō-sə-ten; ko-suh-ten]: (Japanese) intersection

Kiho [kē-hō; kee-ho]: (African, Japanese) fog; hope or beg or sail

Lenora [lə-nòr-ə; luh-nor-uh]: (English, Greek) light; compassion

Loi [lòi; loy]: (Chinese) thunder

Macella [mä-sel-ə; mah-sel-uh]: (French) she who is warlike

Maël [mī-el; my-el]: (French) chief or prince

Maia [mī-ə; my-uh]: (Greek) mother; one who has unconditional love like a
mother

Matthias [mə-tī-əs; muh-tie-us] (Hebrew) gift of God

Meztli [māz-lē; maze-lee] (Aztec/Nahuatl) moon

Orla [òr-lə; or-luh]: (Irish) golden princess

Omari [ō-mär-ē; o-mar-ee]: (Swahili, Egyptian) God the highest; highborn

Rhiannon [rē-an-in; ree-an-in]: (Welsh) divine queen

Shamira [shə-mi-rə; shuh-mere-uh]: (Hebrew) guardian, protector

Tuwile [tū-wē-lā; too-wee-lay]: (Kenyan) death is invincible

Valen [vä-lən; vah-luhn]: (Latin) healthy, strong

Vespera [ves-per-ə; ves-pair-uh]: (Latin) evening star

Zahra [zä-rə; zah-ruh]: (Arabic) bright, brilliant, radiant

SERIES INFORMATION

Macella and Aithan's story continues in...

A SAGA OF
SOVEREIGNS
AND
SECRETS

Darkness gathers, trouble brews. Predator or protector, one must choose.

Fate has led Macella of Shively and Aithan of Auburndale to the seat of Kōsaten's power. As newly appointed Protector of the Crown, Aithan is bound to the kingdom's rulers, particularly its mercurial sovereign, King Khari. Thus, confined to life in the capital, they must learn to navigate complicated court politics and the Crown's dangerous games. Most of all, they must determine how to fulfill prophecy and save the kingdom.

As they discover truths both beautiful and horrifying, sinister forces continue to gather just beyond their realm. Rifts between the realms are appearing with greater frequency, unleashing monsters only the Aegises can destroy. And, if the prophecy is to be believed, only Macella and Aithan ultimately stand between Kōsaten and the forces of hell.

With threats on all sides, Macella and Aithan have to rely on each other and their love to survive. Little do they know, King Khari has plans for them both—sinister, secret plans. But they have their own secrets to protect. Secrets about who they are and what they must do. Secrets that the Crown would kill for.

It seems everyone wants to shape Macella's story to their will. But Macella has always been the author of her life. She's determined to reclaim her story—no matter how it's Fated to end.

ACKNOWLEDGEMENTS

Though it feels like a solitary endeavor at times, writing a book requires a support system, and I have one of the best. First and foremost, I want to thank my partner in crime and in life, the Jay to my Missy, my own personal Aegis, and my number one fan. I love you, husband. To the grandmothers who nurtured my creativity, shaped me, and inspired my nom de plume, I love you both so much. Special thanks to the friends who read early drafts, especially B, the vice president of my fan club. My undying gratitude goes to Shannon McKelden Cave, editor extraordinaire, whose tireless efforts made my book so much better. Thanks to the folks at writers-journey.com for helping me get my map finished when the original artist was incapacitated. And finally, thank everyone who has read any of my words, encouraged me, offered tips, and just generally supported me. Y'all rock.

ABOUT THE AUTHOR

A.J. grew up voraciously reading her grandmother's Harlequin romance novels alongside Madeline L'Engle and R.L. Stine. She has remained an avid reader, whose book choices are as eclectic as her personality. As an anxious, Black, chaotic bisexual, A.J. Shirley writes steamy fantasy romance that is unapologetically inclusive. For the women like A.J. who were fans of the *Twilight* books in their early twenties (but wished for way more sex) and grew up to love shows and books like *Supernatural* for the lore and monsters, *Game of Thrones* for the world-building and intrigue, and *The Witcher* for atmosphere and attractive protagonists, her stories offer another fantasy world to get lost in.

Learn more at https://ajshirleyauthor.com and follow A.J. on social media for updates on *The Aegis Saga*.

instagram.com/ajshirleyauthor/

facebook.com/ajshirleyauthor/

Milton Keynes UK
Ingram Content Group UK Ltd.
UKHW041820140224
437823UK00001B/32